Anne Bradstreet, John Harvard Ellis

The Works of Anne Bradstreet in Prose and Verse

Anne Bradstreet, John Harvard Ellis

The Works of Anne Bradstreet in Prose and Verse

ISBN/EAN: 9783741186110

Manufactured in Europe, USA, Canada, Australia, Japa

Cover: Foto ©Andreas Hilbeck / pixelio.de

Manufactured and distributed by brebook publishing software
(www.brebook.com)

Anne Bradstreet, John Harvard Ellis

The Works of Anne Bradstreet in Prose and Verse

THE WORKS OF

Anne Bradstreet

IN PROSE AND VERSE

EDITED BY

JOHN HARVARD ELLIS

Charlestown

ABRAM E. CUTTER

1867

Two Hundred and Fifty Copies Printed.

CAMBRIDGE:
PRESS OF JOHN WILSON AND SON.

PREFACE.

THIS volume is believed to contain all the extant works of ANNE BRADSTREET. Three editions of her "Poems" have been printed. The first edition appeared in London in 1650, under the title of "The Tenth Muſe, lately ſprung up in America;" a neatly-printed volume in small 16mo, xiv and 207 pages.

The second edition was printed in Boston, by John Foster, in 1678. It contained the additions and corrections of the author, and several poems found amongst her papers after her death; together with some verses in praise of her poems by President Rogers, of Harvard College, and "A Funeral Elogy," upon the author, by the Rev. John Norton, of Hingham. Like the first edition, it is a 16mo; but the page and type are larger. The second edition has two hundred and fifty-five pages, preceded by fourteen pages unnumbered. Copies of the titlepages of the first and second editions, as exact as modern-antique type can make them, are given on pages 79 and 81.

The third edition, in crown 8vo, xiv and 233 pages, was published in Boston in 1758, without bearing the name of its publisher or printer. It had the following titlepage:—

SEVERAL
POEMS

Compiled with great Variety of WIT and LEARNING, full of DELIGHT;

Wherein especially is contained, a compleat Discourse and Description of

The Four { ELEMENTS,
CONSTITUTIONS,
AGES of MAN,
SEASONS of the Year.

Together with an exact EPITOME of the three first MONARCHIES, *viz.* the

ASSYRIAN, *PERSIAN*, *GRECIAN*, and *ROMAN* COMMON WEALTH, from its begin-ging, to the End of their last KING.

With divers other pleasant and serious POEMS.

By a GENTLEWOMAN in *New-England.*

The THIRD EDITION, *corrected by the Author, and enlarged by an Addition of several other* POEMS *found amongst her Papers after her Death.*

Re-printed from the second Edition, in the Year M.DCC.LVIII.

Although it was reprinted from the second edition, there were numerous omissions of words, changes in the spelling, and other alterations of little importance.

In the present edition of the "Poems," the spelling and punctuation, and even the typographical mistakes, of the second edition have been retained. The headings to the pages are new, and the catch-words have been omitted. The paging of that edition is preserved in brackets in the margin. The corrections in the second edition were extensive. The spelling was, as a rule, modernized; although some words, especially proper names, have an older or more incorrect form of spelling in that than in the first edition. Grammatical mistakes were corrected; capitals were omitted from common nouns which had them in the first; the punctuation was improved; and a great many words, enclosed in brackets in the first edition, were without them in the second edition. But no rule is uniformly adhered to in any of these particulars. There is, in both editions, as Charles Lamb's old friend said of a black-letter text of Chaucer, "a deal of very indifferent spelling." A proper name is sometimes, on the same page, spelt in two different ways. I have marked the most important alterations in foot-notes. Mere transpositions of words, changes in punctuation and in the spelling of words other than proper names, and trifling corrections, not materially affecting the sense of a passage, have not been noted. I hope that I have let nothing pass which would have been of interest to any reader.

Some of these alterations may have been made by the publishers, after the author's death. In order to have shown all the changes, it would have been necessary to have presented the text of the first edition entire. There are no foot-notes in either of the early editions.

The miscellaneous writings, which, under the titles of "Religious Experiences and Occasional Pieces" and "Meditations," precede the "Poems" in this volume, are printed from a small manuscript book, which belonged to the author, and which has been kept, since her death, as a precious relic by her descendants. It is about six inches high and three and three-quarters inches broad. The covers are of common sheep-skin, and are very much soiled and worn. The remnants of two small brass clasps still adhere to them. The paper is yellow, stained with water, blotted with ink, and bears marks of having been much read and handled. It has ninety-eight pages, the first forty-one of which are taken up with the "Meditations Diuine and morall," in Mrs. Bradstreet's handwriting. The forty-second page is blank; but, from the forty-third to the sixty-seventh page inclusive, her son Simon has copied in the contents of another manuscript book left by her, which is now probably lost. Mrs. Bradstreet's handwriting is large and distinct; while that of her son is very small and delicate, though clear, and marred by few erasions or alterations. The sixty-eighth page is blank, and then follows a Latin translation of the first four "Meditations" and their dedication, by her great-grandson, the Rev. Simon Bradstreet, of Marblehead, Massachusetts. This covers only four pages. Six pages have been at some time cut out after these. The next twenty-four pages are blank; and on the two sides of the last leaf there are some verses in Mrs. Bradstreet's handwriting, beginning, "As weary pilgrim, now at rest." Several leaves, how many it is uncertain, have been torn out at the end of the book. All the contents of this book are printed in this volume: the order, however, of the separate parts of which it is composed, has been changed. The portion in her son's handwriting, and the verses which I have mentioned as being at the end of the book, being in their nature biographical, I have placed first. The "Meditations," and the fragment of their translation into Latin by her great-grandson, come next.

The manuscript has been closely followed, except that abbreviations, such as "&," "wth," "y^{e}," "y^{t}," and some of longer words, have been printed in full. These are very common in the portion written by her son, who probably tried to shorten his work of copying as much as possible. The author herself rarely uses any abbreviations. Punctuation has been supplied where it was defective; and in some of the poems, whose rhyme required it, the alternate verses have been indented, and some poems have been broken into stanzas. The manuscript has been scribbled over, apparently by a child; and a few corrections have been made since she wrote, in ink fresher than the original: these, of course, have been disregarded.

With these exceptions, the reader has an exact copy of the manuscript. A fac-simile of the first leaf of the volume may be found between pages 46 and 47.

Extracts from the manuscript, with some appropriate remarks on the author's life and character, were published by the Rev. William I. Budington, D.D., for many years pastor of the First Church in Charlestown, in his history of that church; and almost the whole of it appeared in a series of articles, under the title of "The Puritan Mother," contributed by the same gentleman to the first volume of "The Congregational Visiter," a small monthly magazine published in Boston, in 1844, by the Massachusetts Sabbath-School Society. Several extracts have also been published, at various times, in newspapers, by Mr. Dean Dudley, who has written some very interesting pieces concerning the author and her works, and who is known as the indefatigable genealogist of the Dudley and Bradstreet families. A good notice of Mrs. Bradstreet is contained in Duyckinck's "Cyclopædia of American Literature."

The contents of the manuscript book are now, for the first time, printed entire. For the use of it, in preparing this volume for the press, and also for copies of the first three editions of the "Poems," all of which are now extremely rare, I am indebted to the kindness of Mr. Samuel Bradstreet, of Dorchester.

The engraving of Governor Bradstreet, in this volume, is taken from a plate belonging to Mr. S. G. Drake, which he was so good as to allow to be used for this purpose.

In editing Mrs. Bradstreet's works, I have had the benefit of the advice and suggestions of several of my friends; but I am especially obliged, for such favors, to Dr. John Appleton, Assistant Librarian of the Massachusetts Historical Society.

JOHN H. ELLIS.

CHARLESTOWN, MASS.,
Jan. 31, 1867.

INTRODUCTION.

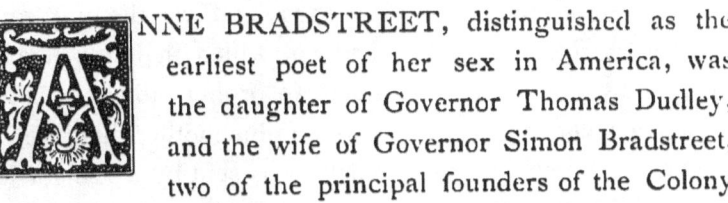

ANNE BRADSTREET, distinguished as the earliest poet of her sex in America, was the daughter of Governor Thomas Dudley, and the wife of Governor Simon Bradstreet, two of the principal founders of the Colony of Massachusetts Bay. The ancestry of that branch of the Dudley family to which Mrs. Bradstreet belonged is now simply a matter of conjecture. Many attempts have been made to trace it, but without success.* "There is a tradition among the descendants of Governor Dudley, in the eldest branch of the family," says Mr. Moore, "that he was descended from John Dudley, Duke of Northumberland, who was beheaded 22 February, 1553."† Mrs. Bradstreet seems to have shared this belief, if we may judge from the following verses from her "Elegy upon Sir

* "The Dudley Genealogies and Family Records." By Dean Dudley. Boston: Published by the Author. 1848. N. E. Hist. Gen. Register, Vol. x. p. 133. — "The Sutton-Dudleys of England, and the Dudleys of Massachusetts." By George Adlard. New York: 1862. — "The Herald and Genealogist," Vol. ii. London: 1865. pp. 409–426, and 494–499.

† Lives of the Governors of New Plymouth and Massachusetts Bay. By Jacob Bailey Moore. New York: 1846. p. 273

Philip Sidney," whose mother was the Lady Mary, eldest daughter of that Duke of Northumberland: —

> "Let then, none dis-allow of these my straines,
> Which have the self-same blood yet in my veines."

But she retracts this claim to relationship, in the second edition of her poems, where the verses appear as follows: —

> "Then let none disallow of these my straines
> Whilst English blood yet runs within my veins." *

Thomas Dudley, her father, was born at Northampton, in England, in the year 1576 or 1577, and was the only son of Captain Roger Dudley, who was killed in battle about the year 1586. He was thus left an orphan, together with a sister, concerning whom, as well as his mother, nothing is known. At a school, to which he was sent by a charitable lady of his native town, he acquired a good knowledge of Latin. But, while still young, he was taken from school, and became a page in the family of William Lord Compton, afterwards Earl of Northampton. He was subsequently a clerk of a kinsman "Judge Nichols," probably Thomas Nicolls, a serjeant-at-law. He next appears at the head of a company of eighty volunteers, raised in and about Northampton, and forming part of the force collected by order of Queen Elizabeth, to assist Henry IV. of France, in the war against Philip II. of Spain. He is said to have been at the siege of Amiens in 1597, and to have returned home to England soon after. From each of these various occupations, of page, lawyer's clerk, and soldier, he derived some benefit, — courtesy of manners, considerable legal skill and acumen, straightforwardness, honesty, and courage. He established himself at Northampton, and married "a Gentle-

* See pages 346, note, and 347.

woman whofe Extract and Eftate were Confiderable." Under the preaching of the well-known Puritan ministers, Dodd and Hildersham, and others of less note, he became a Nonconformist, and ever after adhered most strictly to the views which he thus adopted.

In 1616 Henry de Clinton, Earl of Lincoln, died, his title descending to his son Thomas. The latter survived but three years to enjoy his honors, and left to his son Theophilus, a young man, a large estate heavily encumbered with his father's debts. In this emergency, Dudley was recommended to the young Earl as steward, by Lord Saye and Sele, Lord Compton, and others who had satisfied themselves of his worth and ability. He accordingly took the entire charge of the Earl's large estate, and, by his skilful management, in the space of a few years entirely freed the estate from the debts with which it was laden. By many important services which he rendered, and also by his fidelity and constancy in the discharge of his duties, he greatly endeared himself to the family. For nine or ten years, he continued to be the Earl's steward; but, after that, growing weary of his laborious position, he left the Earl's service, and removed to Boston, in Lincolnshire. He there formed an intimate acquaintance with the vicar of that town, the Rev. John Cotton, who was to be his companion at Boston, in the New World. As his services were again much needed by the Earl of Lincoln, he was obliged to return to his family, and there he remained most of the time, until he left the country.*

* Mather's Magnalia. London: 1702. Bk. ii. pp. 15–17. — Old manuscript life, printed in "The Sutton-Dudleys," pp. 24–38. — "Dudley Genealogies." Hutchinson's History of Massachusetts Bay. Boston: 1795. Vol. i. p. 21, note *. — "Herald and Genealogist," Vol. ii. pp. 409–426; Historic

In Isaac Johnson's will, dated March, 1629, O.S., of which Dudley is constituted one of the executors, he is described as of Clipsham in the county of Rutland;* but it is not known how long he lived there. Dudley's first child was a son, Samuel, born in 1610.

His second child was Anne, the subject of this sketch. She was born in 1612–13, probably at Northampton.† Of her youth and of her bringing up, we know but little. We can infer, however, from what she wrote of herself, later in life, that she was strictly and religiously trained; while it is evident from her poems, that she had read and studied, with unusual diligence, for one of her age and sex. She gives the following account of her early religious experiences:—

"In my yovng years, about 6 or 7 as I take it, I began to make confcience of my wayes, and what I knew was finfull, as lying, difobedience to Parents, &c. I avoided it. If at any time I was overtaken with the like evills, it was a great Trouble. I could not be at reft 'till by prayer I had confeft it vnto God. I was alfo troubled at the neglect of Private Dutyes, tho: too often tardy that way. I alfo fovnd much comfort in reading the Scriptures, efpecially thofe places I thought moft concerned my Condition, and as I grew to haue more vnderftanding, fo the more folace I took in them.

"In a long fitt of ficknes wch I had on my bed I often commvned with my heart, and made my fupplication to the moft High who fett me free from that affliction.

"But as I grew vp to bee about 14 or 15 I fovnd my heart more carnall and fitting loofe from God, vanity and the follyes of youth take hold of me.

Peerage of England, by Sir H. Nicolas, p. 289; Mass. Hist. Soc. Coll., 4th series, Vol. viii. p. 342.

* Mass. Hist. Soc. Coll., 3d series, Vol. viii. p. 245.

† See page 391; "Dudley Genealogies," p. 18; "Sutton-Dudleys," p. 97.

"About 16, the Lord layd his hand fore upon me and fmott mee with the fmall pox. When I was in my affliction, I befovght the Lord, and confeffed my Pride and Vanity and he was entreated of me, and again reftored me. But I rendered not to him according to ye benefitt received.

"After a fhort time I changed my condition and was marryed, and came into this Covntry, where I fovnd a new world and new manners, at which my heart rofe. But after I was convinced it was the way of God, I fubmitted to it and joined to the church at Bofton." *

In her poem, "In Honour of Du Bartas," she has left a very pleasant reminiscence of her childhood, in these verses: —

"My mufe unto a Child I may compare,
Who fees the riches of fome famous Fair,
He feeds his Eyes, but underftanding lacks
To comprehend the worth of all thofe knacks:
The glittering plate and Jewels he admires,
The Hats and Fans, the Plumes and Ladies tires,
And thoufand times his mazed mind doth wifh
Some part (at leaft) of that brave wealth was his,
But feeing empty wifhes nought obtain,
At night turns to his Mothers cot again,
And tells her tales, (his full heart over glad)
Of all the glorious fights his Eyes have had:
But finds too foon his want of Eloquence,
The filly prattler fpeaks no word of fenfe;
But feeing utterance fail his great defires,
Sits down in filence, deeply he admires." †

Notwithstanding the gloom which over-conscientiousness threw over her youth, we can easily imagine the pleasure with which she perused the many new books which were then appearing in such unwonted numbers, and the zest

* See pages 4 and 5. † See page 354.

with which she devoured their delicious contents. The quarter of a century preceding the departure of the Massachusetts Company for New England was one of the most remarkable in the history of English literature. Coming, as it did, at the close of the great Elizabethan Age, the more peaceful reign of James was better fitted for the quiet and considerate study and cultivation of literature than the more glorious and splendid, though more warlike and disturbed, reign of the "Virgin Queen." The impulse given by the great minds of her epoch had not yet died out, but had transmitted much of its vigor to their successors of the Jacoban Age; many renowned writers of the one living late into the other. Spenser had died, near the close of the century, leaving his great poem unfinished; having written enough, however, to charm posterity ever after, and to found a new school of poetry. His patron, the accomplished writer, the elegant poet, and knightly soldier, Sir Philip Sidney, had fallen, some fifteen years before, on the bloody field before Zutphen. One year, 1616, had been rendered famous, by the death of two of the most brilliant names in the world's literature,—Shakespeare and Cervantes; one in the prime of life, and the other at threescore and ten, summoned hence within ten days of each other. To Don Quixote and his squire, Mrs. Bradstreet may have been introduced by Shelton's translation. With the plays of Shakespeare, as well as those of Ben Jonson, Beaumont and Fletcher, Middleton, Webster, Massinger, and the other dramatists, we may well presume that she was not familiar, and that she rather shunned them, as irreligious. There are some passages in her "Poems," however, which seem as if they must have been suggested by a reading of

Shakespeare. The Puritans were bitter enemies of the stage, and all connected with it; and their dislike was reciprocated most heartily by the playwrights and players. Mrs. Lucy Hutchinson, speaking of the treatment of the Puritans, says, —

"every stage, and every table, and every puppet-play, belched forth profane scoffs upon them, the drunkards made them their songs, and all fiddlers and mimics learned to abuse them, as finding it the most gameful way of fooling." *

In 1611, the common version of the Bible was published. We have already seen how early Mrs. Bradstreet began to find comfort in this volume, which was to be the solace of her lonely and melancholy hours, for the rest of her life. The charming essays of Montaigne, with their varied learning and keen insight into human nature, had been "done into Englifh" by John Florio, and had attracted the attention of the immortal dramatist himself. Burton had tried in vain to drive away his melancholy, by writing its "Anatomy." Chapman had given to the world his grand version of Homer. Sir Thomas North had translated "Plutarch's Lives" in a manner most aptly suited to the easy story-telling style of the original; and his book was to be "a household book, for the whole of the seventeenth century." † The "silver-tongued" Sylvester, who was himself the author of many poems, had translated the works of the favorite French poet, the "divine" Du Bartas, of whom we shall hear more farther on. The poets of this period were numerous, and the writings of many of them are even now read. Some of them are noted for their sensuousness,

* Life of Col. Hutchinson, Bohn's ed. p. 82.

† Hooper's Introduction to Chapman's Homer's Iliad, p. ix.

and for their delicious descriptions of the beautiful in nature. Following upon the poets more distinctively belonging to the Elizabethan Age, with their fancifulness, their pretty, tiresome conceits, their quaint analogies, and far-fetched similes, the poets of the reign of James, while they retained many of their faults, were much less artificial. These poets, who have been classified as pastoral, satirical, theological, metaphysical, and humorous, indicate by their number, and by the excellence of many of their writings, the literary spirit of the age. They were generally anti-Puritans, and we may well doubt if Mrs. Bradstreet could have read them with much pleasure, as her scruples and belief would have received many a rude shock over their pages. Wither and Quarles, however, were peculiarly Calvinistic; the former becoming afterwards one of Cromwell's major-generals, and the latter being in manner and matter, if not in spirit, a Puritan. Their works were extremely popular with the Puritans, not only at the period of which we are now speaking, but also long after. Quarles' "Emblems," to be sure, did not appear in print until 1635, but his gloomy poems must have already saddened the heart of many an honest Nonconformist. Quarles appears to have had some correspondence with the New-England men. Josselyn, in his account of his visit to Boston in 1638, speaks of "prefenting my refpects to Mr. *Winthorpe* the Governour, and to Mr. *Cotton*, the Teacher of *Boston* Church, to whom I delivered from Mr. *Francis Quarles* the poet, the Tranflation of the 16, 25, 51, 88, 113, and 137. Pfalms into *Englifh* Meeter for his approbation." *

This period, so prolific in versifiers, was not without its

* Josselyn's "Two Voyages," p. 20.

historians and antiquaries. Speed, Archbishop Usher, the learned primate of Ireland, Sir Robert Cotton, and Sir Henry Spelman, flourished about this time. Knolles published his history of the Turks in 1603, to whom Johnson, in one of his "Ramblers" (122), has awarded the first place among English historians, being borne out in his judgment by Hallam.* The illustrious Camden's "Brittannia" and "Annales Rerum Anglicarum regnante Elizabetha" had appeared early in the century, and the learned author had been long numbered with the dead. There was also the Latin historian and poet of Scotland, Buchanan, who had been the tutor of King James. Sir Walter Raleigh had occupied twelve weary years of imprisonment in writing his "History of the World," published in 1614, the most important of the works of that distinguished soldier and navigator. Bacon, the great philosopher, the able historian, the accomplished orator, who combined in himself most of the varied powers of his noted contemporaries, had been degraded from the exalted post of Lord Chancellor. Shorn of his honors, after devoting the leisure which his retirement afforded to his favorite studies, he died on the 9th of April, 1626, in the sixty-sixth year of his age, a victim of the science he loved so fondly.†

A recent English writer has remarked: "In one sense the reign of James is the most religious part of our history; for religion was then fashionable. The forms of state, the king's speeches, the debates in parliament, and the current literature, were filled with quotations from scripture and quaint allusions to sacred things."‡ Super-

* Craik's English Literature. New York: 1863. Vol. I. p. 619.

† Life pref. to "Essays." Boston: 1856. p. 27.

‡ Marsden's "Early Puritans." London: 1860. p. 382.

ficial as the current of real piety is acknowledged to have been, we find, in addition to all the secular books above referred to, a mass of sermons, books of devotion, religious tracts, and controversial pamphlets. Many productions, too, of more importance and of greater size and pretensions, were the results of deeper delvings in theology and divinity. The "Ecclesiastical Polity" of the illustrious Hooker had been in part published, the whole work complete not appearing until 1632, the author himself having died at the beginning of the century. There were also, besides Archbishop Usher, Andrews, and Donne, the "humble and heavenly minded" Dr. Richard Sibbs, whose sermons, collected under the title of "The Saint's Cordial," were highly prized by the Puritans; the "Englifh Seneca," Bishop Hall, a thorough Calvinist, whose "pious Meditations are still a household volume read by all classes, published in all forms." * One reason for the small number of strictly sectarian, Puritan, or Calvinistic works during this period was, that the censorship of the press, the right of licensing books, was almost entirely arrogated to himself by the untiring enemy of the Nonconformists, Laud, Bishop of London, whose watchful eye few heretical writings could escape. Some such, however, managed to satisfy some of the more liberal censors, and thus appeared with the "cum privilegio;" while many of the most ultra pamphlets and tracts were the fruits of foreign presses, secretly introduced into the country without the form of a legal entry at Stationers' Hall. †

* Marsden's "Early Puritans," p. 393.

† Craik's English Literature. New York: 1863. — Masson's Life of Milton. London: 1859. Vol. I. ch. vi. — Bohn's Bibliographer's Manual, &c., &c.

I have thus, at the risk of trying the patience of the reader, given a very imperfect summary of what the years immediately preceding and including those in which our author was growing up produced in the way of writers. It must not be forgotten either, that it was in the early part of this century that the circulation of the blood was discovered by Dr. Harvey, and logarithms were introduced by Napier; creating new eras in medicine and mathematics. In such an age of literary activity, Mrs. Bradstreet passed the first eighteen years of her life. With literary tastes and the advantages which, without doubt, she enjoyed at the Earl of Lincoln's castle of Sempringham, she must have felt, and, at the same time, been able easily to satisfy, a craving for poetical and historical studies. It should be remembered, however, that she was only eighteen when she was called to leave her native country, with its manifold attractions, and her pleasant home, with its tender associations, to take up her abode in a wilderness. Even then she would be exposed to all the cares consequent upon her position as a wife, and that, too, the wife of a busy magistrate who was frequently called to be absent from home, leaving her no solace except her meditations on what she had once read or experienced.

At the early age of sixteen, she was married to Simon Bradstreet, the son of a Nonconformist minister of the same name, of Lincolnshire. Bradstreet's father was the son of a well-to-do Suffolk gentleman, was one of the first Fellows of Emmanuel College, had preached at Middleburgh, in the Netherlands, and was, like Dudley, a friend of the Rev. Mr. Cotton and Dr. Preston. Young Bradstreet was born at Horbling, March, 1603, and was educated at the grammar school, where he studied until the death of his father, when he was fourteen years old, made it necessary for him to leave. Two or three years after this he was taken into the family of the Earl of Lincoln, where he was under the care of Dudley. He remained there, until, at the suggestion of Dr. Preston, who had been the Earl's tutor, he was sent by the Earl to Emmanuel College, in the capacity of governor to Lord Rich, son of the Earl of Warwick. As the young lord gave up the idea of acquiring an education at the University, Bradstreet continued there only a year; having had, as he himself wrote, a very pleasant but unprofitable time, in the society of the Earl of Lincoln's brother, and of other companions. Notwithstanding, he took his bachelor's degree in 1620, and his master's four years later.* On the removal of Dudley to Boston, Bradstreet succeeded to his place as steward. He afterwards became steward of the Countess of Warwick, and was in that position at the time of his marriage. †

Under Bancroft, as Archbishop of Canterbury, the Nonconformists had suffered severely, many of the ministers being silenced and deprived of their livings, while others were driven into exile. The effect of this harsh treatment was to strengthen the sufferers in their belief, and to bind them more closely together by the common tie of affliction. The succession of the austere Abbot, who had much of the Puritan in his creed and manners, gave them some respite; although the canons requiring the due observance of those forms and ceremonies in worship to which the Nonconformists most strongly objected, were as rigidly enforced as

* Young's Chronicles of Massachusetts. Boston: 1846. p. 125, note.

† Mather's Magnalia. Bk. ii. p. 19.

ever in some places. Bishop Williams, the Lord Keeper, the favorite and confidential adviser both of the King and of Buckingham, was a great power in religious affairs. He was inclined to be tolerant alike of Puritans and Romanists, and it was only those breaches of the canons too flagrant to be overlooked which provoked him to harsh treatment. On the death of James and the accession of Charles, Williams lost the power which he had up to that time enjoyed in church and state, and retired in disgrace to his diocese of Lincoln. Buckingham, who held the same place in the affections of the new King which he had gained in those of his father,* committed to Dr. Laud, his great confidant, then Bishop of Bath and Wells, and sworn a member of the Privy Council, the sole presentation of church promotions and the vacancies which should happen. King Charles, after the assassination of Buckingham, continued that trust in the same hands, infinitely to the benefit and honor of the Church, in Clarendon's opinion, † but greatly to the sorrow and discomfort of the Nonconformists, whose bitter opponent Laud had been from the very first. Slowly but surely this intolerant prelate got into his hands the power which would enable him to indulge his malevolent feelings towards the Puritans. He thus did all he could to kindle the flame which was to break out before long into the dreadful fire of civil war, and in which he was to lose his life. Besides the Romanists, whose numbers cannot be estimated, there was the extreme class of Puritans known as Separatists, who comprised in their ranks only a trifling proportion of the population. The Established

* Clarendon's History of the Rebellion, Bk. i. p. 48.

† *Ibid.*, p. 145.

Church of England was divided into two great parties, the Prelatical or Hierarchical, headed by the zealous Laud, and the Nonconformist or Puritan. This latter party embraced at once the severe doctrines, and the plain and simple forms, inculcated by their great teacher, Calvin. They were still included in the Church; and their preachers were estimated, as early as 1603, at the time of the Hampton Court Conference, to have numbered about a ninth part of the whole parish clergy. The teachers and disciples had both largely increased in numbers during the score of years preceding the time of which we are now treating. What at first had been a mere variance about church government and ritual came to involve important points of doctrine. A strife arose between Calvinism and Arminianism, the Calvinistic or Nonconformist party growing and strengthening as the Arminian or Hierarchical party became more hostile and vehement. The breach constantly widened, severity on the one side being met by persistence and a resolution to endure on the other.*

Such was the state of religious affairs in England, when, at a meeting of the Massachusetts Company on the 28th of July, 1629, Mr. Cradock, the Governor, made the bold proposition to transfer the government and patent of the Plantation to America.† After debating the question thoroughly and weighing the arguments which could be adduced on both sides, legal advice was taken, and they at once commenced preparing to transport themselves and their families to America. Deplorable as was then the condition of religious matters, that of affairs of state was

* Masson's Milton, Vol. i. ch. v.

† Massachusetts Colony Records, Vol. i. p. 49.

equally unpromising, and boded ill for the future. In the first four years of his reign, Charles had summoned three Parliaments, which he had speedily dissolved, because they so scantily supplied him with the money which he demanded, but preferred rather to occupy themselves with the rehearsal of their wrongs, which they finally embodied in the Petition of Right. Once more only after that did the Parliament meet, (in January, 1629,) to be then abruptly dissolved, and to remain in abeyance for nearly twelve years.

The position of those who proposed to go over to America was more disagreeable than dangerous. Their peril, if any, was prospective, not present. In this respect their case was very unlike that of the Separatists who colonized Plymouth. The Massachusetts men professed many years later that "our libertie to walke in the faith of the gofpell with all good confcience, according to the order of the gofpell, . . . was the caufe of our tranfporting ourfelves with our wives, little ones, and our fubftance, from that pleafant land over the Atlantick ocean into the vaft wildernefs."* But it is evident from the character of the first colonists, and the nature of their public acts, that they had a great politico-religious scheme to carry out. They came here to form a state which should be governed according to their own peculiar religious ideas; not solely to seek an asylum from oppression.

On the 26th of August, 1629, Dudley, with eleven others, signed an agreement at Cambridge, whereby they pledged themselves to remove with their families to New England by the first of the next March, provided the whole government, together with the patent, should be legally transferred

* Hutchinson's Collection, p. 326.

before the last of September, to remain with such plantation.* Although Dudley had been, as early as 1627, interested in the proposition to plant a colony for the propagation of the gospel in New England, and had been active in the measures which preceded the departure of the Company itself,† yet he does not appear by the records to have had any connection with the Company until the 15th of October, 1629. On that day, he and Winthrop were, for the first time, present at a meeting.‡ On the 20th of the same month, Dudley was chosen an Assistant; and, on the 18th of the following March, Bradstreet was elected to the same office, in place of Mr. Thomas Goffe. § From that time, they devoted their lives to the interests of the Company, holding the various high offices in the gift of their associates and fellow-colonists. They were the depositaries of the most important trusts, and had at times committed to them the conduct of business of vital consequence to the Colony. A thorough history of the lives of these two men would embrace the history of Massachusetts, if not of all New England, down to the close of the seventeenth century. Dudley was soon elected to the responsible position of "undertaker,"—that is, to be one of those having "the sole managinge of the ioynt stock, wth all things incydent thervnto, for the space of 7 yeares." ‖ At a Court of Assistants held aboard the "Arbella" on the 23d of March he was chosen Deputy-Governor, in place of Mr. John Humphrey, who was to stay behind in England.¶ It would seem as if, before leav-

* Hutchinson's Collections, pp. 25, 26.

† Dudley's Letter in Young's Chronicles of Massachusetts, pp. 309–10.

‡ Mass. Colony Records, Vol. i. p. 54.

§ *Ibid.*, p. 69. ‖ *Ibid.*, p. 65. ¶ *Ibid.*, p. 70.

ing England, Dudley had visited Winthrop at his house at Groton, in Suffolk. The latter, writing from London to his wife on the 5th of February, says in a postscript, "Lett M[r] Dudleys thinges be sent up next week." * While Winthrop was waiting for the arrival of the ships at Southampton, in a letter to his son John he writes, "M[r] Dudlye was gone to the Wight before we came." †

On Monday, the 29th of March, the little band of colonists embarked in their four small vessels, the "Arbella," "Talbot," "Ambrose," and "Jewell." Most of the prominent people were on the "Arbella." Among them were Mr. Isaac Johnson and his wife, the Lady Arbella, sister of the Earl of Lincoln, in whose honor the name of the vessel had been changed from that of "Eagle." There, too, was the Governor, John Winthrop, whom Dudley describes as a man "well known in his own country, and well approved here for his piety, liberality, wisdom, and gravity," ‡ and others whose names are familiar to the readers of our history. With them, we have no doubt, were Mrs. Bradstreet and her nearest relations, her father, mother, and husband. § On the same day they weighed anchor, and sailed down the English Channel; but, on account of the adverse winds by which they were detained, they put into the port of Yarmouth, a small place on the Isle of Wight. From this place they addressed their affectionate and touching farewell to their "Brethren in and of the Church of England," of which Dudley was one of the signers. Charity prompts the sug-

* Life and Letters of John Winthrop. By R. C. Winthrop. Boston: 1864. Vol. i. p. 373.

† *Ibid.*, p. 386.

‡ Dudley's Letter in Young's Chronicles of Massachusetts, p. 310.

§ This is Mr. Savage's opinion. Winthrop's History of New England. Boston: 1853. Vol. i. p. 12, note 3.

gestion that they insensibly merged their sorrow at leaving England in that of leaving the "Church." The genuineness of their affection for the latter was too clearly shown by their conduct on arriving in New England; for "the very first church planted by them was independent in all its forms, and repudiated every connection with Episcopacy or a liturgy."* On the 8th of April, the vessels set sail. Two days before the ladies had gone ashore to refresh themselves; but, from that day until the 12th of the following June, they did not again set foot on dry land; and then it was to tread the soil of the New World. After a stormy voyage, with much cold and rainy weather, the monotony being alleviated by preaching, singing, fasts, and thanksgivings, on the seventy-second day passed aboard ship the sea-worn voyagers came in sight of the rocky but welcome shores of Mount Desert. A modern pleasure-seeker has spoken in the following glowing and perhaps rather exaggerated terms of the appearance of this picturesque spot from the sea: "It is difficult to conceive of any finer combination of land and water than this view. . . . Certainly only in the tropics can it be excelled, only in the gorgeous islands of the Indian and Pacific Oceans. On the coast of America it has no rival, except, perhaps, at the Bay of Rio Janeiro."† What an enchanting sight it must have been to those who had gazed on the blank surface of the broad sea so long! "We had now fair sunshine weather, and so pleasant a sweet air as did much refresh us, and there came a smell off the shore like the smell of

* Story's Commentaries on the Constitution, Vol. i. § 64.

† A Summer Cruise on the Coast of New England. By Robert Carter. Boston: 1865. p. 252.

a garden," writes Winthrop.* The more substantial blessings of the main land rejoiced the hearts of the rest of the party on the following Saturday, 12th June, who, going ashore at Salem, "supped with a good venison pasty and good beer."† Some, wandering along the shore, feasted on the wild strawberries which grew there in abundance. But at night, when it became time to return to the ship, Winthrop remarks that "some of the women stayed behind," doubtless very reasonably cautious about again trusting themselves to the floating prison in which they had been so long pent up. They did not, like the wretched settlers of Plymouth, arrive in a cold and cheerless season of the year, to perish miserably in the ice and snow; but the green hills, clad in the rich verdure of opening summer, smiled a genial welcome to our weary voyagers, their beauty heightened by that indescribable charm which any land has for the sea-tossed adventurer. Higginson, who arrived about a year before, speaks of Ten-pound "island, whither four of our men with a boat went, and brought back again ripe strawberries and gooseberries, and sweet single roses. Thus God," he continues, "was merciful to us in giving us a taste and smell of the sweet fruit as an earnest of his bountiful goodness to welcome us at our first arrival."‡

But the attractions of the scene to Winthrop and his company must have been more than offset by the melancholy condition in which they found the little settlement. They could have had little time to consider the beauties of nature, amid their own cares and the misery around

* Winthrop's New England, Vol. i. p 23, and note 1.

† *Ibid.*, p. 26.

‡ Young's Chronicles of Massachusetts, p. 234.

them. John Endicott had been sent over by the Patentees of the Massachusetts territory. He reached Salem in September, 1628, where he established a post, his own men and those whom he found there making, in all, a company of not much more than fifty or sixty persons.* The Rev. Mr. Higginson followed the next year with two hundred more colonists, finding with Endicott then about one hundred. Of these, two hundred settled at Salem, and the rest established themselves at Charlestown with the intention of founding a town there. † Dudley, in his letter to the Countess of Lincoln, says "We found the Colony in a sad and unexpected condition, above eighty of them being dead the winter before; and many of those alive weak and sick; all the corn and bread amongst them all hardly sufficient to feed them a fortnight, insomuch that the remainder of a hundred and eighty servants we had the two years before sent over, coming to us for victuals to sustain them, we found ourselves wholly unable to feed them, by reason that the provisions shipped for them were taken out of the ship they were put in, and they who were trusted to ship them in another failed us and left them behind; whereupon necessity enforced us, to our extreme loss, to give them all liberty, who had cost us about £16 or £20 a person, furnishing and sending over." ‡

As Salem was not to their taste, after exploring the Charles and Mystic Rivers, they unshipped their goods at Salem into other vessels, and brought them in July to Charlestown. They made a settlement there to the number of fifteen hundred people, § Dudley and Bradstreet, per-

* Young's Chronicles of Massachusetts, p. 13.

† *Ibid.*, p. 259. ‡ *Ibid.*, p. 311-12. § *Ibid.*, p. 378.

haps with their families, being among them. "The Governor and several of the Patentees dwelt in the great house, which was last year built in this town by Mr. Graves and the rest of their servants. The multitude set up cottages, booths and tents about the Town Hill." * From the sad state of things above described, it is easy to see that the new comers had to give rather than receive assistance from those whom they found already at Charlestown. On Friday, July 30, Winthrop, Dudley, Johnson, and Wilson entered into a church covenant, which was signed two days after by Increase Nowell and four others, — Sharpe, Bradstreet, Gager, and Colborne; † the subscribers soon numbering sixty-four men and half as many women. ‡ The next on the list are William Aspinwall and Robert Harding, and then follow the names of "Dorothy Dudley ye wife of Tho: Dudley" and "Anne Bradftreete ye wife of Simon Bradftreete." § Johnson says, in his "Wonder-working Providence," ‖ that, after the arrival of the company at Salem, "the Lady *Arrabella* and fome other godly Women aboad at *Salem*, but their Husbands continued at *Charles* Town, both for the fettling the civill Government and gathering another Church of *Christ*."

It may be that Mrs. Bradstreet was one of those who remained at Salem, and that she was not in Charlestown when the covenant was first signed; but, as her name is

* Charlestown Records in Young's Chronicles of Massachusetts, p. 378.

† Prince's Chronology. Boston: 1826. p. 311. — Bradford's History of Plymouth Plantation. Boston: 1856. p. 278. — Bradford's Letter Book, in Mass. Hist. Soc. Coll., Vol. iii. p. 76. — Budington's History of the First Church in Charlestown. pp. 13–15.

‡ Budington, p. 15.

§ MS. Records of the First Church in Boston.

‖ London: 1654. p. 37.

only the thirteenth on the list, she must have joined her husband in Charlestown soon after.

"Many people arrived sick of the scurvy, which also increased much after their arrival, for want of houses, and by reason of wet lodging in their cottages, &c. Other distempers also prevailed; and, although [the] people were generally very loving and pitiful, yet the sickness did so prevail, that the whole were not able to tend the sick, as they should be tended; upon which many perished and died and were buried about the Town Hill." * In addition to all this trouble, their provisions ran short, and, as it was too late in the season to think of raising any more, they were obliged to despatch a ship to Ireland to buy some. The hot weather, the want of running water, and the general sickness, which they attributed to the situation, made them discontented. Although they had intended to remain and found a town, they moved away, scattering about the neighborhood, the majority of them, including the Governor, Deputy-Governor, and all the Assistants except Mr. Nowell, going across the river to Boston, at the invitation of Mr. Blaxton, who had until then been its only white inhabitant.†

They did not remain long in Boston, as they were apprehensive that the Indians would attack them, now that they were dispersed and so much reduced by sickness; but looked about for a suitable situation for a fortified town, and in December, 1630, decided upon the spot which was afterwards called Cambridge.‡ Fortunately, the winter of 1630 was mild, § or their suffering would have been intense. As

* Young's Chronicles of Massachusetts, pp. 378-9.

† *Ibid.*, pp. 379-81. Budington, p. 18.

‡ Winthrop's New England, Vol. i. p. 39.

§ Wood's "New-England's Profpect," p. 5.

it was, it is not hard to realize how wretchedly the poorer portion must have fared, when we look at the picture which Dudley, one of the richest of the party, writing nine months after their arrival, so vividly presents to us of the condition of himself and his family. He says that he writes "rudely, having yet no table, nor other room to write in than by the fireside upon my knee, in this sharp winter; to which my family must have leave to resort, though they break good manners, and make me many times forget what I would say, and say what I would not."* The new settlement at Cambridge was begun in the spring of the next year; and it was the intention of the settlers to make this place, which they called Newtown, the principal town of the Colony. The Governor, Deputy-Governor, and Bradstreet were among those who moved out and established themselves there. The town was laid out in squares, the streets intersecting each other at right angles. Dudley's house stood on the west side of Water Street, near its southern termination at Marsh Lane, at the corner of the present Dunster and South Streets. Bradstreet's was at the corner of "Brayntree" and Wood Streets, where the University Bookstore of Messrs. Sever & Francis now is, on Harvard Square, at the corner of Brighton Street. Dudley's lot was half an acre in size, and Bradstreet's measured "aboute one rood." †

Governor Winthrop decided not to remain at Newtown,

* Dudley's Letter to the Countess of Lincoln, in Young's Chronicles of Massachusetts, p. 305. This letter is the most vivid and authentic narrative of the labor and sufferings attendant on the planting of the Colony.

† "The Regeſtere Booke of the Lands and Houſes in the Newtowne. 1635." MS. pp. 1 and 27.—Holmes' History of Cambridge. Mass. Hist. Soc. Coll., Vol. vii. pp. 7-8.

and in the autumn took down the frame of his house, and moved it to Boston. This caused much dissatisfaction, as many thought that the prospects of the town would be thereby injured. Dudley was especially displeased, and followed up this and other charges which he had against Winthrop, so as to produce a temporary alienation between them. The matter was afterwards amicably settled, having been referred to a conference of ministers; * and the town continued to grow, notwithstanding the loss of the Governor. In August, 1632, it was largely increased by the arrival of those who had composed the congregation of the Rev. Thomas Hooker at Chelmsford, county of Essex, England. They left Mount Wollaston, where they had established themselves, for Newtown, by order of the General Court.† At their urgent solicitation, their pastor, Mr. Hooker, eluding with difficulty the officers of the High Commission, came to New England in the "Griffin." He reached Boston on the 4th of September, 1633, ‡ and went immediately to Newtown, where he was soon after chosen minister. Many of the people were poor, and there was, at times, a scarcity of food. But the town flourished, the inhabitants being fortunately spared by the Indians, who had them at their mercy. Wood, who visited it before his return to England in August, 1633, thus describes it:—

"This is one of the neateſt and beſt compacted Townes in *New England*, having many faire ſtructures, with many handſome contrived ſtreets. The inhabitants moſt of them are very rich, and well ſtored with Cattell of all ſorts." §

* Holmes' Cambridge, pp. 8 and 11. Winthrop's Life and Letters, Vol. ii. pp. 91–102.

† Winthrop's New England, Vol i. pp. 87–8.

‡ *Ibid.*, pp 108–9.

§ N. E. Proſpect, p. 43.

At length there was a complaint of want of room. Men were accordingly sent to visit Ipswich, with a view to removing there. After much discussion, however, the town was enlarged, and the people remained.

In 1635 Dudley and Bradstreet are found entered among the inhabitants of Ipswich.* As early as Jan. 17, 1632, O.S., fearing some trouble from their French neighbors, among other precautions, it was agreed at a General Court, "that a plantation should be begun at Agawam, (being the best place in the land for tillage and cattle,) least an enemy, finding it void, should possess and take it from us. The governour's son (being one of the assistants) was to undertake this, and to take no more out of the bay than twelve men; the rest to be supplied at the coming of the next ships." † This was done in March, and the little settlement was called Ipswich in August, 1634.‡ The ninth church in the Colony, being the next to that at Cambridge, was gathered there in the same year.§ Mr. Nathaniel Ward was made pastor of the Church, his place being supplied in 1636 by Mr. Nathaniel Rogers.‖ Ipswich was included in the order of the General Court passed September 3d, 1635, that no dwelling-house should be above half a mile from the meeting-house.¶ This precautionary measure, owing to greater danger from the Indians, was followed in the spring of 1636–7 by orders that watches should be kept, that people should travel with

* Felt's History of Ipswich, Essex, and Hamilton, 1834, pp. 10–11.

† Winthrop's New England, Vol. i. pp. 98–9.

‡ Mass. Colony Records, Vol. i. p. 123.

§ Winthrop's New England, Vol. i. p. 94. n. 2.

‖ Johnson's Wonder-working Providence, p. 88.

¶ Mass. Colony Records. Vol i p. 157

arms, and should bring them to the public assemblies. Mr. Daniel Dennison, Mrs. Bradstreet's brother-in-law, was chosen captain for Ipswich.* Mrs. Bradstreet mentions her residing there, but we have no particulars respecting her stay in that town.

On the 4th of March, 1634-5, "It is ordered, that the land aboute Cochichowicke shalbe reserved for an inland plantačon, & that whosoeuer will goe to inhabite there shall haue three yeares im̄unity from all taxes, levyes, publique charges & services whatsoeuer (millitary dissipline onely excepted)," &c., &c.† This is the first mention that we find of what was afterwards the town of Andover. In September, 1638, Mr. Bradstreet, Mr. Dudley, Junior, Captain Dennison, Mr. Woodbridge, and eight others, "are alowed (vpon their petition) to begin a plantation at Merrimack."‡

They do not appear to have left Ipswich immediately, nor do we know the exact year when they went to Andover. It is certain, however, that these and others had already established themselves at Andover before the year 1644,§ in the September of which year two churches were appointed to be gathered,—one at Haverhill, and the other at Andover.‖

Mrs. Bradstreet's son Simon, afterwards minister at New London, Conn., says in his manuscript diary:—

"1640. I was borne in N. England, at Ipſwitch Septem. 28, being Munday 1640.

* Mass. Colony Records, Vol. i. pp. 190-1.

† *Ibid.*, p. 141. ‡ *Ibid.*, p. 237.

§ Abbot's History of Andover. 1829, p. 13.

‖ Winthrop's New England, Vol. ii. p. 194.

"1651. I had my Education in the same Town at the free School, the master of w'ch was my ever respected ffreind Mr. Ezekiell Cheevers. My Father was removed from Ipsw. to Andover, before I was putt to school, so y^t my schooling was more chargeable."

This, though not exact, helps us to fix the time of their removal.

This tract of land was bought of Cutshamache, "Sagamore of ye Massachusets" by John Woodbridge, in behalf of the inhabitants of Cochichewick, "for ye sume of 6£ & a coate;" and in 1646 the town was incorporated by the name of Andover.* The first settlements were made near Cochichewick Brook, the principal part of the town being near the meeting-house, though the houses were too far apart to form much of a village. This is that portion of the town now called North Andover. Not far from the site of the first meeting-house is a large old-fashioned house, the oldest in the town. There is a tradition that this house was built and occupied by Governor Bradstreet, and it is certain that it was the residence of his son, Dudley Bradstreet.† Governor Bradstreet's house was burnt to the ground in July, 1666;‡ and, if the present house was built to supply the place of the old one, Mrs. Bradstreet may have lived in it for a few years, as she did not die until September, 1672, and then in Andover. It has always been believed in the town, that this was the Governor's house; and its size, the solidity of its construction, and its position, certainly tend to strengthen this conclusion. It stands on the old Haverhill and Boston road, within a

* Mass. Colony Records, Vol. ii. p. 159; Abbot's Andover, p. 11.

† Abbot's Andover, pp. 19 and 98. ‡ See page 40.

few feet of the way, and has a southerly aspect. It has two full stories in front, but slopes to a single one in the rear. The rooms on both sides of the front door are high-studded, the floor having been sunk not long since. The doors are small, and very low. The walls of some of the rooms are wainscotted, while others are papered in the modern style. The frame of the house is very heavy, with massive old timbers; and an immense chimney, strongly buttressed on its four sides, runs up in the centre. On the lawn in front of the house are some beautiful elms, one of which is noted for its unusual size.* The ground, falling abruptly from the easterly side of the house into a deep hollow where there is a little brook, rises again into a hill on the slope of which once stood the meeting-house, not a vestige of which is now left. Opposite its site is the old burying-ground, an irregular lot, sparsely covered with ancient moss-grown stones, in all positions straggling, broken, and neglected, and overrun with tall grass and weeds. Some few, including several tombs with horizontal slabs, are more modern and better preserved. The Merrimac is but a mile and a quarter distant, and the Cochichewick is quite near.

The views from the hill-tops in the vicinity are charming, though it is difficult to imagine the appearance the town presented when it was first settled, and there was an unbroken circle of woods in every direction. Now the visitor has to gaze on the smooth sides of the green hills, the country sparsely covered with houses, and the long line of the

* This tree, more than twenty-five years ago, measured sixteen and a half feet in circumference, at one foot above the ground. Abbot's Andover, p. 195. A view of the house is given in the frontispiece.

great mills of Lawrence in the distance, which last, more than any thing else, tell of the wonderful change wrought by two centuries of progress. Dr. Timothy Dwight, who had an opportunity (in 1810) to see this town before it lost so much of its native beauty, gives the following description of it:—

"North Andover is a very beautiful piece of ground. Its surface is elegantly undulating, and its soil in an eminent degree fertile. The meadows are numerous, large, and of the first quality. The groves, charmingly interspersed, are tall and thrifty. The landscape, every where varied, neat, and cheerful, is also; everywhere rich.

"The Parish is a mere collection of plantations, without any thing like a village.

"Upon the whole, Andover is one of the best farming Towns in Eastern Massachusetts." *

Mr. John Woodbridge was ordained pastor of the church at Andover in October, 1645.† He was the husband of Mrs. Bradstreet's sister Mercy. He was born at Stanton, near Highworth, in Wiltshire, about 1613, of which parish his father was minister. He had been some time at Oxford, but was unable to complete the course there, owing to his own and his father's unwillingness that he should take the oath of conformity required of him. About the year 1634, he came to New England, with his uncle, Mr. Thomas Parker, and settled at Newbury.‡ From that place, as we have seen, he moved to Andover. In 1647 he sailed for the old country, probably taking with him

* Travels. New Haven: 1821. Vol. i. p. 401.

† Winthrop's New England, Vol. ii. pp. 252-3.

‡ Mather's Magnalia, Bk. iii. p. 219.

the manuscript poems of our author. These he caused to be published in London in 1650, under the title of "The Tenth Muſe Lately ſprung up in America. Or Severall Poems, compiled with great variety of VVit and Learning, full of delight. . . . By a Gentlewoman in thoſe parts." *

They were introduced to the reader in a short preface in which the author is described as "a VVoman, honoured, and eſteemed where ſhe lives, for her gracious demeanour, her eminent parts, her pious converſation, her courteous diſpoſition, her exact diligence in her place, and diſcreet mannaging of her family occaſions." The poems were said to be "the fruit but of ſome few houres, curtailed from her ſleep, and other refreſhments." He also adds: "I feare the diſpleaſure of no perſon in the publiſhing of theſe Poems but the Authors, without whoſe knowledge, and contrary to her expectation, I have preſumed to bring to publick view what ſhe reſolved ſhould never in ſuch a manner ſee the Sun; but I found that divers had gotten ſome ſcattered papers, affected them wel, were likely to have ſent forth broken pieces to the Authors prejudice, which I thought to prevent, as well as to pleaſure thoſe that earneſtly deſired the view of the whole." †

That Woodbridge was principally concerned in their publication appears yet more fully from a poetical epistle signed "I. W." and addressed "To my deare Siſter the Author of theſe Poems" which follows soon after.‡

Besides this, there are other commendatory verses, in which her poems are praised most extravagantly, by the Rev. N.

* See page 79. † First edition, pp. iii–iv. See pages 83–4.
‡ See page 86.

Ward, who had been one of her neighbors and her minister at Ipswich; by the Rev. Benjamin Woodbridge, and other friends and admirers of hers. There are some anagrams on her name, a poetical dedication by her of the whole to her father,* and a prologue. The first four pieces in the book, "The Foure Elements," "The Foure Humours in Man's Conftitution," "The Four Ages of Man," and "The Four Seafons of the Year," are really four parts of one entire poem. In this the sixteen personified characters —Fire, Earth, Water, Aire, Choler, Blood, Melancholy, Flegme, Childhood, Youth, Middle Age, Old Age, Spring, Summer, Autumne, and Winter—like the embodied abstractions of the old English moral plays, appear upon the stage, where each sets forth successively his various qualities, and boasts of the great power which he exerts for good or evil in the world.† Next comes the poem on "The Four Monarchies of the World," the Assyrian, Persian, Grecian, and Roman, which takes up more than half of the whole volume. To these are added, "A Dialogue between Old-

* The date, March 20, 1642, attached to this Dedication in the second edition, may have led to a mistake as to the time when the first edition was published. Mr. Allibone, in his "Dictionary of Authors," and Mr. Griswold, in his "Female Poets of America," state it to have been in 1640; and in Appleton's "Cyclopædia of Biography" it is given as 1642. Both dates are wrong, the first edition being published in 1650.

† The Percy Society have reprinted, in the twenty-second volume of their "Publications," "one of the earliest moral plays in the English language known to exist," called "The Interlude of the Four Elements." Some of the "dyvers matters whiche be in this Interlude conteynyd," are "Of the sytuacyon of the iiij. elementes, that is to say, the Yerth, the Water, the Ayre, and Fyre, and of their qualytese and propertese, and of the generacyon and corrupcyon of thynges made of the commyxton of them."

But none of the Elements themselves are players, and there is nothing contained in the play similar to what we find in Mrs. Bradstreet's verses.

England and New, Concerning their prefent troubles. Anno 1642;" elegies upon Sir Philip Sidney and Queen Elizabeth; a poem "In honour of *Du Bartas*, 1641;" "*David's* Lamentation for *Saul*, and *Jonathan*," versified from the second book of Samuel; and another, and the last, "*Of the vanity of all worldly creatures.*"

Of the merit of these productions, I will say but little, leaving the reader to judge for himself on this point. I can hardly expect, however, that, after 'twice drinking the nectar of her lines,' he will "welter in delight," like the enthusiastic President Rogers.* Yet I am confident, that, if it is denied that they evince much poetic genius, it must, at least, be acknowledged that they are remarkable, when the time, place, and circumstances under which they were composed, are taken into consideration. They are quaint and curious; they contain many beautiful and original ideas, not badly expressed; and they constitute a singular and valuable relic of the earliest literature of the country. It is important that the reader should bear in mind the peculiarly unpropitious circumstances under which they were written. No genial coterie of gifted minds was near to cheer and inspire her, no circle of wits to sharpen and brighten her faculties; she had no elegant surroundings of rich works of art to encourage and direct her tastes: but the country was a wilderness, and the people among whom she dwelt were the last in the world to stimulate or appreciate a poet.

Notwithstanding her assurance to her father that

"My goods are true (though poor) I love no flealth," †

Mrs. Bradstreet's longer poems appear to be, in many places,

* See pages 93-96. † See page 98, last line.

simply poetical versions of what she had read. Accordingly, her facts and theories are often discordant with what the more accurate and thorough investigation of recent years has made certain or probable. To point out these differences wherever they occur would be at once a difficult and a useless task. Her poems make it evident that she had been a faithful student of history, an assiduous reader, and a keen observer of nature and of what was transpiring both at home and abroad. She mentions many of the principal Greek and Latin authors, such as Hesiod, Homer, Thucydides, Xenophon, and Aristotle, Virgil, Ovid, Quintus Curtius, Pliny, and Seneca; but there is no reason to suppose that she had read their works, either in the originals or in translations. A few scraps of Latin are to be found scattered through her writings; but they are such as any one might have picked up without knowing the language. "The Exact Epitomie of the Four Monarchies," which takes up considerably more than half of the volume of "Poems," was probably derived almost entirely from Sir Walter Raleigh's "History of the World," Archbishop Usher's "Annals of the World," the Hebrew writings, Pemble's "Period of the Persian Monarchie,"* and perhaps from other historical treatises. She frequently

* See page 250, note.

William Pemble, a learned divine, was born in Sussex, or at Egerton, in Kent, in 1591, and died April 14, 1623. One of his works was entitled "THE PERIOD OF THE PERSIAN MONARCHIE, Wherein sundry places of *Ezra*, *Nehemiah*, and *Daniel* are cleered. Extracted, contracted, and englished, (much of it out of Doctor *Raynolds*) by the late learned and godly Man Mr. WILLIAM Pemble, of *Magdalen Hall in* OXFORD." This is doubtless the book which Mrs. Bradstreet had seen. All of his works were separately printed after his death, and then collected in one volume, folio, in 1635, and reprinted four or five times.

refers to Raleigh and Usher; but it was to Raleigh that she was chiefly indebted, and she follows him very closely. A few parallel passages from her "Poems" and from Raleigh's "History of the World" will prove this, and will show, that, when she apparently gives the result of her own researches among the writers of antiquity, she is only quoting them indirectly through the English historians of her own time.

She thus describes the murder of the philosopher Callisthenes by Alexander the Great, in her account of the Grecian Monarchy:—

"The next of worth that ſuffered after theſe,
Was learned, virtuous, wiſe *Caliſthenes*,
VVho lov'd his Maſter more then did the reſt,
As did appear, in flattering him the leaſt;
In his eſteem a God he could not be,
Nor would adore him for a Diety:
For this alone and for no other cauſe,
Againſt his Sovereign, or againſt his Laws,
He on the Rack his Limbs in pieces rent,
Thus was he tortur'd till his life was ſpent.
Of this unkingly act doth *Seneca*
This cenſure paſs, and not unwiſely ſay,
Of *Alexander* this th' eternal crime,
VVhich ſhall not be obliterate by time.
VVhich virtues fame can ne're redeem by far,
Nor all felicity of his in war.
VVhen e're 'tis ſaid he thouſand thouſands ſlew,
Yea, and *Caliſthenes* to death he drew.
The mighty *Perſian* King he overcame,
Yea, and he kill'd *Caliſtthenes* of fame.
All Countryes, Kingdomes, Provinces, he wan
From *Helliſpont*, to th' farthest Ocean.
All this he did, who knows' not to be true?
But yet withal, *Caliſthenes* he ſlew.

From *Macedon*, his Empire did extend
Unto the utmoſt bounds o' th' orient:
All this he did, yea, and much more, 'tis true,
But yet withal, *Caliſthenes* he ſlew." *

This passage, the quotation from Seneca included, is taken directly from Raleigh, whose words are as follows: —

"Alexander stood behind a partition, and heard all that was spoken, waiting but an opportunity to be revenged on Callisthenes, who being a man of free speech, honest, learned, and a lover of the king's honour, was yet soon after tormented to death, not for that he had betrayed the king to others, but because he never would condescend to betray the king to himself, as all his detestable flatterers did. For in a conspiracy against the king, made by one Hermolaus and others, (which they confessed,) he caused Callisthenes, without confession, accusation, or trial, to be torn asunder, upon the rack. This deed, unworthy of a king, Seneca thus censureth: [He gives the Latin, and thus translates it.] 'This is the eternal crime of Alexander, which no virtue nor felicity of his in war shall ever be able to redeem. For as often as any man shall say, He slew many thousand Persians; it shall be replied, He did so, and he slew Callisthenes: when it shall be said, He slew Darius; it shall be replied, And Callisthenes: when it shall be said, He won all as far as to the very ocean, thereon also he adventured with unusual navies, and extended his empire from a corner of Thrace to the utmost bounds of the orient; it shall be said withal, But he killed Callisthenes. Let him have outgone all the ancient examples of captains and kings, none of all his acts makes so much to his glory, as Callisthenes to his reproach.'" †

* See pages 284-5.

† "History of the World." Oxford: 1829. Bk. iv. ch. 2. sec. 19.

Again, speaking of Cyrus, she says : —

"But *Zenophon* reports, he dy'd in's bed,
In honour, peace, and wealth, with a grey head,
And in his Town of *Pasargada* lyes,
Where *Alexander* fought, in hope of prize,
But in this Tombe was only to be found
Two *Sythian* bowes, a sword, and target round;
Where that proud Conquereur could doe no lesse,
Then at his Herse great honours to expresse;"*

using almost the same words as Raleigh : —

"Wherefore I rather believe Xenophon, saying, that Cyrus died aged, and in peace. . . .

"This tomb was opened by Alexander, as Quintus Curtius, l 1. reporteth, either upon hope of treasure supposed to have been buried with him, (or upon desire to honour his dead body with certain ceremonies,) in which there was found an old rotten target, two Scythian bows, and a sword. The coffin wherein the body lay, Alexander caused to be covered with his own garment, and a crown of gold to be set upon it." †

Her account of the quarrel of Alexander and Cleitus, which resulted in the death of the latter, is evidently taken from Raleigh : —

"The next that in untimely death had part,
Was one of more esteem, but lesse desart;
Clitus, belov'd next to *Ephestion*,
And in his cups, his chief Companion;
When both were drunk, *Clitus* was wont to jeere;
Alexander, to rage, to kill, and sweare,
Nothing more pleasing to mad *Clitus* tongue,
Then's Masters god-head, to defie, and wrong;

* First edition, p. 89. See page 211.

† "History of the World," Bk. iii., ch. 3, sec. 6.

Nothing toucht *Alexander* to the quick
Like this, againſt his deity to kick:
Upon a time, when both had drunken well,
Upon this dangerous theam fond *Clitus* fell;
From jeaſt, to earneſt, and at laſt ſo bold,
That of *Parmenio's* death him plainly told.
Alexander now no longer could containe,
But inſtantly commands him to be ſlaine;
Next day, he tore his face, for what he'd done,
And would have ſlaine himſelf, for *Clitus* gone.
This pot companion he did more bemoan,
Then all the wrong to brave *Parmenio* done." *

Raleigh says: —

. . . "we read of Alexander . . . how he slew him [Clytus] soon after, for valuing the virtue of Philip the father before that of Alexander the son, or rather because he objected to the king the death of Parmenio, and derided the oracle of Hammon; for therein he touched him to the quick, the same being delivered in public and at a drunken banquet. Clytus, indeed, had deserved as much at the king's hands as any man living had done, and had in particular saved his life, which the king well remembered when he came to himself, and when it was too late. Yet, to say the truth, Clytus's insolency was intolerable. As he in his cups forgat whom he offended, so the king in his (for neither of them were themselves) forgat whom he went about to slay; for the grief whereof he tore his own face, and sorrowed so inordinately, as, but for the persuasions of Callisthenes, it is thought he would have slain himself." †

In her sketch of Semiramis, we find this: —

"The River *Indus* ‡ ſwept them half away,
The reſt *Staurobates* in fight did ſlay;

* First edition, pp 145–6. See pages 283–4.

† "History of the World," Bk. iv. ch. 2, sec. 19.

‡ See page 186, note *l*.

This was laſt progreſs of this mighty Queen,
Who in her Country never more was ſeen.
The Poets ſeign'd her turn'd into a Dove,
Leaving the world to *Venus* ſoar'd above:
Which made the *Aſſyrians* many a day,
A Dove within their Enſigns to diſplay:" *

Now, Raleigh says:—

"But of what multitude soever the army of Semiramis consisted, the same being broken and overthrown by Staurobates upon the banks of Indus, *canticum cantavit extremum*, she sang her last song; and (as antiquity hath feigned) was changed by the gods into a dove; (the bird of Venus;) whence it came that the Babylonians gave a dove in their ensigns." †

She says of Xerxes:—

"He with his Crown receives a double war,
The *Egyptians* to reduce, and *Greece* to marr,
The firſt begun, and finiſh'd in ſuch haſte,
None write by whom, nor how, 'twas over paſt.
But for the laſt, he made ſuch preparation,
As if to duſt, he meant, to grinde that nation;
Yet all his men, and Inſtruments of ſlaughter,
Produced but deriſion and laughter." ‡

Raleigh has the same in these words:—

"Xerxes received from his father, as hereditary, a double war, one to be made against the Egyptians, which he finished so speedily that there is nothing remaining in writing how the same was performed; the other against the Grecians, of which it is hard to judge whether the preparations were more terrible, or the success, ridiculous." §

* See page 186.

† "History of the World," Bk. i. ch. 12, sec. 4.

‡ See page 223.

§ "History of the World," Bk. iii. ch. 6, sec. 1.

Speaking of the state of things after the death of Alexander the Great, she uses the following very apt illustration, which, however, she found in Raleigh: —

"Great *Alexander* dead, his Armyes left,
Like to that Giant of his Eye bereft;
When of his monftrous bulk it was the guide,
His matchlefs force no creature could abide.
But by *Uliffes* having loft his fight,
All men began ftreight to contemn his might;
For aiming ftill amifs, his dreadful blows
Did harm himfelf, but never reacht his Foes." *

Now, Raleigh: —

"The death of Alexander left his army (as Demades the Athenian then compared it) in such case, as was that monstrous giant Polyphemus, having lost his only eye. For that which is reported in fables of that great Cyclops might well be verified of the Macedonians: their force was intolerable, but for want of good guidance uneffectual, and harmful chiefly to themselves." †

After the publication of the first edition of her "Poems," Mrs. Bradstreet appears to have read Sir Thomas North's translation of Plutarch's Lives, and to have incorporated some of the facts which she thus obtained into the second edition. She does not mention Plutarch in the first edition; while, in the second, she refers to him twice by name. I will give a single instance of the way in which she made these additions. In place of the lines in the first edition, already quoted, —

"*Alexander* now no longer could containe,
But inftantly commands him to be flaine;" —

* See page 289.

† "History of the World," Bk. iv. ch. 3. sec. 1.

are substituted in the second, the following: —

> "Which *Alexanders* wrath incens'd ſo high,
> Nought but his life for this could ſatisfie;
> From one ſtood by he ſnacht a partizan,
> And in a rage him through the body ran." *

These last two lines must have come from Plutarch.

"Then *Alexander* taking a partiſan from one of his guard, as *Clitus* was coming towards him, and had lift vp the hanging before the doore, he ranne him through the body, ſo that *Clitus* fell to the ground, and ſetching one grone, died preſently." †

So, notwithstanding her allusion to Galen and Hippocrates, ‡ it is almost certain that she obtained her wonderfully exact description of human anatomy from the "curious learned Crooke," § whose "Description of the Body of Man" had gone through three editions in London in 1631.

Mrs. Bradstreet's familiarity with the Bible is apparent all through her writings. There are traces of her having used the Genevan Version, which, for many reasons, was more acceptable to the Puritans than the authorized one of King James.

* See pages 283 and 284, note *i*, and page xlvii.

† North's Plutarch. London: 1631. p. 700.

‡ See page 143.

§ See page 144. Probably Helkiah Crooke, M.D., of whose works Watt has the following in his "Bibliotheca Britannica," Vol. i. p. 272, w.: —

"*Μικροκοσμογραφία*, or a Description of the Body of Man. collected and translated out of all the best Authors of Anatomy, especially out of Gaspar, Bauchinus, and A. Sourentius. Lond. 1615, 1618, 1631. fol. A large work, illustrated with the plates of Vesalius and others. — An Explanation of the fashion and use of three and fifty Instruments of Chirurgery. Lond. 1631, fol. The same Lond. 1634, 8vo. Taken chiefly from Parey." [Ambrose Paré, a French surgeon.]

Du Bartas, as translated by Joshua Sylvester, was her favorite author. However distasteful his writings may be to readers of the present day, they were then exceedingly popular, and we are told that Milton not only found pleasure in reading them, but was to some extent indebted to them.* Mrs. Bradstreet, besides her special tribute to his memory, constantly displays her admiration for Du Bartas. This liking was known to her friends; and in her dedication of her "Poems" to her father, she felt it necessary expressly to disclaim having copied from him at all. How much she really owed to him it is hard to tell. The general idea of her longer poems may have been suggested by reading his works, and her style and manner may have been affected in the same way.†

* Craik's English Literature, Vol. i. p. 569, and note 2. Bohn's Bibliographer's Manual. *sub* Du Bartas.

† Guillaume de Saluste du Bartas, born of noble parents near Auch about 1544, and brought up to the profession of war, distinguished himself as a soldier and a negotiator. Holding the same religious views as Henry IV. before he became King of France, and attached to the person of that prince in the capacity of gentleman in ordinary of his bed-chamber, he was successfully employed by him on missions to Denmark, Scotland. and England. He was at the battle of Ivry, and celebrated in song the victory which he had helped to gain. He died four months after, in July, 1590, at the age of forty-six. in consequence of some wounds which had been badly healed. He passed all the leisure which his duties left him at his château du Bartas. It was there that he composed his long and numerous poems: *La Première Semaine*, that is, the Creation in seven days; *L'Uranie*, *Judith*, *Le Triomphe de la Foi*, *Les Neuf Muses*, and *La Seconde Semaine*. The last work is very strangely entitled, as it comprehends a great part of the Old Testament histories. His principal poem, *La Semaine*, went through more than thirty editions in less than six years, and was translated into Latin, Italian, Spanish, English, German, and Dutch. MICHAUD; BIOGRAPHIE UNIVERSELLE, *sub* Bartas.

Sylvester's translation of Du Bartas's works was first published in a

Sir Philip Sidney was also a great favorite with Mrs. Bradstreet, but she was not able to praise his works in such unqualified terms as she does those of Du Bartas. Her criticisms are quite entertaining. She refers to the "Historie of Great Britaine" by Speed, and to Camden's "Annales,"* as if she had read them, and she probably derived some of the facts used in the "Dialogue between Old-England and New" from the former. She was not ignorant of the works of Spenser,† but she does not discuss their merits.

The earliest date attached to any of Mrs. Bradstreet's writings is that of a posthumous poem entitled "Upon a Fit of Sicknefs, *Anno.* 1632. *Ætatis ſuæ*, 19."‡ This was written at a time of great despondency, and certainly does not show the signs of much poetic genius. The elegy upon Sir Philip Sidney bears date 1638; the poem in honor of Du Bartas, 1641; the Dialogue between Old-England and New, 1642; the Dedication of the "Poems" to her father (in the second edition), March 20, 1642; and the poem in honor of Queen Elizabeth, 1643. All the "Poems," in the first edition at least, were thus apparently written by the time she was thirty years old.

Of her mother, who died on the 27th of December, 1643, scarcely any thing is known, not even her maiden

quarto volume in London in 1605, the parts of which it was composed having previously appeared separately. The title of the edition of 1621 was "DU BARTAS. HIS DIUINE WEEKES AND WORKES, with a Compleate Collection of all the other most delightfull Workes. Translated and Written by y[t] famous Philomusus Josvah Sylvester, Gent." Others had also competed with Sylvester in this work.

* See page 358. † See pages 348 and 358.

‡ See page 391.

name. Her homely virtues are thus simply recorded by her daughter: —

"An EPITAPH

On my dear and ever honoured Mother

Mrs. Dorothy Dudley,

who deceafed Decemb. 27. 1643. *and of her age*, 61:

Here lyes,

A Worthy Matron of unfpotted life,
A loving Mother and obedient wife,
A friendly Neighbor, pitiful to poor,
Whom oft fhe fed, and clothed with her ftore;
To Servants wifely aweful, but yet kind,
And as they did, fo they reward did find:
A true Inftructer of her Family,
The which fhe ordered with dexterity.
The publick meetings ever did frequent,
And in her Clofet conftant hours fhe fpent;
Religious in all her words and wayes,
Preparing ftill for death, till end of dayes:
Of all her Children, Children, liv'd to fee,
Then dying, left a bleffed memory." *

After the death of this lady, Governor Dudley married, on the 14th of the following April, Catherine, widow of Samuel Hackburne.† He died on the 31st of July, 1653,

* See page 369.

† Governor Dudley had the following children by his first wife: —

1. Samuel; born in England, in 1610. Married three times, first in 1632 or '33, Mary, daughter of Governor Winthrop. Settled minister at Exeter, N.H., in 1650, where he died in January, 1682, O.S. Had eighteen children.

2. Anne; married Governor Bradstreet.

3. Patience; married Major-General Daniel Denison. Died Feb. 8, 1690, O.S. Had two children.

in the seventy-seventh year of his age.* He moved from Ipswich to Roxbury about the year 1639,† and resided there during the rest of his life. From the time of his arrival in America he had been a magistrate; he had held the offices of Governor, Deputy-Governor, Assistant, and Justice of the Peace; he was in May, 1636, together with Winthrop, chosen Councillor for life; in 1644 he was elected the first Major-General; he had been appointed to hold court in various places, and had received many other tokens of the regard and confidence of the people.‡ He has been charged with bigotry and intolerance, faults which certainly did not distinguish him from most of his contemporaries,

4. Sarah; baptized July 23, 1620, at Sempringham; married Major Benjamin Keayne, of Boston, and was divorced from him in 1647. She afterwards married —— Pacye, and died Nov. 3, 1659.

5. Mercy; born Sept. 27, 1621; married the Rev. John Woodbridge in 1639; and died in July, 1691. Had twelve children.

6. Dorothy; died Feb. 27, 1643.

By his second wife he had, —

1. Deborah; born Feb. 27, 1644-5; died unmarried Nov. 1, 1683.

2. Joseph; born Sept. 23, 1647; married in 1668 Rebecca, daughter of Edward Tyng, and died April 2, 1720. He was Governor of Massachusetts, Lieutenant-Governor of the Isle of Wight, and first Chief-Justice of New York. He had thirteen children, one of whom, Paul, was also a distinguished man; being Attorney-General, and afterwards Chief-Justice of Massachusetts, Fellow of the Royal Society, and founder of the Dudleian Lectures at Harvard College.

3. Paul; born Sept. 8, 1650, married Mary, daughter of Governor John Leverett, and died 1681-82. Had three children.[a]

* See page 365.

† Felt's Ipswich, p. 72.

‡ Massachusetts Colony Records, Vols. I.-III.

[a] "Sutton-Dudleys," p. 97. Dudley Genealogies, p. 18. N. E. Hist. Gen. Register, Vol. i. pp. 71-2; Vol. x. pp. 130-6. Mass. Hist. Soc. Proceedings (1860-62), pp. 93, 95.

either here or in England. If he was stern, blunt, and overbearing, he was at the same time placable, generous, and hospitable. He was a faithful and an able magistrate, and conscientiously discharged all his duties. He had some knowledge of law, and was a shrewd business man, but honest in all his dealings. In short, he presented that varied phase of character that one might expect to find in a man who had had such a rough experience in life. He left fifty or sixty books, principally on history and divinity, some of them in Latin, and forming what was then a large library.* Mather has preserved a Latin epitaph in his "Magnalia," signed "E. R." [Ezekiel Rogers], in which Dudley is described as a

> "*Helluo Librorum, Lectorum Bibliotheca*
> *Communis, Sacrae Syllabus Historiae.*" †

Mrs. Bradstreet, too, calls him "a magazine of history," and acknowledges that he was her "guide" and "instructor," ‡ and that it was to him that she owed her love of books. In some verses to her father, she says: —

> "Moſt truly honoured, and as truly dear,
> If worth in me, or ought I do appear,
> Who can of right better demand the ſame?
> Then may your worthy ſelf from whom it came." §

If we may judge from a reference in her "Dedication," it is probable that he had written a poem "On the Four Parts of the World," ‖ which might even have been printed. But, if it was similar to the oft-quoted verses said to have

* Suffolk Probate Records, Lib. ii. Fol. 133. N. E. Hist. Gen. Register, Vol. xii. pp. 355–6.

† Magnalia, Bk. ii. p. 17.

‡ See pages 365 and 368.

§ See page 398.

‖ See page 97.

been found in his pocket after his death,* we ought not to complain that the poem is among the lost books of the world. Having had £500 left to him when he was very young,† he had always been prosperous, being the wealthiest man in Roxbury, where the people were generally well-to-do. He was the owner of a large quantity of land, and at the time of his death his property was appraised at £1560. 10*s.* 1*d.*,‡ which was a considerable sum in this country at that early date. He interested himself in town affairs, and headed the list of those who entered into an

* These verses are thus given by Mather (MAGNALIA, Bk. ii. p. 17.) In the old manuscript life in "The Sutton Dudleys," p. 37, there is a somewhat different version:—

"*Dim Eyes, Deaf Ears, Cold Stomach, ſhew*
My Diſſolution is in View.
Eleven times Seven near liv'd have I,
And now God calls, I willing Die.
My Shuttle's ſhot, my Race is run,
My Sun is ſet, my Day is done.
My Span is meaſur'd, Tale is told,
My Flower is faded, and grown old.
My Dream is vaniſh'd, Shadow's fled,
My Soul with Chriſt, my Body Dead.
Farewel Dear Wife, Children and Friends,
Hate Hereſie, make Bleſſed Ends.
Bear Poverty, live with good Men;
So ſhall we live with Joy agen.
Let Men of God in Courts and Churches watch
O're ſuch as do a Toleration *hatch,*
Leſt that Ill Egg bring forth a Cockatrice,
To poiſon all with Hereſie and Vice.
If Men be left, and otherwiſe Combine,
My Epitaph's, I Dy'd no Libertine."

† "Sutton-Dudleys," p. 24.

‡ Suffolk Probate Records, Lib. ii. Fol. 134.

agreement in August, 1645, to support a free school in Roxbury.*

Mrs. Bradstreet had eight children, four sons and four daughters; a fact which she has recorded in some fanciful verses, beginning, —

"I had eight birds hatcht in one neſt,
Four Cocks there were, and Hens the reſt,
I nurſt them up with pain and care,
Nor coſt, nor labour did I ſpare,
Till at the laſt they felt their wing,
Mounted the Trees, and learn'd to ſing;"†

She goes on at some length, carrying out the simile, and describes their past life, their condition at that time, and her solicitude for their future health and happiness. Prompted by her love for her children, she wrote out her religious experiences, in a little book in which she also kept a record, partly in prose and partly in verse, of her sicknesses, her religious feelings, and the most important incidents in her life.‡ The earliest date in it is July 8, 1656,§ but it was undoubtedly begun before that.

Having had from her birth a very delicate constitution, prostrated when only sixteen years old by the small-pox, troubled at one time with lameness, subject to frequent attacks of sickness, to fevers, and to fits of fainting, she bore these numerous inflictions with meekness and resignation. Recognizing the inestimable blessing of health, she regarded it as the reward of virtue, and looked upon

* History of Roxbury Town, by Charles M. Ellis. Boston: 1847, p. 37. Mr. Ellis has given the best sketch of Dudley's life which I have seen (pp. 97–104).

† See page 400. ‡ See pages 2–39. § See page 17.

her various maladies as tokens of the divine displeasure at her thoughtlessness or wrong-doing. She says that her religious belief was at times shaken; but her doubts and fears were soon banished, if, indeed, they were not exaggerated in number and importance by her tender conscience. Her children were constantly in her mind. It was for them that she committed to writing her own religious experiences, her own feelings of joy or sorrow at the various changes which brightened or darkened her life. Her most pointed similes are drawn from the familiar incidents of domestic life, especially the bringing-up of children. From some of these references it would seem as if she had found among her own children the most diverse traits of character; that some of them were obedient and easily governed, while others were unruly and headstrong; and that she derived an intense satisfaction from contemplating the virtues of some, while she deplored the failings of others. Notwithstanding the comfort she took in her children, notwithstanding the happiness of her married life, she continually dwells on the vanity of all worldly delights, the shortness of life, and the great ills to which humanity is subject. She found, however, a never-failing solace for all her troubles in prayer. "I have had," she writes, "great experience of God's hearing my Prayers, and returning comfortable Anſwers to me, either in granting y[e] Thing I prayed for, or elſe," she adds, with a charming frankness, "in ſatiſſying my mind without it." *

In November, 1657, her son Samuel, her eldest child, sailed for England.† He graduated at Harvard College

* See page 7. † See page 24.

in the year 1653, but his age is not known, though at that time he could not have been more than twenty. Mrs. Bradstreet says, "It pleafed God to keep me a long time without a child, which was a great grief to me, and coft mee many prayers and tears before I obtaind one."* Samuel was,—

> "The Son of Prayers, of vowes, of teares,
> The child I ftay'd for many yeares." †

and she was very loth to part with him, but she committed him at last to the care of Providence, and was rewarded by welcoming him home safe, in July, 1661.‡

Her husband's mission to England in January, 1661–2, must have been an event of great importance in her life. Devotedly attached to him as she was, and unhappy when separated from him for even a short time, the circumstances under which he went were such as to make her particularly anxious during his absence. The news of the restoration of Charles II. to the throne had been somewhat coldly received by the Massachusetts colonists. They were justly apprehensive that their indifference, if not actual hostility, to his cause during the Civil War, their severe treatment of the Quakers, and their assumption of the powers of an independent state, might now be brought up against them, and result in a serious diminution of the privileges they had up to that time enjoyed. The complaints of the Quakers, and the exertions of those who had suffered by or who were disaffected with the Massachusetts men, were so violent, and met with such success, that the latter were obliged, by the order of the King, to send agents to plead

* See page 5. † See page 24. ‡ See page 28.

their cause and repel these attacks at Court. The unwillingness of the Government to send these Commissioners was only equalled by the distaste of those upon whom their choice had fallen — Mr. Bradstreet and the Rev. Mr. Norton — for this delicate and unpleasant duty. Mr. Norton was particularly disinclined to have any thing to do with the matter, but his scruples were finally overcome. Having recovered from a severe attack of sickness, whose sudden approach delayed their departure, Norton embarked with Bradstreet on the 10th of February. On the following morning they set sail for England, John Hull, the mint-master of the Colony, being a fellow-passenger with them. They arrived in London the last of March, and were successful in their endeavors, — to divert the anger of the king, to put a favorable construction on the past acts of the Colony, and to secure for it an extension of the royal favor. On the 3d of September, they returned in the ship "Society," bringing with them a letter from the King, in which the charter-privileges were confirmed, and all past errors pardoned. The satisfaction which this gave was more than counterbalanced by the rest of the letter, which enjoined a fuller establishment of the King's authority, and contained other matter equally distasteful to the people. The consequence was, that the two agents became extremely unpopular, and this cold treatment was thought to have hastened the death of Norton, who grew very melancholy, and died on the 5th of the following April. While they were in England, fears were entertained for their safety, and reports came in private letters that they had been detained, and that Mr. Norton was in the Tower. And, according to Sewel, the Quaker historian, who gives no very flattering account of their conduct in London, they were really in some danger.*

Mrs. Bradstreet had from time to time been writing under the name of "Meditations" some apothegms, suggested mainly by the homely events of her own experience. This was done at the request of her son Simon, to whom they were dedicated March 20, 1664.† The "Meditations" display much more ability, much greater cultivation of mind, and a deeper thoughtfulness than most of her other works. She shows in them a more correct taste than in her "Poems." We must take her word for their originality. "I have avoyded," she says, "incroaching upon others conceptions becaufe I would leave you nothing but myne owne, though in value they fall fhort of all in this kinde." And again she reminds him that "There is no new thing vnder ye fun, there is nothing that can be fayd or done, but either that or fomething like it hath been both done and fayd before." ‡

In July, 1666, by the burning of the house at Andover, her papers, books, and many other things of great value to her, were destroyed. She had intended to complete her poetical account of "The Roman Monarchy," and had spent much time in preparing a continuation of it, but the loss of what she had already finished made her abandon the work altogether. § Her son Simon thus notices this disaster in his diary, and represents his father's loss as very great: —

"July. 12. 1666. Whilft I was at N. London my fathers houfe at Andover was burnt, where I loft my Books, and many of my

* See pages 32-9. Hutchinson's History, Vol. i. pp. 201-5; Hull's Diaries, Arch. Amer., Vol. iii. pp. 153-4, and 204-8; History of the Quakers, by William Sewel. London: 1725, pp. 279-80.

† See page 47. ‡ See page 53. § See pages 40 and 329.

clothes, to the valeiu of 50 or 60 lb at leaſt; The Lord gaue, and the Lord hath taken, bleſſed bee the Name of the Lord. Tho: my own loſſe of books (and papers eſpec.) was great and my fathers far more being about 800, yet yᵉ Lord was pleaſed gratiouſly many wayes to make up yᵉ ſame to us. It is therefore good to truſt in the Lord."

There could have been little of variety to call Mrs. Bradstreet aside from the daily routine of her quiet country life. Attendance on the frequent and long-protracted religious meetings, and the duties of her household, must have occupied her time when she was well. She had evidently exposed herself to the criticism of her neighbors by studying and writing so much. The fact of a woman's being able to compose any thing possessing any literary merit was regarded with the greatest surprise by her contemporaries, and was particularly dwelt upon by her admirers.* In the "Prologue" she says: —

"I am obnoxious to each carping tongue
Who ſays my hand a needle better fits,
A Poets pen all ſcorn I ſhould thus wrong,
For ſuch deſpite they caſt on Female wits:
If what I do prove well, it won't advance,
They'l ſay it's ſtoln, or elſe it was by chance." †

* See pages 83–92. There is a paragraph in Mr. and Mrs. S. C. Hall's sketch of Miss Hannah More (probably written by *Mrs.* Hall) which shows that public opinion changed quite slowly on this point.

"In this age, when female talent is so rife, — when, indeed, it is not too much to say women have fully sustained their right to equality with men in reference to all the productions of the mind, — it is difficult to comprehend the popularity, almost amounting to adoration, with which a woman writer was regarded little more than half a century ago. Mediocrity was magnified into genius, and to have printed a book, or to have written even a tolerable poem, was a passport into the very highest society." "Art Journal." London: 1866. p. 187.

† See page 101.

The forests were still stocked with wild beasts, and there was constant fear of assaults and depredations by the Indians. She wandered in the woods, however, and found great pleasure in meditating on their ever winning charms, their grand and quiet beauty. By far the best of all her "Poems" was the result of one of these rambles. It appeared for the first time in the second edition, under the name of "Contemplations." * She describes with great spirit the sights and sounds of the forest, the fields and the stream, and makes us wish that she had done more in this style, for which many of the poets of her time were distinguished. It was doubtless by the side of the untamed Merrimac, before its rushing waters were made to pour through the immense structures which now line its banks, that she sat and pondered. The great dam which now spans the river at Lawrence is only two miles from the spot where the first settlement of Andover was made, and where Mrs. Bradstreet lived when she wrote, —

> "Under the cooling ſhadow of a ſtately Elm
> Cloſe ſate I by a goodly Rivers ſide,
> Where gliding ſtreams the Rocks did overwhelm;
> A lonely place, with pleaſures dignifi'd." †

This "Poem" proves that she had true poetic feeling, and shows to what she could rise when she was willing to throw aside her musty folios and read the fresh book of nature.

> "And Wisdom's self
> Oft seeks to sweet retired solitude,
> Where, with her best nurse Contemplation,
> She plumes her feathers, and lets grow her wings,
> That in the various bustle of resort,
> Were all-to ruffled, and sometimes impair'd." ‡

* See page 370. † See page 377. ‡ Milton's Comus, 375-80.

The revision of her "Poems" must have been no small undertaking, and from some of the references in the many additions which she made, it is evident that she was engaged upon this work as late at least as 1666. Sympathizing, as she naturally did, with Parliament and the Puritans, she said much in the first edition, written at the outbreak of the Civil War, which she felt obliged to omit or modify to suit the state of things existing under the Restoration. Although she speaks of a "*Brittish* bruitish Cavaleer," and dignifies him with the titles of "wretch" and "monster," yet she has to come down to calling Cromwell a "Usurper." Indeed, these alterations form one of the most diverting features of the book. It must be confessed, however, that she rather inclined from the first to be a Monarchist, and that her hatred of Papists admitted of not the slightest compromise.

She had never set a very great value on the pleasures of this world, and had always been ready to abandon them for the joys which she expected to find in another. In the last piece which we have in her writing, dated Aug. 31, 1669,* she represents herself as positively weary of life and longing to die. Three years after, her wish was granted, and she was released from suffering. Her son Simon's sad account of her sickness and death proves that it must have been in reality a blessing to her: —

"September 16. 1672. My ever honoured & most dear Mother was translated to Heaven. Her death was occasioned by a consumption being wasted to skin & bone & She had an issue made in her arm bec: she was much troubled with rheum, & one of y[e] women y[t] tended herr dressing her arm, s'd shee never saw

* See pages 42-4.

such an arm in her Life, I, ſ'd my most dear Mother, but y^t arm ſhall bee a Glorious Arm.

I being abſent fro her lost the opportunity of comitting to memory her pious & memorable xpreſsions vttered in her ſickneſſe. O y^t the good Lord would give vnto me and mine a heart to walk in her steps, cōnſidering what the end of her Converſation was, y^t ſo wee might one day haue a happy & glorious greeting."

Mrs. Bradstreet's burial-place is unknown. No stone bearing her name can be found in the old graveyard at Andover, and it is not at all improbable that her remains were deposited in her father's tomb at Roxbury. As no portrait of her is in existence, the reader will have to contemplate her image in her works, where she will reveal to him all the graces of a loving mother, a devoted wife, and a devout Christian.

Three years after her death, Edward Phillips, the nephew of Milton, has this brief notice of her in his "Theatrum Poetarum:"—

"*Anne Bradstreet*, a *New-England* poetess, no less in title; viz. before her *Poems, printed in Old-England anno* 1650; then [than] *The tenth Muse sprung up in America;* the memory of which poems, consisting chiefly of Descriptions of the *Four Elements*, the *Four Humours;* the *Four Ages*, the *Four Seasons*, and the *Four Monarchies*, is not yet wholly extinct." *

Quite different from this is the pompous eulogy of Cotton Mather:—

"But when I mention the *Poetry* of this Gentleman [Gov. Dudley] as one of his Accompliſhments, I muſt not leave unmen-

* First published in London in 1675. Third Edition. Reprinted by Sir Egerton Brydges, Bart. etc. Geneva: 1824. p. (48). § 108.

tioned the Fame with which the *Poems* of one defcended from him have been Celebrated in both *Englands.* If the rare Learning of a *Daughter*, was not the leaft of thofe bright things that adorn'd no lefs a Judge of *England* than Sir *Thomas More*; it must now be said, that a Judge of *New England*, namely, *Thomas Dudley*, Esq; had a *Daughter* (befides other Children) to be a *Crown* unto him. Reader, *America* juftly admires the Learned Women of the other *Hemifphere.* She has heard of thofe that were *Tutoreffes* to the Old Profeffors of all Philofophy: She hath heard of *Hippatia*, who formerly taught the Liberal Arts; and of *Sarocchia*, who more lately was very often the Moderatrix in the Difputations of the Learned Men of *Rome*: She has been told of the Three *Corinnæ's*, which equall'd, if not excell'd, the moft Celebrated *Poets* of their Time. She has been told of the Emprefs *Eudocia*, who Compofed Poetical Paraphrafes on Divers Parts of the Bible; and of *Rofuida*, who wrote the *Lives* of Holy Men; and of Pamphilia, who wrote other Hiftories unto the Life: The Writings of the most Renowned *Anna Maria Schurnian*, have come over unto her. But fhe now prays, that into fuch Catalogues of *Authoreffes*, as *Beverovicius*, *Hottinger*, and *Voetius*, have given unto the World, there may be a room now given unto Madam **Ann Bradftreet**, the Daughter of our Governour *Dudley*, and the Confort of our Governour Bradftreet, whofe *Poems*, divers times Printed, have afforded a grateful Entertainment unto the Ingenious, and a Monument for her Memory beyond the Stateliest *Marbles*." *

Six years after her death, in 1678, the second edition of her "Poems" was brought out in Boston,† being one of the earliest volumes of poems printed in America. It was the work of John Foster, who had set up a press in

* Magnalia, Bk. ii. p. 17.

† See pages v, vii–viii, 81 *et seq.*

Boston in 1675 or '76, and who issued the first book ever printed in that town.*

Of Mrs. Bradstreet's eight children,† all but one, Dorothy,

* Thomas's History of Printing, Vol. i. p. 275; History of Dorchester, Mass., pp. 244 and 493.

† They were, —

1. Samuel; graduated at Harvard College in 1653. He went to England in November, 1657, and returned in July, 1661. He was a fellow of Harvard College, and represented Andover in the General Court in 1670. He practised as a physician in Boston for many years, but afterwards removed to the island of Jamaica, where he died in August, 1682. He was twice married; first to Mercy, daughter of William Tyng, by whom he had five children, only one of whom survived him. He had three children, who were living with their grandfather, Governor Bradstreet, at the time of the latter's death, by a second wife, whose name is unknown. N. E. Hist. Gen. Register, Vol. viii. pp. 312-14; Vol. ix. pp. 113-4; Governor Bradstreet's will, Suffolk Probate Records, Lib. xi. Fol. 276.

2. Dorothy; married the Rev. Seaborn Cotton, eldest son of the Rev. John Cotton, of Boston, June 25, 1654. She had nine children, and died Feb. 26, 1672. Her husband was ordained pastor of the church at Hampton, N.H., May 4, 1659, and died April 19, 1686, at the age of fifty-two, having survived her and married again. N. E. Hist. Gen. Register, Vol. i. pp. 325-6; Vol. viii. p. 321; Vol. ix. p. 114; Hull's Diaries, pp. 187-8.

3. Sarah; married Richard Hubbard, of Ipswich, brother of the Rev. William Hubbard, the historian. She had five children by him. He died May 3, 1681, and she afterwards married Major Samuel Ward, of Marblehead. N. E. Hist. Gen. Register, Vol. viii. p. 323; Felt's Ipswich, p. 164; Essex Institute Collections, Vol. iii. p. 66; Vol. iv. pp. 66, 71; Vol. v. pp. 92-3.

4. Simon; was born at Ipswich, Sept. 28, 1640, and graduated at Harvard College in 1660. He went to New London, Connecticut, to preach in May, 1666, and was ordained pastor of the church there Oct. 5, 1670. He was married Oct. 2, 1667, at Newbury, by his uncle, Major-General Daniel Denison, to his cousin Lucy, daughter of the Rev. John Woodbridge. They had five children. He died in the fall of 1683. His own MS. Diary; Caulkins's History of New London, *passim*; N. E. Hist. Gen. Register, Vol. viii. pp. 316-17, and 378; Vol. ix. pp. 117-18.

5. Hannah; married Andrew Wiggin, of Exeter, N.H., June 14, 1659,

were living at the time of her death. Her descendants have been very numerous, and many of them have more than made up by the excellence of their writings for whatever beauty or spirit hers may have lacked. Her grandson, the Rev. Simon Bradstreet, of Charlestown, son of the Rev. Simon of New London, Conn., although very eccentric, was one of the most learned men of his

and died in 1707. She had five sons and five daughters. N. E. Hist. Gen. Register, Vol. viii. pp. 167 and 324; Vol. ix. p. 143.

6. Mercy: married Major Nathaniel Wade, of Medford, Oct. 31, 1672. She died Oct. 5, 1715, in her sixty-eighth year. She had eight children. N. E. Gen. Hist. Register, Vol. iii. p. 66; Vol. viii. p. 324; Vol. ix. p. 121; Brooks's History of Medford, p. 558; Essex Institute Collections, Vol. iv. pp. 68–69; Felt's Ipswich. p. 153.

7. Dudley; was born in 1648, and married Ann Wood, widow of Theodore Price, Nov. 12, 1673. He resided in Andover, which town he represented in the General Court, besides holding many municipal offices in its gift. He was one of the Council of Safety between 1689 and 1692, was a colonel in the militia, and for many years a magistrate. During the witchcraft delusion in 1692, he granted thirty or forty warrants for the apprehension and imprisonment of the supposed witches; but, refusing afterwards to grant any more, he himself fell a victim to the same charge, and was obliged for a time to secrete himself. At the time of the attack of the Indians on Andover in 1698, he and his family were made prisoners, but immediately afterwards released. He died Nov. 13, 1702, having won the respect and confidence of his fellow-townsmen. He had three children. Abbot's Andover, pp. 18–19, 133, 154 *et seq.*; N. E. Hist. Gen. Register, Vol. iii. p. 66; Vol. viii. p. 320; Savage's Genealogical Dictionary, Vol. i. p. 235: Butler's History of Groton, pp. 165–70.

8. John; was born in Andover, July 22, 1652, and resided in Topsfield. He married Sarah, daughter of the Rev. William Perkins of that town, June 11, 1677. He died at Topsfield, Jan. 11, 1718. He had five children, and perhaps more. N. E. Hist. Gen. Register, Vol. viii. pp. 320–21; Vol. ix. p. 120; "Sutton-Dudleys," p. 101.

In her poem "*In reference to her Children*" (p. 401), Mrs. Bradstreet speaks of her *fifth* child as being a son. This must be a misprint for *seventh*, as a comparison of the above dates will show.

day.* Among her descendants may be counted the celebrated divine, Dr. Wm. E. Channing; the Rev. Joseph Buckminster, of Portsmouth, N.H., his accomplished son, the Rev. J. S. Buckminster, and his daughter, Mrs. Eliza B. Lee, who has so gracefully recorded her father's and her brother's lives; Mr. Richard H. Dana, the poet, and his son, the Hon. R. H. Dana, Jr., eminent as a man of letters, a lawyer, and a jurist; Dr. Oliver Wendell Holmes, the poet and humorist; Mr. Wendell Phillips, the orator; and Mrs. Eliza G. Thornton, of Saco, Maine, whose verses were once highly esteemed.†

After Mrs. Bradstreet's death, her husband married, June 6, 1676, the widow of Captain Joseph Gardner, of Salem, who was killed in the storming of the Narragansett fort in December, 1675. She was a daughter of Emanuel Downing, and sister of Sir George Downing, Bart., who graduated in the first class of Harvard College, and became afterwards Ambassador from Cromwell and Charles II. successively at the Hague. She was born in London, but came to New England when very young. Her step-son Simon describes her as "a Gentl. of very good birth & education, and of great piety & prudence."‡

* Budington. pp. 111–16 and 125; Sprague's Annals. Vol. i. pp. 241–43; Mass. Hist. Coll. Vol. viii. p. 75; Vol. x. p. 170: Caulkins's New London. p. 193.

† See the "Pedigree of Bradstreet." in Drake's folio History of Boston, and the "Descendants of Governor Bradstreet," in N. E. Hist. Gen. Register, Vol. viii. pp. 312–25, and Vol. ix. pp. 113–21. A book was published in London in 1858, with the title of "Six Legends of King Golden-Star, a poem by Anna Bradstreet." Whether this lady is a descendant or not I cannot say.

‡ MS. Diary.

She died at Salem, April 19, 1713, leaving no children by either husband. N. E. Hist. Gen. Register. Vol. xii. p. 219. Her will, with notes, is printed in the Essex Institute Collections. Vol. iv. pp. 185–90.

Upon the death of Mr. Symonds, in October, 1678, Mr. Bradstreet succeeded him as Deputy-Governor, and the Governor himself, John Leverett, dying in the following March, he was elected Governor in May, 1679, being then about seventy-six years of age.* He continued to be Governor until the dissolution of the Charter and the establishment of the Provisional Government in May, 1686, under his brother-in-law, Joseph Dudley, as President.† Governor Bradstreet and his son, Dudley Bradstreet, were named as Counsellors in the royal commission, but they both refused to act.‡ On the 20th of December of that year, Sir Edmund Andros landed in Boston, and on the same day his commission was read as "Governor in Chief in and over the territory and dominion of New England."§ After a little more than two years of oppression under his administration, on the receipt of the news of the landing of the Prince of Orange in England, there was a rising in Boston in April, 1689. On the morning of the 18th, the Royal Governor and his adherents were made prisoners, and the officers who had been elected under the charter in 1686, with the venerable Bradstreet at their head, were called upon to act as a "Council of Safety." On the assembling of the representatives of the towns a month later, he was confirmed in his position, and acted as Governor under the temporary re-establishment of the old charter government until the 14th of May, 1692. On that day Sir William Phipps arrived in Boston with the new charter and a commission as Governor of the Province of the Massachusetts

* Mass. Colony Records, Vol. v. pp. 209-10; Hutchinson's History, Vol. i. p. 291.

† Hutchinson's History, Vol. i. pp. 306-8.

‡ *Ibid.*, p. 314. note.

§ *Ibid.*, p. 316.

Bay. Thereupon Governor Bradstreet, whose name was the first on the list of Counsellors appointed by the New Charter, resigned his office to him.*

He died at Salem, March 27, 1697, at the age of ninety-four, thus closing a long, exemplary, and honorable life, sixty years of which had been devoted to constant and faithful public service.†

* Hutchinson's History, Vol. i. pp. 332-45; Vol. ii. pp. 19, 20; Palfrey's History of New England. Vol. iii. pp. 574-98; Ancient Charters, p. 27.

† He was buried in Salem, where his tomb is still to be seen in the old Charter Street burying-ground. The inscription on the horizontal slab which covers it is now totally obliterated. His epitaph, however, was preserved by some antiquary in the following communication to "The Boston Chronicle" for March 7-14, 1768 (p. 119): —

"By giving the inclofed a place in your Chronicle, it being now fcarce legible on the monument, you'll oblige a number of your friends, who think it worth preferving.

Infcription upon Governor BRADSTREET'S *Tomb Stone, in Salem.*

"SIMON BRADSTREET. Armiger ex Ordine Senatorio in Colonia Maffachufettenfi ab Anno 1630 ufq; ad Annum 1673 Deinde ad Annum 1679 Vice Gubernator Deniq; ad Annum 1686 ejufdem Coloniæ Communi & Conftanti Populi Suffragio Gubernator Vir Judicis Lynceato præditus Quem nec Minæ nec Honos allexit Regis Authoritatem & Populi Libertatem æqua Lance libravit Religione Cordatus Via innocuus Mundum et vicit et deferuit Die XXVII. Marcij Anno Dom: MDCXCVII Annoq; R. R's Gullielmi tertii IX. et Ætatis fuæ XCIV."

Mr. Robert Peele, of Salem, has a copy of this paper, with this marginal note in the handwriting of the old loyalist, Sam. Curwen, whose Journal and Letters were so ably edited by the late Mr. Geo. A. Ward: —

"Ben son of Col B. Pickman sold ye tomb, being claimed by him for a small expence his father was at in repairing it abt ye yr 1793 or 1794 to one Daniel Hathorne who now holds it."

I am told that the tomb was accordingly cleaned out, and the remains of the honored Governor and his family thrown into a hole not far off.

CONTENTS.

Religious Experiences and Occasional Pieces.

Meditations, Divine and Moral.

Poems.

Posthumous Poems.

RELIGIOUS EXPERIENCES

AND

OCCASIONAL PIECES.

All that is included under the title "Religious Experiences and Occasional Pieces," with the exception of the verses beginning "As weary pilgrim now at reſt," is printed from a manuscript copy in the handwriting of Mrs. Bradstreet's son, the Rev. Simon Bradstreet, of New London, Connecticut. The following note is prefixed by him: "A true copy of a Book left by my hon'd & dear mother to her children & found among ſome papers after her Death."

To my Dear Children.

THIS Book by Any yet vnread,
I leaue for yov when I am dead,
That, being gone, here yov may find
What was your liueing mother's mind.
Make vſe of what I leaue in Loue
And God ſhall bleſſe yov from above.

A. B.

MY DEAR CHILDREN, —

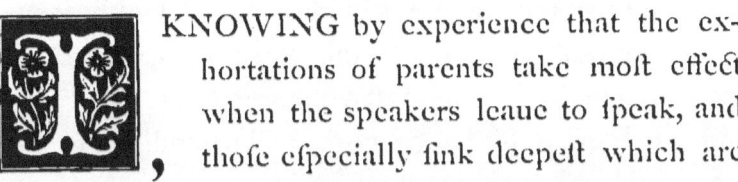

I, KNOWING by experience that the exhortations of parents take moſt effect when the ſpeakers leaue to ſpeak, and thoſe eſpecially ſink deepeſt which are ſpoke lateſt — and being ignorant whether on my death bed I ſhall haue opportvnity to ſpeak to any of yov, much leſſe to All — thought it the beſt, whilſt I was able to compoſe ſome ſhort matters, (for what elſe to call them I know not) and bequeath to yov, that when I am no more with yov, yet I may bee dayly in your remembrance, (Although that is the leaſt in my aim in what I now doe) but that yov may gain ſome ſpiritual Advantage by my experience. I haue not ſtudyed in this yov read to ſhow my ſkill, but to declare the Truth—not to ſett forth myſelf, but the Glory of God. If I had minded the former, it had been perhaps better pleaſing to yov,—but ſeing the laſt is the beſt, let it bee beſt pleaſing to yov.

The method I will obſerve ſhall bee this—I will begin with God's dealing with me from my childhood to this Day. In my yovng years, about 6 or 7 as I take it, I began to make conſcience of my wayes, and what I knew was ſinfull, as lying, diſobedience to Parents, &c. I avoided it. If at any time I was overtaken with the like evills, it was a great Trouble. I could not be at reſt 'till by prayer I had confeſt it vnto God. I was alſo troubled at the neglect of Private Dutyes, tho: too often tardy that way. I alſo fovnd much comfort in reading the Scriptures, eſpecially thoſe places I thought moſt concerned my Condition, and as I grew to haue more vnderſtanding, ſo the more ſolace I took in them.

In a long fitt of ſicknes which I had on my bed I often commvned with my heart, and made my ſupplication to the moſt High who ſett me free from that affliction.

But as I grew vp to bee about 14 or 15 I fovnd my heart more carnall, and ſitting looſe from God, vanity and the follyes of youth take hold of me.

About 16, the Lord layd his hand sore vpon me and smott mee with the small pox. When I was in my affliction, I besovght the Lord, and confessed my Pride and Vanity and he was entreated of me, and again restored me. But I rendered not to him according to the benefitt received.

After a short time I changed my condition and was marryed, and came into this Covntry, where I fovnd a new world and new manners, at which my heart rose. But after I was convinced it was the way of God, I submitted to it and joined to the church at Boston.*

After some time I fell into a lingering sicknes like a consvmption, together with a lamenesse, which correction I saw the Lord sent to humble and try me and doe mee Good: and it was not altogether ineffectuall.

It pleased God to keep me a long time without a child, which was a great greif to me, and cost mee many prayers and tears before I obtaind one, and after him † gave mee many more, of whom I now take the care, that as I have brovght yov into the world, and with great paines, weaknes, cares, and feares brovght yov to this, I now travail in birth again of yov till Christ bee formed in yov.

Among all my experiences of God's gratious Dealings with me I haue constantly observed this, that he hath never suffered me long to sitt loose from him,

* See Introduction. † See page 24.

but by one affliction or other hath made me look home, and ſearch what was amiſſe — ſo vſually thvs it hath been with me that I haue no ſooner felt my heart out of order, but I haue expected correction for it, which moſt commonly hath been vpon my own perſon, in ſickneſſe, weaknes, paines, ſometimes on my ſoul, in Doubts and feares of God's diſpleaſure, and my ſincerity towards him, ſometimes he hath ſmott a child with ſicknes, ſometimes chaſtened by loſſes in eſtate, — and theſe Times (thro: his great mercy) haue been the times of my greateſt Getting and Advantage, yea I haue fovnd them the Times when the Lord hath manifeſted the moſt Love to me. Then haue I gone to ſearching, and haue ſaid with David, Lord ſearch me and try me, ſee what wayes of wickednes are in me, and lead me in the way everlaſting: and ſeldome or never but I haue fovnd either ſome ſin I lay vnder which God would haue reformed, or ſome duty neglected which he would haue performed. And by his help I haue layd Vowes and Bonds vpon my Soul to perform his righteous commands.

If at any time yov are chaſtened of God, take it as thankfully and Joyfully as in greateſt mercyes, for if yee bee his yee ſhall reap the greateſt benefitt by it. It hath been no ſmall ſupport to me in times of Darknes when the Almighty hath hid his face from me, that yet I haue had abundance of ſweetnes and refreſhment after affliction, and more circumſpection in my walking after I haue been afflicted. I haue been with God like an vntoward child, that no longer then the rod has been on my back (or at leaſt in ſight) but I haue been apt to forgett him and myſelf too. Before I was afflicted I went aſtray, but now I keep thy ſtatutes.

I haue had great experience of God's hearing my Prayers, and returning comfortable Anſwers to me, either in granting the Thing I prayed for, or elſe in ſatiſfying my mind without it; and I haue been confident it hath been from him, becavſe I have fovnd my heart through his goodnes enlarged in Thankfullnes to him.

I haue often been perplexed that I haue not found that conſtant Joy in my Pilgrimage and refreſhing which I ſuppoſed moſt of the ſervants of God haue; althovgh he hath not left me altogether without the wittnes of his holy ſpirit, who hath oft given mee his word and ſett to his Seal that it ſhall bee well with me. I haue ſomtimes taſted of that hidden Manna that the world knowes not, and haue ſett vp my Ebenezer, and haue reſolved with myſelf that againſt ſvch a promis, ſvch taſts of ſweetnes, the Gates of Hell ſhall never prevail. Yet haue I many Times ſinkings and droopings, and not enjoyed that felicity that ſomtimes I haue done. But when I haue been in darknes and ſeen no light, yet haue I deſired to ſtay my ſelf upon the Lord.

And, when I haue been in ſicknes and pain, I haue

thovght if the Lord would but lift vp the light of his Covntenance vpon me, altho: he grovnd me to powder, it would bee but light to me; yea, oft haue I thovght were it hell itself, and could there find the Love of God toward me, it would bee a Heaven. And, could I haue been in Heaven without the Love of God, it would haue been a Hell to me; for, in Truth, it is the absence and presence of God that makes Heaven or Hell.

Many times hath Satan troubled me concerning the verity of the scriptures, many times by Atheisme how I could know whether there was a God; I never saw any miracles to confirm me, and those which I read of how did I know but they were feigned. That there is a God my Reason would soon tell me by the wondrous workes that I see, the vast frame of the Heaven and the Earth, the order of all things, night and day, Summer and Winter, Spring and Autvmne, the dayly providing for this great hovshold vpon the Earth, the preserving and directing of All to its proper end. The consideration of these things would with amazement certainly resolve me that there is an Eternall Being.

But how should I know he is such a God as I worship in Trinity, and such a Saviour as I rely upon? tho: this hath thovsands of Times been svggested to mee, yet God hath helped me over. I haue argved thvs with myself. That there is a God I see. If ever this God hath revealed himself, it mvst bee in his word, and this mvſt bee it or none. Haue I not ſovnd that operation by it that no humane Invention can work vpon the Soul? hath not Judgments befallen Diverſe who haue ſcorned and contemd it? hath it not been preſerved thro: All Ages maugre all the heathen Tyrants and all of the enemyes who haue oppoſed it? Is there any ſtory but that which ſhowes the beginnings of Times, and how the world came to bee as wee ſee? Doe wee not know the propheceyes in it fullfilled which could not haue been ſo long foretold by any but God himſelf?

When I haue gott over this Block, then haue I another pvtt in my way, That admitt this bee the trve God whom wee worſhip, and that bee his word, yet why may not the Popiſh Religion bee the right? They haue the ſame God, the ſame Chriſt, the ſame word: they only enterprett it one way, wee another.

This hath ſomtimes ſtuck with me, and more it would, but the vain fooleries that are in their Religion, together with their lying miracles and cruell perſecutions of the Saints, which admitt were they as they terme them, yet not ſo to bee dealt withall.

The conſideration of theſe things and many the like would ſoon turn me to my own Religion again.

But ſome new Troubles I haue had ſince the world has been filled with Blaſphemy, and Sectaries, and ſome who haue been accounted ſincere Chriſtians haue been carryed away with them, that ſomtimes I haue ſaid,

Is there ffaith vpon the earth? and I haue not known what to think. But then I haue remembred the words of Christ that so it must bee, and that, if it were possible, the very elect should bee deceived. Behold, saith our Saviour, I have told yov before. That hath stayed my heart, and I can now say, Return, O my Soul, to thy Rest, vpon this Rock Christ Jesus will I build my faith; and, if I perish, I perish. But I know all the Powers of Hell shall neuer prevail against it. I know whom I haue trvsted, and whom I haue beleived, and that he is able to keep that I haue committed to his charge.

Now to the King, Immortall, Eternall, and invisible, the only wise God, bee Honoure and Glory for ever and ever! Amen.

This was written in mvch sicknesse and weaknes, and is very weakly and imperfectly done; but, if yov can pick any Benefitt out of it, it is the marke which I aimed at.

Here follow feverall occafionall meditations.

I.

BY night when others foundly flept,
And had at once both eafe and Reft,
My waking eyes were open kept,
And fo to lye I fovnd it beft.

II.

I fovght him whom my Soul did Love,
With tears I fovght him earneftly;
He bow'd his ear down from Above,
In vain I did not feek or cry.

III.

My hungry Soul he fill'd with Good,
He in his Bottle putt my teares,*
My fmarting wounds wafht in his blood,
And banifht thence my Doubts and feares.

IV.

What to my Saviour fhall I giue,
Who freely hath done this for me?
I'le ferve him here whilft I fhall liue,
And Loue him to Eternity.

* "Put thou my tears into thy bottle: *are they* not in thy book?"—PSALM lvi. 8.

For Deliverance from a feaver.

WHEN Sorrowes had begyrt me rovnd,
And Paines within and out,
When in my flesh no part was fovnd,
Then didst thou rid me out.

My burning flesh in sweat did boyle,
My aking head did break;
From side to side for ease I toyle,
So faint I could not speak.

Beclouded was my Soul with fear
Of thy Displeasure sore,
Nor could I read my Evidence
Which oft I read before.

Hide not thy face from me, I cry'd,
From Burnings keep my soul;
Thov know'st my heart, and hast me try'd;
I on thy Mereyes Rowl.

O, heal my Soul, thov know'st I said,
Tho' flesh consume to novght;
What tho' in dust it shall bee lay'd,
To Glory't shall bee brovght.

Thou heardst, thy rod thou didst remove,
  And spar'd my Body frail,
Thou shew'st to me thy tender Love,
  My heart no more might quail.

O, Praises to my mighty God,
  Praise to my Lord, I say,
Who hath redeem'd my Soul from pitt:
  Praises to him for Aye!

ffrom another sore ffitt.

IN my distresse I soght the Lord,
  When nought on Earth could comfort giue;
And when my Soul these things abhor'd,
Then, Lord, thou said'st vnto me, Liue.

Thou knowest the sorrowes that I felt,
My plaints and Groanes were heard of Thee,
And how in sweat I seem'd to melt;
Thov help'st and thov regardest me.

My wasted flesh thou didst restore,
My feeble loines didst gird with strenght; *

* "She girdeth her loins with strength, and strengtheneth her arms." Prov. xxxi. 17.

Yea, when I was moſt low and poor,
I ſaid I ſhall praiſe thee at lenght.

What ſhall I render to my God
For all his Bovnty ſhew'd to me,
Even for his mercyes in his rod,
Where pitty moſt of all I ſee?

My heart I wholly giue to Thee:
O make it frvitfull, faithfull Lord!
My life ſhall dedicated bee
To praiſe in thought, in Deed, in Word.

Thou know'ſt no life I did require
Longer then ſtill thy Name to praiſe,
Nor ovght on Earth worthy Deſire,
In drawing out theſe wretched Dayes.

Thy Name and praiſe to celebrate,
O Lord! for aye is my requeſt.
O, gravnt I doe it in this ſtate,
And then with thee which is the Beſt.

Deliverance from a fitt of ffainting.

WORTHY art Thou, O Lord of praiſe!
But ah! it's not in me;
My ſinking heart I pray thee raiſe,
So ſhall I giue it Thee.

My life as Spider's webb's cutt off,
Thvs fainting haue I ſaid,
And liueing man no more ſhall ſee,
But bee in ſilence layd.

My feblee Spirit thou didſt reviue,
My Doubting thou didſt chide,
And tho: as dead mad'ſt me aliue,
I here a while might 'bide.

Why ſhould I liue but to thy Praiſe?
My life is hid with Thee;
O Lord, no longer bee my Dayes,
Then I may frvitfull bee.

Meditations when my Soul hath been refreſhed with the Conſolations which the world knowes not.

LORD, why ſhould I doubt any more when thov haſt given me ſuch aſſured Pledges of thy Loue? Firſt, thov art my Creator, I thy creature; thov my maſter, I thy ſervant. But hence ariſes not my comfort: Thov art my ffather, I thy child. Yee ſhall [be] my Sons and Daughters, ſaith the Lord Almighty. Chriſt is my Brother; I aſcend vnto my ffather and your ffather, vnto my God and your God. But leaſt this ſhould not bee enough, thy maker is thy huſband. Nay, more, I am a member of his Body; he, my head. Such Priviledges, had not the Word of Truth made them known, who or where is the man that durſt in his heart haue preſumed to haue thought it? So wonderfull are theſe thoughts that my ſpirit failes in me at the conſideration thereof; and I am confovnded to think that God, who hath done ſo much for me, ſhould haue ſo little from me. But this is my comfort, when I come into Heaven, I ſhall vnderſtand perfectly what he hath done for me, and then ſhall I bee able to praiſe him as I ovght. Lord, haueing this hope, let me purefie myſelf as thou art Pure, and let me bee no more affraid of Death, but even deſire to bee diſſolved, and bee with thee, which is beſt of All.

July 8th, 1656.

I had a ſore fitt of fainting, which laſted 2 or 3 dayes, but not in that extremity which at firſt it took me, and ſo mvch the ſorer it was to me becauſe my dear huſband was from home (who is my cheifeſt comforter on Earth); but my God, who never failed me, was not abſent, but helped me, and gratiouſly manifeſted his Love to me, which I dare not paſſe by without Remembrance, that it may bee a ſupport to me when I ſhall haue occaſion to read this hereafter, and to others that ſhall read it when I ſhall poſſeſſe that I now hope for, that ſo they may bee encourag^{d} to truſt in him who is the only Portion of his Servants.

O Lord, let me neuer forgett thy Goodnes, nor queſtion thy faithfullnes to me, for thov art my God: Thou haſt ſaid, and ſhall not I beleiue it?

Thou haſt given me a pledge of that Inheritance thou haſt promiſed to beſtow upon me. O, never let Satan prevail againſt me, but ſtrenghten my faith in Thee, 'till I ſhall attain the end of my hopes, even the Salvation of my Soul. Come, Lord Jeſus; come quickly.

WHAT God is like to him I ſerve,
What Saviour like to mine?
O, never let me from thee ſwerue,
For truly I am thine.

My thankfull mouth ſhall ſpeak thy praiſe,
My Tongue ſhall talk of Thee:
On High my heart, O, doe thou raiſe,
For what thou'ſt done for me.

Goe, Worldlings, to your Vanities,
And heathen to your Gods;
Let them help in Adverſities,
And ſanctefye their rods.

My God he is not like to yours,
Your ſelves ſhall Judges bee;
I find his Love, I know his Pow'r,
A Succourer of mee.

He is not man that he ſhould lye,
Nor ſon of man to vnſay;
His word he plighted hath on high,
And I ſhall liue for aye.

And for his ſake that faithfull is,
That dy'd but now doth liue,
The firſt and laſt, that liues for aye,
Me laſting life ſhall giue.

MY ſoul, rejoice thou in thy God,
Boaſt of him all the Day,
Walk in his Law, and kiſſe his Rod,
Cleaue cloſe to him alway.

What tho: thy outward Man decay,
  Thy inward ſhall waxe ſtrong;
Thy body vile it ſhall bee chang'd,
  And gloriovs made ere-long.

With Angels-wings thy Soul ſhall movnt
  To Bliſſe vnſeen by Eye,
And drink at vnexhauſted fovnt
  Of Joy vnto Eternity.

Thy teares ſhall All bee dryed vp,
  Thy Sorrowes all ſhall flye;
Thy Sinns ſhall ne'r bee ſummon'd vp,
  Nor come in memory.

Then ſhall I know what thov haſt done
  For me, vnworthy me,
And praiſe thee ſhall ev'n as I ovght,
  ffor wonders that I ſee.

Baſe World, I trample on thy face,
  Thy Glory I deſpiſe,
No gain I find in ovght below,
  For God hath made me wiſe.

Come, Jeſvs, qvickly, Bleſſed Lord,
  Thy face when ſhall I ſee?
O let me covnt each hour a Day
  'Till I diſſolved bee.

August 28, 1656.

AFTER mvch weaknes and ſicknes when my ſpirits were worn out, and many times my faith weak likewiſe, the Lord was pleaſed to vphold my drooping heart, and to manifeſt his Loue to me; and this is that which ſtayes my Soul that this condition that I am in is the beſt for me, for God doth not afflict willingly, nor take delight in greiving the children of men: he hath no benefitt by my adverſity, nor is he the better for my proſperity; but he doth it for my Advantage, and that I may bee a Gainer by it. And if he knowes that weaknes and a frail body is the beſt to make me a veſſell fitt for his vſe, why ſhould I not bare it, not only willingly but joyfully? The Lord knowes I dare not deſire that health that ſomtimes I haue had, leaſt my heart ſhould bee drawn from him, and ſett vpon the world.

Now I can wait, looking every day when my Saviour ſhall call for me. Lord gravnt that while I live I may doe that ſervice I am able in this frail Body, and bee in continuall expectation of my change, and let me never forgett thy great Love to my ſoul ſo lately expreſſed, when I could lye down and bequeath my Soul to thee, and Death ſeem'd no terrible Thing. O let me ever ſee Thee that Art inviſible, and I ſhall not bee vnwilling to come, tho: by ſo rovgh a Meſſenger.

May 11, 1657.

I HAD a fore ficknes, and weaknes took hold of me, which hath by fitts lafted all this Spring till this 11 May, yet hath my God given me many a refpite, and fome ability to perform the Dutyes I owe to him, and the work of my famely.

Many a refrefhment haue I fovnd in this my weary Pilgrimage, and in this valley of Baca* many pools of water. That which now I cheifly labour for is a contented, thankfull heart vnder my affliction and weaknes, feing it is the will of God it fhould bee thus. Who am I that I fhould repine at his pleafure, efpe-

* "Blessed *is* the man whose strength *is* in thee; in whose heart *are* the ways *of them. Who*, passing through the valley of Baca, make it a well; the rain also filleth the pools." — PSALM lxxxiv. 5, 6.

"Blessed is the man whose strength is in thee: in whose heart are thy ways. Who, going through the vale of misery, use it for a well; and the pools are filled with water." — PSALTER.

"*Εἰς τὴν κοιλάδα τοῦ κλαυθμῶνος.*" — SEPTUAGINT.

"*In valle lacrymarum.*" — VULGATE.

The old Genevan Bible (London, 1599) has the following translation and note: —

"They going through the vale of [e] Baca, make welles therein: the rain alfo couereth the pooles."

— "[e] That is, of mulbery trees, which was a barren place: fo that they which paffed through muft dig pits for water," &c., &c.

The old "Bay Pfalm Book," which she must often have read and sung from, thus quaintly renders the verse: —

"Who as they paffe through Baca's Vale,
doe make it a fountaine:
alfo the pooles *that are therin*
are filled full of raine."

cially feing it is for my spirituall advantage? for I hope my soul shall flourish while my body decayes, and the weaknes of this outward man shall bee a meanes to strenghten my inner man.

Yet a little while and he that shall come will come, and will not tarry.

May 13. 1657.

AS spring the winter doth succeed,
And leaues the naked Trees doe dresse,
The earth all black is cloth'd in green;
At svn-shine each their joy expresse.

My Svns returned with healing wings,
My Soul and Body doth rejoice;
My heart exvlts, and praises sings
To him that heard my wailing Voice.

My winters past, my stormes are gone,
And former clowdes seem now all fled;
But, if they mvst eclipse again,
I'le rvn where I was succoured.

I haue a shelter from the storm,
A shadow from the fainting heat;
I haue accesse vnto his Throne,
Who is a God so wondrous great.

O haſt thou made my Pilgrimage
Thvs pleaſant, fair, and good;
Bleſſ'd me in Youth and elder Age,
My Baca made a ſpringing flood? *

I ſtudiovs am what I ſhall doe,
To ſhow my Duty with delight;
All I can giue is but thine own,
And at the moſt a ſimple mite.

Sept. 30. 1657.

IT pleaſed God to viſet me with my old Diſtemper of weaknes and fainting, but not in that ſore manner ſomtimes he hath. I deſire not only willingly, but thankfully, to ſubmitt to him, for I trvſt it is out of his abvndant Love to my ſtraying Soul which in proſperity is too much in love with the world. I haue fovnd by experience I can no more liue without correction then without food. Lord, with thy correction giue Inſtrvction and amendment, and then thy ſtroakes ſhall bee welcome. I haue not been refined in the furnace of affliction as ſome haue been, but haue rather been preſerved with ſugar then brine, yet will he preſerve me to his heavenly kingdom.

Thus (dear children) haue yee ſeen the many ſick-

* See page 21 and note.

neſſes and weakneſſes that I haue paſſed thro: to the end that, if you meet with the like, yov may haue recourſe to the ſame God who hath heard and deliuered me, and will doe the like for yov if you trvſt in him; And, when he ſhall deliuer yov out of diſtreſſe, forget not to giue him thankes, but to walk more cloſely with him then before. This is the deſire of your Loving mother, A. B.

In the ſame book were vpon ſpeciall occaſions the Poems, &c., which follow added.

*Vpon my Son Samuel his goeing for England, Novem. 6, 1657.**

THOU mighty God of Sea and Land,
I here reſigne into thy hand
The Son of Prayers, of vowes, of teares,
The child I ſtay'd for many yeares.†
Thou heard'ſt me then, and gav'ſt him me;
Hear me again, I giue him Thee.
He's mine, but more, O Lord, thine own,
For ſure thy Grace on him is ſhown.
No freind I haue like Thee to truſt,
For mortall helpes are brittle Dvſt.

* He was her eldest child. See Introduction. † See page 5.

Preſerve, O Lord, from ſtormes and wrack,
Protect him there, and bring him back;
And if thou ſhalt ſpare me a ſpace,
That I again may ſee his face,
Then ſhall I celebrate thy Praiſe,
And Bleſſe the for't even all my Dayes.
If otherwiſe I goe to Reſt,
Thy Will bee done, for that is beſt;
Perſwade my heart I ſhall him ſee
For ever happefy'd with Thee.

May 11, 1661.

IT hath pleaſed God to giue me a long Time of reſpite for theſe 4 years that I haue had no great fitt of ſicknes, but this year, from the middle of January 'till May, I haue been by fitts very ill and weak. The firſt of this month I had a feaver ſeat'd vpon me which, indeed, was the longeſt and foreſt that ever I had, laſting 4 dayes, and the weather being very hott made it the more tedious, but it pleaſed the Lord to ſupport my heart in his goodnes, and to hear my Prayers, and to deliuer me out of adverſity. But, alas! I cannot render vnto the Lord according to all his loving kindnes, nor take the cup of ſalvation with Thankſgiving as I ought to doe. Lord, Thou that knoweſt All things know'ſt that I deſire to teſtefye my

4

thankfullnes not only in word, but in Deed, that my Conversation may speak that thy vowes are vpon me.

MY thankfull heart with glorying Tongue
Shall celebrate thy Name,
Who hath restor'd, redeem'd, recur'd
From sicknes, death, and Pain.

I cry'd thov seem'st to make some stay,
I sovght more earnestly;
And in due time thou succour'st me,
And sent'st me help from High.

Lord, whilst my fleeting time shall last,
Thy Goodnes let me Tell.
And new Experience I haue gain'd,
My future Doubts repell.

An humble, faitefull life, O Lord,
For ever let me walk;
Let my obedience testefye,
My Praise lyes not in Talk.

Accept, O Lord, my simple mite,
For more I cannot giue;
What thou bestow'st I shall restore,
For of thine Almes I liue.

For the restoration of my dear Husband from a burning Ague, June, 1661.

WHEN feares and sorrowes me besett,
Then did'st thou rid me out;
When heart did faint and spirits quail,
Thou comforts me about.*

Thou rais'st him vp I feard to loose,
Regau'st me him again:
Distempers thou didst chase away;
With strenght didst him sustain.

My thankfull heart, with Pen record
The Goodnes of thy God;
Let thy obedience testefye
He taught thee by his rod.

And with his staffe did thee support,
That thou by both may'st learn;
And 'twixt the good and evill way,
At last, thou mig'st discern.

Praises to him who hath not left
My Soul as destitute;
Nor turnd his ear away from me,
But graunted hath my Suit.

* Ps. lxxi. 21.

Vpon my Daughter Hannah Wiggin her recouery from a dangerous feaver.*

BLES'T bee thy Name, who did'ſt reſtore
To health my Daughter dear
When death did ſeem ev'n to approach,
And life was ended near.

Gravnt ſhee remember what thov'ſt done,
And celebrate thy Praiſe;
And let her Converſation ſay,
Shee loues thee all thy Dayes.

On my Sons Return out of England, July 17, 1661.†

ALL Praiſe to him who hath now turn'd
My feares to Joyes, my ſighes to song,
My Teares to ſmiles, my ſad to glad:
He's come for whom I waited long.

Thou di'ſt preſerve him as he went;
In raging ſtormes did'ſt ſafely keep:

* She married Andrew Wiggin, of Exeter, N.H., June 14, 1659, and died in 1707.

† He sailed for England in November, 1657. See page 24.

Did'ſt that ſhip bring to quiet Port.
The other ſank low in the Deep.*

From Dangers great thou did'ſt him free
Of Pyrates who were neer at hand;
And order'ſt ſo the adverſe wind,
That he before them gott to Land.

* Gookin, in his "Historical Collections," pp. 62–63, tells the story of these ships: —

"But An. 1657, in the month of November, Mr. Mayhew, the ſon, took ſhipping at Boſton, to paſs for England, ... He took his paſſage for England in the beſt of two ſhips then bound for London, whereof one James Garrett was maſter. The other ſhip, whereof John Pierſe was commander, I went paſſenger therein, with Mr. Hezekiah Uſher ſenior of Boſton, and ſeveral other perſons. Both theſe ſhips ſailed from Boſton in company. Mr. Garrett's ſhip, which was about four hundred tons, had good accommodations, and greater far than the other: and ſhe had aboard her a very rich lading of goods, but moſt eſpecially of paſſengers, about fifty in number; whereof divers of them were perſons of great worth and virtue, both men and women; eſpecially Mr. Mayhew, Mr. Davis, Mr. Ince, and Mr. Pelham, all ſcholars, and maſters of art, as I take it, moſt of them. The ſecond of theſe, viz. Mr. Davis, ſon to one of that name at New Haven, was one of the beſt accompliſhed perſons for learning, as ever was bred at Harvard college in Cambridge in New England. Myſelf was once intended and reſolved to paſs in that ſhip: but the maſter, who ſometimes had been employed by me, and from whom I expected a common courteſy, carried it ſomething unkindly, as I conceived, about my accommodations of a cabin; which was an occaſion to divert me to the other ſhip, where I alſo had good company, and my life alſo preſerved, as the ſequel proved: For this ſhip of Garrett's periſhed in the paſſage, and was never heard of more. And there good Mr. Mayhew ended his days, and finiſhed his work."

John Hull also mentions the loss of Garrett's ship, in his Diary (Arch. Amer. iii. 184.): —

"4th month [June, 1658]. We heard, by two ships that came in from England, that Master James Garret's ship was not arrived, and looked as foundered in the sea, and so persons and estates lost. There was sundry

In covntry ſtrange thou did'ſt provide,
And freinds raiſ'd him in euery Place;
And courteſies of ſvndry ſorts
From ſuch as 'fore nere ſaw his face.

In ſicknes when he lay full ſore,
His help and his Phyſitian wer't;
When royall ones that Time did dye,*
Thou heal'dſt his fleſh, and cheer'd his heart.

persons of pretty note: Mr. Mejo (Mayhew), a godly minister, that taught the Indians at Martha's Vineyard; and sundry young students, and some very hopeful; sundry women also, two of which were sisters in our own church. . . . . . . One of the ketches, likewise, that went hence for England, was taken by a pirate of Ostend, and therein much estate lost."

* Henry, Duke of Gloucester, third son of Charles I., died of small-pox 13th September, 1660, only a few months after the restoration of his brother, Charles II., to the throne. Mary, their sister, the Princess of Orange, returned from Holland soon after his death, and fell a victim to the same disease on the 24th December following.

"This punishment of declared enemies interrupted not the rejoicings of the court; but the death of the Duke of Gloucester, a young prince of promising hopes, threw a great cloud upon them. The king, by no incident in his life, was ever so deeply affected. Gloucester was observed to possess united the good qualities of both his brothers; the clear judgment and penetration of the king, the industry and application of the Duke of York. He was also believed to be affectionate to the religion and constitution of his country. He was but twenty years of age when the small-pox put an end to his life. The Princess of Orange, having come to England, in order to partake of the joy attending the restoration of her family, with whom she lived in great friendship, soon after sickened and died."—HUME'S "History of England," chap. lxiii.

Under date of Sept. 13, Evelyn writes in his Diary, "In the midst of all this joy and jubilee the Duke of Gloucester died of ye small pox in the prime of youth, and a prince of extraordinary hopes." And again, on the 21st [24th] of December, "This day died the Princesse of Orange, of y^e

From troubles and Incūbers Thov,
Without (all fraud),* did'ſt ſett him free,
That, without ſcandall, he might come
To th' Land of his Nativity.

On Eagles wings him hether brovght †
Thro: Want and Dangers manifold;
And thvs hath graynted my Reqveſt,
That I thy Mercyes might behold.

O help me pay my Vowes, O Lord!
That ever I may thankfull bee,
And may putt him in mind of what
Tho'ſt done for him, and ſo for me.

In both our hearts erect a frame
Of Duty and of Thankfullnes,
That all thy favours great receiv'd,
Oure vpright walking may expreſſe.

O Lord, gravnt that I may never forgett thy Loving kindnes in this Particular, and how gratiovſly thov haſt anſwered my Deſires.

small pox, wch entirely alter'd ye face and gallantry of the whole court." —MEMOIRS, vol. ii. pp. 155 and 159–60.

These sad events were probably fresh in Mrs. Bradstreet's mind.

* *Sic.*

† Ex. xix. 4.

Vpon my dear and loving husband his goeing into England, Jan. 16, 1661.*

O THOV most high who rulest All,
And hear'st the Prayers of Thine;
O hearken, Lord, vnto my suit,
And my Petition signe.

Into thy everlasting Armes
Of mercy I commend
Thy servant, Lord. Keep and preserve
My husband, my dear freind.

At thy command, O Lord, he went,
Nor novght could keep him back;

* This was in 1662 (N. S.), on occasion of Bradstreet's mission to England with the Rev. John Norton (see Introduction). They did not sail until the 11th of February. John Hull, who was their companion out and back, says, in his Diary (Arch. Amer. iii. 205-6), "10th of Feb., Mr. Norton, Mr. Broadstreet, Mr. Davis, and myself, went on shipboard. Next morning, set sail; and, by the 28th March, we saw the Lizard; and, 22d of 1st, we arrived in the Downs. After a few days, the messengers addressed themselves to the Court, delivered their letters to the Lord Chancellor, received good words from him. After their minds, by several comings, fully known, they had fair promises of a full grant to their whole desire in the country's behalf. But their writing, which they drew in order thereunto, at last unsigned; and another letter, wherein was sundry things ordered for the country to attend which seemed somewhat inconsistent with our patent and former privileges, in the beginning of said letter confirmed, and which some endeavor to take advantage from to the change [of] our good laws and customs."

Then let thy promis joy his heart:
  O help, and bee not ſlack.

Vphold my heart in Thee, O God,
  Thou art my ſtrenght and ſtay;
Thou ſee'ſt how weak and frail I am,
  Hide not thy face Away.

I, in obedience to thy Will,
  Thov knoweſt, did ſubmitt;
It was my Duty ſo to doe,
  O Lord, accept of it.

Vnthankfullnes for mercyes Paſt,
  Impute thov not to me;
O Lord, thov know'ſt my weak deſire
  Was to ſing Praiſe to Thee.

Lord, bee thov Pilott to the ſhip,
  And ſend them proſperous gailes;
In ſtormes and ſicknes, Lord, preſerve.
  Thy Goodnes never failes.

Vnto thy work he hath in hand,
  Lord, gravnt Thov good Succeſſe
And favour in their eyes, to whom
  He ſhall make his Addreſſe.

Remember, Lord, thy folk whom thou
To wildernesse hast brovght;
Let not thine own Inheritance
Bee sold away for Novght.

But Tokens of thy favour Give —
With Joy send back my Dear,
That I, and all thy servants, may
Rejoice with heavenly chear.

Lord, let my eyes see once Again
Him whom thov gavest me,
That wee together may sing Praise
ffor ever vnto Thee.

And the Remainder of oure Dayes
Shall consecrated bee,
With an engaged heart to sing
All Praises vnto Thee.

In my Solitary houres in my dear husband his Absence.

O LORD, thov hear'st my dayly moan,
And see'st my dropping teares:
My Troubles All are Thee before,
My Longings and my feares.

Thou hetherto hast been my God;
  Thy help my soul hath fovnd:
Tho: losse and sicknes me assail'd,
  Thro: the I've kept my Grovnd.

And thy Abode tho'st made with me;
  With Thee my Soul can talk
In secrett places, Thee I find,
  Where I doe kneel or walk.

Tho: husband dear bee from me gone,
  Whom I doe loue so well;
I haue a more beloued one
  Whose comforts far excell.

O stay my heart on thee, my God,
  Vphold my fainting Soul!
And, when I know not what to doe,
  I'll on thy mercyes roll.*

* This singular expression has been used once before (page 12). It is probably taken from Ps. xxii. 8, — "He trusted on the Lord *that* he would deliver him: let him deliver him, seeing he delighted in him"; or from Ps. xxxvii. 5, — "Commit thy way unto the Lord; trust also in him; and he shall bring *it* to pass." The marginal reading for "trusted on" is "*rolled* himself," and for "Commit thy way unto," "*roll thy way upon.*"

The "Bay Psalm Book" translates the former verse as follows:

"Vpon the Lord he rold him'selfe,
let him now rid him quite:
let him deliver him, becaufe
in him he doth delight."

My weaknes, thou do'ſt know full well,
  Of Body and of mind.
I, in this world, no comfort haue,
  But what from Thee I find.

Tho: children thou haſt given me,
  And freinds I haue alſo:
Yet, if I ſee Thee not thro: them,
  They are no Joy, but woe.

O ſhine vpon me, bleſſed Lord,
  Ev'n for my Saviour's ſake;
In Thee Alone is more then All,
  And there content I'll take.

O hear me, Lord, in this Reqveſt,
  As thov before ha'ſt done:
Bring back my huſband, I beſeech,
  As thov didſt once my Sonne.

So ſhall I celebrate thy Praiſe,
  Ev'n while my Dayes ſhall laſt;
And talk to my Beloued one
  Of all thy Goodnes paſt.

Winthrop uses the same expression in a letter to his son ("Life and Letters," p. 250).

"But such as will roll their ways upon the Lord, do find him always as good as his word."

So both of vs thy Kindnes, Lord,
  With Praises shall recovnt,
And serve Thee better then before,
  Whose Blessings thvs surmovnt.

But give me, Lord, a better heart,
  Then better shall I bee,
To pay the vowes which I doe owe
  For ever vnto Thee.

Vnlesse thou help, what can I doe
  But still my frailty show?
If thov assist me, Lord, I shall
  Return Thee what I owe.

In thankfull acknowledgment for the letters I received from my husband ovt of England.

O THOU that hear'st the Prayers of Thine,
And 'mongst them hast regarded Mine,
Hast heard my cry's, and seen my Teares;
Hast known my doubts and All my ffeares.

Thov hast releiv'd my fainting heart,
Nor payd me after my desert;

Thov hast to shore him safely brovght
For whom I thee so oft besovght.

Thov wast the Pilott to the ship,
And rais'd him vp when he was sick;
And hope thov'st given of good successe,
In this his Buisnes and Addresse;

And that thov wilt return him back,
Whose presence I so much doe lack.
For All these mercyes I thee Praise,
And so desire ev'n all my Dayes.

*In thankfull Remembrance for my dear husbands safe Arrivall Sept. 3, 1662.**

WHAT shall I render to thy Name,
Or how thy Praises speak;
My thankes how shall I testefye?
O Lord, thov know'st I'm weak.

I ow so mvch, so little can
Return vnto thy Name,

* "Sept. 3. Master Clark, in the ship 'Society,' brought in the country's messengers in safety; viz., Mr. Broadstreet and Mr. Norton."—HULL's Diary; Arch. Amer. iii. 206.

Confusiōn seases on my Soul,
  And I am fill'd with shame.

O thov that hearest Prayers, Lord,
  To Thee shall come all fflesh;
Thou hast me heard and answered,
  My 'Plaints haue had accesse.

What did I ask for but thov gav'st?
  What could I more desire?
But Thankfullnes, even all my dayes,
  I humbly this Require.

Thy mercyes, Lord, haue been so great,
  In nvmber nvmberles,
Impossible for to recovnt
  Or any way expresse.

O help thy Saints that sovght thy fface,
  T' Return vnto thee Praise,
And walk before thee as they ought,
  In strict and vpright wayes.

This was the last Thing written in that Book by my dear and hon'd Mother.

Here followes ſome verſes vpon the burning of our houſe, July 10th, 1666. Copyed ovt of a looſe Paper.

IN ſilent night when reſt I took,
For ſorrow neer I did not look,
I waken'd was with thundring nois
And Piteovs ſhreiks of dreadfull voice.
That fearfull ſound of fire and fire,
Let no man know is my Deſire.

I, ſtarting vp, the light did ſpye,
And to my God my heart did cry
To ſtrengthen me in my Diſtreſſe
And not to leaue me ſuccourleſſe.
Then coming ovt beheld a ſpace,
The flame conſvme my dwelling place.

And, when I could no longer look,
I bleſt his Name that gave and took,
That layd my goods now in the dvſt:
Yea ſo it was, and ſo 'twas jvſt.
It was his own: it was not mine;
ffar be it that I ſhould repine.

He might of All iuſtly bereſt,
But yet ſufficient for us left.

When by the Ruines oft I past,
My sorrowing eyes aside did cast,
And here and there the places spye
Where oft I sate, and long did lye.

Here stood that Trunk, and there that chest;
There lay that store I covnted best:
My pleasant things in ashes lye,
And them behold no more shall I.
Vnder thy roof no gvest shall sitt,
Nor at thy Table eat a bitt.

No pleasant tale shall 'ere be told,
Nor things recovnted done of old.
No Candle 'ere shall shine in Thee,
Nor bridegroom's voice ere heard shall bee.
In silence ever shalt thou lye;
Adeiu, Adeiu; All's vanity.

Then streight I 'gin my heart to chide,
And did thy wealth on earth abide?
Didst fix thy hope on mouldring dvst,
The arm of flesh didst make thy trvst?
Raise vp thy thovghts above the skye
That dunghill mists away may flie.

Thou hast an house on high erect,
Fram'd by that mighty Architect,

With glory richly furniſhed,
Stands permanent tho: this bee fled.
'Its purchaſéd, and paid for too
By him who hath enovgh to doe.

A Priſe ſo vaſt as is vnknown,
Yet, by his Gift, is made thine own.
Ther's wealth enovgh, I need no more;
Farewell my Pelf, farewell my Store.
The world no longer let me Love,
My hope and Treaſure lyes Above.

AS weary pilgrim, now at reſt,
Hugs with delight his ſilent neſt
His waſted limbes, now lye full ſoft
That myrie ſteps, haue troden oft
Bleſſes himſelf, to think vpon
his dangers paſt, and travailes done
The burning ſun no more ſhall heat
Nor ſtormy raines, on him ſhall beat.
The bryars and thornes no more ſhall ſcratch
nor hungry wolues at him ſhall catch
He erring pathes no more ſhall tread
nor wild fruits eate, in ſtead of bread,

for waters cold he doth not long
  for thirst no more shall parch his tongue
No rugged stones his feet shall gaule
  nor stumps nor rocks cause him to fall
All cares and feares, he bids farwell
  and meanes in safity now to dwell.
A pilgrim I, on earth, perplext
  wth sinns wth cares and sorrows vext
By age and paines brought to decay
  and my Clay house mouldring away
Oh how I long to be at rest
  and soare on high among the blest.
This body shall in silence sleep
  Mine eyes no more shall ever weep
No fainting fits shall me assaile
  nor grinding paines my body fraile
W^th^ cares and fears ne'r cumbred be
  Nor losses know, nor sorrowes see
What tho my flesh shall there consume
  it is the bed Christ did perfume
And when a few yeares shall be gone
  this mortall shall be cloth'd vpon
A Corrupt Carcasse downe it lyes
  a glorious body it shall rise
In weaknes and dishonour sowne
  in power 'tis rais'd by Christ alone
Then soule and body shall vnite
  and of their maker haue the sight

Such laſting ioyes ſhall there behold
  as eare ne'r heard nor tongue e'er told
Lord make me ready for that day
  then Come deare bridgrome Come away.*

Aug: 31, 69.

* These verses are printed from the original in Mrs. Bradstreet's handwriting. Her spelling and punctuation are carefully followed.

MEDITATIONS,

DIVINE AND MORAL.

The "Meditations" are printed from the original in Mrs. Bradstreet's handwriting.

For my deare sonne
Simon Bradstreet

Parents perpetuate their lives
in their posterity, and their
maners in their imitation
Children do naturally rather
follow the failings then the ver
tues of their predecessors, but I
am perswaded better things of yo
you once desired me to leave some
thing for you in writeing that
you might look upon, when you
should see me no more, I could
think of nothing more fit for you
nor of more ease to my self then
these short meditations following. Such as they are I bequeath
to you, small legacys are accepted
by true friends much more by
duty full children, I have avoyded
incroaching upon others conceptions
because I would leave you nothing

but myne owne, though in value
they fall short of all in this kinde
yet I presume they will be
better pris'd by you, for the
Authors sake. the lord blesse
you wth grace heer. and crown
you wth glory heerafter. that I
may meet you wth rejoyceing
at that great day of appearing, wch is the continuall pray
er, of

your affectionate
mother, A B

March 20
1664

For my deare ſonne Simon Bradſtreet.

PARENTS perpetuate their liues in their poſterity, and their mañers in their imitation. Children do naturally rather follow the failings then the vertues of their predeceſſors, but I am perſwaded better things of you. You once deſired me to leaue ſomething for you in writeing that you might look vpon when you ſhould ſee me no more. I could think of nothing more fit for you, nor of more eaſe to my ſelf, then theſe ſhort meditations following. Such as they are I bequeath to you: ſmall legacys are accepted by true friends, much more by duty full children. I haue avoyded incroaching upon others conceptions, becauſe I would leaue you nothing but myne owne, though in value they fall ſhort of all in this kinde, yet I preſume they will be better priſ'd by you for the Authors ſake. the Lord bleſſe you with grace heer, and crown you with glory heerafter, that I may meet you with rejoyceing at that great day of appearing, which is the continuall prayer, of

your affectionate mother,

March 20, 1664. A. B.

Meditations Diuine and morall.

I.

THERE is no obiect that we see; no action that we doe; no good that we inioy; no evill that we feele, or fear, but we may make some spiritu[a]ll aduantage of all: and he that makes such improvment is wise, as well as pious.

II.

MANY can speak well, but few can do well. We are better scholars in the Theory then the practique part, but he is a true Christian that is a proficient in both.

III.

YOUTH is the time of getting, middle age of improuing, and old age of spending; a negligent youth is vsually attended by an ignorant middle age, and both by an empty old age. He that hath nothing to feed on but vanity and lyes must needs lye down in the Bed of sorrow.

IV.

A SHIP that beares much saile, and little or no ballast, is easily ouerset; and that man, whose head hath great abilities, and his heart little or no grace, is in danger of foundering.

V.

IT is reported of the peakcock that, prideing himfelf in his gay feathers, he ruffles them vp; but. fpying his black feet, he foon lets fall his plumes, fo he that glorys in his gifts and adornings, fhould look vpon his Corruptions, and that will damp his high thoughts.

VI.

THE fineft bread hath the leaft bran; the pureft hony, the leaft wax; and the fincereft chriftian, the leaft felf loue.

VII.

THE hireling that labours all the day, comforts himfelf that when night comes he fhall both take his reft, and receiue his reward; the painfull chriftian that hath wrought hard in Gods vineyard, and hath born the heat and drought of the day, when he perceiues his fun apace to decline, and the fhadowes of his euening to be ftretched out, lifts vp his head with joy, knowing his refrefhing is at hand.

VIII.

DOWNNY beds make drofey perfons, but hard lodging keeps the eyes open. A profperous ftate makes a fecure Chriftian, but adverfity makes him Confider.

IX.

SWEET words are like hony, a little may refresh, but too much gluts the stomach.

X.

DIUERSE children haue their different natures; some are like flesh which nothing but salt will keep from putrefaction; some again like tender fruits that are best preserued with sugar: those parents are wise that can fit their nurture according to their Nature.

XI.

THAT town which thousands of enemys without hath not been able to take, hath been deliuered vp by one traytor within; and that man, which all the temptations of Sathan without could not hurt, hath been foild by one lust within.

XII.

AUTHORITY without wisedome is like a heavy axe without an edg, fitter to bruise then polish.

XIII.

THE reason why christians are so loth to exchang this world for a better, is because they haue more sence then faith: they se what they inioy, they do but hope for that which is to Come.

XIV.

IF we had no winter the ſpring would not be ſo pleaſant: if we did not ſometimes taſt of adverſity, proſperity would not be ſo welcome.

XV.

A LOW man can goe vpright vnder that door, wher a taller is glad to ſtoop; ſo a man of weak faith and mean abilities, may vndergo a croſſe more patiently then he that excells him, both in gifts and graces.

XVI.

THAT houſe which is not often ſwept, makes the cleanly inhabitant ſoone loath it, and that heart which is not continually purificing it ſelf, is no fit temple for the ſpirit of god to dwell in.

XVII.

FEW men are ſo humble as not to be proud of their abilitys; and nothing will abaſe them more then this, — What haſt thou, but what thou haſt receiued? come giue an account of thy ſtewardſhip.

XVIII.

HE that will vntertake to climb vp a ſteep mountain with a great burden on his back, will finde it a wearyſome, if not an impoſſible taſk; ſo he that thinkes to mount to heaven clog'd with the Cares and riches of this Life, 'tis no wonder if he faint by the way.

XIX.

CORNE, till it haue paſt through the Mill and been ground to powder, is not fit for bread. God ſo deales with his ſervants: he grindes them with greif and pain till they turn to duſt, and then are they fit manchet * for his Manſion.

XX.

GOD hath ſutable comforts and ſupports for his children according to their ſeuerall conditions if he will make his face to ſhine vpon them: he then makes them lye down in green paſtures, and leades them beſides the ſtill waters; if they ſtick in deepe mire and clay, and all his waues and billows goe ouer their heads, he then leads them to the Rock which is higher then they.

XXI.

HE that walks among briars and thorns will be very carefull where he ſets his foot. And he that paſſes through the wildernes of this world, had need ponder all his ſteps.

* The finest white rolls. *Nares.*

XXII.

WANT of prudence, as well as piety, hath brought men into great inconveniencys; but he that is well ſtored with both, ſeldom is ſo inſnared.

XXIII.

THE ſkillfull fiſher hath his ſeverall baits for ſeverall fiſh, but there is a hooke vnder all; Satan, that great Angler, hath his ſundry baits for ſundry tempers of men, which they all catch grēdily at, but few perceiues the hook till it be to late.

XXIV.

THERE is no new thing vnder the ſun, there is nothing that can be ſayd or done, but either that or ſomething like it hath been both done and ſayd before.

XXV.

AN akeing head requires a ſoft pillow; and a drooping heart a ſtrong ſupport.

XXVI.

A SORE finger may diſquiet the whole body, but an vlcer within deſtroys it: ſo an enemy without may diſturb a Commonwealth, but diſſentions within ouer throw it.

XXVII.

IT is a pleaſant thing to behold the light, but ſore eyes are not able to look vpon it; the pure in heart ſhall ſe God, but the defiled in conſcience ſhall rather chooſe to be buried vnder rocks and mountains then to behold the preſence of the Lamb.

XXVIII.

WISEDOME with an inheritance is good, but wiſedome without an inheritance is better then an inheritance without wiſedome.

XXIX.

LIGHTENING doth vſually preceed thunder, and ſtormes, raine; and ſtroaks do not often fall till after threat'ning.

XXX.

YELLOW leaues argue want of ſap, and gray haires want of moiſture; ſo dry and ſapleſſe performances are ſimptoms of little ſpiritall vigor.

XXXI.

IRON till it be throughly heat is vncapable to be wrought; ſo God ſees good to caſt ſome men into the furnace of affliction, and then beats them on his anuile into what frame he pleaſes.

XXXII.

AMBITIOUS men are like hops that neuer rest climbing soe long as they haue any thing to stay vpon; but take away their props and they are, of all, the most deiected.

XXXIII.

MUCH Labour wearys the body, and many thoughts oppresse the minde: man aimes at profit by the one, and content in the other; but often misses of both, and findes nothing but vanity and vexation of spirit.

XXXIV.

DIMNE eyes are the concomitants of old age; and short sightednes, in those that are eyes of a Republique, foretels a declineing State.

XXXV.

WE read in Scripture of three sorts of Arrows,— the arrow of an enemy, the arrow of pestilence, and the arrow of a slanderous tongue; the two first kill the body, the last the good name; the two former leaue a man when he is once dead, but the last mangles him in his graue.

XXXVI.

SORE labourers haue hard hands, and old ſinners haue brawnie Conſciences.

XXXVII.

WICKEDNES comes to its height by degrees. He that dares ſay of a leſſe ſin, is it not a little one? will ere long ſay of a greater, Tuſh, God regards it not!

XXXVIII.

SOME Children are hardly weaned, although the teat be rub'd with wormwood or muſtard, they wil either wipe it off, or elſe ſuck down ſweet and bitter together; ſo is it with ſome Chriſtians, let God imbitter all the ſweets of this life, that ſo they might feed vpon more ſubſtantiall food, yet they are ſo childiſhly ſottiſh that they are ſtill huging and ſucking theſe empty breſts, that God is forced to hedg vp their way with thornes, or lay affliction on their loynes, that ſo they might ſhake hands with the world before it bid them farwell.

XXXIX.

A PRUDENT mother will not cloth her little childe with a long and cumberſome garment; ſhe eaſily foreſees what euents it is like to produce, at the beſt but falls and bruiſes, or perhaps ſomewhat worſe, much more will the alwiſe God proportion his diſpenſations according to the ſtature and ſtrength of the perſon he beſtowes them on. Larg indowments of honour, wealth, or a helthfull body would quite ouerthrow ſome weak Chriſtian, therefore God cuts their garments ſhort, to keep them in ſuch a trim that they might run the wayes of his Commandment.

XL.

THE ſpring is a liuely emblem of the reſurrection, after a long winter we ſe the leavleſſe trees and dry ſtocks (at the approach of the ſun) to reſume their former vigor and beavty in a more ample manner then what they loſt in the Autumn; ſo ſhall it be at that great day after a long vacation, when the Sun of righteouſnes ſhall appear, thoſe dry bones ſhall ariſe in far more glory then that which they loſt at their creation, and in this tranſcends the ſpring, that their leafe ſhall neuer faile, nor their ſap decline.

XLI.

A WISE father will not lay a burden on a child of ſeven yeares old, which he knows is enough for one of twice his ſtrength, much leſſe will our heauenly father (who knowes our mould), lay ſuch afflictions vpon his weak children as would cruſh them to the duſt, but according to the ſtrength he will proportion the load, as God hath his little children ſo he hath his ſtrong men, ſuch as are come to a full Stature in Chriſt;

and many times he impoſes waighty burdens on their ſhoulders, and yet they go vpright vnder them, but it matters not whether the load be more or leſſe if God afford his help.

XLII.

I HAUE ſeen an end of all perfection (ſayd the royall prophet);* but he never ſayd, I haue ſeen an end of all ſinning: what he did ſay, may be eaſily ſayd by many; but what he did not ſay, cannot truly be vttered by any.

XLIII.

FIRE hath its force abated by water, not by wind; and anger muſt be alayed by cold words, and not by bluſtering threats.

XLIV.

A SHARP appetite and a through concoction, is a ſigne of an healthfull body; ſo a quick reception, and a deliberate cogitation, argues a ſound mind.

XLV..

WE often ſe ſtones hang with drops, not from any innate moiſture, but from a thick ayre about them; ſo may we ſometime ſe marble-hearted ſinners ſeem full of contrition; but it is not from any dew of

* Psalm cxix. 96.

grace within, but from ſome black Clouds that impends them, which produces theſe ſweating effects.

XLVI.

THE words of the wiſe, ſaith Solomon,* are as nailes, and as goads, both vſed for contrary ends, — the one holds faſt, the other puts forward; ſuch ſhould be the precepts of the wiſe maſters of aſſemblys to their heareres, not only to bid them hold faſt the form of ſound Doctrin, but alſo, ſo to run that they might obtain.

XLVII.

A SHADOW in the parching ſun, and a ſhelter in a bluſtering ſtorme, are of all ſeaſons the moſt welcom; ſo a faithfull friend in time of adverſity, is of all other moſt comfortable.

XLVIII.

THERE is nothing admits of more admiration, then Gods various diſpenſation of his gifts among the ſons of men, betwixt whom he hath put ſo vaſt a diſproportion that they ſcarcely ſeem made of the ſame lump, or ſprung out of the loynes of one Adam; ſome ſet in the higheſt dignity that mortality is capable off; and ſome again ſo baſe, that they are viler

* "The words of the wise *are* as goads, and as nails fastened *by* the masters of assemblies, *which* are given from one shepherd." — Eccl. xii. 11.

then the earth: ſome ſo wiſe and learned, that they ſeeme like Angells among men: and ſome againe ſo ignorant and ſotiſh, that they are more like beaſts then men: ſome pious ſaints; ſome incarnate Deuils: ſome exceeding beautyfull; and ſome extreamly deformed: ſome ſo ſtrong and healthfull that their bones are full of marrow, and their breaſts of milk: and ſome againe ſo weak and feeble, that, while they liue, they are accounted among the dead,—and no other reaſon can be giuen of all this, but ſo it pleaſed him, whoſe will is the perfect rule of righteouſneſſe.

XLIX.

THE treaſures of this world may well be compared to huſkes, for they haue no kernell in them, and they that feed vpon them, may ſoon ſtuffe their throats, but cannot fill their bellys; they may be choaked by them, but cannot be ſatisfied with them.

L.

SOMTIMES the ſun is only ſhadowed by a cloud that wee cannot ſe his luſter, although we may walk by his light, but when he is ſet we are in darknes till he ariſe againe; ſo God doth ſomtime vaile his face but for a moment, that we cannot behold the light of his Countenance as at ſome other time, yet he affords ſo much light as may direct our way, that we may go forwards to the Citty of habitation, but when he ſeemes to ſet and be quite gone out of ſight, then must we needs walk in darknesse and se no light, yet then must we trust in the Lord, and stay vpon our God, and when the morning (which is the appointed time) is come, the Sun of righteousnes will arise with healing in his wings.

LI.

THE eyes and the eares are the inlets or doores of the soule, through which innumerable objects enter, yet is not that spacious roome filled, neither doth it euer say it is enough, but like the daughters of the horsleach, crys giue, giue! * and which is most strang, the more it receius, the more empty it finds it self, and sees an impossibility, euer to be filled, but by him in whom all fullnes dwells.

LII.

HAD not the wisest of men taught vs this lesson, that all is vanity and vexation of spirit, yet our owne experience would soon haue speld it out; for what do we obtaine of all these things, but it is with labour and vexation? when we injoy them it is with vanity and vexation; and, if we loose them, then they are lesse then vanity and more then vexation: so that we haue good cause often to repeat that sentence, vanity of vanityes, vanity of vanityes, all is vanity.

* "The horseleach hath two daughters, *crying*, Give, give."—PROV. XXX. 15.

LIII.

HE that is to saile into a farre country, although the ship, cabbin, and prouision, be all convenient and comfortable for him, yet he hath no desire to make that his place of residence, but longs to put in at that port wher his bussines lyes: a christian is sailing through this world vnto his heauenly country, and heere he hath many conueniences and comforts; but he must beware of desire[ing] to make this the place of his abode, lest he meet with such tossings that may cause him to long for shore before he sees land. We must, therfore, be heer as strangers and pilgrims, that we may plainly declare that we seek a citty aboue, and wait all the dayes of our appointed time till our chang shall come.

LIV.

HE that neuer felt what it was to be sick or wounded, doth not much care for the company of the phisitian or chirurgian; but if he perceiue a malady that threatens him with death, he will gladly entertaine him, whom he slighted before: so he that neuer felt the sicknes of sin, nor the wounds of a guilty Conscience, cares not how far he keeps from him that hath skill to cure it; but when he findes his diseases to distrest him, and that he must needs perish if he haue no remedy, will vnfeignedly bid him welcome that brings a plaifter for his fore, or a cordiall for his fainting.

LV.

WE read of ten lepers that were Cleanfed, but of one that returned thanks: we are more ready to receiue mercys then we are to acknowledg them: men can vfe great importunity when they are in diftreffes, and fhew great ingratitude after their fucceffes; but he that ordereth his conuerfation aright, will glorifie him that heard him in the day of his trouble.

LVI.

THE remembrance of former deliuerances is a great fupport in prefent deftreffes: he that deliuered me, fath Dauid, from the paw of the Lion and the paw of the Beare, will deliuer mee from this vncircumcifed Philiftin; and he that hath deliuered mee, faith Paul, will deliuer me: God is the fame yefterday, to day, and for euer; we are the fame that ftand in need of him, today as well as yefterday, and fo fhall for euer.

LVII.

GREAT receipts call for great returnes, the more that any man is intrufted withall, the larger his accounts ftands vpon Gods fcore: it therfore behoues euery man fo to improue his talents, that when his great maſter ſhall call him to reckoning he may receiue his owne with advantage.

LVIII.

SIN and ſhame euer goe together. He that would be freed from the laſt, muſt be ſure to ſhun the company of the firſt.

LIX.

GOD doth many times both reward and puniſh for one and the ſame action: as we ſee in Jehu, he is rewarded with a kingdome to the fourth generation, for takeing veangence on the houſe of Ahab; and yet a little while (ſaith God), and I will avenge the blood of Jezerel vpon the houſe of Jehu: he was rewarded for the matter, and yet puniſhed for the manner, which ſhould warn him, that doth any ſpeciall ſeruice for God, to fixe his eye on the command, and not on his own ends, leſt he meet with Jehu's reward, which will end in puniſhment.

LX.

HE that would be content with a mean condition, muſt not caſt his eye vpon one that is in a far better eſtate then himſelf, but let him look vpon him that is lower then he is, and, if he ſe that ſuch a one beares pouerty comfortably, it will help to quiet him; but if that will not do, let him look on his owne vnworthynes, and that will make him ſay with Jacob, I am leſſe then the leaſt of thy mercys.

LXI.

CORNE is produced with much labour (as the huſbandman well knowes), and ſome land aſkes much more paines then ſome other doth to be brought into tilth, yet all muſt be ploughed and harrowed; ſome children (like ſowre land) are of ſo tough and moroſe a diſpo[ſi]tion, that the plough of correction muſt make long furrows on their back, and the Harrow of diſcipline goe often ouer them, before they bee fit ſoile to ſow the ſeed of morality, much leſſe of grace in them. But when by prudent nurture they are brought into a fit capacity, let the ſeed of good inſtruction and exhortation be ſown in the ſpring of their youth, and a plentifull crop may be expected in the harueſt of their yeares.

LXII.

AS man is called the little world, ſo his heart may be cal'd the little Commonwealth: his more fixed and reſolued thoughts are like to inhabitants, his ſlight and flitting thoughts are like paſſengers that trauell to and fro continvally; here is alſo the great Court of iuſtice erected, which is alway kept by conſcience who is both accuſer, excuſer, witnes, and Judg, whom no bribes can pervert, nor flattery cauſe to favour, but as he finds the evidence, ſo he abſolues or condemnes: yea, ſo Abſolute is this Court of Judicature, that there is no appeale from it,—no, not to the Court of heaven itſelf,—for if our conſcience condemn vs, he, alſo, who is greater then our conſcience, will do it much more; but he that would haue boldnes to go to the throne of grace to be accepted there, muſt be ſure to carry a certificate from the Court of conſcience, that he ſtands right there.

LXIII.

HE that would keep a pure heart, and lead a blamleſſe life, muſt ſet himſelf alway in the awefull preſence of God, the conſideration of his all-ſeeing eye will be a bridle to reſtrain from evill, and a ſpur to quicken on to good dutys: we certainly dream of ſome remotnes betwixt God and vs, or elſe we ſhould not ſo often faile in our whole Courſe of life as we doe; but he, that with David, ſets the Lord alway in his ſight, will not ſinne againſt him.

LXIV.

WE ſee in orchards ſome trees ſoe fruitfull, that the waight of their Burden is the breaking of their limbes; ſome again are but meanly loaden; and ſome haue nothing to ſhew but leaues only; and ſome among them are dry ſtocks: ſo is it in the church, which is Gods orchard, there are ſome eminent Chriſtians that are ſoe frequent in good dutys, that many times the waight therof impares both their bodys and eſtates; and there are ſome (and they ſincere ones too) who haue not attained to that fruitfullnes, altho they aime at perfection: And again there are others that haue nothing to commend them but only a gay proffession, and these are but leavie christians, which are in as much danger of being cut down as the dry stock, for both cumber the ground.

LXV.

WE see in the firmament there is but one Sun among a multitude of starres, and those starres also to differ much one from the other in regard of bignes and brightnes, yet all receiue their light from that one Sun: so is it in the church both militant and triumphant, there is but one Christ, who is the Sun of righteousnes, in the midest of an innumerable company of Saints and Angels; those Saintes haue their degrees euen in this life, some are Stars of the first magnitude, and some of a lesse degree; and others (and they indeed the most in number), but small and obscure, yet all receiue their luster (be it more or lesse) from that glorious sun that inlightens all in all; and, if some of them shine so bright while they moue on earth, how transcendently splendid shall they be, when they are fixt in their heauenly spheres!

LXVI.

MEN that haue walked very extrauagantly, and at last bethink themselues of turning to God, the first thing which they eye, is how to reform their wayes rather then to beg forgiuenes for their sinnes: nature lookes more at a Compensation then at a pardon; but he that will not Come for mercy without mony and without price, but bring his filthy raggs to barter for it, shall meet with miserable disapointment, going away empty, beareing the reproch of his pride and folly.

LXVII.

ALL the works and doings of God are wonderfull, but none more awfull then his great worke of election and Reprobation; when we consider how many good parents haue had bad children, and againe how many bad parents haue had pious children, it should make vs adore the Soueraínty of God, who will not be tyed to time nor place, nor yet to persons, but takes and chuses when and where and whom he pleases: it should alsoe teach the children of godly parents to walk with feare and trembling, lest they, through vnbeleif, fall short of a promise: it may also be a support to such as haue or had wicked parents, that, if they abide not in vnbeleif, God is able to graffe them in: the vpshot of all should makes vs, with the Apostle, to admire the iustice and mercy of God, and say, how vnsearchable are his wayes, and his footsteps past finding out.

LXVIII.

THE gifts that God beftows on the fons of men, are not only abufed, but moft Commonly imployed for a Clean Contrary end, then that which they were giuen for, as health, wealth, and honour, which might be fo many fteps to draw men to God in confideration of his bounty towards them, but haue driuen them the further from him, that they are ready to fay, we are lords, we will come no more at thee. If outward bleffings be not as wings to help vs mount vpwards, they will Certainly proue Clogs and waights that will pull vs lower downward.

LXIX.

ALL the Comforts of this life may be compared to the gourd of Jonah, that notwithftanding we take great delight for a feafon in them, and find their fhadow very comfortable, yet there is fome worm or other of difcontent, of feare, or greife that lyes at the root, which in great part withers the pleafure which elfe we fhould take in them; and well it is that we perceiue a decay in their greennes, for were earthly comforts permanent, who would look for heauenly?

LXX.

ALL men are truly fayd to be tenants at will, and it may as truly be fayd, that all haue a leafe of their liues,—fome longer, fome fhorter,—as it pleafes our great landlord to let. All haue their bounds set, ouer which they cannot passe, and till the expiration of that time, no dangers, no ficknes, no paines nor troubles, shall put a period to our dayes; the certainty that that time will come, together with the vncertainty how, where, and when, should make vs so to number our dayes as to apply our hearts to wisedome, that when wee are put out of these houses of clay, we may be sure of an euerlasting habitation that fades not away.

LXXI.

ALL weak and diseased bodys haue hourly mementos of their mortality. But the soundest of men haue likwise their nightly monitor by the embleam of death, which is their sleep (for so is death often calld), and not only their death, but their graue is liuely represented before their eyes, by beholding their bed; the morning may mind them of the resurrection; and the sun approaching, of the appearing of the Sun of righteousnes, at whose comeing they shall all rise out of their beds, the long night shall fly away, and the day of eternity shall neuer end: seeing these things must be, what manner of persons ought we to be, in all good conversation?

LXXII.

AS the brands of a fire, if once severed, will of themselues goe out, altho you vse no other meanes to extinguish them, so distance of place, together with length of time (if there be no intercourſe) will coole the affectiones of intimate friends, though there ſhould be no diſpleaſence betweene them.

LXXIII.

A GOOD name is as a precious oyntment, and it is a great favour to haue a good repute among good men; yet it is not that which Commends vs to God, for by his ballance we muſt be weighed, and by his Judgment we muſt be tryed, and, as he paſſes the ſentence, ſo ſhall we ſtand.

LXXIV.

WELL doth the Apoſtle call riches deceitfull riches, and they may truely be compared to deceitfull friends who ſpeake faire, and promiſe much, but perform nothing, and ſo leaue thoſe in the lurch that moſt relyed on them: ſo is it with the wealth, honours, and pleaſures of this world, which miſerably delude men and make them put great confidence in them, but when death threatens, and diſtreſſe lays hold vpon them, they proue like the reeds of Egipt that peirce inſteed of ſupporting,* like empty wells in the time of drought, that thoſe that go to finde water in them, return with their empty pitchers aſhamed.

* "Now, behold, thou trustest upon the staff of this bruised reed, *even* upon Egypt, on which if a man lean, it will go into his hand, and pierce it." —2 KINGS xviii. 21.

LXXV.

IT is admirable to consider the power of faith, by which all things are (almost) possible to be done: it can remoue mountaines (if need were) it hath stayd the course of the sun, raised the dead, cast out divels, reversed the order of nature, quenched the violence of the fire, made the water become firme footing for Peter to walk on; nay more then all these, it hath ouercome the Omnipotent himself, as when Moses intercedes for the people, God sath to him, let me alone that I may destroy them, as if Moses had been able, by the hand of faith, to hold the everlasting armes of the mighty God of Jacob ; yea, Jacob himself, when he wrestled with God face to face in Peniel: let me go! sath that Angell. I will not let thee go, replys Jacob, till thou blesse me! faith is not only thus potent, but it is so necessary that without faith there is no salvation, therfore, with all our seekings and gettings, let vs aboue all seek to obtain this pearle of prise.

LXXVI.

SOME christians do by their lusts and Corruptions as the Isralits did by the Canaanites, not destroy them, but put them vnder tribute, for that they could do (as they thought) with lesse hazard, and more profit; but what was the Issue? they became a snare vnto them, prickes in their eyes, and thornes in their sides, and at laſt ouercame them, and kept them vnder ſlauery: ſo it is moſt certain that thoſe that are diſobedient to the Command of God, and endeavour not to the vtmoſt to drive out all their accurſed inmates, but make a league with them, they ſhall at laſt fall into perpetuall bondage vnder them vnleſſe the great deliuerer, Chriſt Jeſus, come to their reſcue.

LXXVII.

GOD hath by his prouidence ſo ordered, that no one Covntry hath all Commoditys within it ſelf, but what it wants, another ſhall ſupply, that ſo there may be a mutuall Commerce through the world. As it is with Covntrys ſo it is with men, there was neuer yet any one man that had all excellences, let his parts, naturall and acquired, ſpirituall and morall, be neuer ſo large, yet he ſtands in need of ſomething which another man hath, (perhaps meaner then himſelf,) which ſhews vs perfection is not below, as alſo, that God will haue vs beholden one to another.

MY hon[d] and dear mother intended to haue filled up this Book with the like obſervations, but was prevented by Death.*

* This note is in the handwriting of the Rev. Simon Bradstreet.

Ad Sim. Bradſtreet filium chariſsimum meum.

IN posteris Parentes vitam perpetuam faciunt, & in liberorum imitatione, mores diuturnos.

Naturaliter tamen posteritati ineſt diſpositio magis, defectus majorum quam vertutes imitari. Sed a te, meliora, mi Fili, expecto. Tu enim, petiisti, ut scriptioni tibi legendum, aliquid, cum ab oculis detraherer, committerem. His igitur sequentibus meditatiunculis, nihil venit in mentem, tibi idoneus, mihi nihil facilius. Qualia ſunt addico tibi. Parva ab amicis acceptabilia ſunt dona, multo magis, a filiis piis. Cogitationes aliorum quo nullas niſi verè maternas darem, studiosé vitavi; quas, magni estimandas, credo, mei cauſâ, futuras, licet seipsis, parvas fuerint. Largiatur tibi in hac vitâ gratiam suam Jehovah, & posthâc gloriæ coronam donet, ut in Die judicii, gaudio te summo, aſpiciam.—Sic Deum continuò ſupplicè rogat

Tua amantiſsima Parens,

Ann Bradstreet.

Mar. 20. 1664.

Hæc Epiſtola Romano Sermone verſus eſt à Simone Bradſtreet hujus Excellentiſsimæ Fæminæ Pronepote, cum ſequentibus meditatiunculis.*

* "This epistle was translated into the Roman Language by Simon Bradstreet, this most excellent woman's great-grandson, together with the following short meditations."

This Simon Bradstreet was son of the Rev. Simon Bradstreet, of

Meditationes Divinæ & Ethicæ.

I.

EST nihil occulis visibile, hominum nullæ actiones, nullum acquisitum bonum, nullum præsens uel futurum malum, a quibus omnibus animi salutem & utilitatem promovere non possimus — Et ille homo, non minus sapiens, quàm pius est, qui tales fructus ab eis carpit.

II.

PLURIMI queant bene loqui, at paucis bene agere. Majores in speculatione, quam sumus in actione. Ipse autem reverà Christianus est qui in utrisque proficit.

III.

JUVENTUS est capiendi, ampliandi ætas media & utendi senectus, optima opportunitas. Juventus remissa, ignorantem facit mediam ætatem, & ferè, senectutem, utræque vacuam reduat. Et cujus est tantum vanitate & mendaciis cibus, cubitum mæstus est eundum.

Charlestown, Mass., and grandson of the Rev. Simon Bradstreet, of New London, Conn. He was graduated at Harvard College in 1728, and was ordained minister of the Second Church in Marblehead, Mass., Jan. 4, 1738, to fill the place of the Rev. Edward Holyoke, who had been elected President of Harvard College. He is described as "a most worthy, pious, devout christian, and faithful pastor," and also as "an excellent scholar." — MASS. HIST. COLL., viii. 75–76.

This Latin translation was probably made in his youth. He died Oct. 5, 1771.

IV.

UT navis quæ nimium vela petit ſubtimia,* nullamq; habens vel levem ſuburram,† citò evertitur, sic homo multa scientia ac doctrina, ſed gratia & prudentia parva præditus, ab imis ruinæ profunditatibus non procul abest.

* *Sublimia.* † *Saburram.*

P O E M S.

THE "POEMS" are printed from the second edition, which was published in Boston, in 1678, and which contained the author's corrections, and some unpublished pieces. Fac-similes of the title-pages of the first and second editions are given.

THE TENTH MUSE

Lately ſprung up in AMERICA.

OR

Severall Poems, compiled with great variety of VVit and Learning, full of delight.

Wherein eſpecially is contained a compleat diſcourſe and deſcription of

The Four { *Elements,* *Conſtitutions,* *Ages of Man,* *Seaſons of the Year.*

Together with an Exact Epitomie of the Four Monarchies, *viz.*

The { *Aſſyrian,* *Perſian,* *Grecian,* *Roman.*

Alſo a Dialogue between Old *England* and New, concerning the late troubles.

With divers other pleaſant and ſerious Poems.

By a Gentlewoman in thoſe parts.

Printed at *London* for *Stephen Bowtell* at the ſigne of the Bible in Popes Head-Alley. 1650.

SEVERAL
POEMS

Compiled with great variety of Wit and Learning, full of Delight;

Wherein especially is contained a compleat Discourse, and Description of

The Four { ELEMENTS. CONSTITUTIONS, AGES of Man, SEASONS of the Year.

Together with an exact Epitome of the three first *Monarchyes*

Viz. The { *ASSYRIAN, PERSIAN, GRECIAN.*

And beginning of the Romane Common-wealth *to the end of their last King:*

With diverse other pleasant & serious *Poems*,

By a Gentlewoman in *New-England.*

The second Edition, Corrected by the Author, and enlarged by an Addition of several other Poems found amongst her Papers after her Death.

Boston, Printed by *John Foster*, 1678.

Kind Reader:

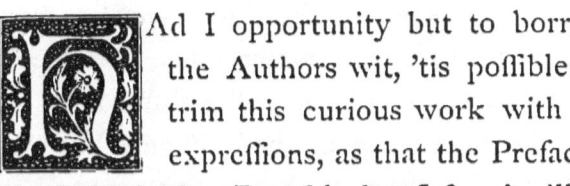

HAd I opportunity but to borrow ſome of the Authors wit, 'tis poſſible I might ſo trim this curious work with ſuch quaint expreſſions, as that the Preface might beſpeak thy further Peruſal; but I fear 'twill be a ſhame for a Man that can ſpeak ſo little, To be ſeen in the title-page of this Womans Book, leſt by comparing the one with the other, the Reader ſhould paſs his ſentence that it is the gift of women not only to ſpeak moſt but to ſpeak beſt; I ſhal leave therefore to commend that, which with any ingenious Reader will too much commend the Author, unleſs men turn more peeviſh then women, to envy the excellency of the inferiour Sex. I doubt not but the Reader will quickly find more then I can ſay, and the worſt effect of his reading will be unbelief, which will make him queſtion whether it be a womans work, and aſke, Is is poſſible? If any do, take this as an anſwer from him that dares avow it; It is the Work of a Woman, honoured, and eſteemed where ſhe lives, for her gracious demeanour, her eminent parts, her pious converſation, her courteous diſpoſition, her exact diligence in her place, and diſcreet managing of her Family [iv] occaſions, and more then ſo, theſe Poems are the fruit but of ſome few houres, curtailed from her ſleep and other refreſhments. I dare adde little leſt I keep thee too long; if thou wilt not believe the worth of theſe things (in their kind) when a man ſayes it, yet believe it from a woman when thou ſeeſt it. This only I ſhall annex, I fear the diſpleaſure of no perſon in the publiſhing of theſe Poems but the Author, without whoſe knowledg, and contrary to her expectation, I have preſumed to bring to publick view, what ſhe reſolved in ſuch a manner ſhould never ſee the Sun; but I found that diverſe had gotten ſome ſcattered Papers, affected them well, were likely to have ſent forth broken pieces, to the Authors prejudice, which I thought to prevent, as well as to pleaſure thoſe that earneſtly deſired the view of the whole.

MErcury ſhew'd *Apollo*, *Bartas* Book,
Minerva this, and wiſht him well to look,
And tell uprightly which did which excell,
He view'd and view'd, and vow'd he could not tel.
They bid him Hemiſphear his mouldy noſe,
With's crackt leering glaſſes, for it would poſe
The beſt brains he had in's old pudding-pan,
Sex weigh'd, which beſt, the Woman, or the Man?
He peer'd and por'd, & glar'd, & ſaid for wore,
I'me even as wiſe now, as I was before:
They both 'gan laugh, and ſaid it was no mar'l
The Auth'reſs was a right *Du Bartas* Girle.
Good ſooth quoth the old *Don*, tell ye me ſo,
I muſe whither at length theſe Girls will go;
It half revives my chil froſt-bitten blood,
To ſee a Woman once, do ought that's good;
And chode by *Chaucers* Boots, and *Homers* Furrs,
Let Men look to't, leaſt Women wear the Spurrs.

*N. Ward.**

* This clergyman, well known as the eccentric author of "The Simple Cobbler of Agawam," had been a neighbor of Mrs. Bradstreet in Ipswich. He returned to England in 1647, and may have been concerned in the publication of her poems.

To my dear Siſter, the Author of these Poems. [vi]

THough moſt that know me, dare (I think) affirm
I ne're was born to do a Poet harm,
Yet when I read your pleaſant witty ſtrains,
It wrought ſo ſtrongly on my addle brains;
That though my verſe be not ſo finely ſpun,
And ſo (like yours) cannot ſo neatly run,
Yet am I willing, with upright intent,
To ſhew my love without a complement.
There needs no painting to that comely face,
That in its native beauty hath ſuch grace;
What I (poor ſilly I) prefix therefore,
Can but do this, make yours admir'd the more;
And if but only this, I do attain
Content, that my diſgrace may be your gain.
If women, I with women may compare,
Your works are ſolid, others weak as Air;
Some Books of Women I have heard of late,
Peruſed ſome, ſo witleſs, intricate,
So void of ſenſe, and truth, as if to erre
Were only wiſht (acting above their ſphear)
And all to get, what (ſilly Souls) they lack,
Eſteem to be the wiſeſt of the pack;

Though (for your ſake) to ſome this be permitted, [vii]
To print, yet wiſh I many better witted;
Their vanity make this to be enquired,
If Women are with wit and ſence inſpired:
Yet when your Works ſhall come to publick view,
'Twill be affirm'd, 'twill be confirm'd by you:
And I, when ſeriouſly I had revolved
What you had done, I preſently reſolved,
Theirs was the Perſons, not the Sexes failing,
And therefore did be-ſpeak a modeſt vailing.
You have acutely in *Eliza*'s ditty,*
Acquitted Women, elſe I might with pitty,
Have wiſht them all to womens Works to look,
And never more to meddle with their book.
What you have done, the Sun ſhall witneſs bear,
That for a womans Work 'tis very rare;
And if the Nine, vouchſafe the Tenth a place,
I think they rightly may yield you that grace.
But leaſt I ſhould exceed, and too much love,
Should too too much endear'd affection move,
To ſuper-adde in praiſes, I ſhall ceaſe,
Leaſt while I pleaſe myſelf I ſhould diſpleaſe
The longing Reader, who may chance complain,
And ſo requite my love with deep diſdain;
That I your ſilly Servant, ſtand i' th' Porch,
Lighting your Sun-light, with my blinking Torch;
Hindring his minds content, his ſweet repoſe,
Which your delightful Poems do diſcloſe,

* See her Elegy "In Honour of that High and Mighty Princeſs Queen Elizabeth of Happy Memory."

When once the Caſkets op'ned; yet to you
Let this be added, then I'le bid adieu,
If you ſhall think, it will be to your ſhame [viii]
To be in print, then I muſt bear the blame:
If't be a fault, 'tis mine, 'tis ſhame that might
Deny ſo fair an Infant of its right,
To look abroad; I know your modeſt mind,
How you will bluſh, complain, 'tis too unkind:
To force a womans birth, provoke her pain,
Expoſe her labours to the Worlds diſdain.
I know you'l ſay, you do defie that mint,
That ſtampt you thus, to be a fool in print.
'Tis true, it doth not now ſo neatly ſtand,
As if 'twere polliſht with your own ſweet hand;
'Tis not ſo richly deckt, ſo trimly tir'd,
Yet it is ſuch as juſtly is admir'd.
If it be folly, 'tis of both, or neither,
Both you and I, we'l both be fools together;
And he that ſayes, 'tis fooliſh, (if my word
May ſway) by my conſent ſhall make the third,
I dare out-face the worlds diſdain for both,
If you alone profeſs you are not wroth;
Yet if you are, a Womans wrath is little,
When thouſands elſe admire you in each Tittle.

*I. W.**

* Both this and the address to the reader were undoubtedly written by the Rev. John Woodbridge, first minister of Andover. He was Mrs. Bradstreet's brother-in-law, having married her sister Mercy. He sailed for England in 1647, and was there when the first edition of these poems was published. A more particular account of him is given in the Introduction.

Vpon the Author; by a known Friend. [ix]

NOw I believe Tradition, which doth call
The Muſes, Virtues, Graces, Females all;
Only they are not nine, eleven nor three;
Our Auth'reſs proves them but one unity.
Mankind take up ſome bluſhes on the ſcore;
Monopolize perfection no more;
In your own Arts, confeſs your ſelves out-done,
The Moon hath totally eclips'd the Sun,
Not with her ſable Mantle muffling him;
But her bright ſilver makes his gold look dim:
Juſt as his beams force our pale lamps to wink,
And earthly Fires, within their aſhes ſhrink.

B. W.*

* These initials, which appeared for the first time in the second edition, are thought to be those of the Rev. Benjamin Woodbridge, D.D., brother of the Rev. John Woodbridge. He was born in England, and after having studied at Magdalen College, Oxford, came to join his brother, and some other relations, in this country. He entered Harvard College, and his name stands first on the list of graduates. He was among the first settlers of the town of Andover; but he soon returned to England, where he succeeded the Rev. William Twiss, D.D., as minister of Newbury, in

I cannot wonder at Apollo *now,*
That he with Female Laurel crown'd his brow,
That made him witty: had I leave to choſe,
My Verſe ſhould be a page unto your Muſe

C. B.*

Berkshire. He held that position until his death in 1684, a period of about forty years. His learning, ability, and goodness have been highly eulogized.

I have been unable to discover to whom the initials belong attached to the other verses.

* In the first edition, immediately after these, are the following verses: —

ARME, arme, Soldado's arme, Horſe,
Horſe, ſpeed to your Horſes,
Gentle-women, make head, they vent
their plots in Verſes;
They write of Monarchies, a moſt ſe-
ditious word,
It ſignifies Oppreſſion, Tyranny, and
Sword:
March amain to *London*, they'l riſe, for
there they flock,
But ſtay a while, they ſeldome riſe till
ten a clock.

R. Q.

In praise of the Author, Mistris *Anne Bradstreet*, [x]
Virtues true and lively Pattern, Wife of the
Worshipfull *Simon Bradstreet* Esq;

At present residing in the Occidental parts of the World in America, Alias
NOV-ANGLIA.

VV*Hat golden splendent STAR is this so bright,*
One thousand Miles twice told, both day and night,
(From th' Orient first sprung) now from the West
That shines; swift-winged Phœbus, *and the rest*
Of all Jove's *fiery flames surmounting far*
As doth each Planet, every falling Star;
By whose divine and lucid light most clear
Natures dark secret mysteryes appear;
Heavens, Earths, admired wonders, noble acts
Of Kings and Princes most heroick facts,
And what e're else in darkness seem'd to dye,
Revives all things so obvious now to th' eye,
That he who these its glittering rayes views o're,
Shall see what's done in all the world before.

N. H.

Upon the Author. [xi]

'TWere extream folly ſhould I dare attempt,
To praiſe this Authors worth with complement;
None but her ſelf muſt dare commend her parts,
Whoſe ſublime brain's the Synopſis of Arts.
Nature and ſkill, here both in one agree,
To frame this Maſter-piece of Poetry:
Falſe Fame, belye their Sex no more, it can
Surpaſs, or parallel, the beſt of Man.

C. B.

Another to Mrs. *Anne Bradſtreet*, Author of this Poem.

I'Ve read your Poem (Lady) and admire,
Your Sex to ſuch a pitch ſhould e're aſpire;
Go on to write, continue to relate,
New Hiſtoryes, of Monarchy and State:
And what the *Romans* to their Poets gave,
Be ſure ſuch honour, and eſteem you'l have.

H. S.

An Anagram.

Anna Bradeſtreate Deer neat *An Bartas.*

SO *Bartas* like thy fine ſpun Poems been,
That *Bartas* name will prove an Epicene.

Another.

Anna Bradſtreate Artes bred neat *An.*

VPON

Mrs. Anne Bradſtreet

Her Poems, &c.

MADAM, twice through the Muſes Grove I walkt,
Under your bliſsfull bowres, I ſhrowding there,
It ſeem'd with Nymphs of *Helicon* I talkt:
For there thoſe ſweet-lip'd Siſters ſporting were,
Apollo with his ſacred Lute ſate by,
On high they made their heavenly Sonnets flye,
Poſies around they ſtrow'd, of ſweeteſt Poeſie.

2

Twice have I drunk the Nectar of your lines,
Which high ſublim'd my mean born phantaſie,
Fluſht with theſe ſtreams of your *Maronean* wines
Above my ſelf rapt to an extaſie:
Methought I was upon Mount *Hiblas* top,
There where I might thoſe fragrant flowers lop,
Whence did ſweet odors flow, and honey ſpangles drop.

3

To *Venus* ſhrine no Altars raiſed are,
Nor venom'd ſhafts from painted quiver fly,
Nor wanton Doves of *Aphrodites* Carr,
Or fluttering there, nor here forlornly lie,
Lorne Paramours, not chatting birds tell news
How ſage *Apollo*, *Daphne* hot purſues,
Or ſtately *Jove* himſelf is wont to haunt the ſtews.

4

Nor barking Satyrs breath, nor driery clouds [xiii]
Exhal'd from *Styx*, their diſmal drops diſtil
Within theſe *Fairy*, flowry fields, nor ſhrouds
The ſcreeching night Raven, with his ſhady quill:
But Lyrick ſtrings here *Orpheus* nimbly hitts,
Orion on his ſadled Dolphin ſits,
Chanting as every humour, age & ſeaſon fits.

5

Here ſilver ſwans, with Nightingales ſet ſpells,
Which ſweetly charm the Traveller, and raiſe
Earths earthed Monarchs, from their hidden Cells,
And to appearance ſummons lapſed dayes,
There heav'nly air, becalms the ſwelling frayes,
And fury fell of Elements allayes,
By paying every one due tribute of his praiſe.

6

This ſeem'd the Scite of all thoſe verdant vales,
And purled ſprings, whereat the Nymphs do play,
With lofty hills, where Poets rear their tales,
To heavenly vaults, which heav'nly ſound repay
By ecchoes ſweet rebound, here Ladyes kiſs,
Circling nor ſongs, nor dances circle miſs;
But whilſt thoſe Syrens ſung, I ſunk in ſea of bliſs.

7

Thus weltring in delight, my virgin mind
Admits a rape; truth ſtill lyes undiſcri'd,
Its ſingular, that plural ſeem'd, I find,
'Twas Fancies glaſs alone that multipli'd;
Nature with Art ſo cloſely did combine,
I thought I ſaw the Muſes trebble trine,
Which prov'd your lonely Muſe, ſuperiour to the nine.

8

Your only hand thoſe Poeſies did compoſe, [xiv]
Your head the ſource, whence all thoſe ſprings did flow,
Your voice, whence changes ſweeteſt notes aroſe,
Your feet that kept the dance alone, I trow:
Then vail your bonnets, Poetaſters all,
Strike, lower amain, and at theſe humbly fall,
And deem your ſelves advanc'd to be her Pedeſtal.

9

Should all with lowly Congies Laurels bring,
Waſte *Floraes* Magazine to find a wreathe;
Or *Pineus* Banks 'twere too mean offering,
Your Muſe a fairer Garland doth bequeath
To guard your fairer front; here 'tis your name
Shall ſtand immarbled; this your little frame
Shall great *Coloſſus* be, to your eternal fame.

I'le pleaſe my ſelf, though I my ſelf diſgrace,
What errors here be found, are in *Erratæs* place.

J. Rogers.*

* These verses were not in the first edition. Their author was the son of the Rev. Nathaniel Rogers, of Ipswich. He was born in England in 1630, and came to America, with his father, in 1636. He graduated at Harvard College in 1649, and studied both divinity and medicine. He preached at Ipswich for some time, but afterwards devoted himself altogether to the practice of medicine. In 1682, he succeeded the Rev. Urian Oakes as President of Harvard College. He died suddenly, July 2, 1684, the day after Commencement, during an eclipse of the sun. He had requested, in the previous December, that the Commencement exercises should be held a day earlier than usual, as he feared the eclipse might interfere with them.—MATHER PAPERS. Cotton Mather says, "He was One of ſo ſweet a Temper, that the Title of *Deliciæ humani Generis* might have on that Score been given him; and his Real *Piety* ſet off with the Accompliſhments of a *Gentleman*, as a *Gem* ſet in *Gold*."—MAGNALIA, iv. p. 130.

His wife, Elizabeth Denison, was the only daughter of Major-General Daniel Denison and Patience Dudley, and therefore Mrs. Bradstreet's niece.

To her most Honoured Father *Thomas Dudley* Esq; *these humbly presented.* [1]

DEar Sir of late delighted with the sight
Of your four Sisters cloth'd* in black and white,
Of fairer Dames the Sun, ne'r saw the face;
Though made a pedestal for *Adams* Race;
Their worth so shines in these rich lines you show
Their paralels to finde I scarcely know
To climbe their Climes, I have nor strength nor skill
To mount so high requires an Eagles quill;
Yet view thereof did cause my thoughts to soar;
My lowly pen might wait upon these four

T. D. *On the four parts of the world.*†

* We have in the first edition, instead of this, "deckt." The readings of the first edition will be designated hereafter, without further comment, by notes distinguished by the letters of the alphabet.

† This was probably a manuscript poem. Nothing further is known of it.

I bring my four times four,[a] now meanly clad
To do their homage, unto yours, full[b] glad:
Who for their Age, their worth and quality
Might ſeem of yours to claim precedency:
But by my humble hand, thus rudely pen'd
They are, your bounden handmaids to attend
Theſe ſame are they, from whom we being have [2]
Theſe are of all, the Life, the Nurſe, the Grave,
Theſe are the hot, the cold, the moiſt, the dry,
That ſink, that ſwim, that fill, that upwards fly,
Of theſe conſiſts our bodies, Cloathes and Food,
The World, the uſeful, hurtful, and the good,
Sweet harmony they keep, yet jar oft times
Their diſcord doth[c] appear, by theſe harſh rimes
Yours did conteſt for wealth, for Arts, for Age,
My firſt do ſhew their good, and then their rage.
My other foures[d] do intermixed tell
Each others faults, and where themſelves excell;
How hot and dry contend with moiſt and cold,
How Air and Earth no correſpondence hold,
And yet in equal tempers, how they 'gree
How divers natures make one Unity
Something of all (though mean) I did intend
But fear'd you'ld judge *Du*[e] *Bartas* was my friend
I honour him, but dare not wear his wealth
My goods are true (though poor) I love no ſtealth

[a] my four; and four. [b] moſt. [c] may.
[d] four. [e] one.

But if I did I durſt not ſend them you
Who muſt reward a Thief, but with his due.
I ſhall not need, mine innocence to clear
Theſe ragged lines, will do't, when they appear:
On what they are, your mild aſpect I crave
Accept my beſt, my worſt vouchſafe a Grave.

From her that to your ſelf, more duty owes
Then water in the boundeſs Ocean flows.

March 20. 1642.*

ANNE BRADSTREET.

* This date does not appear in the first edition.

THE PROLOGUE.

1.

TO ſing of Wars, of Captains, and of Kings,
Of Cities founded, Common-wealths begun,
For my mean pen are too ſuperiour things:
Or how they all, or each their dates have run
Let Poets and Hiſtorians ſet theſe forth,
My obſcure Lines/ ſhall not ſo dim their worth.

2.

But when my wondring eyes and envious heart
Great *Bartas* ſugar'd lines, do but read o're
Fool I do grudg the Muſes did not part
'Twixt him and me that overfluent ſtore;
A *Bartas* can, do what a *Bartas* will
But ſimple I according to my ſkill.

3.

From ſchool-boyes tongue no rhet'rick we expect
Nor yet a ſweet Conſort from broken ſtrings,
Nor perfect beauty, where's a main defect:
My fooliſh, broken, blemiſh'd Muſe ſo ſings

/ Verſe.

And this to mend, alas, no Art is able,
'Cause nature, made it so irreparable.

4.

Nor can I, like that fluent sweet tongu'd Greek,
Who lisp'd at first, in future times speak plain[g]
By Art he gladly found what he did seek
A full requital of his, striving pain
Art can do much, but this maxime's most sure [4]
A weak or wounded brain admits no cure.

5.

I am obnoxious to each carping tongue
Who says my hand a needle better fits,
A Poets pen all scorn I should thus wrong,
For such despite they cast on Female wits:
If what I do prove well, it won't advance,
They'l say it's stoln, or else it was by chance.

6.

But sure the Antique Greeks were far more mild
Else of our Sexe, why feigned they those Nine
And poesy made, *Calliope's* own Child;
So 'mongst the rest they placed the Arts Divine,
But this weak knot, they will full soon untie,
The Greeks did nought, but play the fools & lye.

[g] speake afterwards more plaine.

7.

Let Greeks be Greeks, and women what they are
Men have precedency and ſtill excell,
It is but vain unjuſtly to wage warre;
Men can do beſt, and women know it well
Preheminence in all and each is yours;
Yet grant ſome ſmall acknowledgement of ours.

8.

And oh ye high flown quills that ſoar the Skies,
And ever with your prey ſtill catch your praiſe,
If e're you daigne theſe lowly lines your eyes
Give Thyme or [h] Parſley wreath, I ask no bayes,
This mean and unrefined ure [i] of mine
Will make you gliſtring gold, but more to ſhine.*

[h] Give wholſome. [i] ſtuffe.

* The initials, "A. B.," are appended in the first edition.

The

Four Elements.

THe Fire, Air, Earth and water did conteſt[j]
Which was the ſtrongeſt, nobleſt and the beſt,
Who was of greateſt uſe and might'eſt force;
In placide Terms they thought now to diſcourſe,[k]
That in due order each her turn ſhould ſpeak;
But enmity this amity did break
All would be chief, and all ſcorn'd to be under
Whence iſſu'd winds & rains, lightning & thunder
The quaking earth did groan, the Sky lookt black
The Fire, the forced Air, in ſunder crack;
The ſea did threat the heav'ns, the heavn's the earth,
All looked like a Chaos or new birth:
Fire broyled Earth, & ſcorched Earth it choaked
Both by their darings, water ſo provoked
That roaring in it came, and with its ſource
Soon made the Combatants abate their force

[j] Fire, Aire, Earth, and Water, did all conteſt.

[k] Who the moſt good could ſhew, & who moſt rage
For to declare, themſelves they all ingage.

The rumbling hiſſing, puffing was ſo great
The worlds confuſion, it did ſeem to threat
Till gentle Air,[l] Contention ſo abated
That betwixt hot and cold, ſhe arbitrated
The others difference,[m] being leſs did ceaſe
All ſtorms now laid, and they in perfect peace
That Fire ſhould firſt begin, the reſt conſent, [6]
The nobleſt and moſt active Element.[n]

Fire.

WHAT is my worth (both ye) and all men[o] know,
In little time[p] I can but little ſhow,
But what I am, let learned Grecians ſay
What I can do well skil'd Mechanicks may:
The benefit all living[q] by me finde,
All ſorts of Artiſts, here[r] declare your mind,
What tool was ever fram'd, but by my might?
Ye Martiliſts, what weapons[s] for your fight
To try your valour by, but it muſt feel
My force? your ſword, & Gun,[t] your Lance of ſteel

[l] But Aire at length. [m] enmity. [n] Being the moſt impatient Element.
[o] things. [p] Where little is. [q] Beings. [r] Come firſt ye Artiſts, and.
[s] O Martialiſt! what weapon. [t] your Pike, your flint and ſteele.

Your Cannon's bootlefs and your powder too
Without mine aid, (alas) what can they do:
The adverfe walls not fhak'd, the Mines not blown
And in defpight the City keeps her own;
But I with one Granado or Petard
Set ope thofe gates, that 'fore fo ftrong were bar'd
Ye Hufband-men, your Coulters made by me
Your Hooes[u] your Mattocks, & what e're you fee
Subdue the Earth, and fit it for your Grain
That fo it might in time requite your pain:
Though ftrong limb'd Vulcan forg'd it by his skill
I made it flexible unto his will;
Ye Cooks, your Kitchen implements I frame
Your Spits, Pots, Jacks, what elfe I need not name
Your dayly[v] food I wholfome make, I warm [7]
Your fhrinking Limbs, which winter's cold doth harm
Ye *Paracelfians* too in vain's your skill
In Chymiftry, unlefs I help you Still.
And you Philofophers, if e're you made
A tranfmutation it was through mine aid.
Ye filver Smiths, your Ure I do refine
What mingled lay with Earth I caufe to fhine;
But let me leave thefe things, my flame afpires
To match on high with the Celeftial fires:
The Sun an Orb of fire was held of old,
Our Sages new another tale have told:
But be he what they will,[w] yet his afpect
A burning fiery heat we find reflect

[u] fhares. [v] dainty. [w] lift.

And of the ſelf ſame nature is with mine
Cold[x] ſiſter Earth, no witneſs needs but thine:
How doth his warmth, refreſh thy frozen back[y]
And trim thee brave,[z] in green, after thy black.[a]
Both man and beaſt rejoyce at his approach,
And birds do ſing, to ſee his glittering Coach
And though nought, but *Salmander's* live in fire
And fly Pyrauſta call'd, all elſe expire,
Yet men and beaſt Aſtronomers will tell
Fixed in heavenly Conſtellations dwell,
My Planets of both Sexes whoſe degree
Poor Heathen judg'd worthy a Diety:
There's *Orion* arm'd attended by his dog;
The *Theban* ſtout *Alcides* with his Club;
The valiant *Perſeus*, who *Meduſa* ſlew,
The horſe that kil'd *Belerophon*, then flew.
My Crab, my Scorpion, fiſhes you may ſee [8]
The Maid with ballance, wain with horſes three,
The Ram, the Bull, the Lion, and the Beagle,
The Bear, the Goat, the Raven, and the Eagle,
The Crown the Whale, the Archer, Bernice Hare
The Hidra, Dolphin, Boys that water bear,
Nay more, then theſe, Rivers 'mongſt ſtars are found
Eridanus, where *Phaeton* was drown'd.
Their magnitude, and height, ſhould I recount
My ſtory to a volume would amount;
Out of a multitude theſe few I touch,
Your wiſdome out of little gather much.

[x] Good. [y] backs. [z] gay. [a] blacks.

I'le here let paſs, my choler, cauſe of wars
And influence of divers of thoſe ſtars
When in Conjunction with the Sun do more
Augment his heat, which was too hot before.
The Summer ripening ſeaſon I do claim
And man from thirty unto fifty frame.
Of old when Sacrifices were Divine,
I of acceptance was the holy ſigne,
'Mong all my wonders which I might recount,
There's none more ſtrange then *Ætna*'s Sulphry mount
The choaking flames, that from *Veſuvius* flew
The over curious ſecond *Pliny** flew,
And with the Aſhes that it ſometimes ſhed
Apulia's 'jacent parts were covered.
And though I be a ſervant to each man
Yet by my force, maſter, my maſters can.
What famous Towns, to Cinders have I turn'd?
What laſting forts my kindled wrath hath burn'd?
The ſtately Seats of mighty Kings by me [9]
In confuſed heaps, of aſhes may you ſee.
Wher's *Ninus* great wall'd Town, & *Troy* of old
Carthage, and hundred more in ſtories told
Which when they could not be o'recome by foes
The Army, through my help victorious roſe
And ſtately *London*, (our great *Britain*'s glory)
My raging flame did make a mournful ſtory,

* She does not mean, by mistake, the *Younger* Pliny, but translates the cognomen of *Secundus*, which belonged to both Plinys.

But maugre all, that I, or foes could do
That *Phœnix* from her Bed, is riſen New.*
Old ſacred *Zion*, I demoliſh'd thee.
Lo great *Diana*'s Temple was by me,
And more then bruitiſh *Sodom*, for her luſt
With neighbouring Towns, I did conſume to duſt
What ſhall I ſay of Lightning and of Thunder
Which Kings & mighty ones amaze with wonder,
Which made a *Cæſar*, (*Romes*) the worlds proud head,
Fooliſh *Caligula* creep under's bed.
Of *Meteors, ignis fatuus* and the reſt,
But to leave thoſe to th'wiſe, I judge it beſt.
The rich I oft make poor, the ſtrong I maime,
Not ſparing Life when I can take the ſame;
And in a word, the world I ſhall conſume
And all therein, at that great day of Doom;
Not before then, ſhall ceaſe, my raging ire
And then becauſe no matter more for fire
Now Siſters pray proceed, each in your Courſe
As I, impart your uſefulneſs and force.

* This and the three preceding lines were not in the first edition. The Great Fire of London did not take place until September, 1666.

Earth. [10]

THE next in place Earth judg'd to be her due,
Sifter (quoth fhee)[b] I come not fhort of you,
In wealth and ufe I do furpafs you all,
And mother earth of old men did me call:
Such is[c] my fruitfulnefs, an Epithite,
Which none ere gave, or you could claim of right
Among my praifes this I count not leaft,
I am th'original of man and beaft.
To tell what fundry fruits my fat foil yields
In Vineyards, Gardens, Orchards & Corn-fields,
Their kinds, their tafts, their colors & their fmells
Would fo pafs time I could fay nothing elfe:
The rich the poor, wife, fool, and every fort
Of thefe fo common things can make report.
To tell you of my countryes and my Regions,
Soon would they pafs not hundreds but legions:
My cities famous, rich and populous,
Whofe numbers now are grown innumerous.
I have not time to think of every part,
Yet let me name my *Grecia*, 'tis my heart.
For learning arms and arts I love it well,
But chiefly 'caufe the *Mufes* there did dwell.
Ile here skip ore my mountains reaching skyes,
Whether *Pyrenean*, or the *Alpes*, both lyes
On either fide the country of the *Gaules*
Strong forts, from *Spanifh* and *Italian* brawles.

[b] Sifter, in worth. [c] was.

And huge great *Taurus* longer then the rest, [11]
Dividing great *Armenia* from the least;
And *Hemus* whose steep sides none foot upon,
But farewell all for dear mount *Helicon*.
And wondrous high *Olimpus*, of such fame,
That heav'n it self was oft call'd by that name.
Parnassus sweet, I dote too much on thee,
Unless thou prove a better friend to me:
But Ile leap [d] ore these hills, not touch a dale,
Nor will I stay, no not in *Tempe* Vale,[e]
Ile here let go my Lions of *Numedia*,
My Panthers and my Leopards of *Libia*,
The Behemoth and rare found Unicorn,
Poysons sure antidote lyes in his horn,
And my *Hiæna* (imitates mans voice)
Out of great [f] numbers I might pick my choice,
Thousands in woods & plains, both wild & tame,
But here or there, I list now none to name:
No, though the fawning Dog did urge me sore,
In his behalf to speak a word the more,
Whose trust and valour I might here commend;
But time's too short and precious so to spend.
But hark you wealthy [g] merchants, who for prize
Send forth your well-man'd ships where sun doth rise,
After three years when men and meat is spent,
My rich Commodityes pay double rent.
Ye *Galenists*, my Drugs that come from thence,
Do cure your Patients, fill your purse with pence;

[d] skip. [e] Nor yet expatiate, in Temple vale;
[f] huge. [g] ye worthy.

Beſides the uſe of roots,[h] of hearbs and plants,
That with leſs coſt near home ſupply your wants.
But Mariners where got you ſhips and Sails, [12]
And Oars to row, when both my Siſters fails
Your Tackling, Anchor, compaſs too is mine,
Which guids when ſun nor moon nor ſtars do ſhine
Ye mighty Kings, who for your laſting fames
Built Cities, Monuments, call'd by your names,
Were thoſe compiled heaps of maſſy ſtones
That your ambition laid, ought but my bones?
Ye greedy miſers, who do dig for gold
For gemms, for ſilver, Treaſures which I hold,
Will not my goodly face your rage ſuffice
But you will ſee, what in my bowels lyes?
And ye Artificers, all Trades and ſorts
My bounty calls you forth to make reports,
If ought you have, to uſe, to wear, to eat,
But what I freely yield, upon your ſweat?
And Cholerick Siſter, thou for all thine ire
Well knowſt my fuel, muſt maintain thy fire.
As I ingenuouſly with thanks confeſs,
My cold thy fruitfull heat doth crave no leſs:
But how my cold dry temper works upon
The melancholy Conſtitution;
How the autumnal ſeaſon I do ſway,
And how I force the grey-head to obey,
I ſhould here make a ſhort, yet true Narration,
But that thy method is mine imitation.

[h] uſe you have.

Now muſt I ſhew mine adverſe quality,
And how I oft work mans mortality:
He ſometimes finds, maugre his toiling pain
Thiſtles and thorns where he expected grain.
My ſap to plants and trees I muſt not grant, [13]
The vine, the olive, and the figtree want:
The Corn and Hay do fall before the're mown,
And buds from fruitfull trees as ſoon as[i] blown;
Then dearth prevails, that nature to ſuffice
The Mother on her tender infant flyes;[j]
The huſband knows no wife, nor father ſons,
But to all outrages their hunger runs:
Dreadfull examples ſoon I might produce,
But to ſuch Auditors 'twere of no uſe.
Again when Delvers dare in hope of gold
To ope thoſe veins of *Mine*, audacious bold:
VVhile they thus in mine entrails love[k] to dive,
Before they know, they are inter'd alive.
Y'affrighted wights appal'd, how do ye ſhake,
VVhen once you feel me your foundation quake?
Becauſe in the Abbyſſe of my dark womb
Your cities and your ſelves I oft intomb:
O dreadfull Sepulcher! that this is true
Dathan * and all his company well knew,

[i] before they'r. [j] The tender mother on her Infant flyes. [k] ſeem.

* The first edition has "Korah" instead of "Dathan." It does not appear clearly from the account in Numbers, ch. xvi., whether Korah was swallowed up in the earth with Dathan and Abiram, or whether he was among those destroyed by the fire. See Patrick's "Commentary," and Smith's "Bible Dictionary."

So did that Roman, far more ſtout then wiſe,
Bur'ing himſelf alive for honours prize.[l]
And ſince fair *Italy* full ſadly knowes
What ſhe hath loſt by theſe remed'leſs[m] woes.[n]
Again what veins of poyſon in me lye,
Some kill outright, and ſome do ſtupifye:
Nay into herbs and plants it ſometimes creeps,
In heats & colds & gripes & drowzy ſleeps:
Thus I occaſion death to man and beaſt
When food they ſeek, & harm miſtruſt the leaſt.
Much might I ſay of the hot *Libian* ſand[o] [14]
Which riſe like tumbling[p] Billows on the Land[q]
Wherein *Cambyſes* Armie was o'rethrown[r]
(but windy Siſter, 'twas when you have blown)
I'le ſay no more, but this thing add I muſt
Remember Sons, your mould is of my duſt
And after death whether interr'd or burn'd
As Earth at firſt ſo into Earth return'd.

[l] This and the preceding line were not in the first edition.

[m] my dreadfull.

[n] After this we find in the first edition, —

> And *Rome*, her *Curtius*, can't forget I think;
> Who bravely rode into my yawning chinke.
> Again, what veines of poyſon in me lye;
> As *Stibium* and unfixt *Mercury*:
> With divers moe, nay, into plants it creeps;
> In hot, and cold, and ſome benums with ſleeps,

[o] the *Arabian* ſands; [p] mighty. [q] lands:

[r] Wherein whole Armies I have overthrown;

Water.

SCARCE Earth had done, but th'angry water mov'd
Siſter (quoth ſhe) it had full well behov'd
Among your boaſtings to have praiſed me
Cauſe of your fruitfulneſs as you ſhall ſee:
This your neglect ſhews your ingratitude
And how your ſubtilty, would men delude
Not one of us (all knows) that's like to thee
Ever in craving, from the other three;
But thou art bound to me, above the reſt
Who am thy drink, thy blood, thy ſap and beſt:
If I withhold what art thou? dead dry lump
Thou bearſt nor graſs or plant nor tree, nor ſtump
Thy extream thirſt is moiſtned by my love
With ſprings below, and ſhowres from above
Or elſe thy Sun-burnt face, and gaping chops
Complain to th' heavens, if I withhold my drops
Thy Bear, thy Tyger, and thy Lion ſtout,
When I am gone, their fiercenes none needs doubt
Thy Camel hath no ſtrength, thy Bull no force [15]
Nor mettal's found, in the couragious Horſe
Hinds leave their calves, the Elephant the Fens
The wolves and ſavage beaſts, forſake their Dens
The lofty Eagle, and the Stork fly low,
The Peacock and the Oſtrich, ſhare in woe,
The Pine, the Cedar, yea, and *Daphne*'s Tree
Do ceaſe to flouriſh in this miſery,

Man wants his bread and wine, & pleaſant fruits
He knows, ſuch ſweets, lies not in Earths dry roots
Then ſeeks me out, in river and in well
His deadly malady I might expell:
If I ſupply, his heart and veins rejoyce,
If not, ſoon ends his life, as did his voyce;
That this is true, Earth thou canſt not deny
I call thine *Egypt*, this to verifie,
Which by my fatting *Nile*, doth yield ſuch ſtore
That ſhe can ſpare, when nations round are poor
When I run low, and not o'reflow her brinks
To meet with want, each woful man be-thinks:
And ſuch I am, in Rivers, ſhowrs and ſprings
But what's the wealth, that my rich Ocean brings
Fiſhes ſo numberleſs, I there do hold
If thou ſhouldſt buy, it would exhauſt thy gold:
There lives the oyly Whale, whom all men know
Such wealth but not ſuch like, Earth thou maiſt ſhow
The Dolphin loving muſick, *Arians* friend
The witty[s] Barbel, whoſe craft[t] doth her commend
With thouſands more, which now I liſt not name
Thy ſilence of thy Beaſts doth cauſe the ſame
My pearles that dangle at thy Darlings ears, [16]
Not thou, but ſhel-fiſh yield, as *Pliny* clears.
Was ever gem ſo rich found in thy trunk,
As *Egypts* wanton, *Cleopatra* drunk?
Or haſt thou any colour can come nigh
The Roman purple, double *Tirian* Dye?

[s] crafty. [t] wit.

Which *Cæſars* Conſuls, Tribunes all adorn,
For it to ſearch my waves they thought no ſcorn.
Thy gallant rich perfuming Amber-greece
I lightly caſt aſhore as frothy fleece:
With rowling grains of pureſt maſſie gold,
Which *Spains Americans* do gladly hold.
Earth thou haſt not moe countrys vales & mounds
Then I have fountains, rivers lakes and ponds.
My ſundry ſeas, black, white and *Adriatique*,
Ionian, *Baltique* and the vaſt *Atlantique*,
Ægean,[u] *Caſpian*, golden Rivers five,
Aſphaltis lake where nought remains alive:
But I ſhould go beyond thee in my[v] boaſts,
If I ſhould name[w] more ſeas then thou haſt Coaſts.
And be thy mountains n'er ſo high and ſteep,
I ſoon can match them with my ſeas as deep.[x]
To ſpeak of kinds of waters I neglect,
My diverſe fountains and their ſtrange effect:
My wholſome bathes, together with their cures;
My water Syrens with their guilefull lures.
Th'uncertain cauſe of certain ebbs and flows,
Which wondring *Ariſtotles* wit n'er knows.
Nor will I ſpeak of waters made by art,
Which can to life reſtore a fainting heart.
Nor fruitfull dews, nor drops diſtil'd from[y] eyes, [17]
Which pitty move, and oft deceive the wiſe:

[u] The *Ponticke*. [v] thy. [w] ſhew.

[x] But note this maxime in Philoſophy:
Then Seas are deep, mountains are never high.

[y] drops from weeping.

Nor yet of falt and fugar, fweet and fmart,
Both when we lift to water we convert.
Alas thy fhips and oars could do no good
Did they but want my Ocean and my flood.
The wary merchant on his weary beaft
Tranffers his goods from fouth to north and eaft,
Unlefs I eafe his toil, and do tranfport
The wealthy fraight unto his wifhed port.
Thefe be my benefits, which may fuffice:
I now muft fhew what ill[z] there in me lies.
The flegmy Conftitution I uphold,
All humors, tumors which are bred of cold:
O're childhood and ore winter I bear fway,
And *Luna* for my Regent I obey.
As I with fhowers oft times refrefh the earth,
So oft in my excefs I caufe a dearth,
And with abundant wet fo cool the ground,
By adding cold to cold no fruit proves found.
The Farmer and the Grafier do[a] complain
Of rotten fheep, lean kine, and mildew'd grain.
And with my wafting floods and roaring torrent,
Their cattel hay and corn I fweep down current.
Nay many times my Ocean breaks his bounds,
And with aftonifhment the world confounds,
And fwallows Countryes up, n'er feen again,
And that an ifland makes which once was Main:
Thus *Britain* fair[b] (tis thought) was cut from *France*
Scicily from *Italy* by the like chance,

[z] force. [a] Plowman both. [b] Thus *Albion*.

And but one land was *Africa* and *Spain* [18]
Untill proud[c] *Gibrallar* did make them twain.
Some ſay I ſwallow'd up (ſure tis a notion)
A mighty country in th' *Allantique Ocean.*
I need not ſay much of my hail and ſnow,
My ice and extream cold, which all men know,
Whereof the firſt ſo ominous I rain'd,
That *Iſraels* enemies therewith were brain'd:
And of my chilling ſnows[d] ſuch plenty be,
That *Caucaſus* high mounts are ſeldome free.
Mine ice doth glaze *Europes* great[e] rivers o're,
Till ſun releaſe, their ſhips can ſail no more.
All know that[f] inundations I have made,
Wherein not men, but mountains ſeem'd to wade;
As when *Achaia*, all under water ſtood,
That for two hundred years it n'er prov'd good.
Deucalions great Deluge with many moe,
But theſe are trifles to the flood of *Noe*,
Then wholly periſh'd Earths ignoble race,
And to this day impairs her beauteous face,
That after times ſhall never feel like woe,
Her confirm'd ſons behold my colour'd bow.
Much might I ſay of wracks, but that Ile ſpare,
And now give place unto our Siſter *Air*,

[c] ſtraight. [d] colds. [e] big'ſt. [f] what.

Air. [19]

CONTENT (quoth Air) to ſpeak the laſt of you,
Yet am not ignorant[g] firſt was my due:
I do ſuppoſe you'l yield without controul
I am the breath of every living ſoul.
Mortals, what one of you that loves not me
Abundantly more then my Siſters three?
And though you love Fire, Earth and Water well
Yet Air beyond all theſe you know t'excell.
I ask the man condemn'd, that's neer his death,
How gladly ſhould his gold purchaſe his breath,
And all the wealth that ever earth did give,
How freely ſhould it go ſo he might live:
No earth,[h] thy witching traſh were all but vain,
If my pure air thy ſons did not ſuſtain.
The famiſh'd thirſty man that craves ſupply,
His moving reaſon is, give leaſt I dye,
So loth he is to go though nature's ſpent
To bid adieu to his dear Element.
Nay what are words which do reveal the mind,
Speak who or what they will they are but wind.
Your drums your trumpets & your organs ſound,
What is't but forced air which doth[i] rebound,
And ſuch are ecchoes and report ofth' gun
That tells afar th'exploit which it hath done.
Your Songs and pleaſant tunes they are the ſame,
And ſo's the notes which Nightingales do frame.

[g] Though not through ignorance. [h] world. [i] muſt.

Ye forging Smiths, if bellows once were gone [20]
Your red hot work more coldly would go on.
Ye Mariners, tis I that fill your ſails,
And ſpeed you to your port with wiſhed gales.
When burning heat doth cauſe you faint, I cool,
And when I ſmile, your ocean's like a pool.
I help to ripe the corn, I turn the mill,[j]
And with my ſelf I every *Vacuum* fill.
The ruddy ſweet ſanguine is like to air,
And youth and ſpring, Sages to me compare,
My moiſt hot nature is ſo purely thin,
No place ſo ſubtilly made, but I get in.
I grow more pure and pure as I mount higher,
And when I'm throughly rarifi'd turn fire:
So when I am condens'd, I turn to water,
Which may be done by holding down my vapour.
Thus I another body can aſſume,
And in a trice my own nature reſume.
Some for this cauſe of late have been ſo bold
Me for no Element longer to hold,
Let ſuch ſuſpend their thoughts, and ſilent be,
For all Philoſophers make one of me:
And what thoſe Sages either[k] ſpake or writ
Is more authentick then our[l] modern wit.
Next of my fowles ſuch multitudes there are,
Earths beaſts and waters fiſh ſcarce can compare.
Th'Oſtrich with her plumes, th'Eagle with her eyn
The Phœnix too (if any be) are mine,

[j] I ripe the corne, I turne the grinding mill;
[k] Sages did, or. [l] their.

The ſtork, the crane, the partridg, and the pheſant
The Thruſh, the wren,[m] the lark a prey to'th' peſant.
With thouſands more which now I may omit [21]
Without impeachment to my tale or wit.
As my freſh air preſerves all things in life,
So when corrupt, mortality is rife:
Then Fevers, Purples, Pox and Peſtilence,
With divers moe, work deadly conſequence:
Whereof ſuch multitudes have di'd and fled,
The living ſcarce had power to bury dead;
Yea ſo contagious countryes have we known
That birds have not 'ſcapt death as they have flown
Of murrain, cattle numberleſs did fall,
Men fear'd deſtruction epidemical.
Then of my tempeſts felt at ſea and land,
Which neither ſhips nor houſes could withſtand,
What wofull wracks I've made may well appear,
If nought were known but that before *Algere*,
Where famous *Charles the fifth* more loſs ſuſtaind
Then in his long hot war which *Millain* gain'd.[n]
Again what furious ſtorms and Hurricanoes[o]
Know weſtern Iſles, as *Chriſtophers*, *Barbadoes*,

[m] The Pye, the Jay.

[n] After this the first edition has,—

> How many rich fraught veſſells, have I ſplit?
> Some upon ſands, ſome upon rocks have hit.
> Some have I forc'd, to gaine an unknown ſhoare;
> Some overwhelm'd with waves, and ſeen no more.

Again what tempeſts, and what hericanoes.

Where neither houſes, trees nor plants I ſpare;
But ſome fall down, and ſome fly up with air.
Earthquakes ſo hurtfull, and ſo fear'd of all,
Impriſon'd I, am the original.
Then what prodigious ſights I ſometimes ſhow,
As battles pitcht in th' air, as countryes know,
Their joyning fighting, forcing and retreat,
That earth appears in heaven, O wonder great!
Sometimes red[p] flaming ſwords and blazing ſtars,
Portentous ſigns of famines, plagues and wars.
Which make the mighty Monarchs fear their fates [22]
By death or great mutation of their States.
I have ſaid leſs then did my Siſters three,
But what's their wrath[q] or force, the ſame's[r] in me.
To adde to all I've ſaid was my intent,
But dare not go beyond my Element.

[p] ſtrange. [q] worth. [r] but more's.

Of the four Humours *in Mans* Conſtitution.

THe former four now ending their diſcourſe,
Ceaſing to vaunt their good, or threat their force.
Lo other four ſtep up, crave leave to ſhow
The native qualityes that from them[s] flow:
But firſt they wiſely ſhew'd their high deſcent,
Each eldeſt daughter to each Element.
Choler was own'd by fire, and Blood by air,
Earth knew her black ſwarth child, water her fair:
All having made obeyſance to each Mother,
Had leave to ſpeak, ſucceeding one the other:
But 'mongſt themſelves they were at variance,
Which of the four ſhould have predominance.
Choler firſt[t] hotly claim'd right by her mother,
Who had precedency of all the other:
But Sanguine did diſdain what ſhe requir'd,
Pleading her ſelf was moſt of all deſir'd.
Proud Melancholy more envious then the reſt,
The ſecond, third or laſt could not digeſt.

[s] each. [t] "firſt" not in the firſt edition.

She was the ſilenteſt of all the four, [23]
Her wiſdom ſpake not much, but thought the more
Mild[u] Flegme did not conteſt for chiefeſt[v] place,
Only ſhe crav'd to have a vacant ſpace.
Well, thus they parle and chide; but to be brief,
Or will they, nill they, Choler will be chief.
They ſeing her impetuoſity[w]
At preſent yielded to neceſſity.

Choler.

TO ſhew my high[x] deſcent and pedegree,
Your ſelves would judge but vain prolixity;
It is acknowledged from whence I came,
It ſhall ſuffice to ſhew[y] you what I am,
My ſelf and mother one, as you ſhall ſee,
But ſhee in greater, I in leſs degree.
We both once Maſculines, the world doth know,
Now Feminines awhile, for love we owe
Unto your Siſterhood, which makes us render
Our noble ſelves in a leſs noble gender.
Though under Fire we comprehend all heat,
Yet man for Choler is the proper ſeat:
I in his heart erect my regal throne,
Where Monarch like I play and ſway alone.

[u] Cold. [v] higheſt. [w] imperioſity.
[x] great. [y] tel.

Yet many times unto my great diſgrace
One of your ſelves are my Compeers in place,
Where if your rule prove once= predominant,
The man proves boyiſh, ſottiſh, ignorant:
But if you yield ſubſervience unto me, |24|
I make a man, a man in th'high'ſt degree:
Be he a ſouldier, I more fence his heart
Then iron Corſlet 'gainſt a ſword or dart.
What makes him face his foe without appal,
To ſtorm a breach, or ſcale a city wall,
In dangers to account himſelf more ſure
Then timerous Hares whom Caſtles do immure?
Have you not heard of worthyes, Demi-Gods?
Twixt them and others what is't makes the odds
But valour? whence comes that? from none of you,
Nay milkſops at ſuch brunts you look but blew.
Here's ſiſter ruddy, worth the other two,
Who much will talk, but little dares ſhe do,
Unleſs to Court and claw, to dice and drink,
And there ſhe will out-bid us all, I think,
She loves a fiddle better then a drum,
A Chamber well, in field ſhe dares not come,
She'l ride a horſe as bravely as the beſt,
And break a ſtaff, provided 'be in jeſt;
But ſhuns to look on wounds, & blood that's ſpilt,
She loves her ſword only becauſe its gilt.
Then here's our ſad black Siſter, worſe then you.
She'l neither ſay ſhe will, nor will ſhe doe;

= once grow.

But peeviſh Malecontent, muſing ſits,
And by miſpriſſions like to looſe her witts:
If great perſwaſions cauſe her meet her foe,
In her dull reſolution ſhe's ſo ſlow,
To march her pace to ſome is greater pain
Then by a quick encounter to be ſlain.
But be ſhe beaten, ſhe'l not run away, [25]
She'l firſt adviſe if't be not beſt to ſtay.
Now[a] let's give cold white ſiſter flegme her right,
So loving unto all ſhe ſcorns to fight:
If any threaten her, ſhe'l in a trice
Convert from water to congealed ice:
Her teeth will chatter, dead and wan's her face,
And 'fore ſhe be aſſaulted, quits the place.
She dares not challeng, if I ſpeak amiſs,
Nor hath ſhe wit or heat to bluſh at this.
Here's three of you all ſee now what you are,
Then yield to me preheminence in war.
Again who fits for learning, ſcience, arts?
Who rarifies the intellectual parts:
From whence fine ſpirits flow and witty notions:
But tis[b] not from our dull, ſlow ſiſters motions:
Nor ſiſter ſanguine, from thy moderate heat,
Poor ſpirits the Liver breeds, which is thy ſeat.
What comes from thence, my heat refines the ſame
And through the arteries ſends it o're the frame:
The vital ſpirits they're call'd, and well they may
For when they fail, man turns unto his clay.

[a] But. [b] "But tis" not in the first edition.

The animal I claim as well as theſe,
The nerves, ſhould I not warm, ſoon would they freeze
But flegme her ſelf is now provok'd at this
She thinks I never ſhot ſo far amiſs.
The brain ſhe challengeth, the head's her ſeat;
But know'ts a fooliſh brain that wanteth heat.
My abſence proves it plain, her wit then flyes
Out at her noſe, or melteth at her eyes.
Oh who would miſs this influence of thine [26]
To be diſtill'd, a drop on every Line?
Alas,[c] thou haſt no Spirits, thy Company
Will feed a dropſy, or a Tympany,
The Palſy, Gout, or Cramp, or ſome ſuch dolour:
Thou waſt not made, for Souldier or for Scholar;
Of greazy paunch, and bloated[d] cheeks go vaunt,
But a good head from theſe are diſſonant.
But Melancholy, wouldſt have this glory thine,
Thou ſayſt thy wits are ſtaid, ſubtil and fine;
'Tis true, when I am Midwife to thy birth
Thy ſelf's as dull, as is thy mother Earth:
Thou canſt not claim the liver, head nor heart
Yet haſt the[e] Seat aſſign'd, a goodly part
The ſinke of all us three, the hateful Spleen
Of that black Region, nature made thee Queen;
Where pain and ſore obſtruction thou doſt work,
Where envy, malice, thy Companions lurk.
If once thou'rt great, what follows thereupon
But bodies waſting, and deſtruction?

[c] No, I.O. [d] palled. [e] thy.

So baſe thou art, that baſer cannot be,
Th' excrement aduſtion of me.
But I am weary to dilate your ſhame,
Nor is't my pleaſure thus to blur your name,
Only to raiſe my honour to the Skies,
As objects beſt appear by contraries.
But[f] Arms, and Arts I claim, and higher things.
The princely qualities befitting Kings,
Whoſe profound[g] heads I line with policies,
They'r held for Oracles, they are ſo wiſe,
Their wrathful looks are death their words are laws [27]
Their Courage it foe, friend, and Subject awes;
But one of you, would make a worthy King
Like our ſixth *Henry* (that ſame virtuous[h] thing)
That when a Varlet ſtruck him o're the ſide,
Forſooth you are to blame, he grave reply'd.
Take Choler from a Prince, what is he more
Then a dead Lion, by Beaſts triumph'd o're.
Again you know, how I act every part
By th' influence, I ſtill ſend from the heart:
It's nor your Muſcles, nerves, nor this nor that
Do's ought without my lively heat, that's flat:[i]
Nay th' ſtomack magazine to all the reſt
Without my boyling heat cannot digeſt:
And yet to make my greatneſs, ſtill more great
What differences, the Sex? but only heat.

[f] Thus. [g] Serene. [h] worthy.

[i] After this the first edition has, —

The ſpongy Lungs, I feed with frothy blood.
They coole my heat, and ſo repay my good.

And one thing more, to clofe up my narration
Of all that lives, I caufe the propagation.
I have been fparings what I might have faid
I love no boafting, that's but Childrens trade.
To what you now fhall fay I will attend,
And to your weaknefs gently condefcend.

Blood.

GOOD Sifters, give me leave, as is my place
To vent my grief, and wipe off my difgrace:
Your felves may plead your wrongs are no whit lefs
Your patience more then mine, I muft confefs
Did ever fober tongue fuch language fpeak, [28]
Or honefty fuch tyes unfriendly break?
Doft know thy felf fo well us fo amifs?
Is't arrogance [j] or folly caufeth this?
Ile only fhew the wrong thou'ft done to me,
Then let my fifters right their injury.
To pay with railings is not mine intent,
But to evince the truth by Argument:
I will analyfe this thy proud relation
So full of boafting and prevarication,
Thy foolifh [k] incongruityes Ile fhow,
So walk thee till thou'rt cold, then let thee go.

[j] ignorance. [k] childifh.

There is no Souldier but thy ſelf (thou ſayeſt,)
No valour upon Earth, but what thou haſt
Thy ſilly [l] provocations I deſpiſe,
And leave't to all to judge, where valour lies
No pattern, nor no pattron will I bring
But *David*, *Judah*'s moſt heroick King,
Whoſe glorious deeds in Arms the world can tell,
A roſie cheek Muſitian thou know'ſt well;
He knew well how to handle Sword and Harp,
And how to ſtrike full ſweet, as well as ſharp,
Thou laugh'ſt at me for loving merriment,
And ſcorn'ſt all Knightly ſports at Turnament.
Thou ſayſt I love my Sword, becauſe it's gilt,
But know, I love the Blade, more then the Hilt,
Yet do abhor ſuch temerarious deeds,
As thy unbridled, barbarous Choler breeds: [m]
Thy rudeneſs counts good manners vanity,
And real Complements baſe flattery.
For drink, which of us twain like it the beſt, [29]
Ile go no further then thy noſe for teſt:
Thy other ſcoffs, not worthy of reply
Shall vaniſh as of no validity:
Of thy black Calumnies this is but part,
But now Ile ſhew what ſouldier thou art.
And though thou'ſt us'd me with opprobrious ſpight
My ingenuity muſt give thee right.
Thy choler is but rage when tis moſt pure,
But uſefull when a mixture can endure;

[l] fooliſh. [m] yeelds.

As with thy mother fire, so tis with thee,
The best of all the four when they agree:
But let her leave the rest, then [n] I presume
Both them and all things else she would [o] consume.
VVhilst us for thine associates thou tak'st,
A Souldier most compleat in all points mak'st:
But when thou scorn'st to take the help we lend,
Thou art a Fury or infernal Fiend.
Witness the execrable deeds thou'st done,
Nor sparing Sex nor Age, nor Sire nor Son;
To satisfie thy pride and cruelty,
Thou oft hast broke bounds of Humanity,
Nay should I tell, thou would'st count me no blab,
How often for the lye, thou'st given the stab.
To take the wall's a sin of so high rate,
That nought but death [p] the same may expiate,
To cross thy will, a challenge doth deserve
So shed'st that blood,[q] thou'rt bounden to preserve
Wilt thou this valour, Courage, Manhood call:
No, know 'tis pride most diabolibal.
If murthers be thy glory, tis no less, [30]
Ile not envy thy feats, nor happiness:
But if in fitting time and place 'gainst foes
For countreys good thy life thou dar'st expose,
Be dangers n'er so high, and courage great,
Ile praise that prowess, fury,[r] Choler, heat:
But such thou never art when all alone,
Yet such when we all four are joyn'd in one.

[n] and. [o] will. [p] blood.
[q] So spils that life. [r] that fury, valour.

And when ſuch thou art, even ſuch are we,
The friendly Coadjutors ſtill of thee.
Nextly the Spirits thou doſt wholly claim,
Which nat'ral, vital, animal we name:
To play Philoſopher I have no liſt,
Nor yet Phyſitian, nor Anatomiſt,
For acting theſe, I have no will nor Art,
Yet ſhall with Equity, give thee thy part
For natural,[s] thou doſt not much conteſt;
For there is [t] none (thou ſayſt) if ſome not beſt;
That there are ſome, and beſt, I dare averre
Of greateſt uſe, if reaſon do not erre: [u]
What is there living, which do'nt firſt [v] derive
His Life now Animal, from vegetive:
If thou giv'ſt life, I give the [w] nouriſhment,
Thine without mine, is not, 'tis evident:
But I without thy help, can give a growth
As plants trees, and ſmall Embryon know'th
And if vital Spirits, do flow from thee
I am as ſure, the natural, from me:
Be [x] thine the nobler, which I grant, yet mine
Shall juſtly claim priority of thine.
I am the fountain which thy Ciſtern fills [31]
Through warm blew Conduits of my venial rills:
What hath the heart, but what's ſent from the liver
If thou'rt the taker, I muſt be the giver.

s th' natural. t are.
u More uſeful then the reſt, don't reaſon erre:
v cannot. w thee. x But.

Then never boaſt of what thou doſt receive:
For of ſuch glory I ſhall thee bereave.
But why the heart ſhould be uſurp'd by thee,
I muſt confeſs ſeems ſomething[y] ſtrange to me:
The ſpirits through thy heat made perfect are,[z]
But the Materials none of thine, that's clear:
Their wondrous mixture is of blood and air,
The firſt my ſelf, ſecond my mother[a] fair.
But Ile not force retorts, nor do thee wrong,
Thy fi'ry yellow froth is mixt among,
Challeng not all, 'cauſe part we do allow;
Thou know'ſt I've there to do as well as thou:
But thou wilt ſay I deal unequally,
Their lives the iraſcible faculty,
Which without all diſpute, is Cholers own;
Beſides the vehement heat, only there known
Can be imputed, unto none but Fire
Which is thy ſelf, thy Mother and thy Sire
That this is true, I eaſily can aſſent
If ſtill you take along my Aliment;
And let me be your partner which is due,
So ſhall I give the dignity to you:
Again, Stomacks Concoction thou doſt claim,
But by what right, nor do'ſt, nor canſt thou name
Unleſs as heat, it be thy faculty,
And ſo thou challengeſt her property.[b]

[y] is ſomewhat. [z] are made perfect there. [a] filler.

[b] It is her own heat, not thy faculty,
Thou do'ſt unjuſtly claime, her property.

The help ſhe needs, the loving liver lends, [32]
Who th' benefit o'th' whole ever intends
To meddle further I ſhall be but ſhent,
Th'reſt to our Siſters is more pertinent;
Your ſlanders thus refuted takes no place,
Nor what you've ſaid, doth argue my diſgrace,[c]
Now through your leaves, ſome little time I'l ſpend
My worth in humble manner to commend
This, hot, moiſt nutritive humour of mine
When 'tis untaint, pure, and moſt genuine
Shall chiefly[d] take the[e] place, as is my[e] due
Without the leaſt indignity to you.
Of all your qualities I do partake,
And what you ſingle are, the whole I make
Your hot, moiſt, cold, dry natures are but four,
I moderately am all, what need I more;
As thus, if hot then dry, if moiſt, then cold,
If this you cann't diſprove,[f] then all I hold
My virtues hid, I've let you dimly ſee
My ſweet Complection proves the verity.
This Scarlet die's a badge of what's within
One touch thereof, ſo beautifies the skin:
Nay, could I be, from all your tangs but pure
Mans life to boundleſs Time might ſtill endure.
But here one thruſts her heat, wher'ts not requir'd
So ſuddenly, the body all is fired,
And of the calme ſweet temper quite bereft,
Which makes the Manſion, by the Soul ſoon left.

[c] Though caſt upon my guiltleſſe bluſhing face;
[d] firſtly. [e] her. [f] If this can't be diſprov'd.

So Melancholy ſeizes* on a man,
With her unchearful viſage, ſwarth and wan,
The body dryes, the mind ſublime doth ſmother, [33]
And turns him to the womb of's earthy mother:
And flegm likewiſe can ſhew her cruel art,
With cold diſtempers to pain every part:
The lungs ſhe rots, the body wears away,
As if ſhe'd leave no fleſh to turn to clay,
Her languiſhing diſeaſes, though not quick
At length demoliſhes the Faberick,
All to prevent, this curious care I take,
In th' laſt concoction ſegregation make
Of all the perverſe humours from mine own,
The bitter choler moſt malignant known
I turn into his Cell cloſe by my ſide
The Melancholy to the Spleen t'abide:
Likewiſe the whey, ſome uſe I in the veins,
The overplus I ſend unto the reins:
But yet for all my toil, my care and skill,
Its doom'd by an irrevocable will
That my intents ſhould meet with interruption,
That mortal man might turn to his corruption.
I might here ſhew the nobleneſs of mind
Of ſuch as to the ſanguine are inclin'd,
They're liberal, pleaſant, kind and courteous,
And like the Liver all benignious.
For arts and ſciences they are the fitteſt;
And maugre Choler ſtill they are the wittieſt:

* ceaſes.

With an ingenious working Phantaſie,
A moſt voluminous large Memory,
And nothing wanting but Solidity.
But why alas, thus tedious ſhould I be, [34]
Thouſand examples you may daily ſee.
If time I have tranſgreſt, and been too long,
Yet could not be more brief without much wrong;
I've ſcarce wip'd off the ſpots proud choler caſt,
Such venome lies in words, though but a blaſt:
No braggs i've us'd, to you I dare appeal,
If modeſty my worth do not conceal.
I've us'd no bitterneſs nor taxt your name,
As I to you, to me do ye the ſame.

Melancholy.

HE that with two Aſſailants hath to do,
Had need be armed well and active too.
Eſpecially when friendſhip is pretended,
That blow's moſt deadly where it is intended.
Though choler rage and rail, I'le not do ſo,
The tongue's no weapon to aſſault a foe:
But ſith we fight with words, we might be kind
To ſpare our ſelves and beat the whiſtling wind,
Fair roſie ſiſter, ſo might'ſt thou ſcape free;
I'le flatter for a time as thou didſt me:

But when the firſt offender I have laid,
Thy ſoothing girds ſhall fully be repaid.
But Choler be thou cool'd or chaf'd, I'le venter,
And in contentions liſts now juſtly enter.[h]
What mov'd thee thus to vilifie my name,
Not paſt all reaſon, but in truth all ſhame:
Thy fiery ſpirit ſhall bear away this prize,
To play ſuch furious pranks I am too wiſe:
If in a Souldier raſhneſs be ſo precious,
Know in a General tis moſt pernicious.
Nature doth teach to ſhield the head from harm,
The blow that's aim'd thereat is latcht by th'arm.
When in Batalia my foes I face
I then command proud Choler ſtand thy place,
To uſe thy ſword, thy courage and thy art
There to defend my ſelf, thy better part.
This warineſs count not for cowardize,
He is not truly valiant that's not wiſe.
It's no leſs glory to defend a town,
Then by aſſault to gain one not our own;
And if *Marcellus* bold be call'd *Romes* ſword,
Wiſe *Fabius* is her buckler all accord:
And if thy haſt my ſlowneſs ſhould not temper,
'Twere but a mad irregular diſtemper;
Enough of that by our ſiſters heretofore,
Ile come to that which wounds me ſomewhat more

[h] After this the first edition has,—

Thy boaſted valour ſtoutly's been repell'd,
If not as yet, by me, thou ſhalt be quell'd:

Of learning, policy thou wouldst bereave me,
But 's not thine ignorance shall thus deceive me:
What greater Clark or Politician lives,
Then he whose brain a touch my humour gives?
What is too hot my coldness doth abate,
What's diffluent I do consolidate.
If I be partial judg'd or thought to erre,
The melancholy snake shall it aver,
Whose [i] cold dry head [j] more subtilty doth yield,
Then all the huge beasts of the fertile field.
Again [k] thou dost confine me to the spleen, [36]
As of that only part I were the Queen,
Let me as well make thy precincts the Gall,
So prison thee within that bladder small:
Reduce the man to's principles, then see
If I have not more part then all you three:
What is within, without, of theirs or thine,
Yet time and age shall soon declare it mine.
When death doth seize the man your stock is lost,
When you poor bankrupts prove then have I most.
You'l say here none shall e're disturb my right,
You high born from that lump then take your flight.
Then who's mans friend, when life & all forsakes?
His Mother mine, him to her womb retakes:
Thus he is ours, his portion is the grave,
But while he lives, I'le shew what part I have:
And first the firm dry bones I justly claim,
The strong foundation of the stately frame:

[i] Those. [j] heads. [k] Thirdly.

Likewiſe the uſefull Slpeen, though not the beſt,
Yet is a bowel call'd well as the reſt:
The Liver, Stomack, owe their[l] thanks of right,
The firſt it drains, of th'laſt quicks appetite.
Laughter (thô thou ſay malice) flows from hence,
Theſe two in one cannot have reſidence.
But thou moſt groſly doſt miſtake to think
The Spleen for all you three was made a ſink,
Of all the reſt thou'ſt nothing there to do,
But if thou haſt, that malice is[m] from you.
Again you often touch my ſwarthy hue,
That black is black, and I am black tis true;
But yet more comely far I dare avow, [37]
Then is thy torrid noſe or brazen brow.
But that which ſhews how high your ſpight is bent
Is charging me to be thy excrement:
Thy loathſome imputation I defie,
So plain a ſlander needeth no reply.
When by thy heat thou'ſt bak'd thy ſelf to cruſt,
And ſo art call'd black Choler or aduſt,
Thou witleſs think'ſt that I am thy excretion,
So mean thou art in Art as in diſcretion:[n]
But by your leave I'le let your greatneſs ſee
What Officer thou art to us all three,
The Kitchin Drudge, the cleanſer of the ſinks
That caſts out all that man e're eats or drinks:

[l] owes it. [m] comes.

[n] Thou do'ſt aſſume my name, wel be it juſt:
This tranſmutation is, but not excretion.
Thou wants Philoſophy, and yet diſcretion.

If any doubt the truth whence this ſhould come,
Shew them thy paſſage to th' Duodenum;
Thy biting[e] quality ſtill irritates,
Till filth and thee nature exonerates:
If there thou'rt ſtopt, to th' Liver thou turn'ſt in,
And thence with jaundies ſaffrons all the skin.
No further time Ile ſpend in confutation,
I truſt I've clear'd your ſlanderous imputation.
I now ſpeak unto all, no more to one,
Pray hear, admire and learn inſtruction.
My virtues yours ſurpaſs without compare,
The firſt my conſtancy that jewel rare:
Choler's too raſh this golden gift to hold,
And Sanguine is more fickle manifold,
Here, there her reſtleſs thoughts do ever fly,
Conſtant in nothing but unconſtancy.
And what Flegme is, we know, like to her mother, [38]
Unſtable is the one, and ſo the other;
With me is noble patience alſo found,
Impatient Choler loveth not the ſound,
What ſanguine is, ſhe doth not heed nor care,
Now up, now down, tranſported like the Air:
Flegme's patient becauſe her nature's tame;
But I, by virtue do acquire the ſame.
My Temperance, Chaſtity is eminent,
But theſe with you, are ſeldome reſident;
Now could I ſtain my ruddy Siſters face
With deeper red,[f] to ſhew you her diſgrace.

[e] bittering. [f] purple dye.

But rather I with ſilence vaile her ſhame
Then cauſe her bluſh, while I relate[q] the ſame.
Nor are ye free from this inormity,
Although ſhe bear the greateſt obloquie,
My prudence, judgement, I might now reveal
But wiſdom 'tis my wiſdome to conceal.
Unto diſeaſes not inclin'd as you,
Nor cold, nor hot, Ague nor Pluriſie,
Nor Cough, nor Quinſey, nor the burning Feaver,
I rarely feel to act his fierce endeavour;
My ſickneſs in conceit chiefly doth lye,
What I imagine that's my malady.
Chymeraes ſtrange are in my phantaſy,
And things that never were, nor ſhall I ſee
I love not talk, Reaſon lies not in length,
Nor multitude of words argues our ſtrength;
I've done pray ſiſter Flegme proceed in Courſe,
We ſhall expect much ſound, but little force.

Flegme. [39]

PATIENT I am, patient i'd need to be,
To bear with the injurious taunts of three,
Though wit I want, and anger I have leſs,
Enough of both, my wrongs now to expreſs

q dilate.

I've not forgot, how bitter Choler ſpake
Nor how her gaul on me ſhe cauſeleſs brake;
Nor wonder 'twas for hatred there's not ſmall,
Where oppoſition is Diametrical.
To what is Truth I freely will aſſent,
Although my Name do ſuffer detriment,
What's ſlanderous repell, doubtful diſpute,
And when I've nothing left to ſay be mute.
Valour I want, no Souldier am 'tis true,
I'le leave that manly Property to you;
I love no thundring guns,[r] nor bloody wars,
My poliſh'd Skin was not ordain'd for Skarrs:
But though the pitched field I've ever fled,
At home the Conquerours have conquered.
Nay, I could tell you what's more true then meet,
That Kings have laid their Scepters at my feet;
When Siſter ſanguine paints my Ivory face:
The Monarchs bend and ſue, but for my grace
My lilly white when joyned with her red,
Princes hath ſlav'd, and Captains captived,
Country with Country, Greece with *Aſia* fights
Sixty nine Princes, all ſtout *Hero* Knights.
Under *Troys* walls ten years will wear[s] away,
Rather then looſe one beauteous *Helena*.
But 'twere as vain, to prove this truth of mine
As at noon day, to tell the Sun doth ſhine.
Next difference that 'twixt us twain doth lye
Who doth poſſeſs the brain, or thou or I?

[r] Drums. [s] walls.

Shame forc'd the ſay, the matter that was mine,
But the Spirits by which it acts are thine:
Thou ſpeakeſt Truth, and I can ſay no leſs,
Thy heat doth much, I candidly confeſs;
Yet without oſtentation I may ſay,
I do as much for thee another way:[t]
And though I grant, thou art my helper here,
No debtor I becauſe it's paid elſe where.
With all your flouriſhes, now Siſters three
Who is't that dare, or can, compare with me,
My excellencies are ſo great, ſo many,
I am confounded; fore I ſpeak of any:
The brain's the nobleſt member all allow,
Its form and Scituation will avow,
Its Ventricles, Membranes and wondrous net,
Galen, *Hippocrates* drive to a ſet;
That Divine Offspring[u] the immortal Soul
Though it in all, and every part be whole,
Within this ſtately place of eminence,
Doth doubtleſs keep its mighty reſidence.
And ſurely, the Soul ſenſitive here lives,
Which life and motion to each creature gives,
The Conjugation of the parts, to th' braine
Doth ſhew, hence flow the pow'rs which they retain
Within this high Built *Cittadel*, doth lye [41]
The Reaſon, fancy, and the memory;

[t] But yet thou art as much, I truly ſay,
Beholding unto me another way.

[u] Eſſence.

The faculty of ſpeech doth here abide,
The Spirits animal, from hence do ſlide:
The five moſt noble Senſes here do dwell;
Of three it's hard to ſay, which doth excell.
This point now to diſcuſs, 'longs not to me,
I'le touch the ſight, great'ſt wonder of the three;
The optick Nerve, Coats, humours all are mine,
The watry, glaſſie, and the Chryſtaline;
O mixture ſtrange! O colour colourleſs,
Thy perfect temperament who can expreſs:
He was no fool who thought the ſoul lay there,
Whence her affections paſſions ſpeak ſo clear.
O good, O bad, O true, O traiterous eyes
What wonderments within your Balls there lyes,
Of all the Senſes ſight ſhall be the Queen;
Yet ſome may wiſh, O had mine eyes ne're ſeen.
Mine, likewiſe is the marrow, of the back,
Which runs through all the Spondles of the rack,
It is the ſubſtitute o'th royal brain,
All Nerves, except ſeven pair, to it retain.
And the ſtrong Ligaments from hence ariſe,
Which joynt to joynt, the intire body tyes.
Some other parts there iſſue from the Brain,
Whoſe worth and uſe to tell, I muſt refrain:
Some curious [v] learned *Crooke*,* may theſe reveal
But modeſty, hath charg'd me to conceal
Here's my Epitome of excellence:
For what's the Brains is mine by Conſequence.

[v] worthy. * See Introduction.

A foolifh brain (quoth [w] Choler) wanting heat [42]
But a mad one fay I, where 'tis too great,
Phrenfie's worfe then folly, one would more glad
With a tame fool converfe then with a mad;
For learning then my brain [x] is not the fitteft,
Nor will I yield [y] that Choler is [z] the wittieft.
Thy judgement is unfafe, thy fancy little,
For memory the fand is not more brittle;
Again, none's fit for Kingly ftate [a] but thou,
If Tyrants be the beft, I le it allow:
But if love be as requifite as fear,
Then thou and I muft make a mixture here.
Well to be brief, I hope now Cholers laid,
And I'le pafs by what Sifter fanguine faid.
To Melancholy I le make no reply,
The worft fhe faid was inftability,
And too much talk, both which I here confefs
A warning good, hereafter I'le fay lefs.
Let's now be friends; its time our fpight were fpent,
Left we too late this rafhnefs do repent,
Such premifes will force a fad conclufion,
Unlefs we agree, all falls into confufion.
Let Sangine with her hot hand Choler hold,
To take her moift my moifture will be bold:
My cold, cold melancholy [b] hand fhall clafp;
Her dry, dry Cholers other hand fhall grafp.

[w] faith.
[x] Then, my head for learning.
[y] Ne're did I heare.
[z] was.
[a] place.
[b] Melanchollies.

Two hot, two moiſt, two cold, two dry here be,
A golden Ring, the Poſey *VNITY.*
Nor jarrs nor ſcoffs, let none hereafter ſee,
But all admire our perfect Amity
Nor be diſcern'd, here's water, earth, air, fire, [43]
But here a compact body, whole intire.
This loving counſel pleas'd them all ſo well
That flegm was judg'd for kindneſs to excell.

Of the four Ages of Man.

LO now four other act[c] upon the ſtage,
Childhood and Youth, the Manly & Old age;
The firſt ſon unto flegm, Grand-child to water,
Unſtable, ſupple, cold and moiſt's his nature.
The ſecond frolick, claims his pedegree
From blood and air, for hot and moiſt is he.
The third of fire and Choler is compos'd
Vindicative and quarrelſome diſpos'd.
The laſt of earth, and heavy melancholy,
Solid, hating all lightneſs and all folly.
Childhood was cloth'd in white & green[d] to ſhow
His ſpring was intermixed with ſome ſnow:
Upon his head nature a Garland ſet
Of Primroſe, Daizy & the Violet.
Such cold mean flowrs the ſpring puts forth[e] betime [44]
Before the ſun hath throughly heat[f] the clime.
His Hobby ſtriding did not ride but run,
And in his hand an hour-glaſs new begun.

[c] acts. [d] given. [e] (as theſe) bloſſome. [f] warm'd.

In danger every moment of a fall,
And when tis broke then ends his life and all:
But if he hold till it have run its laſt,
Then may he live out[g] threeſcore years or paſt.
Next Youth came up in gorgeous attire,
(As that fond age doth moſt of all deſire)
His Suit of Crimſon and his ſcarſe of green,
His pride in's countenance was quickly ſeen,
Garland of roſes, pinks and gilli-flowers
Seemed on's head to grow bedew'd with ſhowers:
His face as freſh as is *Aurora* fair,
When bluſhing ſhe firſt 'gins to light[h] the air.
No wooden horſe, but one of mettal try'd,
He ſeems to fly or ſwim, and not to ride.
Then prancing on the ſtage, about he wheels,
But as he went death waited at his heels.
The next came up in a much[i] graver ſort,
As one that cared for a good report,
His ſword by's ſide, and choler in his eyes,
But neither us'd as yet, for he was wiſe:
Of Autumns fruits a basket on his arm,
His golden God in's purſe, which was his charm.
And laſt of all to act upon this ſtage
Leaning upon his ſtaff came up Old Age,
Under his arm a ſheaf of wheat he bore,
An harveſt of the beſt, what needs he more?
In's other hand a glaſs ev'n almoſt run, [45]
Thus writ about *This out then am I done.*

[g] til. [h] red. [i] more.

His hoary hairs, and grave aſpect made way,
And all gave ear to what he had to ſay.
Theſe being met each in his equipage
Intend to ſpeak according to their age:
But wiſe Old age did with all gravity
To childiſh Childhood give precedency,
And to the reſt his reaſon mildly told,
That he was young before he grew ſo old.
To do as he each one[j] full ſoon aſſents,
Their method was that of the Elements,
That each ſhould tell what of himſelf he knew,
Both good and bad, but yet no more then's true.
With heed now ſtood three ages of frail man,
To hear the child, who crying thus began:

Childhood.

AH me! conceiv'd in ſin and born with ſorrow,
A nothing, here to day and gone to morrow,
VVhoſe mean beginning bluſhing can't reveal,
But night and darkneſs muſt with ſhame conceal.
My mothers breeding ſickneſs I will ſpare,
Her nine moneths weary burthen not declare.
To ſhew her bearing pains,[k] I ſhould do wrong,
To tell thoſe pangs[l] which can't be told by tongue:

[j] the reſt. [k] pangs. [l] that paine.

VVith tears into the world I did arrive,
My mother ſtill did waſte as I did thrive,
Who yet with love and all alacrity, [46]
Spending, was willing to be ſpent for me.
With wayward cryes I did diſturb her reſt,
Who ſought ſtill to appeaſe me with the breaſt:
With weary arms ſhe danc'd and *By By* ſung,
When wretched I ingrate had done the wrong.
When infancy was paſt, my childiſhneſs
Did act all folly that it could expreſs,
My ſillineſs did only take delight
In that which riper age did ſcorn and ſlight.
In Rattles, Baubles and ſuch toyiſh ſtuff,
My then ambitious thoughts were low enough:
My high-born ſoul ſo ſtraightly was confin'd,
That its own worth it did not know nor mind:
This little houſe of fleſh did ſpacious count,
Through ignorance all troubles did ſurmount;
Yet this advantage had mine ignorance
Freedom from envy and from arrogance.
How to be rich or great I did not cark,
A Baron or a Duke ne'r made my mark,
Nor ſtudious was Kings favours how to buy,
With coſtly preſence [m] or baſe flattery:
No office coveted wherein I might
Make ſtrong my ſelf and turn aſide weak right:
No malice bare to this or that great Peer,
Nor unto buzzing whiſperers gave ear:

[m] preſents.

I gave no hand nor vote for death or life,
I'd nought to do 'twixt King[n] and peoples ſtrife.
No Statiſt I, nor Martiliſt in'th field,
Where ere I went mine innocence was ſhield.
My quarrels not for Diadems did riſe, [47]
But for an apple, plum, or ſome ſuch prize:
My ſtrokes did cauſe no blood[o] no wounds or skars,
My little wrath did end[p] ſoon as my Warrs:
My Duel was no challeng nor did ſeek
My foe ſhould weltring in his bowels reek.
I had no ſuits at law neighbours to vex,
Nor evidence for lands did me perplex.
I fear'd no ſtorms, nor all the wind that blowes,
I had no ſhips at ſea; nor fraights to looſe.
I fear'd no drought nor wet, I had no crop,
Nor yet on future things did ſet[q] my hope.
This was mine innocence, but ah! the ſeeds
Lay raked up of all the curſed weeds
Which ſprouted forth in mine enſuing age,
As he can tel that next comes on the ſtage:
But yet let me relate before I go
The ſins and dangers I am ſubject to,
Stained from birth with *Adams* ſinfull fact,
Thence I began to ſin as ſoon as act:
A perverſe will, a love to what's forbid,
A ſerpents ſting in pleaſing face lay hid:
A lying tongue as ſoon as it could ſpeak,
And fifth Commandment do daily break.

[n] Prince. [o] death. [p] ceaſe. [q] place.

Oft ſtubborn, peeviſh, ſullen, pout and cry,
Then nought can pleaſe, and yet I know not why.
As many are [r] my ſins, ſo dangers too;
For ſin brings ſorrow, ſickneſs death and woe:
And though I miſs the toſſings of the mind,
Yet griefs in my frail fleſh I ſtill do find.
VVhat gripes of wind mine infancy did pain, [48]
VVhat tortures I in breeding teeth ſuſtain?
VVhat crudityes my ſtomack cold hath bred,
VVhence vomits, flux and worms have iſſued?
VVhat breaches, knocks and falls I daily have,
And ſome perhaps I carry to my grave,
Sometimes in fire, ſometimes in water fall,
Strangly preſev'd, yet mind it not at all:
At home, abroad my dangers manifold,
That wonder tis, my glaſs till now doth hold.
I've done; unto my elders I give way,
For tis but little that a child can ſay.

Youth.

MY goodly cloathing, and my beauteous skin
Declare ſome greater riches are within:
But what is beſt I'le firſt preſent to view,
And then the worſt in a more ugly hue:

[r] was.

For thus to doe we on this ftage affemble,
Then let not him that hath moft craft diffemble.
My education and my learning fuch,
As might my felf and others profit much;
VVith nurture trained up in virtues fchools
Of fcience, arts and tongues I know the rules,
The manners of the court I alfo[s] know,
And fo likewife[t] what they in'th Country doe.
The brave attempts of valiant knights I prize,
That dare fcale walls and forts[u] rear'd to the skies.
The fnorting Horfe, the trumpet, Drum I like, [49]
The glitt'ring fword, the Piftol and the Pike:[v]
I cannot lye intrench'd before a town,
Nor wait till good fuccefs[w] our hopes doth crown:
I fcorn the heavy Corflet, musket-proof;
I fly to catch the bullet thats aloof.
Though thus in field, at home to all moft kind,
So affable, that I can[x] fuit each mind.
I can infinuate into the breaft,
And by my mirth can raife the heart depreft:
Sweet mufick raps my brave harmonious foul,
My high thoughts elevate beyond the pole:[y]
My wit, my bounty, and my courtefie,
Make all to place their future hopes on me.

[s] likewife, [t] Not ignorant. [u] That dare climbe Battlements.
[v] and wel advanced Pike; [w] advice. [x] do.
[y] Sweet Mufick rapteth my harmonious Soul,
And elevates my thoughts above the Pole.

This is my beſt, but Youth is known, Alas!
To be as wild as is the ſnuffing Aſs:
As vain as froth, or vanity can be,
That who would ſee vain man, may look on me.
My gifts abusd, my education loſt,
My wofull Parents longing hopes are[*] croſt,
My wit evaporates in merriment,
My valour in ſome beaſtly quarrell's ſpent:[a]
My luſt doth hurry me to all that's ill:
I know no law nor reaſon but my will.
Sometimes lay wait to take a wealthy purſe,
Or ſtab the man in's own defence (that's worſe)
Sometimes I cheat (unkind) a female heir
Of all at once, who not ſo wiſe as fair
Truſteth my loving looks and glozing tongue,
Untill her friends, treaſure and honour's gone.
Sometimes I ſit carouſing others health,
Untill mine own be gone, my wit and wealth.
From pipe to pot, from pot to words and blows,
For he that loveth wine, wanteth no woes.
Whole[b] nights with Ruffins, Roarers Fidlers ſpend,
To all obſcenity mine ears I lend:[c]
All Counſell hate, which tends to make me wiſe,
And deareſt friends count for mine enemies.

[*] all.

[a] After this the first edition has, —
Martial deeds I love not, 'cauſe they're vertuous,
But doing ſo, might ſeem magnanimous.

[b] Dayes. [c] bend.

If any care I take tis to be fine,
For fure my fuit, more then my virtues fhine
If time from leud Companions I can fpare,
'Tis fpent to curle, and pounce my new-bought hair.[d]
Some new[e] *Adonis* I do ftrive to be;
Sardanapalus now furvives in me.
Cards, Dice, and Oathes concomitant I love,
To playes, to mafques, to Taverns ftill I move.
And in a word, if what I am you'd hear,
Seek out a *Brittifh* bruitifh Cavaleer:
Such wretch, fuch Monfter am I, but yet more,
I have no heart at all this to deplore,[f]
Remembring not the dreadfull day of doom,
Nor yet that heavy reckoning foon to come.
Though dangers do attend me every hour,
And gaftly Death oft threats me with his[g] power,
Sometimes by wounds in idle Combates taken,
Sometimes with Agues all my body fhaken:
Sometimes by fevers, all my moifture drinking,
My heart lies frying, & mine eyes are finking,
Sometimes the Quinfey,[h] painfull Pleurifie,
With fad affrighrs of death doth menace me:

[d] If any time from company I fpare,
'Tis fpent in curling, frifling up my hair:

[e] young.

[f] I want a heart all this for to deplore.
Thus, thus alas! I have mifpent my time,
My youth, my beft, my ftrength, my bud, and prime:

[g] her. [h] Cough, Stitch.

Sometimes the two ſold Pox me ſore be:marrs [51]
With outward marks, & inward loathſome ſcarrs,[i]
Sometimes the Phrenzy ſtrangly mads my brain,
That oft for it in *Bedlam* I remain.
Too many my diſeaſes to recite,
That wonder tis, I yet behold the light,
That yet my bed in darkneſs is not made,
And I in black oblivions Den now[j] laid.
Of aches full my bones, of woe my heart,
Clapt in that priſon, never thence to ſtart.[k]
Thus I have ſaid, and what I've been,[l] you ſee
Childhood and Youth are vain ye[m] vanity.

Middle Age.

CHILDHOOD and Youth (forgot) I've ſometimes ſeen
And now am grown more ſtaid who have bin green
What they have done, the ſame was done by me,
As was their praiſe or ſhame, ſo mine muſt be.

[i] Sometimes the loathſome Pox, my face be-mars,
With ugly marks of his eternal fears;

[j] long.

[k] Of Marrow ful my bones, of Milk my breaſts,
Ceas'd * by the gripes of Serjeant Death's Arreſts: †

[l] ſaid. [m] yea.

* See p. 135. note *g*.
† "——(as this fell sergeant, death,
Is strict in his arrest)." — HAMLET, v. 2.

Now age is more; more good you may[n] expect,
But more mine age, the more is my defect.[o]
When my wild oates were ſown & ripe and mown
I then receiv'd an harveſt of mine own.
My reaſon then bad judge how little hope
My[p] empty ſeed ſhould yield a better crop:
Then with both hands I graſpt the world together
Thus out of one extream into another:
But yet laid hold on virtue ſeemingly,
Who climbs without hold climbs dangerouſly:
Be my condition mean, I then take pains [52]
My Family to keep, but not for gains.
A Father I, for children muſt provide;
But if none, then for kindred near ally'd.
If rich, I'm urged then to gather more,
To bear a port[q] i'th'world, and feed the poor.
If noble, then mine honour to maintain,
If not, riches[r] nobility can gain.
For time, for place, likewiſe for each Relation
I wanted not, my ready allegation.
Yet all my powers for ſelf ends are not ſpent,
For hundreds bleſs me for my bounty lent.[s]
Whoſe backs[t] I've cloth'd, and bellyes I have fed
With mine own fleece, & with my houſhold bread,

[n] do.

[o] After this the first edition has, —
But what's of worth, your eyes ſhal firſt behold,
And then a world of droſſe among my gold.

[p] Such. [q] me out. [r] yet wealth.

[s] ſent. [t] loynes.

Yea, juſtice have I done, was I in place.
To chear the good, and wicked to deface.
The proud I cruſh't, th'oppreſſed I ſet free.
The lyars curb'd, but nouriſht verity.
Was I a Paſtor, I my Flock did feed,
And gently lead the Lambs as they had need.
A Captain I, with Skill I train'd my Band,
And ſhew'd them how in face of Foes to ſtand.
A Souldier I, with ſpeed I did obey
As readily, as could my leader ſay.
Was I a labourer, I wrought all day
As cheerfully as e're I took my pay.
Thus hath mine Age in all ſometimes done well,
Sometimes again, mine Age[u] been worſe then Hell.
In meanneſs, greatneſs, riches, poverty,
Did toyle, did broyle, oppreſſ'd, did ſteal and lye.
Was I as poor as poverty could be, [53]
Then baſeneſs was Companion unto me.
Such ſcum as hedges and high-ways do yield,
As neither ſow, nor reap, nor plant, nor build,
If to Agriculture I was ordain'd,
Great labours, ſorrows, Croſſes I ſuſtain'd.
The early Cock did ſummon but in vain
My wakeful thoughts up to my painful gain:[v]
My weary Beaſt reſt from his toyle can find,
But if I reſt the more diſtreſt my mind.

[u] Sometimes mine age (in all).

[v] After this the first edition has,—

For reſtleſſe day and night, I'm rob'd of ſleep,
By cankered care, who centinel doth keep.

If happineſs my ſordidneſs hath found,
'Twas in the Crop of my manured ground.
My thriving Cattle and my new-milch-Cow,
My fleeced Sheep, and fruitful farrowing Sow:[w]
To greater things I never did aſpire,
My dunghil thoughts or hopes could reach no higher.
If to be rich or great it was my fate,
How was I broyl'd with envy and with hate?
Greater then was the great'ſt was my deſire,
And thirſt for honour, ſet my heart on fire:[x]
And by Ambition's[y] ſails I was ſo carried,
That over Flats and ſands, and Rocks I hurried,
Oppreſt and ſunk, and ſtav'd[z] all in my way
That did oppoſe me, to my longed Bay.
My thirſt was higher then nobility,
I oft long'd ſore to taſt on Royalty:
Then Kings muſt be depos'd or put to flight,
I might poſſeſs that Throne which was their right;[a]
There ſet, I rid my ſelf ſtraight out of hand
Of ſuch Competitors, as might in time withſtand.[b]

[w] My fatted Oxe, and my exuberous Cow,
My fleeced Ewe, and ever farr owing Sow.

[x] And greater ſtil, did ſet my heart on fire.
If honour was the point, to which I ſteer'd;
To run my hull upon diſgrace I fear'd.

[y] But by ambitious. [z] ſact.

[a] Instead of this and the preceding line, the first edition has, —
Whence poyſon, Piſtols, and dread inſtruments,
Have been curſt furtherers of mine intents.
Nor Brothers, Nephewes, Sons, nor Sires I've ſpar'd,
When to a Monarchy, my way they barr'd.

[b] Of ſuch as might my ſon, or his withſtand.

Then thought my ſtate firm founded ſure to laſt, [54]
But in a trice 'tis ruin'd by a blaſt,
Though cemented with more then noble bloud,
The bottom nought, and ſo no longer ſtood.[c]
Sometimes vain glory is the only baite
Whereby my empty Soul is lur'd and caught.
Be I of wit,[d] of learning, and of parts,
I judge I ſhould have room in all mens hearts.
And envy gnaws if any do ſurmount,
I hate, not to be held in high'ſt account.[e]
If *Bias* like I'm ſtript unto my skin,
I glory in my wealth I have within.*
Thus good and bad, and what I am you ſee,
Now in a word, what my diſeaſes be.
The vexing ſtone in bladder and in reins,
The Strangury torments me with ſore pains.[f]
The windy Cholick oft my bowels rend,
To break the darkſome priſon where it's pen'd.
The Cramp and Gout[g] doth ſadly torture me,
And the reſtraining, lame Sciatica.
The Aſtma, Megrim, Palſy, Lethargie,
The quartan Ague, dropſy, Lunacy:[h]

[c] Instead of this and the three preceding lines, the first edition has, —
Then heapt up gold, and riches as the clay;
Which others ſcatter, like the dew in *May*.

[d] worth.

[e] I hate for to be had, in ſmall account.

[f] Torments me with intollerable paines;

[g] The knotty Gout.

[h] The Quinſie, and the Feavours, oft diſtaſte me,
And the Conſumption, to the bones doth waſte me:

* "Omnia mea porto mecum." — Bias, *apud Cic. Parad.* I. 1. 8.

Subject to all diſtempers [i] (that's the truth)
Though ſome more incident, to Age or Youth.
And to conclude, I may not tedious be,
Man at his beſt eſtate is vanity.

Old Age.

WHAT you have been, ev'n ſuch have I before:
And all you ſay, ſay I, and ſomewhat more.
Babes innocence, youths wildneſs I have ſeen, [55]
And in perplexed middle Age have been:
Sickneſs, dangers, and anxieties have paſt,
And on this ſtage am come to act my laſt.
I have been young, and ſtrong, and wiſe as you:
But now *Bis pueri ſenes*, is too true.
In every Age I've found much vanity,
An end of all perfection now I ſee.
It's not my valour, honour, nor my gold,
My ruin'd houſe now falling can uphold.
It's not my learning Rhetorick wit ſo large,
Hath now the power, death's warfare to diſcharge.
It's not my goodly ſtate, [j] nor bed of downe
That can refreſh, or eaſe, if Conſcience frown.
Nor from Alliance can I now have hope,
But what I have done well, that is my prop;

[i] Diſeaſes. [j] houſe.

He that in youth is godly, wiſe and ſage,
Provides a ſtaff then to ſupport his Age.
Mutations great, ſome joyful and ſome ſad,
In this ſhort pilgrimage I oft have had.
Sometimes the Heavens with plenty ſmil'd on me
Sometime again rain'd all Adverſity.
Sometimes in honour, ſometimes in diſgrace,
Sometime an Abject, then again in place.
Such private changes oft mine eyes have ſeen,
In various times of ſtate I've alſo been.
I've ſeen a Kingdome flouriſh like a tree,
When it was rul'd by that Celeſtial ſhe;*
And like a Cedar, others ſo ſurmount:
That but for ſhrubs they did themſelves account.
Then ſaw I *France* and *Holland*, ſav'd *Cales* won,† [56]
And *Philip* and *Albertus* half undone.
I ſaw all peace at home, terror to foes,
But ah, I ſaw at laſt thoſe eyes to cloſe,
And then methought the day[k] at noon grew dark
When it had loſt that radiant Sun-like Spark:

* Queen Elizabeth.

† It is difficult to explain this reference unless the destruction of the Spanish Armada in 1588 is meant. While it was at anchor before Calais, it was scattered and put to flight by a successful stratagem of the English admiral. The Engliſh thus gained an advantage which they soon followed up to victory. It can hardly refer to the surprise of Calais in 1596, by Albert, Archduke of Austria, who had recently been made Governor of the Netherlands by Philip II. of Spain. The various successes of Elizabeth may, perhaps, be said to have "half undone" Philip and Albert.

k world.

In midſt of griefs I ſaw our [1] hopes revive,
(For 'twas our hopes then kept our hearts alive)
We chang'd our queen for king* under whoſe rayes
We joy'd in many bleſt and proſperous dayes.
I've ſeen a Prince, the glory of our land
In prime of youth ſeiz'd by heavens angry hand,
Which fil'd our hearts with fears, with tears our eyes,
Wailing his fate, & our own deſtinies.†
I've ſeen from *Rome* an execrable thing,
A Plot to blow up Nobles and their King,
But ſaw their horrid fact ſoon diſappointed,
And Land & Nobles ſav'd with their anointed.‡
I've Princes ſeen to live on others lands;
A royal one by gifts from ſtrangers hands
Admired for their magnanimity,
Who loſt a Prince-dome and a Monarchy.§
I've ſeen deſigns for *Ree* and *Rochel* croſt,||
And Poor *Palatinate* for ever loſt.

[1] ſome.

* James I.

† Henry, Prince of Wales, died suddenly Nov. 6, 1612, in his nineteenth year. He was very popular, and his death was greatly lamented, especially by the more religious party, whose friend he was.

‡ Gunpowder Plot.

§ The Elector Palatine Frederick V., who had married the Princess Elizabeth, daughter of James I., accepted the crown from the revolted states of Bohemia in 1619. He did not long enjoy this dangerous honor, but was beaten by the Austrians in the battle of Prague, Nov. 9, 1620, and was obliged, with his family, to take refuge in Holland. He soon after lost also his hereditary possessions, and passed the rest of his life as a needy exile, wandering from court to court. The Reformed Religion in Bohemia fell with him; an event which caused the greatest sorrow to all Protestants.

|| Buckingham made an unsuccessful attempt to take the Isle de Rhé, in

I've ſeen unworthy men advanced high,
(And better ones ſuffer extremity)
But neither favour, riches, title, State,
Could length their dayes or once reverſe their fate
I've ſeen one ſtab'd,* and ſome to looſe their heads †
And others fly, ſtruck both with gilt and dread.
I've ſeen and ſo have you, for tis but late, [57]
The deſolation of a goodly State,
Plotted and acted ſo that none can tell,
VVho gave the counſel, but the Prince of hell,
Three hundred thouſand ſlaughtered innocents,
By bloudy Popiſh, helliſh miſcreants:
Oh may you live, and ſo you will I truſt
To ſee them ſwill in bloud untill they burſt.‡
I've ſeen a King § by force thruſt from his throne,
And an Uſurper‖ ſubt'ly mount thereon.

front of La Rochelle, in 1627. Instead of "*Rochel*," the first edition has "*Cades*," referring to the failure of a naval expedition under the command of Sir Edward Cecil, which sailed in October, 1625, to capture some Spanish treasure ships in the bay of Cadiz.

* Buckingham.

† The Earl of Strafford, Archbishop Laud, and Charles I.

‡ Whoever has read of the massacre and inhuman atrocities connected with the Insurrection in Ireland in 1641 will not be surprised at the strong language of the author. As to the number of those killed, Hume says, "By some computations, those who perished by all these cruelties are supposed to be a hundred and fifty or two hundred thousand: by the most moderate, and probably the most reasonable account, they are made to amount to forty thousand,—if this estimation itself be not, as is usual in such cases, somewhat exaggerated."—History of England, chap. lv.

§ Charles I.

‖ Cromwell.

I've ſeen a ſtate unmoulded, rent in twain,
But ye may live to ſee't made up again.
I've ſeen it plunder'd, taxt and ſoak'd in bloud,
But out of evill you may ſee much good.
What are my thoughts, this is no time to ſay.
Men may more freely ſpeak another day.*

* In the first edition there is a different version of the events related in the passage beginning with line 3, page 163 ("We changed our queen for king," &c.), and ending here. It will be observed in this and many other places, that the author, in preparing her poems for republication, had regard to the political changes which had taken place. Charles II. had been restored, and it was necessary to be loyal or silent.

I ſaw hopes daſht, our forwardneſſe was ſhent,
And ſilenc'd we, by Act of Parliament.
I've ſeen from *Rome*, an execrable thing,
A plot to blow up Nobles, and their King;
I've ſeen deſignes at Ree, and *Cades* croſt,
And poor *Palatinate* for ever loſt;
I've ſeen a Prince, to live on others lands,
A Royall one, by almes from Subjects hands,
I've ſeen baſe men, advanc'd to great degree,
And worthy ones, put to extremity:
But not their Princes love, nor ſtate ſo high
Could once reverſe, their ſhameſull deſtiny.
I've ſeen one ſtab'd, another looſe his head:
And others fly their Country, through their dread.
I've ſeen, and ſo have ye, for 'tis but late,
The deſolation, of a goodly State.
Plotted and acted, ſo that none can tell,
Who gave the counſel, but the Prince of hell.
I've ſeen a land unmoulded with great paine.
But yet may live, to ſee't made up again:
I've ſeen it ſhaken, rent, and ſoak'd in blood.
But out of troubles, ye may ſee much good.

These are no old-wives tales, but this is truth,
We old men love to tell what's done in youth.
But I return from whence I ſtept awry,
My memory is bad,[m] my brain is dry:
Mine Almond tree, grey hairs, doe flouriſh now,
And back once ſtraight, apace begins to bow:
My grinders now are few, my ſight doth fail,
My skin is wrinkled, and my cheeks are pale,
No more rejoyce at muſicks pleaſing noiſe,
But waking glad to hear the cocks ſhrill voice:[n]
I cannot ſcent ſavours of pleaſant meat,
Nor ſapors find in what I drink or eat:
My arms and hands once ſtrong have loſt their might
I cannot labour, much leſs can I fight.[o]
My comely legs as nimble as the Roc * [58]
Now ſtiff and numb, can hardly creep or goe,
My heart ſometimes as fierce as Lion bold,
Now trembling is, all[p] fearful ſad and cold;
My golden Bowl and ſilver Cord e're long
Shall both be broke, by racking death ſo ſtrong:
Then ſhall I go whence I ſhall come no more,
Sons, Nephews, leave my farewel[q] to deplore.
In pleaſures and in labours I have found
That Earth can give no conſolation ſound;

[m] ſhort.

[n] But do awake, at the cocks clanging voyce.

[o] nor I cannot fight.

[p] trembling, and.

* 1 Chron. xii. 8; Cant. ii. 9 and 17.

[q] death for.

To great to rich, to poor, to young, to old,
To mean, to noble, fearful or to bold:
From King to begger, all degrees ſhall find
But vanity vexation of the mind.*
Yea, knowing much, the pleaſants life of all,
Hath yet among thoſe ſweets [r] ſome bitter gall;
Though reading others works doth much refreſh,
Yet ſtudying much brings wearineſs to th' fleſh:
My ſtudies, labours, readings all are done,
And my laſt period now ev'n almoſt run.
Corruption my Father I do call,
Mother and Siſters both, the worms that crawle
In my dark houſe, ſuch kindred I have ſtore,
Where I ſhall reſt till heavens ſhall be no more,
And when this fleſh ſhall rot and be conſum'd,
This body by this Soul ſhall be aſſum'd:
And I ſhall ſee with theſe ſame very eyes,
My ſtrong Redeemer coming in the Skies.
Triumph I ſhall o're ſin, o're death, o're Hell,
And in that hope I bid you all farewel.

* Eccl. xii. 1-8.
[r] that ſweet.

The four Seasons of the Year. [59]

Spring.

ANother four I've left[s] yet to bring on,
Of four times four the last *Quaternion*,
The Winter, Summer, Autumn & the Spring,
In season all these Seasons I shall bring:
Sweet Spring like man in his Minority,
At present claim'd, and had priority.
With smiling face and garments somewhat green,
She trim'd her locks, which late had frosted been,
Nor hot nor cold, she spake, but with a breath,
Fit to revive, the nummed earth from death.[t]

[s] yet for.

[t] Instead of this and the three preceding lines the first edition has.—
With smiling Sun-shine face, and garments green,
She gently thus began, like some fair Queen.

Three months (quoth she)[u] are 'lotted to my share
March, April, May of all the rest most fair.
Tenth of the first, *Sol* into *Aries* enters,
And bids defiance to all tedious winters.
Crosseth the Line, and equals night and day,
(Stil adds to th' last til after pleasant *May*)
And now makes glad the darkned[v] northern wights
Who for some months have seen but starry lights.
Now goes the Plow-man to his merry toyle,
He might[w] unloose his winter locked soyl:
The Seeds-man too, doth lavish out his grain,
In hope the more he casts, the more to gain:
The Gardner now superfluous branches lops,
And poles erects for his young[x] clambring hops.
Now digs then sowes his herbs, his flowers & roots
And carefully manures his trees of fruits.
The *Pleiades their influence* now give,
And all that seem'd as dead afresh doth live.
The croaking frogs, whom nipping winter kil'd
Like birds now chirp, and hop about the field,
The Nightingale, the black-bird and the Thrush
Now tune their layes, on sprayes of every bush.
The wanton frisking Kid, and soft-fleec'd Lambs
Do[y] jump and play before their feeding Dams,
The tender tops of budding grass they crop,
They joy in what they have, but more in hope:

[u] there are. [v] those blinded. [w] For to.
[x] green. [y] Now.

For though the froſt hath loſt his binding power,
Yet many a fleece of ſnow and ſtormy ſhower
Doth darken *Sol*'s bright eye,[z] makes us remember
The pinching North-weſt wind of cold[a] *December*.
My ſecond moneth is *April*, green and fair,
Of longer dayes, and a more temperate Air:
The Sun in *Taurus* keeps his reſidence,[b]
And with his warmer beams glanceth from thence
This is the month whoſe fruitful ſhowrs produces
All ſet and ſown[c] for all delights and uſes:
The Pear, the Plum, and Apple-tree now flouriſh
The graſs grows long the hungry beaſt[d] to nouriſh.
The Primroſe pale, and azure violet
Among the virduous graſs hath nature ſet,
That when the Sun on's Love (the earth) doth ſhine
Theſe might as lace ſet out her garment fine.
The fearfull bird his little houſe now builds [61]
In trees and walls, in Cities and in fields.
The outſide ſtrong, the inſide warm and neat;
A natural Artificer compleat.

[z] face. [a] Nor-weſt cold. of fierce.

[b] The Sun now keeps his poſting reſidence
In *Taurus* Signe, yet haſteth ſtraight from thence:
For though in's running progreſſe he doth take
Twelve houſes of the oblique Zodiack
Yet never minute ſtil was known to ſtand,
But only once at *Joſhua*'s ſtrange command;

All Plants, and Flowers. [d] the tender Lambs.

The clocking hen her chirping chickins[e] leads
With wings & beak defends them from the gleads
. My next and laſt is fruitfull pleaſant *May*,
Wherein the earth is clad in rich aray,
The Sun now enters loving *Gemini*,
And heats us with the glances of his eye,
Our thicker[f] rayment makes us lay aſide
Leſt by his fervor we be torrifi'd.[g]
All flowers the Sun now with his beams diſcloſes,[h]
Except the double pinks and matchleſs Roſes.
Now ſwarms the buſy, witty,[i] honey-Bee,
VVhoſe praiſe deſerves a page from more then me
The cleanly Huſwifes Dary's now in th' prime,
Her ſhelves and firkins fill'd for winter time.
The meads with Cowſlips, Honey-ſuckles dight,
One hangs his head, the other ſtands upright:
But both rejoyce at th' heavens clear ſmiling face,
More at her ſhowers, which water them a ſpace..
For fruits my Seaſon yields the early Cherry,
The haſty Peas, and wholſome cool[j] Strawberry.
More ſolid fruits require a longer time,
Each Seaſon hath his fruit, ſo hath each Clime:
Each man his own peculiar excellence,
But none in all that hath preheminence.

[e] chipping brood now.
[f] Winter. [g] terrifi'd.
[h] All flowers before the ſun-beames now diſcloſes.
[i] buzzing. [j] red.

Sweet fragrant Spring, with thy ſhort pittance fly[k]
Let ſome deſcribe thee better then can I.
Yet above all this priviledg is thine, [62]
Thy dayes ſtill lengthen without leaſt decline:

Summer.

WHEN *Spring* had done, the *Summer* did[l] begin,
With melted tauny face, and garments thin,
Reſembling Fire, Choler, and Middle age,
As *Spring* did Air, Blood, Youth in's equipage.
Wiping the ſweat from of her face[m] that ran,
With hair all wet ſhe puffing thus began;
Bright *June*, *July* and *Auguſt* hot are mine,
In'th firſt *Sol* doth in crabbed *Cancer* ſhine.
His progreſs to the North now's fully done,
Then retrograde muſt be[n] my burning Sun,
Who to his ſouthward Tropick ſtill is bent,
Yet doth his parching heat but more augment
Though he decline, becauſe his flames ſo fair,
Have throughly dry'd the earth, and heat the air.[o]

[k] Instead of this and the following line, the first edition has, —
Some ſubject, ſhallow braines, much matter yeelds,
Sometime a theame that's large, proves barren fields.
Melodious Spring, with thy ſhort pittance flye,
In this harſh ſtrain, I find no melody,

[l] muſt. [m] brow. [n] now is.

[o] The reaſon why, becauſe his flames ſo faire,
Hath formerly much heat, the earth and aire.

Like as an Oven that long time hath been heat,
Whoſe vehemency at length doth grow ſo great,
That if you do withdraw[p] her burning ſtore,
Tis[q] for a time as fervent as before.
Now go thoſe frolick Swains, the Shepherd Lads
To waſh the[r] thick cloth'd flocks with pipes full glad
In the cool ſtreams they labour with delight
Rubbing their dirty coats till they look white:
Whoſe fleece when finely[s] ſpun and deeply dy'd
With Robes thereof Kings have been dignifi'd.
Bleſt ruſtick Swains, your pleaſant quiet life, [63]
Hath envy bred in Kings that were at ſtrife,[t]
Carleſs of worldly wealth you ſing[u] and pipe,
Whilſt they'r imbroyl'd in wars & troubles rife:[v]
VVhich made great *Bajazet* cry out in's woes,
Oh happy ſhepherd which hath not to loſe.
Orthobulus, nor yet *Sebaſtia* great,
But whiſt'leth to thy flock in cold and heat.*

[p] remove. [q] She's. [r] their. [s] purely.

[t] Instead of this and the preceding line, the first edition has,—

'Mongſt all ye ſhepheards never but one man.
Was like that noble, brave *Archadian*.
Yet hath your life, made kings the ſame envy,
Though you repoſe on graſſe under the skye.

[u] ſit. [v] ripe.

* "Moſt of the Latine hiſtories report, that when *Tamerlane* had taken SEBASTIA, hee put all the men to the ſword, and bringing the women and children into the fields without the citie, there ouer-ran them with his horſemen, excepting ſome few which were reſerued for priſoners. As alſo that *Baiazet* there loſt his eldeſt ſonne *Erthogrul* (of ſome called *Orthobules*) whoſe death with the loſſe of the citie ſo much grieued him (as is

Viewing the Sun by day, the Moon by night
Endimions, Dianaes dear delight,
Upon the graſs reſting your healthy limbs.
By purling Brooks looking how fiſhes ſwims.
If pride within your lowly Cells ere haunt.
Of him that was Shepherd then King go vaunt.*
This moneth the Roſes are diſtil'd in glaſſes,
VVhoſe fragrant ſmel[w] all made perfumes ſurpaſſes
The Cherry, Gooſeberry are now in th' prime,
And for all ſorts of Peaſe, this is the time.
July my next, the hott'ſt in all the year,
The ſun through *Leo* now takes[x] his Career.
VVhoſe flaming breath doth melt us from afar,
Increaſed by the ſtar Canicular.
This Month from *Julius Cæſar* took its name,
By Romans celebrated to his fame.
Now go the Mowers to their ſlaſhing toyle,
The Meadowes of their riches[y] to diſpoyle,

reported) that marching with his great armie againſt *Tamerlane*, and by the way hearing a country ſhepheard merrily repoſing himſelf with his homely pipe, as he ſat vpon the ſide of a mountaine feeding his poore flock; ſtanding ſtill a great while liſtening vnto him, to the great admiration of many, at laſt fetching a deepe ſigh, brake forth in theſe words: O happie ſhepheard, which haddeſt neither *Orthobules* nor SEBASTIA to looſe: bewraying therein his owne diſcontentment, and yet withal ſhewing, That worldly bliſſe conſiſteth not ſo much in poſſeſſing of much, ſubject vnto danger, as joying a little contentment deuoid of feare."—THE GENERALL HISTORIE OF THE TURKES, BY RICHARD KNOLLES. Second edition. 1610. p. 216. Bajazet I. became Sultan of the Turks in 1389. and died in 1403.

* This and the three preceding lines are not in the first edition.

[w] ſcent. [x] hath. [y] burden.

VVith weary ſtrokes, they take all in their way,
Bearing the burning heat of the long day.
The forks and Rakes do follow them amain,
VVhich makes the aged fields look young again.
The groaning Carts do bear away this prize. [64]
To Stacks and Barns where it for Fodder lyes.
My next and laſt is *Auguſt* fiery hot
(For much, the *Southward* Sun abateth not)
This Moneth he keeps with *Virgo* for a ſpace,
The dryed Earth is parched with his face.
Auguſt of great *Auguſtus* took its name,
Romes ſecond Emperour of laſting[z] fame,
With ſickles now the bending[a] Reapers goe
The ruſtling treſs of *terra* down to mowe;
And bundles up in ſheaves, the weighty wheat,
Which after Manchet makes[b] for Kings to eat:
The Barly, Rye and Peaſe[c] ſhould firſt had place,
Although their bread have not ſo white a face.
The Carter leads all home with whiſtling voyce,
He plow'd with pain, but reaping doth rejoyce;
His ſweat, his toyle, his careful wakeful nights,
His fruitful Crop abundantly requites.
Now's ripe the Pear, Pear-plumb, and Apricock,
The prince of plumbs, whoſe ſtone's as hard as Rock
The Summer ſeems but ſhort, the Autumn haſts[d]
To ſhake his fruits, of moſt delicious taſts

[z] peaceful. [a] painful.
[b] made. [c] The Barley, and the Rye.
[d] The Summer's ſhort, the beauteous Autumne haſtes.

Like good old Age, whoſe younger juicy Roots
Hath ſtill aſcended, to bear[e] goodly fruits.
Until his head be gray, and ſtrength be gone.
Yet then appears the worthy deeds he'th done:
To feed his boughs exhauſted hath his ſap,
Then drops his fruits into the eaters lap.

Autumn.

[65]

OF *Autumn* moneths *September* is the prime,
Now day and night are equal in each Clime,
The twelfth[f] of this *Sol* riſeth in the Line,
And doth in poizing *Libra* this month ſhine.
The vintage now is ripe, the grapes are preſt,
Whoſe lively liquor oft is curſ'd and bleſt:
For nought ſo good, but it may be abuſed,
But its a precious juice when well its uſed.
The raiſins now in cluſters dryed be,
The Orange, Lemon dangle on the tree:
The Pomegranate, the Fig are ripe alſo,
And Apples now their yellow ſides do ſhow.
Of Almonds,[g] Quinces, Wardens, and of Peach,
The ſeaſon's now at hand of all and each.
Sure at this time, time firſt of all began,
And in this moneth was made apoſtate Man:

[e] up in. [f] tenth. [g] Of Medlar.

For then in *Eden* was not only ſeen,
Boughs full of leaves, or fruits unripe or[h] green,
Or withered ſtocks, which were[i] all dry and dead,
But trees with goodly fruits repleniſhed;
Which ſhews nor Summer, Winter nor the Spring
Our Grand-Sire[j] was of Paradice made King:
Nor could that temp'rate Clime ſuch difference make,
If ſcited as the moſt Judicious take.[k]
October is my next, we hear in this
The Northern winter-blaſts begin to hiſs.
In *Scorpio* reſideth now the Sun, [66]
And his declining heat is almoſt done.
The fruitleſs[l] Trees all withered now do ſtand,
Whoſe ſapleſs yellow leavs, by winds are fan'd,
Which notes when youth and ſtrength have paſt their prime
Decrepit age muſt alſo have its time.
The Sap doth ſlily creep towards the Earth
There reſts, until the Sun give it a birth.
So doth old Age ſtill tend unto his grave,
Where alſo he his winter time muſt have;
But when the Sun of righteouſneſs draws nigh,
His dead old ſtock, ſhall mount again on high.
November is my laſt, for Time doth haſte,
We now of winters ſharpneſs 'gins to taſt.

[h] but raw, and.
[i] "which were" is not in the first edition.
[j] Great *Adam*.
[k] These two lines are not in the first edition.
[l] fruitful.

This moneth the Sun's in *Sagitarius*,
So farre remote, his glances warm not us.
Almoſt at ſhorteſt is the ſhorten'd day,
The *Northern* pole beholdeth not one ray.
Now *Greenland*, *Groanland*,* *Finland*, *Lapland*, ſee
No Sun, to lighten their obſcurity:
Poor wretches that in total darkneſs lye,
With minds more dark then is the dark'ned Sky.[m]
Beaf, Brawn, and Pork are now in great requeſt,
And ſolid meats our ſtomacks can digeſt.
This time warm cloaths, full diet, and good fires,
Our pinched fleſh, and hungry mawes[n] requires:
Old, cold, dry Age and Earth *Autumn* reſembles,
And Melancholy which moſt of all diſſembles.
I muſt be ſhort, and ſhorts, the ſhort'ned day,
What winter hath to tell, now let him ſay.

Winter. [67]

COLD, moiſt, young flegmy winter now doth lye
In ſwadling Clouts, like new born Infancy
Bound up with froſts, and furr'd with hail & ſnows,
And like an Infant, ſtill it[o] taller grows;

* *Groen-land* [or Grönland, *Dan.*] in the first edition.

[m] After this the first edition has, —

This month is timber for all uſes fell'd,
When cold, the ſap to th' roots hath low'ſt repell'd;

[n] empty panch.

[o] he.

December is my firſt, and now the Sun
To th' Southward *Tropick*, his ſwift race doth[p] run:
This moneth he's hous'd in horned *Capricorn*,
From thence he 'gins to length the ſhortned morn,
Through *Chriſtendome* with great Feaſtivity,
Now's held, (but gheſt) for bleſt[q] Nativity.
Cold frozen *January* next comes in,
Chilling the blood and ſhrinking up the skin;
In *Aquarius* now keeps the long wiſht[r] Sun,
And Northward his unwearied Courſe[s] doth run:
The day much longer then it was before,
The cold not leſſened, but augmented more.
Now Toes and Ears, and Fingers often freeze,
And Travellers their noſes ſometimes leeſe.
Moiſt ſnowie *February* is my laſt,
I care not how the winter time doth haſte.
In *Piſces* now the golden Sun doth ſhine,
And Northward ſtill approaches to the Line.
The Rivers 'gin to ope, the ſnows to melt,
And ſome warm glances from his face[t] are felt;
Which is increaſed by the lengthen'd day,
Until by's heat, he drive all cold away,
And thus the year in Circle runneth round: [68]
Where firſt it did begin, in th' end its found.[u]

[p] hath. [q] a Gueſt, (but bleſt). [r] the loved.
[s] race. [t] the Sun.
[u] These two lines are not in the first edition.

My Subjects bare, my Brain is bad,
Or better Lines you ſhould have had:
The firſt fell in ſo nat'rally,
I knew not how to paſs it by;[v]
The laſt, though bad I could not mend,
Accept therefore of what is pen'd,
And all the faults that you ſhall ſpy
*Shall at your feet for pardon cry.**

[v] I could not tell how to paſſe 't by.

* This is signed in the first edition.

Your dutifull Daughter.

A. B.

The four *Monarchyes*, [69]

the *Aſſyrian* being the firſt,

beginning under *Nimrod*, 131. Years aſter the Flood,

WHen time was young, & World in Infancy,
Man did not proudly[w] ſtrive for Soveraignty:
But each one thought his petty Rule was high,
If of his houſe he held the Monarchy.
This was the golden Age, but after came
The boiſterous ſon of *Chus*,[x] Grand-Child to *Ham*,
That mighty Hunter, who in his ſtrong toyles
Both Beaſts and Men ſubjected to his ſpoyles:
The ſtrong foundation of proud *Babel* laid,
Erech, *Accad*, and *Culneh* alſo made.
Theſe were his firſt, all ſtood in *Shinar* land,
From thence he went *Aſſyria* to command,
And mighty *Niniveh*, he there begun,
Not finiſhed till he his race had run.

[w] "Proudly" is not in the first edition.

[x] Sons of Cush.

Reſen, *Caleh*, and *Rehoboth* likewiſe
By him to Cities eminent did riſe.
Of *Saturn*, he was the Original,
Whom the ſucceeding times a God did call,
When thus with rule, he had been dignifi'd,
One hundred fourteen years he after dy'd.

Belus.

GREAT *Nimrod* dead, *Belus* the next his Son
Confirms the rule, his Father had begun;
Whoſe acts and power is not for certainty
Left to the world, by any Hiſtory.
But yet this blot for ever on him lies,
He taught the people firſt to Idolize:
Titles Divine he to himſelf did take,
Alive and dead, a God they did him make.
This is that *Bel* the *Chaldees* worſhiped,
Whoſe Prieſts in Stories oft are mentioned;
This is that *Baal* to whom the *Iſraelites*
So oft profanely offered ſacred Rites:
This is *Beelzebub* God of *Ekronites*,
Likewiſe *Baalpeor* of the *Mohabites*,
His reign was ſhort, for as I calculate,
At twenty five ended his Regal date.

Ninus.

HIS Father dead, *Ninus* begins his reign,
Transfers his ſeat to the *Aſſyrian* plain:
And mighty *Nineveh* more mighty made,
Whoſe Foundation was by his Grand-ſire laid:
Four hundred forty Furlongs wall'd about,
On which ſtood fifteen hundred Towers ſtout.
The walls one hundred ſixty foot upright, [71]
So broad three Chariots run abreſt there might.
Upon the pleaſant banks of *Tygris* floud
This ſtately Seat of warlike *Ninus* ſtood:
This *Ninus* for a God his Father canonized,
To whom the ſottiſh people ſacrificed.
This Tyrant did his Neighbours all oppreſs,
Where e're he warr'd he had too good ſucceſs.
Barzanes the great *Armenian* King
By force and fraud did under Tribute bring.[1]
The *Median* Country he did alſo gain,
Thermus[2] their King he cauſed to be ſlain;
An Army of three millions he led out
Againſt the *Bactrians* (but that I doubt)
Zoreaſter their King he likewiſe ſlew,
And all the greater *Aſia* did ſubdue.
Semiramis from *Menon* did he take
Then drown'd himſelf, did *Menon* for her ſake.
Fifty two years he reign'd, (as we are told)
The world then was two thouſand nineteen old.

[1] By force, his tributary, he did bring. [2] Pharmus.

Semiramis.

THIS great oppreſſing *Ninus*, dead and gone,
His wife *Semiramis* uſurp'd the Throne;
She like a brave *Virago* played the *Rex*
And was both ſhame and glory of her Sex:
Her birth place was Philiſtines *Aſcolan*,[a]
Her mother *Dorceta*[b] a Curtizan.
Others report ſhe was a veſtal *Nun*,
Adjudged to be drown'd for th' crime[c] ſhe'd done.
Tranſform'd into a Fiſh by *Venus* will, [72]
Her beauteous face, (they feign) reteining ſtill.
Sure from this Fiction *Dagon* firſt began,
Changing the[d] womans face into a man:
But all agree that from no lawfull bed,
This great renowned Empreſs iſſued:
For which ſhe was obſcurely nouriſhed,
Whence roſe that Fable, ſhe by birds was fed.
This gallant Dame unto the *Bactrian* warre,
Accompanying her husband *Menon* farr,
Taking a town, ſuch valour ſhe did ſhow,
That *Ninus* amorous of her ſoon did grow,
And thought her fit to make a Monarchs wife,
Which was the cauſe poor *Menon* loſt his life:
She flouriſhing with *Ninus* long did reign,
Till her Ambition caus'd him to be ſlain.

[a] *Philiſtrius Aſcalon.* [b] *Docreta.*
[c] for what. [d] his.

That having no Compeer, ſhe might rule all,
Or elſe ſhe ſought revenge for *Menon's* fall.
Some think the Greeks this ſlander on her caſt,
As on her life Licentious, and unchaſt,
That undeſerv'd, they blur'd her name and fame[e]
By[f] their aſperſions, caſt upon the ſame:
But were her virtues more or leſs, or none,
She for her potency muſt go alone.
Her wealth ſhe ſhew'd in building *Babylon*,
Admir'd of all, but equaliz'd of none;
The Walls ſo ſtrong, and curiouſly was[g] wrought,
That after Ages, Skill by them was[g] taught:
With Towers and Bulwarks made of coſtly ſtone,
Quadrangle was the form it ſtood upon.
Each Square was fifteen thouſand paces long, [73]
An hundred gates it had of mettal ſtrong:
Three hundred ſixty foot the walls in height,
Almoſt incredible, they were in breadth
Some[h] writers ſay, ſix Chariots might affront
With great facility, march ſafe upon't:
About the Wall a ditch ſo deep and wide,
That like a River long it did abide.
Three hundred thouſand men here day by day
Beſtow'd their labour, and receiv'd their pay.
And that which did all coſt and Art excell,
The wondrous Temple was, ſhe rear'd to *Bell*:

[e] And that her worth, deſerved no ſuch blame.
[f] As. [g] were. [h] Moſt.

Which in the midſt of this brave Town was plac'd,
Continuing till *Xerxes* it deſac'd:
Whoſe ſtately top above[i] the Clouds did riſe.
From whence Aſtrologers oft view'd the Skies.
This to deſcribe in each particular,
A ſtructure rare I ſhould but rudely marre.
Her Gardens, Bridges, Arches, mounts and ſpires
All eyes that ſaw, or Ears that hear admires,
In *Shinar* plain on the *Euphratian* flood
This wonder of the world, this *Babel* ſtood.
An expedition to the *Eaſt* ſhe made
Staurobates, his Country to invade:[j]
Her Army of four millions did conſiſt,
Each may believe it as his fancy liſt.
Her Camels, Chariots, Gallyes in ſuch number,
As puzzles beſt Hiſtorians to remember;
But this is wonderful,[k] of all thoſe men,
They ſay, but twenty e're came back agen.
The River *Judas*[l] ſwept them half away, [74]
The reſt *Staurobates* in fight did ſlay;
This was laſt progreſs of this mighty Queen,
Who in her Country never more was ſeen.
The Poets ſeign'd her turn'd into a Dove,
Leaving the world to *Venus* ſoar'd above:
Which made the *Aſſyrians* many a day,
A Dove within their Enſigns to diſplay:
Forty two years ſhe reign'd, and then ſhe di'd
But by what means we are not certifi'd.

[i] beyond.
[j] Great King *Staurobates*, for to invade.
[k] marvelous.
[l] *Indus*.

Ninias or Zamies.

HIS Mother dead, *Ninias* obtains his right,
A Prince wedded to eafe and to delight,
Or elfe was his obedience very great,
To fit thus long (obfcure) rob'd[l] of his Seat.
Some write his Mother put his habit on,
Which made the people think they ferv'd her Son:
But much it is, in more then forty years
This fraud in war nor peace at all appears:
More like it is his luft[m] with pleafures fed,
He fought no rule till fhe was gone and dead.
VVhat then he did of worth can no man tell,
But is fuppof'd to be that *Amraphel*
VVho warr'd with *Sodoms* and *Gomorrahs* King,
'Gainft whom his trained bands *Abram* did bring,
But this is farre unlike, he being Son[n]
Unto a Father, that all Countryes won

[l] wrong'd. [m] being.

[n] Instead of this and the nine lines following, the first edition has.—
Some may object, his Parents ruling all,
How he thus fuddenly fhould be thus fmall?
This anfwer may fuffice, whom it wil pleafe,
He thus voluptuous, and given to eafe;
Each wronged Prince, or childe that did remain,
Would now advantage take, their own to gain;
So Province, after Province, rent away,
Until that Potent Empire did decay.
Again, the Country was left bare (there is no doubt)
Of men, and wealth, his mother carried out;
Which to her neighbors, when it was made known,
Did then incite, them to regain their own.

So ſuddenly ſhould looſe ſo great a ſtate,
VVith petty Kings to joyne Confederate.
Nor can thoſe Reaſons which wiſe *Raileih** finds,
VVell ſatisfie the moſt conſiderate minds:
VVe may with learned *Vſher** better ſay,
He many Ages liv'd after that day.
And that *Semiramis* then flouriſhed
VVhen famous *Troy* was ſo beleaguered:
VVhat e're he was, or[o] did, or how it fell,
VVe may ſuggeſt our thoughts but cannot tell.
For *Ninias* and all his race are left
In deep oblivion, of acts bereſt:
And many[p] hundred years in ſilence ſit,
Save a few Names a new *Beroſus*† writ.
And ſuch as care not what befalls their fames,
May feign as many acts as he did Names;
It may ſuffice,[q] if all be true that's paſt.
T' *Sardanapalas* next, we will make haſte.

* See Introduction.

[o] they. [p] cleav'n. [q] It is enough.

† See Raleigh's "Hiſtory of the World," Bk. I. ch. 8, sec. 5, and Bk. II. ch. 1, sec. 1. "The work entitled *Beroſi Antiquitatum libri quinque cum Commentariis Joannis Annii*, which appeared at Rome in 1498, fol., and was afterwards often reprinted and even translated into Italian, is one of the many fabrications of Giovanni Nanni, a Dominican monk of Viterbo, better known under the name of Annius of Viterbo, who died in 1502." — SMITH's "Dictionary of Greek and Roman Biography and Mythology."

The writings of the real Berosus exist only in a fragmentary condition, as quoted by Josephus and other authors. See page [182.]

Sardanapalas

SARDANAPALAS, Son to *Ocrazapes*,
VVho wallowed in all voluptuoufnefs,
That palliardizing fot that out of dores,
Ne're fhew'd his face but revell'd with his whores
Did wear their garbs, their geftures imitate,
And in their kind, t excel did emulate.
His bafenefs knowing, and the peoples hate
Kept clofe, fearing his well deferved fate;[r]
It chanc'd[s] *Arbaces* brave unwarily,
His Mafter like a Strumpet clad did[t] fpye.
His manly heart difdained (in the leaft)
Longer to ferve this Metamorphos'd Beaft;
Unto *Belofus* then he brake his mind, [76]
Who fick of his difeafe, he foon did find
Thefe two, rul'd *Media* and *Babilon*
Both for their King, held their Dominion;
Belofus promifed *Arbaces* aid,
Arbaces him fully to be repayd.
The laft: The *Medes* and *Perfians* do invite
Againft their monftrous King, to ufe[u] their might.
Belofus, the *Chaldeans* doth require
And the *Arabians*, to further his defire:

[r] Kept ever clofe, fearing fome difmal fate.
[s] At laft. [t] chanc'd to. [u] bring.

Theſe all agree, and forty thouſand make
The Rule, from their unworthy Prince to take:[v]
Theſe Forces muſtered, and in array
Sardanapalus leaves his Apiſh play.
And though of wars, he did abhor the ſight;
Fear of his diadem did force him fight:
And either by his valour, or his fate,
Arbaces Courage he did ſo[w] abate;
That in diſpair, he left the Field and fled,
But with freſh hopes *Beloſus* ſuccoured,
From *Bactria*, an Army was at hand
Preſt for this Service by the Kings Command:
Theſe with celerity *Arbaces* meet,[x]
And with all Terms of amity them greet.[y]
With[z] promiſes their necks now to unyoke,
And their Taxations ſore all to revoke;
T' infranchiſe them, to grant what they could crave,
No priviledge to want, Subjects ſhould have,
Only intreats them, to joyn their Force with his,
And win the Crown, which was the way to bliſs.
Won by his loving looks, more by his[a] ſpeech, [77]
T' accept of what they could, they all[b] beſeech:
Both ſides their hearts their hands, & bands unite,
And ſet upon their Princes Camp that night;

[v] After this the first edition has.—

By prophecie, *Beloſus* ſtrength's their hands.
Arbaces muſt be maſter of their lands.

[w] ſore. [x] meets. [y] he greets.
[z] Makes. [a] more loving. [b] him.

Who revelling in Cups, ſung care away,
For victory obtain'd the other day:
And now[c] ſurpriſ'd, by this unlookt for fright,
Bereft of wits, were ſlaughtered down right.
The King his brother leavs, all to ſuſtain,
And ſpeeds himſelf to *Niniveh* amain.
But *Salmeneus* ſlain, the Army falls;
The King's purſu'd unto the City Walls,
But he once in, purſuers came to late,
The Walls and Gates their haſt[d] did terminate,
There with all ſtore he was ſo well provided:
That what *Arbaces* did, was but derided:
Who there incamp'd, two years for little end,
But in the third, the River prov'd his friend,
For by the rain, was *Tygris* ſo o'reflown,
Part of that ſtately Wall was overthrown.[e]
Arbaces marches in the Town he takes,
For few or none (it ſeems)[f] reſiſtance makes:
And now they ſaw fulfil'd a Propheſy,
That when the River prov'd their Enemy,
Their ſtrong wal'd Town ſhould ſuddenly be taken
By this accompliſhment, their hearts were ſhaken.
Sardanapalas did not ſeek to fly,
This his inevitable deſtiny;
But all his wealth and friends together gets,
Then on himſelf, and them a fire he ſets.

[c] But all. [d] courſe.

[e] Which through much rain, then ſwelling up ſo high,
Part of the wal it level cauſ'd to lye.

[f] did there.

This was laſt Monarch of great *Ninus* race [78]
That for twelve hundred years had held the place;
Twenty he reign'd ſame time, as Stories tell,
That *Amaziah* was King of *Iſrael.*
His Father was then King (as we ſuppoſe)
VVhen *Jonah* for their ſins denounc'd thoſe woes.
He did repent, the threatning[g] was not done,
But now accompliſh'd in his wicked Son.[h]
Arbaces thus of all becoming Lord,
Ingeniouſly with all did keep his word.
Of *Babylon Beloſus* he made King,
VVith overplus of all the wealth[i] therein.
To *Bactrians* he gave their liberty,
Of *Ninivites* he cauſed none to dye.
But ſuffer'd with their goods, to go elſe where,
Not granting them now[j] to inhabit there:
For he demoliſhed that City great,
And unto *Media* transfer'd his Seat.
Such was his promiſe which he firmly made,
To *Medes* and *Perſians* when he crav'd their aid:[k]
A while he and his race aſide muſt ſtand,
Not pertinent to what we have in hand;
And *Belochus* in's progeny purſue,
VVho did this Monarchy begin anew.

[g] therefore it. [h] But was accompliſhed now, in his Son.
[i] treaſures. [j] Yet would not let them.
[k] Thus was the promiſe bound, ſince firſt he crav'd.
Of *Medes*, and *Perſians*, their aſſiſting aide:

Belosus or Belochus.

BELOSUS setled in his new old Seat,
Not so content but aiming to be great,
Incroaching still upon the bordering lands,
Till *Mesopotamia* he got in's hands.
And either by compound or else by strength, [79]
Assyria he gain'd also at length;
Then did rebuild, destroyed *Nineveh*,
A costly work which none could do but he,
VVho own'd the Treasures of proud *Babylon*,
And those that seem'd with *Sardanapal's* gone;
For though his Palace did in ashes lye,
The fire those Mettals could not damnifie;
From[1] these with diligence he rakes,
Arbaces suffers all, and all he takes,
He thus inricht by this new tryed gold.
Raises a Phœnix new, from grave o'th' old:
And from this heap did after Ages see
As fair a Town, as the first *Niniveh*.
VVhen this was built, and matters all in peace
Molests poor *Israel*, his wealth t' increase.
A thousand Talents of *Menahem* had,
(Who to be rid of such a guest was glad;)
In sacrid writ he's known by name of *Pul*,
Which makes the world of difference so full.

[1] From rubbish.

That he and *Belochus* could not one be,
But Circumſtance doth prove the verity;
And times of both computed ſo fall out,
That theſe two made but one, we need not doubt:
What elſe he did, his Empire to advance,
To reſt content we muſt, in ignorance.
Forty eight years he reign'd, his race then run,
He left his new got Kingdome to his Son.

Tiglath Pulaſsar. [80]

BELOSUS dead, *Tiglath* his warlike Son,
Next treads thoſe ſteps, by which his Father won;
Damaſcus ancient Seat, of famous Kings
Under ſubjection, by his Sword he brings.
Reſin their valiant King he alſo ſlew,
And *Syria* t' obedience did ſubdue.
Judas bad King occaſioned this war,
When *Reſins* force his Borders ſore did marre,
And divers Cities by ſtrong hand did ſeaze:
To *Tiglath* then, doth *Ahaz* ſend for eaſe,
The Temple robs, ſo to fulfil his ends,
And to *Aſſyria*'s King a preſent ſends.
I am thy Servant and thy Son, (quoth he)
From *Reſin*, and from *Pekah* ſet me free,

Gladly doth *Tiglath* this advantage take.
And ſuccours *Ahaz*, yet for *Tiglath*'s ſake.
Then *Reſin* ſlain, his Army overthrown,
He *Syria* makes a Province of his own.
Unto *Damaſcus* then comes *Judah*'s King,
His humble thankfulneſs (in haſte) to bring,
Acknowledging th' *Aſſyrians* high deſert,
To whom he ought all loyalty of heart.
But *Tiglath* having gain'd his wiſhed end,
Proves unto *Ahaz* but a feigned friend;
All *Iſraels* lands beyond *Jordan* he takes,
In *Galilee* he woful havock makes.
Through *Syria* now he march'd none ſtopt his way,
And *Ahaz* open at his mercy lay;
Who ſtill implor'd his love, but was diſtreſt; [81]
This was that *Ahaz*, who ſo high [m] tranſ greſt: *
Thus *Tiglath* reign'd, & warr'd twenty ſeven years
Then by his death releas'd was Iſraels fears.

Salmanaſſar or Nabanaſſar.

TIGLATH deceas'd, *Salmanaſſar* was next,
He Iſraelites, more then his Father vext;
Hoſhea their laſt King he did invade,
And him ſix years his Tributary made;

[m] much. * 2 Chron. xxviii. 22.

But weary of his ſervitude, he ſought
To *Egypts* King, which did avail him nought;
For *Salmanaſſar* with a mighty Hoſt,
Beſieg'd his Regal Town, and ſpoyl'd his Coaſt,
And did the people, nobles, and their King,
Into perpetual thraldome that time bring;
Thoſe that from Joſhuah's time had been a ſtate,[n]
Did Juſtice now by him eradicate: [10 *years.*
This was that ſtrange, degenerated brood,
On whom, nor threats, nor mercies could do good;
Laden with honour, priſoners, and with ſpoyle,
Returns triumphant Victor to his ſoyle;
He placed *Iſrael* there,[o] where he thought beſt,
Then ſent his Colonies, theirs to inveſt;
Thus *Jacobs* Sons in Exile muſt remain,
And pleaſant *Canaan* never ſaw again:
Where now thoſe ten Tribes are, can no man tell,
Or how they fare, rich, poor, or ill, or well;
Whether the *Indians* of the Eaſt, or Weſt,
Or wild *Tartarians*, as yet ne're bleſt,
Or elſe thoſe *Chinoes* rare, whoſe wealth & arts [82]
Hath bred more wonder then belief in hearts:
But what, or where they are; yet know we this,
They ſhall return, and *Zion* ſee with bliſs.

[n] been Eſtate. [o] Plac'd *Iſrael* in's Land,

Senacherib.

SENACHERIB *Salmanaſſer* ſucceeds,
Whoſe haughty heart is ſhowne in words[p] & deeds
His wars, none better then himſelf can boaſt,
On *Henah*, *Arpad*, and on *Juahs* coaſt;
On *Hevahs* and on *Shepharvaims* gods,[q]
'Twixt them and *Iſraels* he knew no odds, *[7 *years.*
Untill the thundring hand of heaven he felt,
Which made his Army into nothing melt:
With ſhame then turn'd to *Ninive* again,
And by his ſons in's Idols houſe was ſlain.

Eſſarhadon.

HIS Son, weak *Eſſarhaddon* reign'd in's place,
The fifth, and laſt of great *Belloſus* race.
Brave *Merodach*, the Son of *Baladan*,
In *Babylon* Lieftenant to this man
Of opportunity advantage takes,
And on his Maſters ruines his houſe makes,
As *Beloſus* his Soveraign[r] did onthrone,
So he's now ſtil'd the King of *Babilon*.
After twelve years did *Eſſarhaddon* dye,
And *Merodach* aſſume the Monarchy.

p works.
q *Ivah* leaſt:
On *Hena's*, and on *Sepharvaim's* gods.
r firſt, his.
* In the firſt edition.

Merodach Balladan. [83]

ALL yield to him, but *Niniveh* kept free,
Untill his Grand-child made her bow the knee.
Ambassadors to *Hezekiah* sent, * [21 *years.*
His health congratulates with complement.

Ben Merodach.

BEN MERODACH Successor to this King,
Of whom is little said in any thing, * [22 *years.*
But by conjecture this, and none but he
Led King *Manasseh* to Captivity.

Nebulassar.

BRAVE *Nebulassar* to this King was son,
The famous[s] *Niniveh* by him was won,
For fifty years, or more, it had been free,
Now yields her neck unto captivity: * [12 *years.*

[s] ancient. * In the first edition.

A Vice-Roy from her foe ſhe's glad to accept,
By whom in firm obedience ſhe is kept.
This King's leſs fam'd for all the acts he's done,
Then being Father to ſo great a Son.[t]

Nebuchadnezzar, or *Nebopolaſſar*.

THE famous acts[u] of this heroick King
Did neither *Homer*, *Heſiod*, *Virgil* ſing:
Nor of his Wars[v] have we the certainty
From ſome *Thucidides* grave hiſtory;
Nor's Metamorphoſis from *Ovids* book,
Nor his reſtoriag from old Legends took:
But by the Prophets, Pen-men moſt divine, [84]
This prince in's magnitude doth ever ſhine:
This was of Monarchyes that head of gold,
The richeſt and the dread fulleſt to behold:
This was that tree whoſe branches fill'd the earth,
Under whoſe ſhadow birds and beaſts had birth:
This was that king of kings, did what he pleas'd,
Kil'd, ſav'd, pul'd down, ſet up, or pain'd or eas'd;
And this was he, who when he fear'd the leaſt
Was changed[w] from a King into a beaſt.*

[t] These two lines are not in the first edition.
[u] Wars. [v] acts. [w] turned.
* Dan. ii. 32, 37, 38; iv. 10–12, 33.

This Prince the laſt year of his fathers reign
Againſt *Jehojakim* marcht with his train,
Judahs poor King beſieg'd and ſuccourleſs
Yields to his mercy, and the preſent 'ſtreſs;
His Vaſſal is, gives pledges for his truth,
Children of royal blood, unblemiſh'd youth:
Wiſe *Daniel* and his fellowes, mongſt the reſt,
By the victorious king to *Babel*'s preſt:
The Temple of rich ornaments defac'd,
And in his Idols houſe the veſſels* plac'd.
The next year he with unreſiſted hand
Quite vanquiſh'd *Pharaoh Necho* with his band:
By great *Euphrates* did his army fall,
Which was the loſs of *Syria* withall.
Then into *Egypt Necho* did retire,
Which in few years proves the *Aſſirians* hire.
A mighty army next he doth prepare,
And unto wealthy *Tyre* in haſt repair.
Such was the ſcituation of this place,
As might not him, but all the world out-face,
That in her pride ſhe knew not which to boaſt [85]
Whether her wealth, or yet her ſtrength was moſt
How in all merchandize ſhe did excel,
None but the true *Ezekiel* need to tell.
And for her ſtrength, how hard ſhe was to gain,
Can *Babels* tired ſouldiers tell with pain.
Within an Iſland had this city ſeat,
Divided from the Main by channel great:

* Vaſſal's.

Of coftly fhips and Gallyes fhe had ftore,
And Mariners to handle fail and oar:
But the *Chaldeans* had nor fhips nor skill,
Their fhoulders muft their Mafters mind fulfill,
Fetcht rubbifh from the oppofite old town,
And in the channel threw each burden down;
Where after many effayes, they made at laft
The fea firm land, whereon the Army paft,
And took the wealthy town; but all the gain,
Requited not the lofs,[y] the toyle and pain.
Full thirteen years in this ftrange work he fpent
Before he could accomplifh his intent:
And though a Victor home his Army leads,
With peeled fhoulders, and with balded heads.*
When in the *Tyrian* war this King was hot,
Jehojakim his oath had clean forgot,
Thinks this the fitteft time to break his bands
Whileft *Babels* King thus deep engaged ftands:
But he whofe fortunes all were in the ebbe,[z]
Had all his hopes like to a fpiders web;
For this great King withdraws part of his force,
To *Judah* marches with a fpeedy courfe,
And unexpected finds the feeble Prince [86]
Whom he chaftis'd thus for his proud offence,
Faft bound, intends to *Babel* him to fend,[a]
But chang'd his mind, & caus'd his life there end,[b]

[y] coft. [z] But he (alas) whofe fortunes now i' the ebbe.
[a] intends at *Babel* he fhal flay. [b] and flew him by the way.
* Ezek. xxix. 18.

Then caſt him out like to a naked Aſs,
For this is he for whom none ſaid alas.*
His ſon he ſuffered three months to reign,
Then from his throne he pluck'd[c] him down again,
Whom with his mother he to *Babel* led,
And ſeven and[d] thirty years in priſon fed:
His Uncle he eſtabliſh'd in his place
(Who was laſt King of holy *Davids* race)
But he as perjur'd as *Jehojakim*,
They loſt more now[e] then e're they loſt by him.
Seven years he kept his faith, and ſafe he dwells;
But in the eighth againſt his Prince rebels:
The ninth came *Nebuchadnezzar* with power,
Beſieg'd his city, temple, *Zions* tower,
And after eighteen months he took them all:
The Walls ſo ſtrong, that ſtood ſo long, now fall.
The curſed King by flight could no wiſe fly[f]
His well deſerv'd and foretold miſery:
But being caught to *Babels* wrathfull King
With children, wives and Nobles all they bring,
Where to the ſword all but himſelf were put,
And with that wofull ſight his eyes cloſe ſhut.
Ah! hapleſs man, whoſe darkſome contemplation
Was nothing but ſuch gaſtly meditation.
In midſt of *Babel* now till death he lyes;
Yet as was told ne're ſaw it with his eyes.

[c] pull'd.
[d] And more then.
[e] *Judah* loſt more.
[f] free.
* Jer. xxii. 18, 19.

The Temple's burnt, the veſſels had away. [87]
The towres and palaces brought to decay:
Where late of harp and Lute were heard the noiſe
Now *Zim* & *Jim** liſt up their ſcrieching[g] voice.
All now of worth are Captive led with tears,
And ſit bewailing *Zion* ſeventy years.
With all theſe conqueſts, *Babels* King reſts not,
No not when *Moab*, *Edom* he had got,
Kedar and *Hazar*, the *Arabians* too,
All Vaſſals at his hands for Grace muſt ſue.
A total conqueſt of rich *Egypt* makes,
All rule he from the ancient *Phraohes* takes,
Who had for ſixteen hundred years born ſway,
To *Babilons* proud King now yields the day.
Then *Put* and *Lud*† do at his mercy ſtand.
VVhere e're he goes, he conquers every land.

* These words are explained by the translation and marginal note of Isaiah xiii. 21, 22, in the Genevan Bible (London, 1599): —

"But *p* Zijm ſhall lodge there, & their houſes ſhalbe full of Ohim: Oſtriches ſhall dwell there. and the Satyrs ſhall dance there.

"*p* Which were either wild beaſts. or foules, or wicked ſpirits, whereby Satan deluded man, as by the fairies, goblins, and ſuch like fantaſies.

"And Iim ſhall cry in their palaces, and dragons in their pleaſant palaces: and the time thereof is ready to come, and the dayes thereof ſhal not be prolonged."

Also in Jeremiah l. 39: "Therefore the Ziims with the Iims ſhall dwell *there*."

"Ziim" means literally *inhabitants of the desert*, either men or beasts. The "Iim" were probably jackals. In King James's version of the Bible the words are translated by "wild beasts of the desert" and "wild beasts of the islands."

The first edition has "Sim" instead of "Jim."

† Judith ii. 23.

g ſhriking.

His ſumptuous buildings paſſes all conceit,
Which wealth and ſtrong ambition made ſo great.
His Image *Judahs* Captives worſhip not,
Although the Furnace be ſeven times more hot.
His dreams wiſe *Daniel* doth expound full well,
And his unhappy chang with grief foretell.
Strange melancholy humours on him lay,
Which for ſeven years his reaſon took away,
VVhich from no natural cauſes did proceed,
But for his pride, ſo had the heavens decreed.[g]
The time expir'd, bruitiſh remains[h] no more,
But Goverment reſumes as heretofore:
In ſplendor, and iu Majeſty he ſits,
Contemplating thoſe times he loſt his witts.
And if by words we may gheſs at the heart, [88]
This king among the righteous had a part:
Fourty four years he reign'd, which being run,
He left his wealth and conqueſts to his ſon.

Evilmerodach

BABEL'S great Monarch now laid in the duſt,
His ſon poſſeſſes wealth and rule as juſt:
And in the firſt year of his Royalty
Eaſeth *Jehojakims* Captivity:

g For by the Heavens above it was decreed. h remains a Beaſt

Poor forlorn Prince, who had all ſtate forgot
In ſeven and thirty years had ſeen no jot.
Among the conquer'd Kings that there did ly
Is Judah's King now lifted up on high:
But yet in *Babel* he muſt ſtill remain,
And native *Canaan* never ſee again:
Unlike his Father *Evilmerodach*,
Prudence and magnanimity did lack;
Fair *Egypt* is by his remiſneſs loſt,
Arabia, and all the bordering coaſt.
Warrs with the *Medes* unhappily he wag'd
(Within which broyles rich *Crœſus* was ingag'd)
His Army routed, and himſelf there ſlain:
His Kingdome to *Belſhazzar* did remain.

Belſhazzar.

UNWORTHY *Belſhazzar* next wears the crown,
Whoſe acts profane a ſacred Pen ſets down,
His luſt and crueltyes in ſtoryes [i] find,
A royal State rul d by a bruitiſh mind.
His life ſo baſe, and diſſolute invites [89]
The noble *Perſian* to invade his rights.
Who with his own, and Uncles power anon,
Layes ſiedge to's Regal Seat, proud *Babylon*,

[i] cruelty, in books we.

The coward King, whoſe ſtrength lay in his walls,
To banquetting and revelling now falls,
To ſhew his little dread, but greater ſtore,
To chear his friends, and ſcorn his foes the more.
The holy veſſels thither brought long ſince,
They carrows'd in, and ſacrilegious prince
Did praiſe his Gods of mettal, wood, and ſtone,
Protectors of his Crown, and *Babylon*,
But he above, his doings did deride,
And with a hand ſoon daſhed all this pride.
The King upon the wall caſting his eye,
The fingers of a [i] hand writing did ſpy,
Which horrid ſight, he fears muſt needs portend
Deſtruction to his Crown, to's Perſon end.
With quaking knees, and heart appall'd he cries,
For the Soothſayers, and Magicians wiſe;
This language ſtrange to read, and to unfold;
With gifts of Scarlet robe, and Chain of gold,
And higheſt dignity, next to the King,
To him that could interpret, clear this thing:
But dumb the gazing Aſtrologers ſtand,
Amazed at the writing, and the hand.
None anſwers the affrighted Kings intent,
Who ſtill expects ſome fearful ſad event;
As dead, alive [j] he ſits, as one [k] undone:
In comes the Queen, to chear her heartleſs Son.
Of *Daniel* tells, who in his grand-ſires dayes
VVas held in more account [l] then now he was.

[i] his. [j] As thus amort. [k] all. [l] requeſt.

Daniel in haſte is brought before the King,
VVho doth not flatter, nor once cloak the thing;
Reminds him of his Grand-Sires height and fall,
And of his own notorious ſins withall:
His Drunkenneſs, and his profaneſs high,
His pride and ſottiſh groſs Idolatry.
The guilty King with colour pale and dead
Then hears his *Mene* and his *Tekel* read.*
And one thing did worthy a King (though late)
Perform'd his word to him that told his fate.
That night victorious *Cyrus* took the town,
VVho ſoon did terminate his life and crown;
VVith him did end the race of *Baladan:*
And now the *Perſian* Monarchy began.

* Dan. v. 25–28.

The End of the Aſſyrian Monarchy.

The Second *Monarchy*, [91]
being the *Perſian*, began under

Cyrus, Darius being his Uncle and Father-in-law reigned with him about two years.

C*Yrus Cambyſes* Son of *Perſia* King,
Whom Lady *Mandana* did to him bring,
She daughter unto great *Aſtiages*,
He in deſcent the ſeventh from *Arbaces*.
Cambyſes was of *Achemenes* race,
VVho had in *Perſia* the Lieſtenants place
VVhen *Sardanapalus* was overthrown,
And from that time had held it as his own.
Cyrus, Darius Daughter took to wife,
And ſo unites two Kingdomes without ſtrife.
Darius unto *Mandana* was brother,
Adopts her ſon for his, having no other.
This is of *Cyrus* the true pedegree.
VVhoſe Anceſtors were royal in degree:

His Mothers dream, and Grand-Sires cruelty,
His preservation, in his misery,
His nourishment afforded by a Bitch,
Are fit for such, whose ears for Fables itch.
He in his younger dayes an Army led, [92]
Against great *Cressus* then of *Lidia* head;
Who over-curious of wars event,
For information to *Apollo* went:
And the ambiguous Oracle did trust,
So overthrown by *Cyrus*, as was just;
Who him puasues to *Sardis*, takes the Town,
Where all that dare [m] resist are slaughter'd down;
Disguised *Cressus* hop'd to scape i'th' throng,
Who had no might to save himself from wrong;
But as he past, his Son who was born dumb,
With pressing grief and sorrow overcome:
Among the tumult, bloud-shed, and the strife,
Brake his long silence, cry'd, spare *Cressus* life:
Cressus thus known, it was great *Cyrus* doom,
(A hard decree) to ashes he consume;
Then on a wood-pile [n] set, where all might eye,
He *Solon*, *Solon*, *Solon*, thrice did cry.
The Reason of those words *Cyrus* demands,
Who *Solon* was? to whom he lifts his hands;
Then to the King he makes this true report,
That *Solon* sometimes at his stately Court,
His Treasures, pleasures, pomp and power did see,
And viewing all, at all nought mov'd was he:

[m] doe [n] Pike being.

That *Cressus* angry, urg'd him to express,
If ever King equal'd his happiness.
(Quoth he) that man for happy we commend,
Whose happy life attains an happy end.[o]
Cyrus with pitty mov'd, knowing Kings stand,
Now up and down, as fortune turns her hand,
Weighing the Age, and greatness of the Prince, [93]
(His Mothers Uncle) stories do evince:
Gave him his life, and took him for a friend,
Did to him still his chief designs commend.[p]
Next war the restless *Cyrus* thought upon,
Was conquest of the stately *Babilon*,
Now treble wall'd, and moated so about,
That all the world they need not[q] fear nor doubt;
To drain this ditch, he many Sluces cut,
But till convenient time their heads kept shut;
That night *Belshazzar* feasted all his rout,
He cut those banks, and let the River out,
And to the walls securely marches on,
Not finding a defendant thereupon;
Enters the Town, the sottish King he slayes,
Upon Earths richest spoyles his Souldiers preys;
Here twenty years provision good[r] he found,
Forty five miles this City scarce could round;

[o] Instead of this and the nine preceding lines, the first edition has, —
Upon demand, his minde to *Cyrus* broke,
And told, how *Solon* in his hight had spoke.

[p] Gave him at once, his life, and Kingdom too,
And with the *Lidians*, had no more to doe.

[q] they neither.

[r] "good" not in the first edition.

This head of Kingdomes *Chaldees* excellence,
For Owles and Satyres made a refidence;*
Yet wondrous monuments this ftately Queen,
A thoufand years had after to be feen.[s]
Cyrus doth now the Jewifh Captives free,
An Edict made, the Temple builded be,
He with his Uncle *Daniel* fets on high,
And caus'd his foes in Lions Den to dye.
Long after this he 'gainft the *Scythians* goes,
And *Tomris* Son and[t] Army overthrows;
VVhich to revenge fhe hires a mighty power,
And fets on *Cyrus*, in a fatal hour;
There routs his Hoft, himfelf fhe prifoner takes, [94]
And at one blow (worlds head) fhe headlefs makes
The which fhe bath'd,[u] within a But of bloud,
Ufing fuch taunting words, as fhe thought good.
But *Xenophon* reports he di'd in's bed,
In honour, peace, and wealth, with a grey head;
And in his Town of *Paffagardes*[v] lyes,
VVhere fome long after fought in vain for prize,[w]
But in his[x] Tombe, was only to be found
Two *Scythian* boys,[y] a Sword and Target round:
And *Alexander* coming to the fame,
VVith honours great, did celebrate his fame.[z]

* Is. xiii. 21. [s] Had after thoufand yeares faire to be feen.
[t] an [u] bak'd [v] *Pafargada*,
[w] Where *Alexander* fought, in hope of prize. [x] this [y] bowes.
[z] Instead of this and the preceding line, the first edition has,—

Where that proud Conquereur could doe no leffe.
Then at his Herfe great honours to expreffe;

Three daughters and two Sons he left behind,
Innobled more by birth, then by their mind;[a]
Thirty two years in all this Prince did reign,
But eight whilſt *Babylon*, he did retain:
And though his conqueſts made the earth to groan,
Now quiet lyes under one marble ſtone.
And with an Epitaph, himſelf did make,
To ſhew how little Land he then ſhould take.

Cambyſes.

CAMBYSES no wayes like his noble Sire,
Yet to inlarge his State had ſome deſire,
His reign with bloud and Inceſt firſt begins,
Then ſends to find a Law, for theſe his ſins;
That Kings with Siſters match, no Law they find,
But that the *Perſian* King may act his mind:[b]
He wages war the fifth year of his reign,
'Gainſt *Egypts* King, who there by him was ſlain.
And all of Royal Bloud, that came to hand, [95]
He ſeized firſt of Life, and then of Land,

[a] Instead of the six lines following this, the first edition has, —
Some thirty years this potent Prince did reign,
Unto *Cambyſes* then, all did remain.

[b] After this the first edition has, —
Which Law includes all Lawes, though lawleſſe ſtil,
And makes it lawful Law, if he but wil;

(But little *Narus*[c] ſcap'd that cruel fate,
VVho grown a man, reſum'd again his State.)
He next to *Cyprus* ſends his bloudy Hoſt,
VVho landing ſoon upon that fruitful Coaſt,
Made *Evelthon* their King with bended knee,
To hold his own, of his free Courteſie.
Their Temple[d] he deſtroys, not for his Zeal,
For he would be profeſt, God of their weal;
Yea, in his pride, he ventured ſo farre,
To ſpoyle the Temple of great *Jupiter*:
But as they marched o're thoſe deſert ſands,
The ſtormed duſt o'rewhelm'd his daring bands;
But ſcorning thus, by *Jove* to be outbrav'd,
A ſecond Army he[e] had almoſt grav'd,
But vain he found to fight with Elements,
So left his ſacrilegious bold intents.
The Egyptian *Apis* then he likewiſe flew,
Laughing to ſcorn, that ſottiſh Calviſh Crew:
If all this[f] heat had been for pious[g] end,
Cambyſes to the Clouds we might commend.
But he that 'fore the Gods himſelf prefers,
Is more profane then groſs Idolaters;[h]

[c] *Marus.* [d] The Temples. [e] there. [f] his. [g] a good.

[h] Instead of the four lines following this, the first edition has, —

And though no gods, if he eſteem them ſome,
And contemn them, woful is his doome,
He after this, ſaw in a Viſion,
His brother *Smerdis* ſit upon his throne:
He ſtrait to rid himſelf of cauſleſſe fears,
Complots the Princes death, in his green years.

He after this, upon ſuſpition vain,
Unjuſtly cauſ'd his brother to be ſlain.
Praxaſpes into *Perſia* then is ſent,
To act in ſecret, this his lewd intent:
His Siſter (whom Inceſtuouſly he wed,)
Hearing her harmleſs brother thus was dead.
His wofull death [i] with tears did ſo bemoan, [96]
That by her husbands charge, ſhe caught her own,
She with her fruit at once were both undone
Who would have born a Nephew and a ſon.
Oh helleſh husband, brother, uncle, Sire,
Thy cruelty all [j] ages will [k] admire.
This ſtrange ſeverity he ſometimes us'd [l]
Upon a Judge, for taking bribes [m] accus'd,
Flay'd him alive, hung up his ſtuffed skin
Over his ſeat, then plac'd his ſon therein,
To whom he gave this in remembrance,
Like fault muſt look for the like recompence.
His cruelty was come unto that height,
He ſpar'd nor foe, nor friend, nor favourite. [n]

Who for no wrong, poore innocent muſt dye,
Praraſpes now muſt act this tragedy;
Who into *Perſia* with Commiſſion ſent,
Accompliſhed this wicked Kings intent:

[i] fate. [j] will. [k] ſtill.
[l] one time he us'd. [m] breach of Law.

[n] Instead of this and the preceding line, the first edition has, —
Praraſpes, to *Cambyſes* favourite,
Having one ſon, in whom he did delight,
His cruell Maſter, for all ſervice done,
Shot through the heart of his beloved ſon:

'Twould be no pleasure,[o] but a tedious thing
To tell the facts of this most bloody King,
Feared of all, but lov'd of few or none,
All wisht[p] his short reign past before[q] 'twas done.
At last two of his Officers he hears
Had set one *Smerdis* up, of the same years,
And like in feature to his brother[r] dead,
Ruling, as they thought best[s] under this head.
The people ignorant of what was done,
Obedience yielded as to *Cyrus* son.[t]
Toucht with this news to *Persia* he makes,
But in the way his sword just vengeance takes,
Unsheathes, as he his horse mounted on high,
And with a mortal thrust wounds him ith' thigh,
Which ends before begun his home-bred[u] warr:
So yields[v] to death, that dreadfull Conquerour.
Grief for his brothers death he did express, [97]
And more, because he died Issueless.
The male line of great *Cyrus* now had end,
The Female to many Ages did extend.
A *Babylon* in *Egypt* did he make,
And *Meroe* built for his fair Sisters sake.[w]
Eight years he reign'd, a short, yet too long time
Cut off in's wickedness in's strength and prime.

And only for his fathers faithfullnesse,
Who said but what, the king bad him expresse.

[o] pleasant. [p] thought. [q] long, till. [r] the *Smerdis*.
[s] good. [t] This and the preceding line are not in the first edition.
[u] the *Persian*. [v] Yeelding.
[w] And built fair *Meroe*, for his sisters sake.

The inter regnum between Cambyſes And Darius Hiſtaſpes.

CHILDLESS *Cambyſes* on the ſudden dead,
(The Princes meet, to chuſe one in his ſtead,
Of which the chief was[x] ſeven, call'd *Satrapes*,
Who like to Kings, rul'd Kingdomes as they pleaſe,
Deſcended all of *Achemenes* bloud,
And Kinſmen in account to th' King they ſtood.
And firſt theſe noble *Magi* 'gree upon,
To thruſt th' impoſter *Smerdis* out of Throne:
Then[y] Forces inſtantly they raiſe, and rout
This King with his Conſpirators ſo ſtout,[z]
But yet 'fore this was done much bloud was ſhed,
And two of theſe great Peers in Field[a] lay dead.
Some write that ſorely hurt they ſcap'd away,
But ſo, or no, ſure 'tis they won the day.
All things in peace, and Rebels throughly quell'd,
A Conſultation by thoſe States was held,
What form of government now to erect
The old, or new, which beſt, in what reſpect.
The greater part declin'd a Monarchy [98]
So late cruſht by their Princes tyranny,

[x] were. [y] Their.

[z] After this, the first edition has, —

Who little pleaſure had, in his ſhort reigne,
And now with his accomplyces lye ſlaine.

[a] place.

And thought the people would more happy be
If govern'd by an Ariſtocracy:
But others thought (none of the dulleſt brain)
That better one then many tyrants reign.
What Arguments they us'd, I know not well,
Too politick, its like, for me to tell,
But in concluſion they all agree,
Out of the ſeven a Monarch choſen be.
All envy to avoid, this was thought on
Upon a green to meet by riſing ſun,
And he whoſe horſe before the reſt ſhould neigh,
Of all the Peers ſhould have precedency.
They all attend on the appointed hour,
Praying to fortune for a kingly power.
Then mounting on their ſnorting courſers proud,
Darius luſty Stallion neigh'd full loud.[a]
The Nobles all alight, bow to their King,
And joyfull acclamations ſhrill they ring.
A thouſand times, long live the King they cry,
Let Tyranny with dead *Cambiſes* dye:
Then all[b] attend him to his royall room:
Thanks for all this to's crafty ſtable-groom.

[a] Instead of the four lines following this, the first edition has.—
The Nobles all alight, their King to greet,
And after *Perſian* manner, kiſſe his feet.
His happy wiſhes now doth no man ſpare,
But acclamations ecchoes in the aire:
A thouſand times, God ſave the King, they cry,
Let tyranny now with *Cambyſes* dye.

[b] They then.

Darius Hyſtaſpes.

DARIUS by election made a King,
His title to make ſtrong, omits no thing:
He two of *Cyrus* daughters then doth wed,
Two of his Neeces takes to Nuptial bed,
By which he cuts their hopes for future time, [99]
That by ſuch ſteps to Kingdomes often clime.
And now a King by mariage, choice and blood:
Three ſtrings to's bow, the leaſt of which is good;
Yet firmly more, the peoples hearts to bind.
Made wholſome, gentle laws which pleas'd each mind.
His courteſie and affability.
Much gain'd the hearts of his nobility.[c]
Yet notwithſtanding all he did ſo well,
The *Babylonians* 'gainſt their prince rebell.
An hoſt he rais'd the city to reduce;
But men [d] againſt thoſe walls were of no uſe.[e]
Then brave *Zopirus* for his maſters good,
His manly face diſfigures, ſpares no blood:
With his own hands cutts off his ears and noſe,
And with a faithfull fraud to th' town he goes,

[c] His affability, and milde aſpect,
Did win him loyalty, and all reſpect;

[d] ſtrength.

[e] After this, the first edition has, —
For twice ten months before the town he lay,
And fear'd, he now with ſcorn muſt march away.

tells them how harſhly the proud king had dealt,
That for their ſakes his cruelty he felt,
Deſiring of the Prince to raiſe the ſiege,
This violence was done him by his Liege.
This told, for entrance he ſtood not long;
For they believ'd his noſe more then his tongue.
With all the city's ſtrength they him betruſt,
If he command, obey the greateſt muſt.
When opportunity he ſaw was fit
Delivers up the town, and all in it.
To looſe a noſe, to win a town's no ſhame,
But who dares venture ſuch a ſtake for th' game.
Then thy diſgrace, thine honour's manifold,
Who doth deſerve a ſtatue made of gold.
Nor can *Darius* in his Monarchy, [100]
Scarce find enough to thank thy loyalty:[f]
Yet o're thy glory we muſt caſt this vail,
Thy craft more then thy valour did prevail.[g]
Darius in the ſecond of his reign
An Edict for the Jews publiſh d again:
The Temple to rebuild, for that did reſt
Since *Cyrus* time, *Cambiſes* did moleſt.
He like a King now grants a Charter large,
Out of his own revennues bears the charge,

[f] After this, the first edition has,—
But yet thou haſt ſufficient recompence.
In that thy fame ſhall ſound whilſt men have ſence:

[g] Thy falſhood, not thy valour did prevaile:
Thy wit was more then was thine honeſty.
Thou lov'dſt thy Maſter more then verity.

Gives Sacrifices, wheat, wine, oyle and salt,
Threats punishment to him that through default
Shall let the work, or keep back any thing
Of what is freely granted by the King:
And on all Kings he poures out Execrations
That shall once[h] dare to rase those firm foundations
They thus backt by the King, in spight of foes
Built on and prosper'd till their house they[i] close,
And in the sixth year of his friendly reign,
Set up a Temple (though a less) again:
Darius on the *Scythians* made a war,
Entring that larg and barren Country far:
A Bridge he made, which serv'd for boat & barge
O're *Ister* fair, with labour and with charge.[j]
But in that desert; 'mongst his barbarous foes
Sharp wants, not swords, his valour did oppose,
His Army fought with hunger and with cold,
Which to assail his royal Camp was bold.[k]
By these alone his host was pincht so sore,
He warr'd defensive, not offensive more.
The Salvages did laugh at his distress, [101]
Their minds by Hiroglyphicks they express,
A Frog a Mouse, a bird, an arrow sent,
The King will needs interpret their intent,
Possession of water, earth and air,
But wise *Gobrias* reads not half so fair:[l]

[h] but. [i] walls did.
[j] Over fair *Ister*, at a mighty charge.
[k] Which two then to assaile, his Camp was bold. [l] farre.

(Quoth he) like frogs in water we muſt dive,
Or like to mice under the earth muſt live,
Or fly like birds in unknown wayes full quick,
Or *Scythian* arrows in our ſides muſt ſtick.
The King ſeeing his men and victuals ſpent,
This fruitleſs war began late to repent,
Return'd with little honour, and leſs gain.
His enemies ſcarce ſeen, then much leſs ſlain.
He after this intends *Greece* to invade,
But troubles in leſs *Aſia* him ſtaid,
Which huſht, he ſtraight ſo orders his affairs,
For *Attaca* an army he prepares;
But as before, ſo now with ill ſucceſs
Return'd with wondrous loſs, and honourleſs.
Athens perceiving now their deſperate ſtate
Arm'd all they could, which eleven thouſand made
By brave *Miltiades* their chief being led:
Darius multitudes before them fled.
At *Marathon* this bloudy field was fought,
Where *Grecians* prov'd themſelves right ſouldiers ſtout
The *Perſians* to their gallies poſt with ſpeed
Where an *Athenian* ſhew'd a valiant deed,
Purſues his flying foes then on the ſand,[m]
He ſtayes a lanching[n] gally with his hand,
Which ſoon cut off, inrag'd,* he with his left, [102]
Renews his hold, and when of that bereft,

[m] ſtrand. [n] landing.

* "inrag'd" not in the first edition.

His whetted teeth he claps [o] in the firm wood,
Off flyes his head, down ſhowres his frolick bloud,
Go *Perſians*, carry home that angry piece,
As the beſt Trophe which ye won in *Greece*,
Darius light, yet [p] heavy home returns,
And for revenge, his heart ſtill reſtleſs burnes,
His Queen *Atoſſa* Author of [q] this ſtirr,
For *Grecian* maids ('tis ſaid) to wait on her.
She loſt her aim, her Husband he loſt more,
His men his coyne, his honour, and his ſtore;
And the enſuing year ended his Life,
('Tis thought) through grief of this ſucceſsleſs ſtrife
Thirty ſix years this noble Prince did reign,
Then to his ſecond [r] Son did all remain.

Xerxes,

XERXES. *Darius*, and *Atoſſa*'s Son,
Grand child to *Cyrus*, now ſits on the Throne:
(His eldeſt brother put beſide the place,
Becauſe this was, firſt born of *Cyrus* race.)*
His [s] Father not ſo full of lenity,
As was his [t] Son of pride and cruelty;

[o] ſticks. [p] he. [q] cauſed all.
* This and the preceding line are not in the first edition.
[r] eldeſt. [s] The. [t] is the.

He with his Crown receives a double war,
The *Egyptians* to' reduce, and *Greece* to marr,
The firſt begun, and finiſh'd in ſuch haſte,
None write by whom, nor how, 'twas over paſt.
But for the laſt, he made ſuch preparation,
As if to duſt, he meant, to grinde that nation;
Yet all his men, and Inſtruments of ſlaughter, [103]
Produced but deriſion and laughter.
Sage Artabanus Counſel had he taken,
And's Couzen young *Mardonius* forſaken,
His Souldiers credit, wealth at home had ſtaid,
And *Greece* ſuch wondrous triumphs ne'r had made.
The firſt dehorts[u] and layes before his eyes
His Fathers ill ſucceſs, in's enterprize,
Againſt the *Scythians* and *Grecians* too,
What Infamy to's honour did accrew.
Flatt'ring *Mardonius* on the other ſide,
With conqueſt of all *Europe*,[v] feeds his pride:
Vain *Xerxes* thinks his counſel hath moſt wit,
That his ambitious humour beſt can fit;
And by this choice unwarily poſts on,
To preſent loſs, future ſubverſion.
Although he haſted, yet four years was ſpent
In great proviſions, for this great intent:
His Army of all Nations was compounded,
That the vaſt[w] *Perſian* government ſurrounded.
His Foot was ſeventeen hundred thouſand ſtrong,
Eight hundred thouſand horſe, to theſe belong

[u] deports. [v] With certainty of *Europe*. [w] large.

His Camels, beasts for carriage numberless,
For Truths asham'd, how many to express;
The charge of all, he severally commended
To Princes, of the *Persian* bloud descended:
But the command of these commanders all,
Unto *Mardonius* made their General;[x]
(He was the Son of the fore nam'd *Gobrius*,
Who married the Sister of *Darius*.)
Such[y] his land Forces were, then next a fleet, [104]
Of two and twenty thousand Gallies meet
Man'd with *Phenicians* and *Pamphylians*
Cipriots, *Dorians* and *Cilicians*,
Lycians, *Carians* and *Ionians*,
Eolians and the *Helespontines*.
Besides the vessels for his transportation,
Which to three thousand came[a] (by best relation)
Brave *Artemisia*, *Hallicarnassus* Queen[b]
In person present[c] for his aid[d] was seen,
Whose Gallyes all the rest in neatness pass,
Save the *Zidonians*, where *Xerxes* was:
But hers she kept still seperate from the rest,
For to command alone, she judg'd[e] was best.
O noble Queen, thy valour I commend;
But pitty 'twas thine aid thou[f] here didst lend.
At *Sardis* in *Lydia*, all these do meet,
Whether[g] rich *Pythias* comes *Xerxes* to greet,

[x] To *Mardonius*, Captain Generall. [y] These.
[a] Three thousand (or more). [b] *Artemesia*, *Halicarna's* Queene,
[c] there, now. [d] help. [e] thought. [f] that. [g] Whither.

Feasts all this multitude of his own charge,
Then gives the King a king-like gift full [h] large,
Three thousand talents of the purest gold,
Which mighty sum all wondred to behold:
Then humbly to the king he makes request,
One of his five sons there might be releas'd,
To be to's age a comfort and a stay,
The other four he freely gave away.
The king calls for the youth, who being brought,
Cuts him in twain for whom his Sire besought,
Then laid his parts on both sides of the way,
'Twixt which his souldiers marcht in good array.[i]
For his great love is this thy recompence? [105]
Is this to do like *Xerxes* or a Prince?
Thou shame of kings, of men the detestation,
I Rhetorick want to pour out execration.
First thing he did that's worthy of recount,[j]
A Sea passage cut behind *Athos* mount.
Next o're the *Helespont* a bridge he made
Of Boats together coupled, and there laid:
But winds and waves those iron bands did break;
To cross the sea such strength he found too weak,
Then whips the sea, and with a mind most vain
He fetters casts therein the same to chain.

[h] most.

[i] Instead of this and the preceding line, the first edition has, —
O most inhumain incivility!
Nay, more then monstrous barb'rous cruelty!

[j] *Xerxes* did worthy recount.

The work-men put to death the bridge that made,
Becauſe they wanted skill the ſame to've ſtaid.[k]
Seven thouſand Gallyes chain'd by *Tyrians* skill,
Firmly at laſt[l] accompliſhed his will.
Seven dayes and nights, his hoſt without leaſt ſtay
Was marching o're this new deviſed way.[m]
Then in *Abidus* plains muſtring his forces,
He gloryes in his ſquadrons and his horſes.
Long viewing them, thought it great happineſs,
One king ſo many ſubjects ſhould poſſeſs:
But yet this ſight from him[n] produced tears,
That none of thoſe could[o] live an hundred years.
What after did enſue had he foreſeen,
Of ſo long time his thoughts had never been.
Of *Artubanus* he again demands
How of this enterpriſe his thoughts now ſtands,
His anſwer was, both ſea and land he fear'd,
Which was not vain as after[p] ſoon appear'd.
But *Xerxes* reſolute to *Thrace* goes firſt, [106]
His Hoſt all[q] *Liſſus* drinks, to quench their thirſt;
And for his Cattel, all *Piſſyrus* Lake
Was ſcarce enough, for each a draught to take:
Then marching on to th' ſtreight *Thermopyle*,
The *Spartan* meets him brave *Leonade*:

[k] Inſtead of this and the five preceding lines, the firſt edition has, —
But winds, and waves, theſe couples ſoon diſſever'd,
Yet *Xerxes* in his enterpriſe perſever'd;

[l] length. [m] this interrupting Bay. [n] this goodly ſight.
[o] theſe ſhould. [p] as it. [q] who.

This 'twixt the mountains lyes (half Acre wide)
That pleaſant *Theſſaly* from *Greece* divide
Two dayes and nights, a fight they there maintain,
Till twenty thouſand *Perſians* fell [r] down ſlain;
And all that Army then diſmaid, had fled,
But that a Fugitive diſcovered.
How ſome [s] might o're the mountains go about,
And wound the backs of thoſe brave [t] warriors ſtout
They thus behem'd with multitude of Foes,
Laid on more fiercely their deep mortal blows.
None cries for quarter, nor yet ſeeks to run;
But on their ground they die each Mothers Son.
O noble Greeks, how now degenerate,
Where is the valour of your ancient State?
When as one thouſand could a [u] million daunt,
Alas! it is *Leonades* you want.
This ſhameful victory coſt *Xerxes* dear.
Among the reſt, two brothers he loſt there;
And as at Land, ſo he at Sea was croſt,
Four hundred ſtately Ships by ſtorms was loſt;
Of Veſſels ſmall almoſt innumerable,
The Harbours to contain them was not able,[v]
Yet thinking to out-match his Foes at Sea,
Encloſ'd their Fleet i'th' ſtreight of *Eubea:*
But they as fortunate at [w] Sea as Land, [107]
In this ſtreight, as the other firmly ſtand.

[r] falls. [s] part. [t] bold. [u] ſome Millions.
[v] Them to receive, the Harbour was not able; [w] valiant by.

And *Xerxes* mighty Gallyes battered ſo,
That their ſplit ſides witneſſ'd his overthrow;
Then in the ſtreight of *Salamis* he try'd,
If that ſmall number his great force could 'bide:
But he in daring of his forward Foe,
Received there a ſhameful overthrow.
Twice beaten thus at Sea he warr'd no more,
But then the *Phocians* Country [x] waſted ſore;
They no way able to withſtand his force,
That brave *Themiſtocles* takes this wiſe courſe,
In ſecret manner word to *Xerxes* ſends,
That Greeks to break his Bridg ſhortly intends:
And as a friend warns him what e're he do
For his Retreat, to have an eye thereto,
He hearing this, his thoughts & courſe home bended
Much fearing that [y] which never was intended.
Yet 'fore he went to help out his expence,
Part of his Hoſt to *Delphos* ſent from thence,
To rob the wealthy Temple of *Apollo*,
But miſchief ſacriledge doth ever follow.
Two mighty Rocks brake from *Parnaſſus* hill,
And many thouſands of thoſe men did kill;
VVhich accident the reſt affrighted ſo,
VVith empty hands they to their Maſter go:
He finding all, to tend to his decay,
Fearing his Bridge, no longer there would ſtay.[z]

[x] But *Phocians* Land, he then

[y] Much, that.

[z] He ſeeing all thus tend unto decay,
Thought it his beſt, no longer for to ſtay;

Three hundred thouſand yet he left behind,
VVith his *Mardonius* Index[a] of his mind:
Who for his ſake he knew would venture farre, [108]
(Chief inſtigator of this hapleſs[b] warr.)
He inſtantly to *Athens* ſends for peace,
That all Hoſtility from[c] thence forth ceaſe;
And that with *Xerxes* they would be at one,
So ſhould all favour to their State be ſhown.
The *Spartans* fearing *Athens* would agree,
As had *Macedon*, *Thebes*, and *Theſſaly*,
And leave them out, this Shock now to ſuſtain,
By their Ambaſſador they thus complain,
That *Xerxes* quarrel was 'gainſt *Athens* State,
And they had helpt them as Confederate;
If in their[d] need they ſhould forſake[e] their friends,
Their infamy would laſt till all things ends:
But the *Athenians* this peace deteſt,
And thus reply'd unto *Mardon*'s requeſt.
That whil'ſt the Sun did run his endleſs Courſe
Againſt the *Perſians*, they would bend[f] their force;
Nor could the brave Ambaſſador he[g] ſent,
With Rhetorick gain[h] better Complement:
A *Macedonian* born, and[i] great Commander,
No leſs then grand-Sire to great *Alexander*
Mardonius proud hearing this Anſwer ſtout,
To add more to his numbers layes about;

[a] judex. [b] hopeleſſe. [c] might. [d] If now in.
[e] thus fail. [f] uſe. [g] be. [h] t' gain.
[i] Though of this Nation borne a

And of thoſe Greeks which by his Skill he'd won,
He fifty thouſand joyns unto his own:
The other Greeks which were Confederate
In all one hundred and ten thouſand made.[j]
The *Athenians* could but forty thouſand Arme,
The reſt had weapons would do little harm;
But that which helpt defects, and made them bold, [109]
Was victory by Oracle foretold.
Then for one battel ſhortly all provide,
Where both their Controverſies they'l decide;[k]
Ten dayes theſe Armyes did each other face,
Mardonius finding victuals waſt apace,
No longer dar'd, but bravely[l] on-ſet gave,
The other not a hand nor Sword would wave,
Till in the Intrails of their Sacrifice
The ſignal of their victory did riſe,
Which ſound like Greeks they fight, the *Perſians* fly,
And troubleſome *Mardonius* now muſt dye.
All's loſt, and of three hundred thouſand men,
Three thouſand only can[m] run home agen.

[j] One hundred thouſand, and ten thouſand make.

[k] Instead of this and the five preceding lines, the first edition has, —

The *Beotian* Fields, of war, the ſeats.
Where both ſides exercis'd their manly feats:
But all their controverſies to decide,
For one maine Battell ſhortly, both provide;
The *Athenians* could but forty thouſand arme,
For other Weapons, they had none would harme;
But that which helpt defects, and made them bold.
Was Victory, by Oracle fore-told:

[l] fiercely. [m] ſeapes, for to.

For pitty let thoſe few to *Xerxes* go,
To certifie his final overthrow:
Same day the ſmall remainder of his Fleet,
The Grecians at *Mycale* in *Aſia* meet.
And there ſo utterly they wrackt the ſame,
Scarce one was left to carry home the Fame;
Thus did the Greeks conſume, deſtroy, diſperse
That Army, which did fright the Univerſe.
Scorn'd *Xerxes* hated for his cruelty,
Yet ceaſes not to act his villany.
His brothers wife ſolicites to his will,
The chaſt and beautious Dame refuſed ſtill;
Some years by him in this vain ſuit was ſpent,
Nor prayers,[o] nor gifts could win him leaſt content;
Nor matching of her daughter to his Son,
But ſhe was ſtill as when he[p] firſt begun:
When jealous Queen *Ameſtris* of this knew,
She Harpy like upon the Lady flew,
Cut off her breaſts, her lips,[q] her noſe and ears,
And leavs her thus beſmear'd in bloud and tears.
Straight comes her Lord, and finds his wife thus ly,
The ſorrow of his heart did cloſe his Eye:
He dying to behold that wounding ſight,
Where he had ſometime gaz'd with great delight,
To ſee that face where roſe, and Lillyes ſtood,
O'reflown with Torrent of her guiltleſs[r] bloud,
To ſee thoſe breaſts where Chaſtity did dwell,
Thus cut and mangled by a Hag of Hell:

[o] Yet words. [p] it. [q] Cut off her lilly breaſts. [r] ruby.

With loaden heart unto the King he goes,
Tells as he could his unexpreſſed woes;
But for his deep complaints and ſhowres of tears,
His brothers recompence was nought but jears:
The grieved prince finding nor right, nor love,
To *Bactria* his houſhold did remove.
His brother ſent ſoon after him a crew,[s]
Which him and his moſt barbarouſly there ſlew:
Unto ſuch height did grow his cruelty,
Of life no man had leaſt ſecurity.
At laſt his Uncle did his death conſpire,
And for that end his Eunuch he did hire;
Who privately him[t] ſmother'd in his bed,
But yet by ſearch he was found murthered;
Then *Artabanus*[u] hirer of this deed,
That from ſuſpition he might be fre'd:
Accus'd *Darius Xerxes* eldeſt Son,
To be the Author of the crime[v] was done.
And by his craft order'd the matter ſo, [111]
That the Prince[w] innocent to death did[x] goe:
But in ſhort time this wickedneſs was known,
For which he died, and not he alone,
But all his Family was likewiſe ſlain:
Such Juſtice in the *Perſian* Court did reign.[y]
The eldeſt ſon thus immaturely dead,
The ſecond was inthron'd in's fathers ſtead.

[s] His wicked brother, after ſent a crew.
[t] Which wretch, him privately. [u] The *Artacanus.* [v] deed.
[w] poor. [x] muſt. [y] Such Juſtice then, in *Perſia* did remain,

Artaxerxes Longimanus.

AMONGST the Monarchs, next this prince had place
The beſt that ever ſprung of *Cyrus* race.
He firſt war with revolted[z] *Egypt* made,
To whom the perjur'd *Grecians* lent their aid:
Although to *Xerxes* they not long before
A league of amity had firmly ſwore,[a]
Which had they kept, *Greece* had more nobly done
Then when the world they after overrun.
Greeks and *Egyptians* both he overthrows,
And payes them both[b] according as he owes.
Which done, a ſumptuous feaſt makes like a king
Where ninefcore dayes are ſpent in banquetting.
His Princes, Nobles, and his Captains calls,
To be partakers of theſe Feſtivals:
His hangings white and green, and purple dye,
With gold and ſilver beds, moſt gorgeouſly.
The royal wine in golden cups did paſs,
To drink more then he liſt, none bidden was:
Queen *Vaſthi* alſo feaſts, but 'fore tis ended,
She's from her Royalty (alas) ſuſpended,
And one more worthy placed in her room, [112]
By *Memucans* advice ſo was the doom.
What *Eſther*[c] was and did, the ſtory read,
And how her Country-men from ſpoyle ſhe freed.

[z] revolting. [a] had ſworn before. [b] now. [c] *Heſter.*

Of *Hamans* fall, and *Mordicaes* great Rise.
The might of th' prince, the tribute of the Isles.
Good *Ezra* in the seventh year of his reign,
Did for the Jews commission large obtain,
With gold and silver, and what ere they need:
His bounty did *Darius* far exceed.
And *Nehemiah* in his twentieth year,
Went to *Jerusalem* his city dear,
Rebuilt those walls which long in rubbish lay,
And o're his opposites still got the day,[d]
Unto this King *Themistocles* did fly,
When under *Ostracisme* he did lye:
For such ingratitude did *Athens* show,
(This valiant Knight whom they so much did owe)
Such royal bounty from his[e] prince he found,
That in his[f] loyalty his heart was bound.
The king not little joyfull of this chance,
Thinking his *Gresian* warrs now to advance,
And for that end great preparation made
Fair *Attica* a third time to invade.
His grand-Sires old disgrace did vex him sore.
His Father *Xerxes* loss and shame much more.
For punishment their breach of oath did call
This noble *Greek*, now fit for General.
Provisions then and season being fit,
To *Themistocles* this warr he doth commit,

[d] This and the seven preceding lines are not in the first edition.
[e] Such entertainment with this. [f] all.

Who for his wrong he could not chuſe but deem [113]
His Country nor his Friends would much eſteem:[g]
But he all injury had ſoon forgat,
And to his native land[h] could bear no hate,
Nor yet diſloyal to his Prince would prove,
By[i] whom oblig'd by bounty,[j] and by love;
Either to wrong, did wound his heart ſo ſore,
To wrong himſelf by death he choſe before:
In this ſad conflict marching on his wayes,
Strong poyſon took, ſo put an end to's dayes.
The King this noble Captain having loſt,
Diſperſt again his newly levied hoſt:
Reſt of his time in peace he did remain,
And di'd the two and forti'th of his reign.

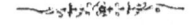

Darius Nothus.

THREE ſons great *Artaxerxes* left behind;
The eldeſt to ſucceed, that was his mind:
His ſecond Brother with him fell at ſtrife,
Stil making war, till firſt had loſt his life:[k]
Then the Surviver is by *Nothus* ſlain,
Who now ſole Monarch doth of all remain.

[g] his Kindred would eſteem. [h] Country-men. [i] To. [j] favour.
[k] But he, with his next brother fell at ſtrife,
That nought appeas'd him, but his brothers life.

The two firſt[l] ſons (are by Hiſtorians thought)
By fair Queen *Eſther*[m] to her husband brought:
If ſo they were,[n] the greater was her moan,
That for ſuch graceleſs wretches ſhe did groan.
Revolting[o] *Egypt* 'gainſt this King rebels,
His Gariſons drives out that 'mongſt them[p] dwells;
Joyns with the *Greeks*, and ſo maintain their right
For ſixty years, maugre the *Perſians* might.
A ſecond trouble after this ſucceeds, [114]
Which from remiſsneſs in *Leſs Aſia* breeds.[q]
Amorges, whom for[r] Vice-Roy he ordain'd,
Revolts, treaſure and people having gain'd,
Plunders[s] the Country, & much miſchief[t] wrought
Before things could to quietneſs be brought.
The King was glad with *Sparta* to make peace,
That ſo he might thoſe troubles[u] ſoon appeaſe:
But they in *Aſia* muſt firſt reſtore
All towns held by his Anceſtors before.
The King much profit reaped by this league,[v]
Regains his own, then doth the Rebel break,
Whoſe ſtrength by *Grecians* help was overthrown,[w]
And ſo each man again poſſeſt his own.
This King *Cambiſes* like his ſiſter wed,
To which his pride, more then his luſt him led:[x]

[l] Theſe two lewd. [m] To be by *Heſter*. [n] If they were hers.
[o] Diſquiet. [p] therein. [q] in *Aſia* proceeds.
[r] their. [s] Invades. [t] trouble.
[u] theſe tumults. [v] reapeth, by theſe leagues.

[w] Whoſe forces by their helpe were overthrown.

[x] The King, his ſiſter, like *Cambyſes*, wed;
More by his pride, then luſt, thereunto led.

For *Perſian* Kings then deem'd[y] themſelves ſo good
No match was high enough but their own blood.
Two ſons ſhe bore, the youngeſt *Cyrus* nam'd,
A Prince whoſe worth by *Xenophon* is fam'd:[z]
His Father would no notice of that take
Prefers his brother for his birthrights ſake.
But *Cyrus* ſcorns his brothers feeble wit,
And takes more on him then was judged fit.
The King provoked ſends for him to th' Court,
Meaning to chaſtiſe him in ſharpeſt ſort,
But in his ſlow approach, e're he came there
His Father di'd, ſo[a] put an end to's fear.
'Bout nineteen years this *Nothus* reigned,[b] which run,
His large Dominions left to's eldeſt Son.

Artaxerxes Mnemon. [115]

MNEMON now ſet upon his Fathers Throne,
Yet fears[c] all he enjoys, is not his own:
Still on his brother caſts a jealous eye,
Judging his[d] actions tends to's injury.
Cyrus on th' other ſide weighs in his mind,
What help in's enterprize he's like to find;

[y] did deem.
[z] A hopefull Prince, whoſe worth is ever fam'd.
[a] fathers death, did.
[b] *Nothus* reign'd nineteen years.
[c] doubts.
[d] all's.

His Intereſt in th' Kingdome now next heir,
More dear to's Mother then his brother farr:
His brothers little love like to be gone,
Held by his Mothers Interceſſion.
Theſe and like motives hurry him amain,
To win by force, what right could not obtain;
And thought it beſt now in his Mothers time,
By lower[e] ſteps towards the top to climbe:
If in his enterprize he ſhould fall ſhort,
She to the King would make a fair report,
He hop'd if fraud nor force, the Crown would gain
Her prevalence, a pardon might obtain.
From the *Lieutenant* firſt he takes away
Some Towns, commodious in leſs *Aſia*,
Pretending ſtill the profit of the King,
Whoſe Rents and Cuſtomes duly he ſent in;
The King finding Revenues now amended,
For what was done ſeemed no whit offended.
Then next he takes the *Spartans* into pay,[f]
One Greek could make ten *Perſians* run away.
Great care was his pretence thoſe Souldiers ſtout,
The Rovers in *Piſidia* ſhould drive out;
But leſt ſome blacker[g] news ſhould fly to Court, [116]
Prepares[h] himſelf to carry the report:
And for that end five hundred Horſe he choſe;
With poſting ſpeed on t'wards the king he goes:
But fame more quick, arrives ere he comes there,
And fills the Court with tumult, and with fear.

[e] leſſer.
[f] Then next, the *Lacedemons* he takes to pay:
[g] worſer.
[h] He meant.

The old Queen and the young at bitter jarrs,
The laſt accus'd the firſt for theſe ſad warrs,[i]
The wife againſt the mother ſtill doth cry
To be the Author of conſpiracy.
The King diſmaid, a mighty hoſt doth raiſe,
Which *Cyrus* hears, and ſo foreſlows his pace:
But as he goes his forces ſtill augments,
Seven hundred *Greeks* repair for[j] his intents,
And others to be warm'd by this new ſun
In numbers from his brother dayly run.
The fearfull King at laſt muſters his forces,
And counts nine hundred thouſand Foot & horſes.
Three hundred thouſand he to *Syria* ſent
To keep thoſe ſtreights his brother to prevent.[k]
Their Captain hearing but of *Cyrus* name,
Forſook his charge to his eternal ſhame.[l]
This place ſo made by nature and by art,
Few might have kept it, had they had a heart.
Cyrus diſpair'd a paſſage there to gain,
So hir'd a fleet to waſt him o're the Main:
The 'mazed King was then about to fly
To *Bactria* and for a time there lye,[m]

[i] The one accus'd the other, for theſe wars: [j] *Greeks* now further.

[k] And yet with theſe, had neither heart, nor grace;
To look his manly brother in the face.
Three hundred thouſand, yet to *Syria* ſent:
To keep thoſe ſtreights, to hinder his intent.

[l] Ran back, and quite abandoned the ſame,
Abrocomes, was this baſe cowards name.
Not worthy to be known, but for his ſhame:

[m] To th' utmoſt parts of *Bactr'a*, and there lye.

Had not his Captains[n] ſore againſt his will
By reaſon and by force detain'd him ſtill.
Up then with ſpeed a mighty trench he throws [117]
For his ſecurity againſt his foes.
Six yards the depth and forty miles in length,
Some fifty or elſe ſixty foot in breadth;
Yet for his brothers coming durſt not ſtay,
He ſafeſt[o] was when fartheſt out of th' way.
Cyrus finding his camp, and no man there,
Was not a little jocund[p] at his fear.
On this he and his ſouldiers careleſs grow,
And here and there in carts their arms they throw
When ſuddenly their ſcouts come in and cry,
Arm, *Arm*, the King with all his hoſt is nigh.[q]
In this confuſion each man as he might
Gets on his arms, arrayes himſelf for fight,
And ranged ſtood by great *Euphrates* ſide
The brunt of that huge multitude to 'bide,
Of whoſe great numbers their intelligence
Was gather'd by the duſt that roſe from thence,
Which like a mighty cloud darkned the sky,
And black and blacker grew, as they drew nigh:
But when their order and their ſilence ſaw,
That, more then multitudes their hearts did awe;
For tumult and confuſion they expected,
And all good diſcipline to be neglected.

[n] a Captain: [o] ſureſt. [p] Rejoyced not a little.
[q] the King is now approaching nigh;

But long under their fears they did not ſtay,
For at firſt charge the *Perſians* ran away,
Which did ſuch courage to the *Grecians* bring,
They all [r] adored *Cyrus* for their King:
So had he been, and got the victory,
Had not his too much valour put him by.
He with ſix hundred on a Squadron ſet, [118]
Of thouſands ſix wherein the King was yet,
And brought his Souldiers on ſo gallantly,
They ready were [s] to leave their King and fly;
Whom *Cyrus* ſpies cryes loud,[t] I ſee the man,
And with a full carreer at him he ran:
And in his ſpeed a dart him hit i'th' eye,
Down *Cyrus* falls, and yields to deſtiny:
His Hoſt in chaſe knows not of this diſaſter,
But treads down all, ſo to advance their maſter;
But when [u] his head they ſpy upon a Lance,
Who knows the ſudden change made by this chance
Senſeleſs & mute they ſtand, yet breath out groans,
Nor *Gorgons* head like [v] this transform'd to ſtones.
After this trance, revenge, new Spirits blew,
And now more eagerly their Foes purſue;
And heaps on heaps ſuch multitudes they laid,
Their Arms grew weary by their ſlaughters made.[w]
The King unto a Country Village flyes,
And for a while unkingly there he lyes.

[r] ſtraight. [s] They were about. [t] out.
[u] At laſt. [v] Nor *Gorgons* like to.
[w] weake, through ſlaughters that they made.

At laft difplays his Enfigne on a Hill,
Hoping by that to make the Greeks ftand ftill;
But was deceiv'd. to him they run[x] amain,
The King upon the fpur runs back again:
But they too faint ftill to purfue their game,
Being Victors oft, now to their Camp they came.
nor lackt they any of their number fmall,
Nor wound receiv'd, but one among them all:
The King with his difperft, alfo incamp'd,
With Infamy upon each Forehead ftamp'd.
His hurri'd thoughts he after recollects,[y] [119]
Of this dayes Cowardize he fears th' effects.
If Greeks in their own Country fhould declare,[z]
What daftards in the Field the *Perfians* are,
They in fhort time might[a] place one in his Throne;
And rob him both of Scepter and of Crown;
To hinder their return by craft or force,
He judg'd his wifeft and his fafeft Courfe.
Then fends, that to his Tent, they ftreight addrefs,[b]
And there all wait, his mercy weaponlefs;
The Greeks with fcorn reject his proud Commands
Asking no favour, where they fear'd no bands:
The troubled King his Herrld fends again,
And fues for peace, that they his friends remain,

[x] it they make. [y] After a while his thoughts he re-collects.
[z] If *Greeks* unto their Country-men declare.
[a] They foone may come, and.
[b] That their return be ftopt, he judg'd was beft.
That fo *Europians* might no more moleft;
Forth-with he fends to's Tent, they ftraight addreffe.

The ſmiling Greeks reply, they firſt muſt bait,
They were too hungry to Capitulate;
The King great ſtore of all proviſion ſends,
And Courteſie to th' utmoſt he pretends,
Such terrour on the *Perſians* then did fall,
They quak'd to hear them, to each other call.
The King perplext, there dares not let them ſtay;
And fears as much, to let them march away,
But Kings ne're want ſuch as can ſerve their will,
Fit Inſtruments t' accompliſh what is ill.
As *Tyſſaphernes* knowing his maſters mind,
Their chief Commanders feaſts and yet more kind,[c]
With all the Oaths and deepeſt Flattery,
Gets them to treat with him in privacy,
But violates his honour and his word,
And Villain like there puts them all to th' Sword.
The *Greeks* ſeeing[d] their valiant Captains ſlain, [120]
Choſe *Xenophon* to lead them home again:
But *Tiſſaphernes* what he could deviſe,
Did ſtop the way in this their enterprize.
But when through difficulties all[e] they brake,
The Country burnt, they no relief might take.[f]
But on they march through hunger & through cold
O're mountains, rocks and hills as lions bold,

[c] Invites their chief Commander. as moſt kinde:
[d] having. [e] ſtill.

[f] He ſought all ſuſtinance from them to take;
Before them burnt the country as they went,
So to deprive them of all nouriſhment;

Nor Rivers courſe, nor *Perſians* force could ſtay,
But on to *Trabeſond* they kept their way:
There was of *Greeks* ſetled a Colony,
Who after all receiv'd them joyfully.
Thus finiſhing their travail, danger, pain,[g]
In peace they ſaw their native ſoyle again.
The *Greeks* now (as the *Perſian* king ſuſpects)
The *Aſiaticks* cowardize detects,
The many victoryes themſelves did gain,
The many thouſand *Perſians* they had ſlain,
And how their nation with facillity,
Might gain[h] the univerſal Monarchy.
They then *Dercilladus* ſend with an hoſt,
Who with the *Spartans* on the *Aſian* coaſt,
Town after town with ſmall reſiſtance take,
Which rumour makes great *Artaxerxes* quake.
The *Greeks* by this ſucceſs encourag'd ſo,
Their King *Ageſilaus* doth over goe,
By *Tiſſaphernes* is encountered,
Lieſtenant to the King, but ſoon he fled.[i]

[g] There for ſome time they were, but whilſt they ſtaid,
Into *Bythinia* often in-rodes made;
The King afraid what further they might doe,
Unto the *Spartan* Admirall did ſue.
Straight to tranſport them to the other ſide,
For theſe incurſions he durſt not abide;
So after all their travell, danger, pain,

[h] win.

[i] *Ageſilaus* himſelf doth over-goe;
By th' Kings Lieutenant is encountered,
But *Tyſſaphernes* with his Army fled:

Which overthrow incens'd the King ſo ſore,
That *Tiſſaphern* muſt be Viceroy no more.
Tythrauſtes then is placed in his ſtead, [121]
Commiſſion hath to[j] take the others head:
Of that perjurious wretch this was the fate,
Whom the old Queen did bear a mortal hate.[k]
Tythrauſtes truſts more to his wit then Arms,
And hopes by craft to quit his Maſters harms;
He knows that many Towns in *Greece* envyes
The *Spartan* State, which now ſo faſt did riſe;[l]
To them he thirty thouſand Tallents ſent
With ſuit, their Arms againſt their[m] Foes be bent;
They to their diſcontent receiving hire,
With broyles and quarrels ſets all *Greece* on fire:
Ageſilaus is call'd home with ſpeed,
To defend, more then offend, there was[n] need,
Their winnings loſt, and peace their glad to take
On ſuch conditions as the King will make.[o]
Diſſention in *Greece* continued ſo long,
Till many a Captain fell, both wiſe and ſtrong,
Whoſe courage nought but death could ever tame
'Mongſt theſe *Epimanondas* wants no fame,
VVho had (as noble *Raileigh* doth evince)
All the peculiar virtues of a Prince;

[j] And hath command, to.

[k] Of that falſe perjur'd wretch, this was the laſt,
Who of his cruelty made many taſt,

[l] height, which now apace doth riſe: [m] force, againſt his. [n] he had.

[o] They now loſt all, and were a peace to make,
The Kings conditions they are forc't to take:

But let us leave theſe Greeks to diſcord bent,
And turn to *Perſia*, as is pertinent.
The King from forreign parts now well[p] at eaſe,
His home-bred troubles ſought how to[q] appeaſe;
The two Queens by his means ſeem[r] to abate,
Their former envy and inveterate hate:
But the old Queen implacable in ſtrife,
By poyſon cauſ'd, the young one loſe her life.
The King highly inrag'd doth hereupon [122]
From Court exile her unto *Babilon*:
But ſhortly calls her home, her counſells prize,
(A Lady very wicked, but yet wiſe)[s]
Then in voluptuouſneſs he leads his life,
And weds his daughter for a ſecond wife.
But long in eaſe and pleaſure did not lye,
His ſons ſore vext him by diſloyalty.
Such as would know at large his warrs and reign,
What troubles in his houſe he did ſuſtain,
His match inceſtuous, cruelties of th' Queen,
His life may read in *Plutarch* to be ſeen.
Forty three years he rul'd, then turn'd to duſt,
A King nor good, nor valiant, wiſe nor juſt.[t]

[p] foes, and all. [q] ſeeketh to. [r] 'gin.

[s] This and the five preceding lines are not in the first edition.

[t] Instead of this and the seven preceding lines, the first edition has the following: —

His Mothers wicked counſell was the cauſe,
Who ſooths him up, his owne deſires are Lawes:
But yet for all his greatneſſe, and long reign,
He muſt leave all, and in the pit remain:

Dorius Ochus.

OCHUS a wicked and Rebellious ſon
Succeeds in th' throne, his father being gone.
Two of his brothers in his Fathers dayes
(To his great grief) moſt ſubtilly he ſlayes:
And being King, commands thoſe that remain,
Of brethren and of kindred to be ſlain.
Then raiſes forces, conquers *Egypt* land,
Which in rebellion ſixty years did ſtand:
And in the twenty third of's cruel raign
Was by his *Eunuch* the proud *Bagoas* ſlain."

Forty three years he rules, then turns to duſt,
As all the mighty ones, have done, and muſt:
But this of him is worth the memory,
He was the Maſter of good *Nehemie.*

" *Darius Ochus.*

GReat *Artaxerxes* dead, *Ochus* ſucceeds,
Of whom no Record's extant of his deeds:
Was it becauſe the *Grecians* now at war,
Made Writers work at home, they fought not far?
Or dealing with the *Perſian*, now no more
Their Acts recorded not, as heretofore?
Or elſe, perhaps the deeds of *Perſian* Kings
In after wars were burnt, 'mongſt other things?
That three and twenty years he reign'd I finde,
The reſt is but conjecture of my minde.

Arsames or Arses, [123]

ARSAMES plac'd now in his fathers stead,
'By him that late his father murthered.
Some write that *Arsames* was *Ochus* brother,
Inthron'd by *Bagoas* in the room of th' other:
But why his brother 'fore his son succeeds
I can no reason give, 'cause none I read.
His brother, as tis said, long since was slain,
And scarce a Nephew left that now might reign:
What acts he did time hath not now left pen'd,
But most suppose in him did *Cyrus* end,
Whose race long time had worne the diadem,
But now's divolved to another stem.
Three years he reign'd, then drank of's fathers cup
By the same Eunuch who first set him up.[v]

[v] *Arsames*, or *Arses.*

WHy *Arsames* his brother should succeed,
I can no reason give, cause none I read;
It may be thought, surely he had no Son,
So fell to him, which else it had not done:
What Acts he did, time hath not now left pend,
But as 'tis thought, in him had *Cyrus* end:
Whose race long time had worn the Diadem,
But now's divolved, to another Stem.
Three years he reign'd, as Chronicles expresse,
Then Natures debt he paid, quite Issue-lesse.

Darius Codomanus.

DARIUS by this *Bagoas* ſet in throne,
(Complotter with him in the murther done)
And was no ſooner ſetled in his reign,
But *Bagoas* falls to's practices again,
And the ſame ſauce had ſerved him no doubt,
But that his treaſon timely was found out,
And ſo this wretch (a puniſhment too ſmall)
Loſt but his life for horrid treaſons all.
This *Codomanus* now upon the ſtage
Was to his Predeceſſors Chamber page.
Some write great *Cyrus* line was not yet run,
But from ſome daughter this new king was ſprung
If ſo, or not, we cannot tell, but find [124]
That ſeveral men will have their ſeveral mind;
Yet in ſuch differences we may be bold,
With learned and judicious ſtill to hold; [w]
And this 'mongſt all's no Controverred thing,
That this *Darius*, was laſt *Perſian* King,

[w] *Darius Codomanus.*

HOw this *Darius* did attain the Crown,
By favour, force, or fraud, is not ſet down:
If not (as is before) of *Cyrus* race,
By one of theſe, he muſt obtain the place.
Some writers ſay, that he was *Arſes* ſon,
And that great *Cyrus* line, yet was not run,
That *Ochus* unto *Arſames* was father,
Which by ſome probabilities (ſeems rather;)

Whoſe Wars, and loſſes we may better tell,
In *Alexander's* reign who did him quell,
How from the top of worlds felicity,
He fell to depth of greateſt miſery.
Whoſe honours, treaſures, pleaſures had ſhort ſtay,
One deluge came and ſwept them all away.
And in the ſixth year of his hapleſs reign,
Of all did ſcarce his winding Sheet retain:
And laſt, a ſad Cataſtrophe to end,
Him to the grave did Traitor *Beſſus* ſend.

That ſon, and father, both were murthered
By one *Bagoas*, an Eunuch (as is ſed.)
Thus learned *Pemble*,* whom we may not ſlight,
But as before doth (well read) *Raleigh* write,
And he that ſtory reads, ſhall often find;
That ſeverall men, will have their ſeverall mind;
Yet in theſe differences, we may behold;
With our judicious learned Knight to hold.

* See Introduction.

The End of the Perſian Monarchy.

The *Third Monarchy*, being the *Grecian*, beginning under *Alexander the Great* in the 112. *Olympiad*.

GReat *Alexander* was wise *Philips* son,
He to *Amyntas*, Kings of *Macedon*;
The cruel proud *Olympias* was his Mother,
She to *Epirus* warlike[x] King was daughter.
This Prince (his father by *Pausanias* slain)
The twenty first of's age began to reign.
Great were the Gifts of nature which he had,
His education much to those did adde:
By art and nature both he was made fit,
To 'complish that which long before was writ.
The very day of his Nativity
To ground was burnt *Dianaes* Temple high:
An Omen to their near approaching woe,
Whose glory to the earth this king[y] did throw.

x Shee to the rich *Molossians*. y Prince.

His Rule to *Greece* he ſcorn'd ſhould be confin'd,
The Univerſe ſcarce bound his proud[z] vaſt mind.
This is the He-Goat which from *Grecia* came,
That ran in Choler[a] on the *Perſian* Ram,
That brake his horns, that threw him on the ground [126]
To ſave him from his might no man was found: *
Philip on this great Conqueſt had an eye,
But death did terminate thoſe thoughts ſo high.
The Greeks had choſe him Captain General,
Which honour to his Son did now befall.
(For as Worlds Monarch now we ſpeak not on,
But as the King of little *Macedon*)
Reſtleſs both day and night his heart then was,
His high reſolves which way to bring to paſs;
Yet for a while in *Greece* is forc'd to ſtay,
Which makes each moment ſeem more then a day.
Thebes and ſtiff[b] *Athens* both 'gainſt him rebel,
Their mutinies by valour doth he quell.[c]
This done againſt both[d] right and natures Laws,
His kinſmen put to death, who gave no[e] cauſe;
That no rebellion[f] in in his abſence be,
Nor making Title unto Soveraignty.
And all whom he ſuſpects or fears will climbe,[g]
Now taſte of death leaſt they deſerv'd[h] in time,

[z] large. [a] fury. * Daniel, chap. viii. [b] old.
[c] But he their mutinies, full ſoon doth quell. [d] all.
[e] without leaſt. [f] combuſtion.
[g] In ſeeking after Soveraignity:
And many more, whom he ſuſpects will climbe.
[h] deſerv't.

Nor wonder is t if he in blood begin,
For Cruelty was his parental ſin,
Thus eaſed now of troubles and of fears,
Next ſpring his courſe to *Aſia* he ſteers;
Leavs *Sage Antipater*, at home to ſway,
And through the *Helliſpont* his Ships made way.
Coming to Land, his dart on ſhore he throws,
Then with alacrity he after goes;
And with a bount'ous heart and courage brave,
His little wealth among his Souldiers gave.
And being ask'd what for himſelf was left, [127]
Reply'd, enough, ſith only hope he kept.[i]
Thirty two thouſand made up his Foot force,
To which were joyn'd five thouſand goodly horſe.
Then on he marcht, in's way he view'd old *Troy*,
And on *Achilles* tomb with wondrous joy
He offer'd, and for good ſucceſs did pray
To him, his Mothers Anceſtors,[j] (men ſay)
When news of *Alexander* came to Court,
To ſcorn at him *Darius* had good ſport;
Sends him a frothy and contemptuous Letter,
Stiles him diſloyal ſervant, and no better;
Reproves him for his proud audacity
To lift his hand 'gainſt ſuch a Monarchy.
Then to's Lieſtenant he in *Aſia* ſends
That he be ta'ne alive, for he intends

[i] This and the three preceding lines are not in the first edition.

[j] Anceſtor.

To whip him well with rods, and ſo to bring
That boy ſo mallipert before the King.
Ah! fond vain man, whoſe pen ere while
In lower terms was taught a higher ſtile.
To River *Granick Alexander* hyes
Which in *Phrygia* near *Propontike* lyes.[k]
The *Perſians* ready for encounter ſtand,
And ſtrive[l] to keep his men from off the land;
Thoſe banks ſo ſteep the *Greeks* yet ſcramble up,
And beat the coward *Perſians* from the top,
And twenty thouſand of their lives bereave,
Who in their backs did all their wounds receive.
This victory did *Alexander* gain,
With loſs of thirty four of his there ſlain;
Then *Sardis* he, and *Epheſus* did gain, [128]
VVhere ſtood of late, *Diana*'s wondrous *Phane*,
And by *Parmenio* (of renowned Fame,)
Miletus and *Pamphilia* overcame.
Hallicarnaſſus and *Piſidia*
He for his Maſter takes with *Lycia*.
Next *Alexander* marcht towards the black Sea,
And eaſily takes old *Gordium* in his way;
Of Aſs ear'd *Midas*, once the Regal Seat,
VVhoſe touch turn'd all to gold, yea even his meat
VVhere the Prophetick knot he cuts in twain,
VVhich who ſo doth, muſt Lord of all remain.
Now news of *Memnon*'s death (the Kings Viceroy)
To *Alexanders* heart's no little joy,

[k] Which twixt *Phrigia*, and *Propontis* lyes. [l] think.

For in that Peer, more valour did abide,
Then in *Darius* multitude beſide:
In's ſtead, was *Arſes* plac'd, but[m] durſt not ſtay,
Yet ſet one in his room, and ran away;
His ſubſtitute as fearfull as his maſter,
Runs after two,[n] and leaves all to Diſaſter.
Then *Alexander* all *Cilicia* takes,
No ſtroke for it he ſtruck, their hearts ſo quakes.
To *Greece* he thirty thouſand talents ſends,
To raiſe more Force to further his[o] intends:
Then o're[p] he goes *Darius* now to meet,
Who came with thouſand thouſands at his feet.
Though ſome there be (perhaps)[q] more likely write
He but four hundred thouſand had to fight,
The reſt Attendants, which made up no leſs,
Both Sexes there was almoſt numberleſs.
For this wiſe King had brought to ſee the ſport, [129]
With him the greateſt Ladyes[r] of the Court,
His mother, his beauteous Queen[s] and daughters,
It ſeems to ſee the *Macedonian* ſlaughters.
Its much[t] beyond my time and little art,
To ſhew how great *Darius* plaid his part;
The ſplendor and the pomp he marched in,
For ſince the world was no ſuch Pageant ſeen.
Sure[u] 'twas a goodly ſight there to behold,
The *Perſians* clad in ſilk, and gliſtering[v] gold,

[m] There *Arſemes* was plac'd, yet. [n] Goes after too.
[o] for what he yet intends. [p] And on. [q] and that.
[r] Along with him, the Ladyes. [s] His mother old, beautious wiſe,
[t] Sure its. [u] Oh. [v] glitt'ring.

The ſtately horſes trapt, the lances gilt,
As if addreſt[u] now all to run a tilt.
The holy fire was borne before the hoſt,
(For Sun and Fire the *Perſians* worſhip moſt)
The Prieſts in their ſtrange habit follow after,
An object, not ſo much of fear as laughter.
The King ſate in a chariot made of gold,
With crown and Robes moſt glorious to behold,
And o're his head his golden Gods on high,
Support a party coloured Canopy.
A number of ſpare horſes next were led,
Leſt he ſhould need them in his Chariots ſtead;
But thoſe that ſaw him in this ſtate to lye,
Suppos'd he neither meant[v] to fight nor flye.
He fifteen hundred had like women dreſt;
For thus[w] to fright the Greeks he judg'd was beſt.
Their golden ornaments how[w] to ſet forth,
Would ask more time then was their bodies worth
Great *Syſigambis* ſhe brought up the Reer,
Then ſuch a world of waggons did appear,
Like ſeveral houſes moving upon wheels,
As if ſhe'd drawn whole *Shuſhan* at her heels:
This brave *Virago* to the King was mother,
And as much good ſhe did as any other.
Now leſt this gold, and all this goodly ſtuff
Had not been ſpoyle and booty rich enough

[u] As if they were.
[v] Would think he neither thought. [w] ſo.

A thouſand mules and Camels ready wait
Loaden with gold, with jewels and with plate:
For ſure *Darius* thought at the firſt ſight,
The *Greeks* would all adore, but none would fight
But when both Armies met, he might behold
That valour was more worth then pearls or gold,
And that his wealth ſerv'd but for baits to 'lure
To make* his overthrow more fierce and ſure.
The *Greeks* came on and with a gallant grace
Let fly their arrows in the *Perſians* face.
The cowards feeling this ſharp ſtinging charge
Moſt baſely ran, and left their king at large:
Who from his golden coach is glad to 'light,
And caſt away his crown for ſwifter flight:
Of late like ſome immoveable he lay,
Now finds both legs and horſe to run away.
Two hundred thouſand men that day were ſlain,
And forty thouſand priſoners alſo tane,
Beſides the Queens and Ladies of the court,
If *Curtius* be true in his report.
The Regal Ornaments were loſt, the treaſure
Divided at the *Macedonians* pleaſure;
Yet all this grief, this loſs, this overthrow,
Was but beginning of his future woe.
The royal Captives brought to *Alexander* [131]
T'ward them demean'd himſelf like a Commander
For though their beauties were unparaled,
Conquer'd himſelf now he had conquered,

* Which made.

Preſerv'd their honour, us'd them bounteouſly,[y]
Commands no man ſhould doe them injury:
And this to *Alexander* is more fame
Then that the *Perſian* King he overcame.
Two hundred eighty Greeks he loſt in fight,
By too much heat, not wounds (as authors write)
No ſooner had this Victor[z] won the field,
But all *Phenicia* to his pleaſure yield,
Of which the Goverment he doth commit
Unto *Parmenio* of all moſt fit.
Darius now leſs lofty[a] then before,
To *Alexander* writes he would reſtore
Thoſe mournfull Ladies from Captivity,
For whom he offers him a ranſome high:
But down his haughty ſtomach could not bring,
To give this Conquerour the Stile of King.
This Letter *Alexander* doth diſdain,
And in ſhort terms ſends this reply again,
A King he was, and that not only ſo,
But of *Darius* King, as he ſhould know.
Next *Alexander* unto *Tyre* doth goe,
His valour and his victoryes they know:
To gain his love the *Tyrians* intend,
Therefore a crown and great Proviſion ſend,
Their preſent he receives with thankſullneſs,
Deſires to offer unto *Hercules*,
Protector of their town, by whom defended, [132]
And from whom he[b] lineally deſcended.

[y] courteouſly. [z] Captaine. [a] more humble. [b] alſo.

But they accept not this in any wife,
Left he intend more fraud then facrifice,
Sent word that *Hercules* his temple ftood
In the old town, (which then lay like a wood)
With this reply he was fo deep[c] enrag'd,
To win the town, his honour he ingag'd:
And now as *Babels* King did once before,
He leaves not till he made the fea firm fhore,
But far lefs time and coft he did expend,
The former Ruines forwarded his end:[d]
Moreover[e] had a Navy at command,
The other by his men fetcht all by land.
In feven months time he took that wealthy[f] town,
Whofe glory now a fecond time's brought down.
Two thoufand of the chief he crucifi'd,
Eight thoufand by the fword then alfo di'd,
And thirteen thoufand Gally flaves he made,
And thus the *Tyrians* for miftruft were paid.
The rule of this he to *Philotas* gave
Who was the fon of that *Parmenio* brave.
Cilicia to *Socrates* doth give,
For now's the time Captains like Kings may live.
Zidon he on *Ephestion* beftowes;
(For that which freely[g] comes, as freely goes)
He fcorns to have one worfe then had the other,
So gives his little Lordfhip to another.

[c] fore. [d] help to him now lend; [e] Befides, he.
[f] fpace he takes this lofty. [g] eafily.

Epheſtion having chief command of th' Fleet,[h]
At *Gaza* now muſt *Alexander* meet.
Darius finding troubles ſtill increaſe, [133]
By his Ambaſſadors now ſues for peace,
And layes before great *Alexanders* eyes
The dangers difficultyes like to riſe,
Firſt at *Euphrates* what he's like to 'bide,
And then at *Tygris* and *Araxis* ſide,
Theſe he may ſcape, and if he ſo deſire,
A league of friendſhip make firm and entire.
His eldeſt daughter he[i] in mariage profers,[j]
And a moſt princely dowry with her offers.[k]
All thoſe rich Kingdomes large that do abide
Betwixt the *Helleſpont* and *Halys* ſide.
But he with ſcorn his courteſie rejects,
And the diſtreſſed King no whit[l] reſpects,
Tells him, theſe proffers great, in truth were none
For all he offers now was but his own.
But quoth *Parmenio* that brave Commander,
Was I as great, as is great *Alexander*,
Darius offers I would not reject,
But th' kingdomes and the Lady[m] ſoon accept.
To which proud[n] *Alexander* made[o] reply,
And ſo if I *Parmenio* was, would I.
He now to *Gaza* goes, and there doth meet,
His Favorite *Epheſtion* with his Fleet,

[h] And therefore gives this Lord-ſhip to another.
Epeſtion now, hath the command o' th' Fleet,

[i] (him). [j] offers. [k] proffers. [l] way.
[m] Ladies. [n] brave. [o] did.

Where valiant *Betis* ftoutly keeps[p] the town,
(A loyal Subject to *Darius* Crown)
For more repulfe the *Grecians* here abide
Then in the *Perfian* Monarchy befide;
And by thefe walls fo many men were flain,
That *Greece* was forc'd to yield[q] fupply again.
But yet this well defended Town was taken, [134]
For 'twas decree'd, that Empire fhould be fhaken;
Thus *Betis* ta'en[r] had holes bor'd through his feet,
And by command was drawn through every ftreet
To imitate *Achilles* in his fhame,
Who did the like to Hector (of more fame)
What haft thou loft thy magnimity,[s]
Can *Alexander* deal thus cruelly?
Sith valour with *Heroicks* is renown'd,
Though in an Enemy it fhould be found;
If of thy future fame thou hadft regard,
Why didft not heap up honours and reward?
From *Gaza* to *Jerufalem* he goes,
But in no hoftile way, (as I fuppofe)
Him in his Prieftly Robes high *Jaddus* meets,
Whom with great reverence *Alexander* greets;
The Prieft fhews him good *Daniel's* Prophefy,
How he fhould overthrow this Monarchy,
By which he was fo much encouraged,
No future dangers he did ever dread.
From thence to fruitful *Egypt* marcht with fpeed,
Where happily in's wars he did fucceed;

[p] doth defend. [q] muft yeeld a frefh.
[r] The Captaine tane. [s] thy late magnanimity?

To ſee how faſt he gain'd was no ſmall wonder,
For in few dayes he brought that Kingdome under.
Then to the *Phane* of *Jupiter* he went,
To be inſtall'd[s] a God, was his intent.
The *Pagan* Prieſt through hire, or elſe miſtake,
The Son of *Jupiter* did ſtreight him make:
He Diobolical muſt needs remain,
That his humanity will not retain.
Thence[t] back to *Egypt* goes, and in few dayes; [135]
Fair *Alexandria* from the ground doth raiſe;
Then ſetling all things in leſs *Aſia*;
In *Syria*, *Egypt*, and *Phenicia*,
Unto *Euphrates* marcht and overgoes,
For no man's there his Army to oppoſe;[u]
Had *Betis* now been there but with his band,
Great *Alexander* had been kept from Land.
But as the King, ſo is the multitude,
And now of valour both are deſtitute.
Yet he (poor prince) another Hoſt doth muſter,
Of *Perſians*, *Scythians*, *Indians* in a cluſter;
Men but in ſhape and name, of valour none
Moſt fit,[v] to blunt the Swords of *Macedon*.
Two hundred fifty thouſand by account,
Of Horſe and Foot his Army did amount;
For in his multitudes his truſt ſtill lay,
But on their fortitude he had ſmall ſtay;
Yet had ſome hope that on the ſpacious[w] plain,
His numbers might the victory obtain.

[s] For to be call'd. [t] Now.
[u] For no man to reſiſt his valour ſhowes; [v] Fit for. [w] that eeven.

About this time *Darius* beautious Queen,
Who had ſore[x] travail and much ſorrow ſeen,
Now bids the world adue, with pain[y] being ſpent,
Whoſe death her Lord full ſadly did lament.[z]
Great *Alexander* mourns as well as he,
The more becauſe not ſet at liberty;[a]
When this ſad news (at firſt *Darius* hears,
Some injury was offered he fears:
But when inform'd how royally the King,
Had uſed her, and hers, in every thing,
He prays the immortal Gods they would reward [136]
Great *Alexander* for this good regard;
And if they down his Monarchy will throw,
Let them on him this dignity beſtow.
And now for peace he ſues as once before,
And offers all he did and Kingdomes more;
His eldeſt daughter for his princely bride,
(Nor was ſuch match in all the world beſide)
And all thoſe Countryes which (betwixt) did lye
Phœniſian Sea, and great *Euphrates* high:
With fertile *Egypt* and rich *Syria*,
And all thoſe Kingdomes in leſs *Aſia*.
With thirty thouſand Talents to be paid,
For the Queen Mother, and the royal maid;
And till all this be well perform'd, and ſure,
Ochus his Son for Hoſtage ſhould[b] endure.

[x] long. [y] her time.
[z] And leaves her wofull Lord for to lament.
[a] For this loſt Queen (though in captivity)
[b] Son a hoſtage ſhall.

To this ſtout *Alexander* gives no ear,
No though *Parmenio* plead, yet will not hear;
Which had he done. (perhaps) his fame he'd kept,
Nor Infamy had wak'd, when he had ſlept,
For his unlimited proſperity
Him boundleſs made in vice and Cruelty.
Thus to *Darius* he writes back again,
The Firmament, two Suns cannot contain.
Two Monarchyes on Earth cannot abide,
Nor yet two Monarchs in one world reſide;
The afflicted King finding him ſet to jar,
Prepares againſt to morrow, for the war,
Parmenio, Alexander, wiſht that night,
To force his Camp, ſo vanquiſh them by flight.[c]
For tumult in the night[d] doth cauſe moſt dread, [137]
And weakneſs of a Foe is covered,
But he diſdain'd to ſteal a victory:
The Sun ſhould witneſs of his valour be,
And careleſs in his bed, next morne he lyes,
By Captains twice is call'd before hee'l riſe,
The Armyes joyn'd a while, the *Perſians* fight,
And ſpilt the Greeks ſome bloud before their flight
But long they ſtood not e're they're forc'd to run,
So made an end, As ſoon as well begun.[e]
Forty five thouſand *Alexander* had,
But is not known what ſlaughter here was made,

[c] ſo put them all to flight; [d] dark.

[e] Instead of this and the five preceding lines, the first edition has,—
Both Armies meet, *Greeks* fight, the *Perſians* run,
So make an end, before they well begun;

Some write th' other had a million, ſome more,
But *Quintus Curtius* as before.[f]
At *Arbela* this victory was gain'd,
Together with[g] the Town alſo obtain'd;
Darius ſtript of all to *Media* came,
Accompan'ed with ſorrow, fear, and ſhame,
At *Arbela* left his Ornaments and Treaſure,
Which *Alexander* deals as ſuits his pleaſure.
This conqueror to *Babylon* then goes,[h]
Is entertain'd with joy and pompous ſhowes,[i]
With ſhowrs of flours the ſtreets along are ſtrown,
And incenſe burnt the ſilver Altars on.
The glory of the Caſtle he admires,
The ſtrong Foundation[j] and the lofty Spires,
In this, a world[k] of gold and Treaſure lay,
Which in few hours was carried all away.
With greedy eyes he views this City round,
Whoſe fame throughout the world was ſo renownd
And to poſſeſs he counts no little bliſs [138]
The towres and bowres of proud *Semiramis*,
Though worne by time, and rac'd[l] by foes full ſore,
Yet old foundations ſhew'd and ſomewhat more.
With all the pleaſures that on earth are[m] found,
This city did abundantly abound,
Where four and thirty dayes he now did ſtay,
And gave himſelf to banqueting and play:

[f] as was ſaid before. [g] And now with it, [h] now goes to *Babylon*, [i] train. [j] The firme foundations, [k] maſſe. [l] raz'd. [m] was.

He and his ſouldiers wax effeminate,
And former diſcipline begin to hate.
Whilſt revelling at *Babylon* he lyes,
Antipater from *Greece* ſends freſh [n] ſupplyes.
He then to *Shuſhan* [o] goes with his new [p] bands,
But needs no force, tis rendred to his hands.
He likewiſe here a world of treaſure found;
For 'twas the ſeat of *Perſian* Kings renownd.
Here ſtood the royal Houſes of delight,
Where Kings have ſhown their glory wealth and might
The ſumptuous palace of Queen *Eſther* [q] here,
And of good *Mordicai*, her kinſman dear,
Thoſe purple hangings, mixt with green and white
Thoſe beds of gold, and couches of delight.
And furniture the richeſt in all lands,
Now fall into the *Macedonians* hands.
From *Shuſhan* to *Perſipolis* he goes,
Which news doth ſtill augment *Darius* woes.
In his approach the governour ſends word,
For his receipt with joy they all accord,
With open gates the wealthy town did ſtand,
And all in it was at his high command.
Of all the Cities that on earth was found, [139]
None like to this in riches did abound:
Though *Babylon* was rich and *Shuſhan* too
Yet to compare with this they might not doe:
Here lay the bulk of all thoſe precious things
That did pertain unto the *Perſian* Kings:

[n] great. [o] "*Suſhan*," here and elſewhere, in the firſt edition.
[p] freſh. [q] *Heſter*.

For when the ſouldiers rifled had their pleaſure,
And taken money plate and golden treaſure,
Statues ſome[r] gold, and ſilver numberleſs,
Yet after all, as ſtoryes do expreſs
The ſhare of *Alexander* did amount
To an hundred thouſand talents by account.
Here of his own he ſets a Gariſon,
(As firſt at *Shuſhan* and at *Babylon*)
On their old Governours titles he laid,
But on their faithfulneſs he never ſtaid,
Their place[s] gave to his Captains (as was[t] juſt)
For ſuch revolters falſe, what King can[u] truſt?
The riches and the pleaſures of this town
Now makes this King his virtues all to drown,
That wallowing[v] in all licentiouſneſs,
In pride and cruelty to high[w] exceſs.
Being inflam'd with wine upon a ſeaſon,
Filled with madneſs, and quite void of reaſon,
He at a bold proud[x] ſtrumpets leud deſire,
Commands to ſet this goodly town on fire.
Parmenio wiſe intreats him to deſiſt
And layes before his eyes if he perſiſt
His fames[y] diſhonour, loſs unto his ſtate,
And juſt procuring of the *Perſians* hate:
But deaf to reaſon, bent to have his will, [140]
Thoſe ſtately ſtreets with raging flame did fill.
Then to *Darius* he directs his way,
Who was retir'd as far as[z] *Media*,

[r] of. [s] charge. [t] moſt. [u] Prince will. [v] He walloweth now,
[w] to th' higheſt. [x] baſe. [y] names. [z] and gone to.

And there with ſorrows, fears & cares ſurrounded
Had now his army fourth and laſt compounded.
Which forty thouſand made, but his intent
Was theſe [a] in *Bactria* ſoon [b] to augment:
But hearing *Alexander* was ſo near,
Thought now this once to try his fortunes here,
And rather choſe an honourable death,
Then ſtill with infamy to draw his breath:
But *Beſſus* falſe, who was his chief Commander
Perſwades him not to fight with *Alexander.*
With ſage advice he ſets [c] before his eyes
The little hope of profit like to riſe:
If when he'd multitudes the day he loſt,
Then with ſo few, how likely to be croſt.
This counſel for his ſafety he pretended,
But to deliver him to's foe intended.
Next day this treaſon to *Darius* known
Tranſported ſore with grief and paſſion,
Grinding his teeth, and plucking off his hair,
Sate overwhelm'd with ſorrow and diſpair:
Then bids his ſervant *Artabaſus* true,
Look to himſelf, and leave him to that crew,
Who was of hopes and comforts quite bereſt,
And by his guard and Servitors all left.
Straight *Beſſus* comes, & with his trait'rous hands
Layes hold on's Lord, and binding him with bands
Throws him into a Cart, covered with hides, [141]
Who wanting means t' reſiſt theſe wrongs abides,

[a] ſtraight. [b] theſe. [c] layes.

Then draws the cart along with chains of gold,
In more despight the thraled prince to hold,
And thus t'ward[d] *Alexander* on he goes,
Great recompence for this,[e] he did propose:
But some detesting this his wicked fact,
To *Alexander* flyes and tells[f] this act,
Who doubling of his march, posts on amain,
Darius from that[g] traitors hands to gain.
Bessus gets knowledg his disloyalty
Had *Alexanders* wrath incensed high,
Whose army now was almost within sight,
His hopes being dasht prepares himself for flight:
Unto *Darius* first he brings a horse,
And bids him save himself by speedy course:
The wofull King his courtesie refuses,
Whom thus the execrable wretch abuses,
By throwing darts gave him his mortal wound,
Then slew his Servants that were faithfull found,
Yea wounds the beasts that drew him unto death,
And leaves him thus to gasp out his last breath.
Bessus his partner in this tragedy,
Was the false Governour of *Media*.
This done, they with their host soon speed away,
To hide themselves remote in *Bactria*.
Darius bath'd in blood, sends out his groans,
Invokes the heav'ns and earth to hear his moans:
His lost felicity did grieve him sore,
But this unheard of treachery[h] much more:

[d] to. [e] in's thoughts, [f] fly, and told. [g] those. [h] injury.

But [i] above all, that neither Ear nor Eye [142]
Should hear nor ſee his dying [j] miſery;
As thus he lay, *Poliſtrates* a Greek,
Wearied with his long march, did water ſeek,
So chanc'd theſe bloudy Horſes to eſpy,
Whoſe wounds had made their skins of purple dye
To them repairs then [k] looking in the Cart,
Finds poor *Darius* pierced to the heart,
Who not a little chear'd to have ſome eye,
The witneſs of this horrid Tragedy; [l]
Prays him to *Alexander* to commend
The juſt revenge of this his woful end:
And not to pardon ſuch diſloyalty,
Of Treaſon, Murther, and baſe Cruelty.
If not, becauſe *Darius* thus did pray,
Yet that ſucceeding Kings in ſafety may
Their lives enjoy, their Crowns and dignity,
And not by Traitors hands untimely dye.
He alſo ſends his humble thankfulneſs,
For all the Kingly grace he did expreſs;
To's Mother, Children dear, and wife now gone.
Which made their long reſtraint ſeem to be none:
Praying the immortal Gods, that Sea and Land
Might be ſubjected to his royal hand,
And that his Rule as far extended be,
As men the riſing, ſetting Sun ſhall ſee,
This ſaid, the Greek for water doth intreat,
To quench his thirſt, and to allay his heat:

[i] Yea. [j] groans, and. [k] he goes, and. [l] of his dying miſery:

Of all good things (quoth he) once in my power,
I've nothing left, at this my dying hour;
Thy ſervice [m] and compaſſion to reward, [143]
But *Alexander* will, for this regard." [n]
This ſaid, his fainting breath did fleet away,
And though a Monarch late, [o] now lyes like clay;
And [p] thus muſt every Son of *Adam* lye,
Though Gods on Earth like Sons of men they [q] dye.
Now to the Eaſt, great *Alexander* goes,
To ſee if any dare his might oppoſe,
For ſcarce the world or any bounds thereon,
Could bound his boundleſs fond Ambition;
Such as ſubmits again he doth reſtore
Their riches, and their honours he makes more,
On *Artabaces* more then all beſtow'd,
For his fidelity to's Maſter ſhow'd.
Thaleſtris Queen of th' *Amazons* now brought
Her Train to *Alexander*, (as 'tis thought.)
Though moſt [r] of reading beſt and ſoundeſt mind,
Such Country there, nor yet ſuch people find.
Then tell her errand, we had better ſpare
To th' ignorant, her title will [s] declare:
As *Alexander* in his greatneſs grows,
So dayly of his virtues doth he loſe.
He baſeneſs counts, his former Clemency,
And not beſeeming ſuch a dignity;
His paſt ſobriety doth alſo bate, [t]
As moſt incompatible to his State;

[m] pitty. [n] Wherefore the gods requite thy kinde regard.
[o] once. [p] Yea. [q] ſhall. [r] ſome. [s] may. [t] hate.

His temperance is but a ſordid thing,
No wayes becoming ſuch a mighty King;
His greatneſs now he takes to repreſent
His fancy'd Gods above the Firmament.
And ſuch as ſhew'd but reverence before, [144]
Now are commanded ſtrictly to adore;
With *Perſian* Robes himſelf doth dignifie,
Charging the ſame on his nobility,
His manners habit, geſtures, all did [u] faſhion
After that conquer'd and luxurious Nation.
His Captains that were virtuouſly inclin'd,
Griev'd at this change of manners and of mind.
The ruder ſort did openly deride,
His feigned Diety and fooliſh pride;
The certainty of both comes to his Ears,
But yet no notice takes of what he hears:
With thoſe of worth he ſtill deſires eſteem,
So heaps up gifts his credit to redeem
And for the reſt new wars and travails [v] finds,
That other matters might take up their minds,
And hearing *Beſſus*, makes himſelf a King,
Intends that Traitor to his end to bring.[w]
Now that his Hoſt from luggage might be free,
And with his burthen no man burthened be;
Commands forthwith each man his fardle bring,
Into the market place before the King;
VVhich done, ſets fire upon thoſe goodly [x] ſpoyles,
The recompence of travails [v] wars and toyles.

[u] now doth. [v] travels.
[w] Intends with ſpeed, that Traitor down to bring; [x] coſtly.

And thus unwiſely in a mading[y] fume,
The wealth of many Kingdomes did[z] conſume,
But marvell 'tis that without mutiny,
The Souldiers ſhould let paſs this injury;
Nor wonder leſs to Readers may it bring,
Here to obſerve the raſhneſs of the King.
Now with his Army doth he poſt[a] away [145]
Falſe *Beſſus* to find out in *Bactria:*
But much[b] diſtreſt for water in their march,
The drought and heat their bodies ſore did[c] parch.
At length they came to th' river *Oxus* brink,
Where ſo[d] immoderately theſe thirſty drink,
Which[e] more mortality to them did bring,
Then all their[f] warrs againſt the *Perſian* King.
Here *Alexander*'s almoſt at a ſtand,
To paſs the River to[g] the other land.
For boats here's none, nor near it any wood,
To make them Rafts to waft them o're the flood:
But he that was reſolved in his mind,
Would without means ſome[h] tranſportation find.
Then from the[i] Carriages the hides he takes,
And ſtuffing them with ſtraw, he bundles makes.
On theſe together ti'd, in ſix dayes ſpace,
They all paſs over to the other place.

[y] one raging. [z] Cities doth. [a] haſt. [b] ſore.
[c] much doth. [d] moſt. [e] This. [f] did their.
[g] How to paſſe over, and gaine.
[h] Would by ſome means a. [i] So from his.

Had *Beſſus* had but valour to his will,
With little pain there might have kept them ſtill:[j]
But Coward durſt not fight, nor could he fly,
Hated of all for's former treachery,
Is by his own now bound in iron chains,
A Coller of the ſame, his neck contains.
And in this ſort they rather drag then bring
This Malefactor vile[k] before the King,
Who to *Darius* brother gives the wretch,
With racks and tortures every limb to ſtretch.
Here was of *Greeks* a town in *Bactria*,
Whom *Xerxes* from their Country led away,
Theſe not a little joy'd, this day to ſee, [146]
Wherein their own had got the ſov'raignty[l]
And now reviv'd, with hopes held up their head
From bondage long to be Enfranchiſed.
But *Alexander* puts them to the ſword
Without leaſt cauſe from[m] them in deed or word;
Nor Sex, nor age, nor one, nor other ſpar'd,
But in his cruelty alike they ſhar'd:
Nor reaſon could he give for this great wrong,
But that they had forgot their mother tongue.
While thus ſome time he ſpent in *Bactria*,
And in his camp ſtrong and ſecurely lay,
Down from the mountains twenty thouſand came
And there moſt fiercely ſet upon the ſame:
Repelling theſe, two marks of honour got
Imprinted in his[n] leg, by arrows ſhot.

[j] He eaſily might have made them ſtay there ſtil; [k] vild.
[l] had ſoveraignity. [m] Without cauſe, given by. [n] deep in's.

The *Bactrians* againſt him now rebel;
But he their ſtubborneſs in time [o] doth quell.
From hence he to *Jaxartis* River goes,
Where *Scythians* rude his army [p] doth oppoſe,
And with their outcryes in an hideous ſort
Beſet his camp, or military court,
Of darts and arrows, made ſo little ſpare,
They flew ſo thick, they ſeem'd to dark the air:
But ſoon his ſouldiers [q] forc'd them to a flight,
Their [r] nakedneſs could not endure their might.
Upon this rivers bank in ſeventeen dayes
A goodly City doth compleatly raiſe,
Which *Alexandria* he doth likewiſe [s] name,
And ſixty furlongs could but [t] round the ſame.
A [u] third Supply *Antipater* now ſent, [147]
Which did his former forces [v] much augment;
And being one hundred twenty thouſand ſtrong;
He enters then the Indian Kings among:
Thoſe that ſubmit, he gives them rule again, [w]
Such as do not, both them and theirs are ſlain.
His warrs with ſundry nations I'le omit,
And alſo of the *Mallians* what is writ.
His Fights, his dangers, and the hurts he had,
How to ſubmit their necks at laſt they're glad. [x]

[o] full ſoone. [p] valour. [q] the *Grecians*. [r] Whoſe.
[s] alſo. [t] not. [u] His. [v] Army. [w] he doth reſtore again.

[x] Instead of this and the three preceding lines, the first edition has, —

To age, nor ſex, no pitty doth expreſſe,
But all fall by his ſword, moſt mercileſſe.

To *Niſa* goes by *Bacchus* built long ſince,
Whoſe feaſts are celebrated by this prince;
Nor had that drunken god one who would take
His Liquors more devoutly for his ſake.
When thus ten days his brain with wine he'd ſoakt,
And with delicious meats his palate choakt:
To th' River *Indus* next his courſe he bends,
Boats to prepare, *Epheſtion* firſt he ſends,
Who coming thither long before his Lord,
Had to his mind made all things to accord,
The veſſels ready were at his command,
And *Omphis* King of that part of the land,
Through his perſwaſion *Alexander* meets,
And as his Sov'raign Lord him humbly greets
Fifty ſix Elephants he brings to's hand,
And tenders him the ſtrength of all his land;
Preſents himſelf firſt[y] with a golden crown,
Then eighty talents to his captains down:
But *Alexander* made[z] him to behold
He glory ſought, no ſilver nor no gold;
His preſents all with thanks he did reſtore, [148]
And of his own a thouſand talents more.
Thus all the Indian Kings to him ſubmit,
But *Porus* ſtout, who will not yeild as yet:
To him doth *Alexander* thus declare,
His pleaſure is that forthwith he repair
Unto his Kingdomes borders, and as due,
His homage to himſelf[a] as Soveraign doe:

[y] there. [z] caus'd. [a] unto him.

But kingly *Porus* this brave anfwer fent,
That to attend him there was his intent,
And come as well provided as he could,
But for the reft, his fword advife him fhould.
Great *Alexander* vext at this reply,
Did more his valour then his crown envy,
Is now refolv'd to pafs *Hydafpes* flood,
And there by force his foveraignty make good.
Stout *Porus* on the banks doth ready ftand[b]
To give him welcome[c] when he comes to land.
A potent army with him like a King,
And ninety Elephants for warr did bring:
Had *Alexander* fuch refiftance feen
On *Tygris* fide, here now he had not been.
Within this fpacious River deep and wide
Did here and there Ifles full of trees abide.
His army *Alexander* doth divide
With *Ptolemy* fends part to th' other fide;
Porus encounters them and thinks all's there,
When covertly the reft get o're elfe where,
And whilft the firft he valiantly affail'd,
The laft fet on his back, and fo prevail'd.
Yet work enough here *Alexander* found, [149]
For to the laft ftout *Porus* kept his ground:
Nor was't difhonour at the length to yield,
When *Alexander* ftrives to win the field.

[b] And there his Soveraignty for to make good;
But on the banks doth *Porus* ready ftand,

[c] For to receive him,

The kingly Captive 'fore the Victor's brought,
In looks or geſture not abaſed ought,
But him a Prince of an undaunted mind
Did *Alexander* by his anſwers find: [d]
His fortitude his royal [e] foe commends,
Reſtores him and his bounds farther extends.
Now eaſtward *Alexander* would goe ſtill,
But ſo to doe his ſouldiers had no will,
Long with exceſſive travails wearied,
Could by no means be farther drawn or led,
Yet that his fame might to poſterity
Be had in everlaſting memory,
Doth for his Camp a greater circuit take,
And for his ſouldiers larger Cabbins make.
His mangers [f] he erected up ſo high
As never horſe his Provender could eye.
Huge bridles made, which here and there he left,
Which might be found, and for great wonders kept
Twelve altars then for monuments he rears,
Whereon his acts and travels long appears.
But doubting wearing time might [g] theſe decay,
And ſo his memory would [h] fade away,
He on the fair *Hydaſpes* pleaſant ſide,
Two Cities built, his name [i] might there abide,
Firſt *Nicea*, the next *Bucephalon*,
Where he entomb'd his ſtately Stalion.

[d] This and the three preceding lines are not in the first edition.
[e] Kingly. [f] Maungers. [g] would.
[h] might. [i] fame.

His fourth and laſt ſupply was hither ſent, [150]
Then down[j] *Hydaspes* with his Fleet he went;
Some time he after ſpent upon that ſhore,
Whether Ambaſſadors, ninety or more,[k]
Came with ſubmiſſion from the Indian Kings,
Bringing their preſents rare, and precious things,
Theſe all he feaſts in ſtate on beds of gold,
His Furniture moſt ſumptuous to behold;
His meat & drink, attendants, every thing,
To th' utmoſt ſhew'd the glory of a King.
With rich rewards he ſent them home again,
Acknowledged their Maſters ſovereign;
Then ſailing South, and coming to that ſhore,
Thoſe obſcure Nations yielded as before:
A City here he built, call'd by his Name,
Which could not ſound too oft with too much fame
Then ſailing by the[l] mouth of *Indus* floud,
His Gallyes ſtuck upon the flats[m] and mud;
Which the ſtout *Macedonians* amazed ſore,
Depriv'd at once the uſe of Sail and Oar:
Obſerving well the nature of the Tide,
In thoſe their fears[n] they did not long abide.
Paſſing fair *Indus* mouth his courſe he ſteer'd
To th' coaſt which by *Euphrates* mouth appear'd;
Whoſe inlets near unto, he winter ſpent,
Unto his ſtarved Souldiers ſmall content,

[j] down t'. [k] Where one hundred Embaſſadours, or more,
[l] Hence ſayling down by th'. [m] ſand. [n] Upon thoſe Flats.

By hunger and by cold ſo many ſlain,
That of them all the fourth did ſcarce remain.
Thus winter, Souldiers, and proviſions ſpent,
From hence he then unto *Gedroſia* went.
And thence he marcht into *Carmania*, [151]
And ſo at length drew near to *Perſia*,
Now through theſe goodly Countryes as he paſt,
Much time in feaſts and ryoting did waſte;
Then viſits *Cyrus* Sepulchre in's way,
Who now obſcure at *Paſſagardis* lay:
Upon his Monument his Robe[o] he ſpread,
And ſet his Crown on his ſuppoſed head.
From hence to *Babylon*, ſome time there ſpent,
He at the laſt to royal *Shuſhan* went;
A wedding Feaſt to's Nobles then he makes,
And *Statyra*, *Darius* daughter takes,
Her Siſter gives to his *Epheſtian* dear,
That by this match he might be yet more near;
He fourſcore *Perſian* Ladies alſo gave,
At this ſame time unto his Captains brave:
Six thouſand gueſts unto this Feaſt invites,
Whoſe Sences all were glutted with delights.
It far exceeds my mean abilities
To ſhadow forth theſe ſhort felicities,
Spectators here could ſcarce relate the ſtory,
They were ſo rapt[p] with this external glory:
If an Ideal Paradiſe a man would frame,
He might this Feaſt imagine by the ſame;

[o] Robes. [p] wrapt.

To every guefs [q] a cup of gold he fends,
So after many dayes the Banquet ends.
Now *Alexanders* conquefts all are done,
And his long Travails [r] paft and overgone;
His virtues dead, buried, and quite [s] forgot,
But vice remains to his Eternal blot.
'Mongft thofe that of his cruelty did taft, [152]
Philotus was not leaft, nor yet the laft,
Accus'd becaufe he did not certifie
The King of treafon and confpiracy:
Upon fufpition being apprehended,
Nothing was prov'd [t] wherein he had offended
But filence, which [u] was of fuch confequence,
He was judg'd guilty of the fame offence, [v]
But for his fathers great deferts the King
His royal pardon gave for this foul [w] thing.
Yet is *Phylotas* unto judgment brought,
Muft fuffer, not for what is prov'd, [x] but thought.
His mafter is accufer, judge and King,
Who to the height doth aggravate each thing,
Inveighs againft his father now abfent,
And's brethren who for him their lives had fpent.
But *Philotas* his unpardonable crime,
No [y] merit could obliterate, or time:
He did the Oracle of *Jove* [z] deride,
By which his Majefty was diefi'd.

[q] Gueft. [r] travells. [s] all. [t] found. [u] guilt.
[v] His death deferv'd, for this fo high offence. [w] fame.
[x] what he did. [y] Which no. [z] *Iupiter*.

Philotas thus o'recharg'd with wrong and grief
Sunk in deſpair without hope of Relief,
Fain would have ſpoke and made his own defence,
The King would give no ear, but went from thence
Tō his malicious Foes delivers him,
To wreak their ſpight and hate on every limb.
Philotas after him ſends out this cry,
O *Alexander*, thy free clemency
My foes exceeds in malice, and their hate
Thy kingly word can eaſily terminate.
Such torments great as wit could worſt[a] invent, [153]
Or fleſh and life could bear, till both were ſpent
Were now inflicted on *Parmenio*'s ſon
He might[b] accuſe himſelf, as they had done,
At laſt he did, ſo they were juſtifi'd,
And told the world, that for his guilt[c] he di'd.
But how theſe Captains ſhould, or yet their maſter
Look on *Parmenio*, after this diſaſter
They knew not, wherefore beſt now to be done,
Was to diſpatch the father as the ſon.
This ſound advice at heart pleas'd *Alexander*,
Who was ſo much ingag'd to this Commander,
As he would ne're confeſs, nor yet[d] reward,
Nor could his Captains bear ſo great regard:
Wherefore at once, all theſe to ſatisfie,
It was decreed *Parmenio* ſhould dye:
Polidamus, who ſeem'd *Parmenio*'s friend
To do this deed they into *Media* ſend:

[a] firſt. [b] For to. [c] for deſert. [d] could.

He walking in his garden to and fro,
Fearing[e] no harm, becaufe he none did doe,[f]
Moft wickedly was flain without leaft crime,
(The moft renowned captain of his time)
This is *Parmenio* who fo much had done
For *Philip* dead, and his furviving fon,
Who from a petty King of *Macedon*
By him was fet upon the *Perfian* throne,
This that *Parmenio* who ftill overcame,
Yet gave his Mafter the immortal fame,
Who for his prudence, valour, care and truft
Had this reward, moft cruel and unjuft.
The next, who in untimely death had part, [154]
Was one of more efteem, but lefs defert;[g]
Clitus belov'd next to *Ephestian*,
And in his cups his chief companion;
When both were drunk, *Clitus* was wont to jeer,
Alexander to rage, to kill, and fwear;
Nothing more pleafing to mad *Clitus* tongue,
Then's Mafters Godhead to defie and wrong;
Nothing toucht *Alexander* to the quick,
Like this againft his Diety to kick:
Both at a Feaft when they had tippled well,[h]
Upon this dangerous Theam fond *Clitus* fell;
From jeft to earneft, and at laft fo bold,
That of *Parmenio*'s death him plainly told.
Which *Alexanders* wrath incens'd fo high,
Nought but his life for this could fatisfie;

[e] Thinking. [f] owe. [g] defart.
[h] Upon a time, when both had drunken well.

From one ſtood by he ſnatcht a partizan,
And in a rage him through the body ran,[i]
Next day he tore his face for what he'd done,
And would have ſlain himſelf for *Clitus* gone:
This pot Companion he did more bemoan,
Then all the wrongs to brave *Parmenio* done.
The next of worth that ſuffered after theſe,
Was learned, virtuous, wiſe *Caliſthenes*,
VVho lov'd his Maſter more then did the reſt,
As did appear, in flattering him the leaſt;
In his eſteem a God he could not be,
Nor would adore him for a Diety:
For this alone and for no other cauſe,
Againſt his Sovereign, or againſt his Laws,
He on the Rack his Limbs in pieces rent, [155]
Thus was he tortur'd till his life was ſpent.
Of this unkingly act[j] doth *Seneca*
This cenſure paſs, and not unwiſely ſay,
Of *Alexander* this th' eternal crime,
VVhich ſhall not be obliterate by time.
VVhich virtues fame can ne're redeem by far,
Nor all felicity of his in war.
VVhen e're 'tis ſaid he thouſand thouſands ſlew,
Yea, and *Caliſthenes* to death he drew.
The mighty *Perſian* King he overcame,
Yea, and he kill'd *Caliſthenes* of fame.[k]

[i] Instead of this and the three preceding lines, the first edition has, —
Alexander now no longer could containe,
But inſtantly commands him to be ſlaine:

[j] deed.

[k] by name.

All Countryes, Kingdomes, Provinces, he wan
From *Hellifpont*, to th' fartheft Ocean.
All this he did, who knows' not to be true?
But yet withal, *Catifthenes* he flew.
From *Macedon*, his Empire did extend
Unto the utmoft[l] bounds o' th' orient:
All this he did, yea, and much more, 'tis true,
But yet withal, *Catifthenes* he flew.
Now *Alexander* goes to *Media*,
Finds there the want of wife *Parmenio*;
Here his chief favourite *Epheftian* dies,
He celebrates his mournful obfequies:[m]
Hangs his Phyfitian, the Reafon why
He fuffered, his friend *Epheftian* dye.[n]
This act (me-thinks) his Godhead fhould a fhame,
To punifh where himfelf deferved blame;
Or of neceffity he muft imply,
The other was the greateft Diety.
The Mules and Horfes are for forrow fhorne, [156]
The battlements from off the walls are torne.
Of ftately *Ecbatane* who now muft fhew,
A rueful face in this fo general woe;
Twelve thoufand Talents alfo did intend,
Upon a fumptuous monument to fpend:

[l] furtheft.

[m] After this the first edition has, —

For him erects a ftately Monument,
Twelve thoufand Tallents on it franckly fpent;

[n] Becaufe he let *Ephestion* to dye.

What e're he did, or thought not ſo content,
His meſſenger to *Jupiter* he ſent,
That by his leave his friend *Epheſtion*,
Among the Demy Gods they might inthrone.[o]
From *Media* to *Babylon* he went,
To meet him there t' *Antipater* he'd ſent,
That he might act alſo[p] upon the Stage,
And in a Tragedy there end his age.
The Queen *Olimpias* bears him deadly hate,
Not ſuffering her to meddle with the State,
And by her Letters did her Son incite,
This great indignity he ſhould[q] requite;
His doing ſo, no whit diſpleaſ'd the King,
Though to his Mother he diſprov'd the thing.
But now *Antipater* had liv'd ſo long,
He might well dye though he had done no wrong;
His ſervice great is ſuddenly forgot,
Or if remembred, yet regarded not:
The King doth intimate 'twas his intent,
His honours and his riches to augment;
Of larger Provinces the rule to give,
And for his Counſel near the King to live.
So to be caught, *Antipater*'s too wiſe,
Parmenio's death's too freſh before his eyes;
He was too ſubtil for his crafty foe. [157]
Nor by his baits could be inſnared ſo:
But his excuſe with humble thanks he ſends,
His Age and journy long he then pretends;

[o] This and the nine preceding lines are not in the first edition.
[p] might next now act.
[q] for to.

And pardon craves for his unwilling ſtay.
He ſhews his grief, he's forc'd to diſobey.
Before his Anſwer came to *Babylon*,
The thread of *Alexanders* life was ſpun;
Poyſon had put an end to's dayes ('twas thought)
By *Philip* and *Caſſander* to him brought,
Sons to *Antipater*, and bearers of his Cup,
Leſt of ſuch like their Father chance to ſup;
By others thought, and that more generally,
That through exceſſive drinking he did dye:
The thirty third of's Age do all agree,
This Conquerour did yield to deſtiny.
When this ſad news came to *Darius* Mother,
She laid it more to heart, then any other,
Nor meat, nor drink, nor comfort would ſhe take,
But pin d in grief till life did her forſake;
All friends ſhe ſhuns, yea, baniſhed the light,
Till death inwrapt her in perpetual night.[r]
This Monarchs fame[s] muſt laſt whilſt world doth[t] ſtand,
And Conqueſts be talkt of whileſt there is land;
His Princely qualities had he retain'd,
Unparalled for ever had remain'd.
But with the world his virtues overcame,
And ſo with black beclouded, all his fame;
Wiſe *Ariſtotle* Tutor to his youth.
Had ſo inſtructed him in moral Truth:
The principles of what he then had learn'd [158]
Might to the laſt (when ſober) be diſcern'd.

[r] This and the five preceding lines are not in the first edition.
[s] Whoſe famous Acts. [t] ſhall.

Learning and learned men he much regarded,
And curious Artiſt [u] evermore rewarded:
The Illiads of *Homer* he ſtill kept,
And under's pillow laid them when he ſlept.
Achilles happineſs he did envy,
'Cauſe *Homer* kept his acts to memory.
Profuſely bountifull without deſert,
For ſuch as [v] pleas'd him had both wealth and heart
Cruel by nature and by cuſtome too,
As oft his acts throughout his reign doth ſhew:
Ambitious ſo, that nought could ſatiſfie, [w]
Vain, thirſting after immortality,
Still fearing that his name might hap to dye,
And fame not laſt unto eternity.
This Conqueror did oft lament (tis ſaid)
There were no more worlds to be conquered.
This folly great *Auguſtus* did deride,
For had he had but wiſdome to his pride,
He would had found enough there to be done,
To govern that he had already won.
His thoughts are periſht, he aſpires no more,
Nor can he kill or ſave as heretofore.
A God alive, him all muſt Idolize,
Now like a mortal helpleſs man he lyes.
Of all thoſe Kingdomes large which he had got,
To his Poſterity remain'd no jot;
For by that hand which ſtill revengeth bloud,
None of his kindred, nor his race long ſtood:

[u] Artiſts. [v] thoſe that. [w] More boundles in ambition then the ſkie,

But as he took delight much bloud to ſpill, [159]
So the ſame cup to his, did others fill.
Four of his Captains now do all divide,
As *Daniel* before had prophyſi'd.
The Leopard down, the[x] four wings 'gan to riſe,
The great horn broke, the leſs did tyranize.*
What troubles and contentions did enſue
We may hereafter ſhew in ſeaſon due.

Aridæus.

GREAT *Alexander* dead, his Armyes left,
Like to that Giant of his Eye bereſt;
When of his monſtrous bulk it was the guide,
His matchleſs force no creature could abide.
But by *Uliſſes* having loſt his ſight,
All men[y] began ſtreight to contemn his might;
For aiming ſtill amiſs, his dreadful blows
Did harm himſelf, but never reacht his Foes.
Now Court and Camp all in confuſion be,
A King they'l have, but who, none can agree;
Each Captain wiſht this prize to bear away,
But none ſo hardy found as ſo durſt ſay:
Great *Alexander* did leave[z] Iſſue none,
Except by *Artabaſus* daughter one;

[x] his. * Dan. vii. 6; viii. 8. 22. [y] Each man. [z] had left.

And *Roxane* ſair whom latç he married,
Was near her time to be delivered.
By natures right theſe had enough to claim,
But meaneſs of their mothers bar'd the ſame,
Alledg'd by thoſe who by their ſubtile Plea
Had hope themſelves to bear the Crown away.
A Siſter *Alexander* had, but ſhe
Claim'd not, perhaps, her Sex might hindrance be.
After much tumult they at laſt proclaim'd
His baſe born brother *Aridæus* nam'd,
That ſo under his feeble wit and reign,
Their ends they might the better ſtill attain.
This choice *Perdiccas* vehemently diſclaim'd,
And Babe unborn of *Roxane* he proclaim'd;
Some wiſhed him to take the ſtyle of King,
Becauſe his Maſter gave to him his Ring,
And had to him ſtill ſince *Epheſtion* di'd
More then to th' reſt his favour teſtifi'd.
But he refus'd, with feigned modeſty,
Hoping to be elect more generally.
He hold on this occaſion ſhould have laid,
For ſecond offer there was never made.
'Mongſt theſe contentions, tumults, jealouſies,
Seven dayes the corps of their great maſter lies
Untoucht, uncovered ſlighted and neglected,
So much theſe princes their own ends reſpected:
A Contemplation to aſtoniſh Kings,
That he who late poſſeſt all earthly things,

And yet not ſo content unleſs that he
Might be eſteemed for a Diety;
Now lay a Spectacle to teſtifie,
The wretchedneſs of mans mortality.
After ſome[a] time, when ſtirs began to calm,
His body did the *Egyptians* embalme;[b]
His countenance ſo lively did appear,
That for a while they durſt not come ſo near:
No ſign of poyſon in his intrails found,[c] [161]
But all his bowels coloured, well and ſound.
Perdiccas ſeeing *Arideus* muſt be King,
Under his name began to rule each thing.
His chief Opponent who Control'd his ſway,
Was *Meleager* whom he would take away,[d]
And by a wile he got him in his power,
So took his life unworthily that hour.
Uſing the name, and the command of th' King
To authorize his acts in every thing.
The princes ſeeing *Perdiccas* power and pride,
For their ſecurity did now provide.[e]
Antigonus for his ſhare *Aſia* takes,
And *Ptolemy* next ſure of *Egypt* makes:
Seleucus afterward held *Babylon*,
Antipater had long rul'd *Macedon*.

[a] this. [b] The next two lines are not in the first edition.

[c] On which, no ſigne of poyſon could be found,

[d] His chief opponents who kept off the Crown,
Was ſtiffe *Meleager*, whom he would take down.

[e] Thought timely for themſelves, now to provide.

Theſe now to govern for the king pretends,
But nothing leſs each one himſelf intends.
Perdiccas took no province like the reſt,
But held command of th' Army (which was beſt)
And had a higher project in his head,
His Maſters ſiſter ſecretly to wed:[f]
So to the Lady, covertly[g] he ſent,
(That none might know, to fruſtrate his intent)
But *Cleopatra* this Suitor did deny,
For *Leonatus* more lovely in her eye,
To whom ſhe ſent a meſſage of her mind,
That if he came good welcome he ſhould find.
In theſe tumultuous dayes the thralled *Greeks*,
Their Ancient Liberty afreſh now ſeeks.
And gladly would the yoke ſhake off, laid on[h] [162]
Sometimes by[i] *Philip* and his conquering ſon.
The *Athenians* force *Antipater* to fly
To *Lamia* where he ſhut up doth lye.
To brave *Craterus*[j] then he ſends with ſpeed
For ſuccours to relieve[k] him in his need.
The like of *Leonatus* he requires,
(Which at this time well ſuited his deſires)
For to *Antipater* he now might goe,
His Lady take in th' way, and no man know.
Antiphilus the *Athenian* General
With ſpeed his Army[l] doth together call;

[f] Which was his Maſters ſiſter for to wed: [g] ſecretly.
[h] Shakes off the yoke, ſometimes before laid on. [i] By warlike.
[j] *Craterus.* [k] To come and to releaſe. [l] forces.

And *Leonatus* ſeeks to ſtop,[m] that ſo
He joyne not with *Antipater* their[n] foe.
The *Athenian* Army was the greater far,
(Which did his Match with *Cleopatra* mar)
For fighting ſtill, while there did hope remain
The valiant Chief amidſt his foes was ſlain.
'Mongſt all the princes[o] of great *Alexander*
For perſonage, none like to this Commander.
Now to *Antipater Craterus* goes,
Blockt up in *Lamia* ſtill by his foes,
Long marches through *Cilicia* he makes,
And the remains of *Leonatus* takes:
With them and his he into *Grecia* went,
Antipater releas'd from priſonment:
After which time the *Greeks* did never more
Act any thing of worth, as heretofore:
But under ſervitude their necks remain'd,
Nor former liberty or glory gain'd.
Now di'd about the end of th' *Lamian* war [163]
Demoſthenes, that ſweet-tongue'd Orator,[p]
Who fear'd *Antipater* would take his life
For animating the *Athenian* ſtrife:
To end his dayes by poiſon rather choſe
Then fall into the hands of mortal foes.
Craterus and *Antipater* now joyne,
In love and in affinity combine,

[m] Striving to ſtop *Leonatus*. [n] that. [o] Captains.
[p] The next four lines are not in the first edition.

Craterus doth his daughter *Phila* [r] wed
Their friendship might the more be strengthened.
Whilst they in *Macedon* do thus agree,
In *Asia* they all asunder be.
Perdiccas griev'd to see the princes bold
So many Kingdomes in their power to hold,
Yet to regain them, how he did not know,
His [s] souldiers 'gainst those captains would not goe
To suffer them go on as they begun,
Was to give way himself might be undone.
With *Antipater* to joyne he sometimes thought,
That by his help, the rest might low be brought,
But this again dislikes; he would remain,
If not in stile,[t] in deed a soveraign; [u]
(For all the princes of great *Alexander*
Acknowledged for Chief that old Commander)
Desires the King to goe to *Macedon*,
Which once was of his Ancestors the throne,
And by his presence there to nullifie
The acts of his Vice-Roy [v] now grown so high.
Antigonus of treason first attaints,
And summons him to answer his [w] complaints.
This he avoids, and ships himself and son, [164]
goes to *Antipater* and tells what's done.
He and *Craterus*, both with him do joyne,
And 'gainst *Perdiccas* all their strength combine.

[r] *Phisa.* [s] For's. [t] word.

[u] The next two lines are not in the first edition.

[v] Vice-royes, [w] these.

Brave *Ptolemy*, to make a fourth then fent
To fave himfelf from danger imminent.[x]
In midft of thefe garboyles, with wondrous ftate
His mafters funeral doth celebrate:
In *Alexandria* his tomb he plac'd,
Which eating time hath fcarcely yet defac'd.[y]
Two years and more, fince natures debt he paid,
And yet till now at quiet was not laid.
Great love did *Ptolemy* by this act gain,
And made the fouldiers on his fide remain.
Perdiccas hears his foes are all[z] combin'd,
'Gainft which to goe, is not refolv'd in mind.[a]
But firft 'gainft *Ptolemy* he judg'd was beft,[b]
Neer'ft unto him, and fartheft from the reft,
Leaves *Eumenes* the *Afian* Coaft to free
From the invafions of the other three,
And with his army unto[c] *Egypt* goes
Brave *Ptolemy* to th' utmoft to oppofe.
Perdiccas furly cariage, and his pride
Did alinate the fouldiers from his fide.
But *Ptolemy* by affability
His fweet demeanour and his courtefie,
Did make his own, firm to his caufe remain,
And from the other fide did dayly gain.

x dangers eminent;

y At *Alexandria*, in *Egypt* Land,
His fumptuous monument long time did ftand;

z now.

a is troubled in his minde;

b With *Ptolomy* for to begin was beft.

c into.

Perdiccas in his pride did ill intreat
Python of haughty mind, and courage great.
Who could not brook ſo great indignity, [165]
But of his wrongs his friends doth certifie;
The ſouldiers 'gainſt *Perdiccas* they incenſe,
Who vow to make this captain recompence,
And in a rage they ruſh into his tent,[d]
Knock out his brains: to *Ptolemy* then went
And offer him his honours, and his place,
With ſtile of the Protector, him to grace.[e]
Next day into the camp came *Ptolemy*,
And is receiv'd of all moſt joyfully.
Their proffers he refus'd with modeſty,
Yields them to *Python* for his courteſie.[f]
With what he held he was now more[g] content,
Then by more trouble to grow eminent.
Now comes there news of a great victory
That *Eumenes* got of the other three.
Had it but in *Perdiccas* life ariv'd,
With greater joy it would have been receiv'd.
Thus *Ptolemy* rich *Egypt* did retain,
And *Python* turn'd to *Aſia* again.
Whilſt *Perdiccas* encamp'd[h] in *Affrica*,
Antigonus did enter *Aſia*,

[d] Instead of this and the six preceding lines, the first edition has, —
Pithon, next *Perdicas*, a Captaine high,
Being entreated by him ſcornfully,
Some of the Souldiers enters *Perdica's* tent,

[e] would him grace;
[f] Confers them *Pithon* on, for's courteſie;
[g] well.
[h] thus ſtaid.

And fain would *Eumenes* draw to their fide,
But he alone moft [i] faithfull did abide:
The other all had Kingdomes in their eye,
But he was true to's mafters family,
Nor could *Craterus*, whom he much did love.
From his fidelity once make him move:
Two Battles fought, and had of both the beft,[j]
And brave *Craterus* flew among the reft:
For this fad [k] ftrife he poures out his complaints, [166]
And his beloved foe full fore laments.
I fhould but fnip a ftory into bits[l]
And his great Acts and glory much eclipfe,
To fhew the dangers *Eumenes* befel,[m]
His ftratagems wherein he did excel:
His Policies, how he did extricate
Himfelf from out of Lab'rinths intricate:[n]
He that at large would fatiffie his mind,
In *Plutarchs Lives* his hiftory may find.
For all that fhould be faid, let this fuffice,
He was both valiant, faithfull, patient, wife.
Python now chofe Protector of the ftate,
His rule Queen *Euridice* begins to hate,
Sees [o] *Arrideus* muft not King it long,
If once young *Alexander* grow more ftrong,

[i] now. [j] Two battells now he fought, and had the beft,

[k] great. [l] verfe.

[m] And much eclipfe his glory to rehearfe
The difficulties *Eumenes* befell.

[n] The next two lines are not in the first edition. [o] Perceives.

But that her huſband ſerve for ſupplement,
To warm his[p] ſeat, was never her intent.
She knew her birth-right gave her *Macedon*,
Grand-child to him who once ſat on that throne
Who was *Perdiccas*, *Philips* eldeſt[q] brother,
She daughter to his ſon, who had no other.[r]
Pythons commands,[s] as oft ſhe countermands;
What he appoints, ſhe purpoſely withſtands.
He wearied out at laſt would needs be gone,
Reſign'd his place, and ſo let all alone:
In's room[t] the ſouldiers choſe *Antipater*,
Who vext the Queen more then the other far.[u]
From *Macedon* to Aſia he came,
That he might ſettle matters in the ſame.
He plac'd, diſplac'd, control'd rul'd as he liſt, [167]
And this no man durſt queſtion or reſiſt;
For all the nobles of King[v] *Alexander*
Their bonnets vail'd to him as chief Commander.

[p] the.

[q] elder.

[r] After this the firſt edition has, —

> Her mother *Cyna* ſiſter to *Alexander*,
> Who had an Army, like a great Commander.
> *Ceria* the *Phrigian* Queen for to withſtand,
> And in a Battell ſlew her hand to hand;
> Her Daughter ſhe inſtructed in that Art,
> Which made her now begin to play her part;

[s] She ever.

[t] ſtead.

[u] The next two lines are not in the firſt edition.

[v] Princes of great.

When to his pleafure all things they had done,
The King and Queen he takes to *Macedon*,[w]
Two fons of *Alexander*, and the reft,
All to be order'd there as he thought beft.
The Army to *Antigonus* doth leave,
And Goverment of Afia to him gave.
And thus *Antipater* the ground-work layes,
On which *Antigonus* his height doth raife,
Who in few years, the reft fo overtops,
For univerfal Monarchy he hopes.
With *Eumenes* he diverfe Battels fought,
And by his flights to circumvent him fought:
But vain it was to ufe his policy,
'Gainft him that all deceits could fcan and try.]
In this Epitome too long to tell
How finely[x] *Eumenes* did here excell,
And by the felf fame Traps the other laid,
He to his coft was righteoufly repaid.[y]
But while thefe Chieftains doe in Afia fight,
To *Greece* and *Macedon* lets turn our fight.
When great *Antipater* the world muft leave,
His place to *Polifperchon* did bequeath,[z]
Fearing his fon *Caffander* was unftaid,
Too rafh[a] to bear that charge, if on him laid.

[w] Acknowledged for chief, this old Commander:
After a while, to *Macedon* he makes;
The King, and Queen, along with him he takes.

[x] neatly. [y] The next two lines are not in the first edition.

[z] Now great *Antipater*, the world doth leave
To *Polifperchon*, then his place he gave,

[a] young.

Antigonus hearing of his deceaſe
On moſt part of *Aſſyria* doth ſeize.
And *Ptolemy* next to incroach begins, [168]
All *Syria* and *Phenicia* he wins.
Then *Poliſperchon* 'gins to act in's place,
Recalls *Olimpias* the Court to grace.
Antipater had baniſh'd her from thence
Into *Epire* for her great turbulence;
This new Protector's of another mind,
Thinks by her Majeſty much help to find.
Caſſander like his Father could not ſee,
This *Poliſperchons* great ability,
Slights his Commands, his actions he diſclaims,
And to be chief[b] himſelf now bends his aims;
Such as his Father had advanc'd to place,
Or by his favours any way had grac'd
Are now at the devotion of the Son,
Preſt to accompliſh what he would have done;
Beſides he was the young Queens favourite,
On whom (t'was thought) ſhe ſet her chief delight:
Unto theſe helps at home[c] he ſeeks out more,
Goes to *Antigonus* and doth implore,
By all the Bonds 'twixt him and's Father paſt,
And for that great gift which he gave him laſt.
By theſe and all to grant him ſome ſupply,
To take down P*oliſperchon* grown ſo high;
For this *Antigonus* did need no ſpurs,
Hoping to gain yet more by theſe new ſtirs,

[b] great. [c] in *Greece*,

Streight furnish'd him with a sufficient aid,[d]
And so he quick returns thus well appaid,
With Ships at Sea, an Army for the Land,
His proud opponent hopes soon to withstand.
But in his absence *Polisperchon* takes [169]
Such friends away as for his Interest makes
By death, by prison, or by banishment,
That no supply by these here might be lent,
Cassander with his Host to *Grecia* goes,
Whom *Polisperchon* labours to oppose;
But beaten was at Sea, and foil'd at Land,
Cassanders forces had the upper hand,
Athens with many Towns in *Greece* beside,
Firm (for his Fathers sake) to him abide.[e]
Whil'st hot in wars these two in *Greece* remain,
Antigonus doth all in *Asia* gain;
Still labours *Eumenes*, would[f] with him side,
But all in vain,[g] he faithful did abide:
Nor Mother could, nor Sons of *Alexander*,
Put trust in any but in this Commander.

[d] Instead of the next seven lines, the first edition has, —
Cassander for return all'speed now made:
Polisperchon, knowing he did relye
Upon those friends, his father rais'd on high,
Those absent, banished, or else he flew
All such as he suspected to him true.

[e] But had the worst at Sea, as well as Land,
And his opponent still got upper hand,
Athens, with many Townes in *Greece* besides,
Firme to *Cassander* at this time abides:

[f] might.

[g] But to the last.

The great ones now began to ſhew their mind,
And act as opportunity they find.
Aridæus the ſcorn'd and ſimple King,
More then he bidden was could act no thing.
Poliſperchon for office hoping long,
Thinks to inthrone the Prince when riper grown;
Euridice this injury diſdains,
And to *Caſſandar* of this wrong complains.
Hateful the name and houſe of *Alexander*,
Was to this proud vindicative *Caſſander*;
He ſtill kept lockt[h] within his memory,
His Fathers danger, with his Family;
Nor thought[i] he that indignity was[j] ſmall,
When *Alexander* knockt his head to th' wall.
Theſe with his love unto the amorous Queen,
Did make him vow her ſervant to be ſeen.
Olimpias, *Aridæus* deadly hates,
As all her Husbands, Children by his mates,
She gave him poyſon formerly ('tis thought)
Which damage both to mind and body brought;
She now with *Poliſperchon* doth combine,
To make the King by force his Seat reſigne:
And her young grand-child in his State inthrone,[k]
That under him, ſhe might rule, all alone.
For aid ſhe goes t' *Epire* among her friends,
The better to accompliſh theſe her ends;
Euridice hearing what ſhe intends,
In haſte unto her friend[l] *Caſſander* ſends,

[h] freſh. [i] counts. [j] but. [k] Nephew in his ſtead t' inthrone,
[l] deare.

To leave his fiege at *Tegea,*[m] and with fpeed,
To fave the King and her in this their need:[n]
Then by intreaties, promifes and Coyne,
Some forces did procure with her to joyn.
Olimpias foon[o] enters *Macedon,*
The Queen to meet her bravely marches on,
But when her Souldiers faw their ancient Queen,
Calling to mind[p] what fometime fhe had been;
The wife and Mother of their famous Kings,
Nor darts, nor arrows, now none fhoots or flings.[q]
The King and Queen feeing their deftiny,
To fave their lives t' *Amphipolis* do fly;
But the old Queen purfues them with her hate,
And needs will have their lives as well as State:
The King by extream torments had his end,
And to the Queen thefe prefents fhe did fend;
A Halter, cup of poyfon, and a Sword, [171]
Bids chufe her death, fuch kindnefs fhe'l afford.
The Queen with many a curfe, and bitter check,
At length yields to the Halter her fair neck;
Praying that fatal day might quickly hafte,
On which *Olimpias* of the like might tafte.
This done the cruel Queen refts not content,
'Gainft all that lov'd *Caffander* fhe was bent;[r]

[m] *Tagra.* [n] To come and fuccour her, in this great need;
[o] now. [p] Remembring.
[q] Inftead of the next four lines, the firft edition has, —
The King, and Queen, to *Amphipolis* doe fly,
But foone are brought into captivity;
[r] Till all that lov'd *Caffander* was nigh fpent;

His Brethren, Kinsfolk and his chiefeſt friends,
That fell [s] within her reach came to their ends:
Dig'd up his brother dead, 'gainſt natures right,
And threw his bones about to ſhew her ſpight:
The Courtiers wondring at her furious mind,
Wiſht in *Epire* ſhe had been ſtill confin'd.
In *Peloponeſus* then *Caſſander* lay,
Where hearing of this news he ſpeeds away,
With rage, and with revenge he's hurried on,
To find this cruel [t] Queen in *Macedon*;
But being ſtopt, at ſtreight *Thermopoly*,
Sea paſſage gets, and lands in *Theſſaly*:
His Army he divides, ſends poſt [u] away,
Poliſperchon to hold a while in play;
And with the reſt *Olimpias* purſues,
For all her cruelty, to give her dues.
She with the chief [v] o' th' Court to *Pydna* flyes,
Well fortifi'd, (and on the Sea it lyes)
There by *Caſſander* ſhe's blockt up ſo long,
Untill the Famine grows exceeding ſtrong,
Her Couzen of *Epire* did what he might,
To raiſe the Siege, and put her Foes to flight.
Caſſander is reſolved there to remain, [172]
So ſuccours and endeavours proves but vain;
Fain would this wretched Queen [w] capitulate,
Her foe would give no Ear, [x] (ſuch is his hate)

[s] were. [t] So goes to ſinde this. [u] part.
[v] ſlow'r. [w] would ſhe come now to.
[x] *Caſſander* will not heare,

The Souldiers pinched with this ſcarcity,
By ſtealth unto *Caſſander* dayly fly;
Olimpias means to hold out[y] to the laſt,
Expecting nothing but of death to taſt:
But his occaſions calling him away,[z]
Gives promiſe for her life, ſo wins the day.
No ſooner had he got her in his hand,
But made in judgement her accuſers ſtand;
And plead the blood of friends and kindreds[a] ſpilt,
Deſiring juſtice might be done for guilt;
And ſo was he acquitted of his word,
For juſtice ſake ſhe being put to th' Sword:
This was the end of this moſt cruel Queen,
Whoſe fury ſcarcely parallel'd[b] hath been.
The daughter, ſiſter, Mother, Wife to Kings,
But Royalty no good conditions brings;[c]
To Husbands death ('tis[d] thought) ſhe gave conſent,
The murtherer[e] ſhe did ſo much lament:
With Garlands crown'd his head, bemoan'd his ſates,
His Sword unto *Apollo* conſecrates.
Her Outrages too tedious to relate,
How for no cauſe but her inveterate hate;
Her Husbands wives[f] and Children after's death,
Some ſlew, ſome fry'd, of others ſtopt the breath:

[y] wills to keep it, [z] But he unwilling longer there to ſtay.
[a] of their deare Kindred. [b] yet unparalleld.
[c] After this the first edition has, —
So boundleſſe was her pride, and cruelty,
She oft forgot bounds of Humanity.
[d] 'twas. [e] The Authours death. [f] Wife.

Now in her Age ſhe's forc'd to taſt that Cup,
Which ſhe had others often made to ſup.
Now many Towns in *Macedon* ſuppreſt, [173]
And *Pellas* fain to yield among the reſt;
The Funerals *Caſſander* celebrates,
Of *Aridæus* and his Queen with State:
Among their Anceſtors by him they're laid,
And ſhews of lamentation for them made.
Old *Thebes* he then rebuilt ſo much of fame,
And *Caſſandria* rais d after his name.
But leave him building, others in their Urne,
Let's for a while, now into *Aſia* turn.
True *Eumenes* endeavours by all Skill,
To keep *Antigonus* from *Shuſhan* ſtill;
Having command o'th' Treaſure he can hire,
Such as no threats, nor favour could acquire.
In divers Battels he had good ſucceſs,
Antigonus came off ſtill honourleſs;
When Victor oft he'd been, and ſo might ſtill,
Peuceſtes[g] did betray him by a wile.
T' *Antigonus*, who took[h] his Life unjuſt,
Becauſe he never would forgoe[i] his truſt;
Thus loſt he all for his fidelity,
Striving t'uphold his Maſters Family.
But to a period as that did haſte,
So *Eumenes* (the prop) of death muſt taſt;

[g] *Peuceſtas.* [h] *Antigonus*, then takes. [i] let go.

All *Perſia* now *Antigonus* doth gain,[i]
And Maſter of the Treaſure ſole remain:[j]
Then with *Seleucus* ſtreight at odds doth fall,
And he for aid to *Ptolomy* doth call,
The Princes all begin now to envy
Antigonus, he growing up ſo high;
Fearing his force,[k] and what might hap e're long, [174]
Enters into a Combination ſtrong,
Seleucus, *Ptolemy*, *Caſſander* joynes,
Lyſimachus to make a fourth combines:
Antigonus deſirous of the *Greeks*,
To make *Caſſander* odious to them ſeeks,
Sends forth his declarations near and far,[l]
And clears what cauſe he had to make this war,[m]
Caſſanders outrages at large doth tell,
Shews his ambitious practiſes as well.[n]
The mother of their King to death he'd put,
His wife and ſon in priſon cloſe had ſhut:
And aiming now to make himſelf a king,
And that ſome title he might ſeem to bring,
Theſſalonica he had newly wed,
Daughter to *Philip* their renowned head:
Had built and call'd a City by his name,
Which none e're did, but thoſe of royal fame:

[i] So *Eumenes* of deſtiny muſt taſte.
Antigonus, all *Perſia* now gains,

[j] he remains; [k] their ſtate, [l] declaration from a farre,

[m] And ſhews what cauſe they had to take up warre.

[n] This and the preceding line are not in the first edition.

And in deſpight of their two famous Kings
Hatefull *Olinthians* to *Greece* rebrings.
Rebellious *Thebes* he had reedified,
Which their late King in duſt had damnified,
Requires them therefore to take up their arms
And to requite this traitor for these harms.
Then P*tolemy* would gain the *Greeks* likewiſe,
And he declares the others injuryes:[o]
Firſt how he held the Empire in his hands,
Seleucus driven[p] from Goverment and lands,
The[q] valiant *Eumenes* unjuſtly ſlain,
And Lord of royal *Shuſhan*[r] did remain;
Therefore requeſts[s] their help to take him down [175]
Before he wear the univerſal Crown.
Theſe princes at the ſea ſoon had a fight,
Where great *Antigonus* was put to flight:[t]
His ſon at *Gaza* likewiſe loſt the field,
So *Syria* to *Ptolemy* did yield:
And *Seleucus* recovers *Babylon*,
Still gaining Countryes eaſtward he goes on.
Demetrius with[u] *Ptolemy* did fight,
And coming unawares, put him to flight;
But bravely ſends the priſoners back again,
With all the ſpoyle and booty he[v] had tane.

[o] For he declares againſt his injuries; [p] drove. [q] Had.
[r] o' th' City *Suſha*. [s] So therefore craves.
[t] *Antigonus* at Sea ſoone had a fight,
Where *Ptolomy*, and the reſt put him to flight:
[u] againe with. [v] they.

Courteous [w] as noble *Ptolemy*, or more,
VVho at *Gaza* did the like to him before.
Antigonus did much rejoyce, his ſon
VVith victory, his loſt repute had won.
At laſt theſe princes tired out with warrs,
Sought for a peace, and laid aſide their jarrs:
The terms of their agreement, thus expreſs
That each ſhould hold what now he did poſſeſs,
Till *Alexander* unto age was grown,
VVho then ſhould be enſtalled in the throne.
This toucht *Caſſander* ſore for what he'd done,
Impriſoning both the mother and the [x] ſon:
He ſees the Greeks now favour their young Prince
Whom he in durance held, now, and long ſince,
That in few years he muſt be forc'd or glad,
To render up ſuch Kingdomes as he had;
Reſolves to quit his fears by one deed done,
So puts [y] to death the Mother and her Son.
This *Roxane* for her beauty all commend, [176]
But for one act ſhe did, juſt was her end.
No ſooner was great *Alexander* dead,
But ſhe *Darius* daughters murthered.
Both thrown into a well to hide her blot,
Perdiccas was her Partner in this plot.
The heavens ſeem'd ſlow in paying her the ſame;
But at the laſt the hand of vengeance came.
And for that double fact which ſhe had done,
The life of her muſt goe, and of her ſon

w *Curtius*, x her. y And put.

Perdiccas had before for his amiss,
But by their hands who thought not once of this.
Cassanders deed the princes do [z] detest,
But 'twas in shew; in heart it pleas'd them best.
That he is odious to the world, they'r glad:
And now they were free Lords of what they had.
When this foul tragedy was past and done,
Polysperchon brings the [a] other son
Call'd *Hercules*, and elder then his brother,
(But *Olimpias* would [b] prefer the other)
The *Greeks* toucht with the murther done of late,
This Orphan prince 'gan [c] to compassionate,
Begin to mutter much 'gainst proud *Cassander*,
And place their hopes on th' heir of *Alexander*.
Cassander fear'd what might of this ensue,
So *Polisperchon* to his counsel drew,
And gives *Peloponesus* for his hire,[d]
Who slew the prince according to desire.
Thus was the race and house of *Alexander*
Extinct by this inhumane wretch *Cassander*.
Antigonus, for all this doth not mourn, [177]
He knows to's profit, this at last [e] will turn,
But that some Title now he might pretend,
To *Cleopatra* doth for marriage send;
Lysimachus and *Ptolemy* the same,
And lewd [f] *Cassander* too, sticks not for shame:
She then in *Lydia* at *Sardis* lay,
Where by Embassage all these Princes pray.

[z] all. [a] up the. [b] thought to. [c] This Prince began for.
[d] Gives *Peloponesus* unto him for hire, [e] all i'th end. [f] vile.

Choice above all, of *Ptolemy* ſhe makes,
With his Embaſſador her journy takes;
Antigonus Lieutenant ſtayes her ſtill,
Untill he further know his Maſters will:
Antigonus now had a Wolf by th' Ears,
To hold her ſtill, or let her go he fears.
Reſolves at laſt the Princeſs ſhould be ſlain,
So hinders him of her, he could not gain;
Her women are appointed for this deed,
They for their great reward no better ſpeed:
For by command, they ſtreight were put to death,
As vile Conſpirators that ſtopt[g] her breath.
And now he hopes,[h] he's order'd all ſo well,
The world muſt needs believe what he doth tell;
Thus *Philips* houſe was quite extinguiſhed,
Except *Caſſanders* wife who yet not dead.
And by their means who thought of nothing leſs,
Then vengeance juſt, againſt them[i] to expreſs;
Now blood was paid with blood for what was done
By cruel Father, Mother, cruel Son:[j]

[g] took. [h] thinks. [i] the ſame.

[j] After this the first edition has, —

Who did erect their cruelty in guilt,
And wronging innocents whoſe blood they ſpilt.
Philip and *Olympias* both were ſlain.
Aridæus and his Queen by ſlaughters ta'ne:
Two other children by *Olympias* kill'd.
And *Cleopatra's* blood, now likewiſe ſpill'd.
If *Alexander* was not poyſoned,
Yet in the flower of's age, he muſt lie dead.
His wife and ſons then ſlain by this *Caſſander*.
And 's kingdomes rent away by each Commander:

Thus may we hear, and fear, and ever say,
That hand is righteous still which doth repay.
These Captains now the stile of Kings do take, [178]
For to their Crowns their's[k] none can Title make;[l]
Demetrius first the royal stile assum'd,
By his Example all the rest presum'd.
Antigonus himself to ingratiate,
Doth promise liberty to *Athens* State;
With Arms and with provision stores them well,
The better 'gainst *Cassander* to rebel.
Demetrius thether goes, is entertain'd
Not like a King, but like some God they feign'd;
Most grosly base was their[m] great Adulation,
Who Incense burnt, and offered oblation:
These Kings afresh fall to their wars again,
Demetrius of *Ptolemy* doth gain.
'Twould be an endless Story to relate
Their several Battels and their several fate,[n]
Their fights by Sea, their victories by Land,
How some when down, straight got the upper hand
Antigonus and *Seleucus* then fight
Near *Ephesus*, each bringing all his[o] might,
And he that Conquerour shall now remain,
The Lordship of all *Asia*[p] shall retain;

[k] there's.

[l] Instead of the next seven lines, the first edition has, —

Demetrius is first, that so assumes,
To do as he, the rest full soon presumes,
To *Athens* then he goes, is entertain'd.

[m] this.

[n] The next two lines are not in the first edition.

[o] their.

[p] Of *Asia* the Lordship.

This day 'twixt theſe two Kings[q] ends all the ſtrife,
For here *Antigonus* loſt rule and life:
Nor to his Son, did e're[r] one ſoot remain
Of thoſe vaſt Kingdomes,[s] he did ſometimes gain.
Demetrius with his Troops to *Athens* flyes,
Hopes to find ſuccours in his miſeries;[t]
But they adoring in proſperity,
Now ſhut their gates in his adverſity:
He ſorely griev'd at this his deſperate State [179]
Tryes Foes, ſith[u] friends will not compaſſionate.
His peace he then with old *Seleucus* makes,
Who his fair daughter *Stratonica* takes,
Antiochus, Seleucus, dear lov'd Son,
Is for this freſh young Lady quite[v] undone;
Falls ſo extreamly ſick, all fear'd his life,
Yet durſt not ſay, he lov'd his Fathers wife,
When his diſeaſe the skill'd[w] Phyſitian found,
His Fathers mind he wittily did ſound,
Who did no ſooner underſtand the ſame,
But willingly reſign'd the beautious Dame:
Caſſander now muſt dye his race is run,
And leaves the ill got Kingdomes he had won.
Two Sons he left, born of King *Philips* daughter,
Who had an end put to their dayes by ſlaughter;
Which ſhould ſucceed at variance they fell,
The Mother would, the youngeſt might[x] excell:

[q] foes. [r] there. [s] Of thoſe dominions.
[t] Hoping to find ſuccour in miſeries. [u] ſince. [v] half.
[w] skilfull. [x] ſhould.

The eld'ſt inrag'd did play the Vipers part,
And with his Sword did run her through the heart:[y]
Rather then *Philips* race ſhould[z] longer live,
He whom ſhe gave his life her death ſhall[a] give.
This by *Lyſimacus* was[b] after ſlain,
Whoſe daughter he not long before had ta'ne;[c]
Demetrius is call'd in by th' youngeſt Son,
Againſt *Lyſimachus* who from him won.
But he a Kingdome more then's friend did eye,
Seaz'd upon that, and ſlew him traitrouſly.[d]
Thus *Philips* and *Caſſander*'s race both[e] gone,
And ſo falls out to be extinct in one;
And[f] though *Caſſander* died in his bed,
His Seed to be extirpt, was deſtined;
For blood, which was decre'd that he ſhould ſpill,
Yet muſt his Children pay for Fathers ill;
Jehu in killing *Ahab*'s houſe did well,
Yet be aveng'd muſt blood of *Jezerel*.
Demetrius thus *Caſſander*'s Kingdoms gains,
And now in *Macedon* as King he reigns;[g]
Though men and mony both he hath at will,
In neither finds content if he ſits ſtill:
That *Seleucus* holds *Aſia* grievs him ſore,
Thoſe Countryes large his Father got before.

[y] did pierce his mothers heart. [z] child muſt. [a] muſt.
[b] ſoon. [c] unto wife, he'd newly ta'n.
[d] Instead of this and the three preceding lines, the first edition has. —
The youngeſt by *Demetrius* kill'd in fight,
Who took away his now pretended right:
[e] is. [f] Yea. [g] The next two lines are not in the first edition.

Theſe to recover, muſters all his might,
And with his Son in Law will needs go fight;[h]
A mighty Navy rig'd, an Army ſtout,
With theſe he hopes to turn the world about:
Leaving *Antigonus* his eldeſt Son,
In his long abſence to rule *Macedon.*
Demetrius with ſo many troubles met,
As Heaven and Earth againſt him had been ſet:
Diſaſter on diſaſter him purſue,
His ſtory ſeems a Fable more then true.
At laſt he's[i] taken and impriſoned
Within an Iſle that was with pleaſures fed,
Injoy'd what ere beſeem'd his Royalty,
Only reſtrained of his liberty:
After three years he died, left what he'd won,
In *Greece* unto *Antigonus* his Son.
For his Poſterity unto this day,
Did ne're regain one foot in *Aſia*;[j]
His Body *Seleucus* ſends to his Son, [181]
Whoſe obſequies with wondrous pomp was done.
Next di'd the brave and noble *Ptolemy*,
Renown'd for bounty, valour, clemency,
Rich *Egypt* left, and what elſe he had won,
To *Philadelphus* his more worthy Son.
Of the old *Heroes*, now but two remain,
Seleucus and *Lyſimachus* theſe twain,

[h] The next eight lines are not in the first edition. [i] There was he.
[j] The next two lines are not in the first edition.

Muſt needs go try their ſortune and their might,
And ſo *Lyſimachus* was ſlain in fight;
'Twas no ſmall joy unto *Seleucus* breaſt,
That now he had out-lived all the reſt:
Poſſeſſion of *Europe* thinks to take,
And ſo himſelf the only Monarch make;
Whilſt with theſe hopes in *Greece* he did remain,
He was by *Ptolemy Ceraunus* ſlain.
The ſecond Son of the firſt *Ptolemy*,
Who for Rebellion unto him did fly;
Seleucus was a[k] Father and a friend,
Yet by him had this moſt unworthy end.
Thus with theſe Kingly Captains have we done,
A little now how the Succeſſion run,
Antigonus, *Seleucus* and *Caſſander*,
With *Ptolemy*, reign'd after *Alexander*;
Caſſander's Sons ſoon after's death were ſlain,
So three Succeſſors only did remain:
Antigonus his Kingdomes loſt and life,
Unto *Seleucus*, Author of that ſtrife.
His Son *Demetrius*, all *Caſſanders* gains,
And his poſterity, the ſame retains;
Demetrius Son was call'd *Antigonus*, [182]
And his again was nam'd[l] *Demetrius*.
I muſt let paſs thoſe many Battels fought,
Betwixt[m] thoſe Kings, and noble *Pyrrhus* ſtout,
And his Son *Alexander* of *Epire*,
Whereby immortal honour they acquire;

[k] as. [l] againe, alſo. [m] Between.

Demetrius had *Philip* to his Son,[n]
(Part of whofe Kingdomes *Titus Quintius* won)
Philip had *Perfeus,* who was made a Thrale
T[e] *Emilius* the Roman General;
Him with his Sons in Triumph lead did he,
Such riches too as *Rome* did never fee:
This of *Antigonus,* his Seed's the Fate,
VVhofe Empire was fubdu'd to[o] th' Roman State.
Longer *Seleucus* held the royalty,
In *Syria* by his Pofterity;
Antiochus Soter his Son was nam'd,
To whom the old[p] *Berofus* (fo much fam'd,)
His Book of *Affurs* Monarchs dedicates,
Tells of their names, their wars, their riches, fates;
But this is perifhed with many more,
VVhich oft we wifh was extant as before.*
Antiochus Theos was *Soter*'s Son,
VVho a long war with *Egypts* King begun;
The Affinityes and Wars *Daniel* fets forth,
And calls them there the Kings of South & North, †
This *Theos* murther'd was by his lewd wife,[q]
Seleucus reign'd, when he had loft his life.

[n] Instead of the next five lines, the first edition has. —
He *Perfeus,* from him the kingdom's won,
Emillius the *Roman* Generall,
Did take his rule, his fons, himfelf and all.

[o] kingdomes were fubdu'd by.

[p] whom Ancient.

* See page 188 and note.

† Daniel, chap. xi.

[q] This *Theos* he was murthered by his wife,

A third *Seleucus* next ſits on the Seat,
And then *Antiochus* ſirnam'd the great,[r]
VVhoſe large Dominions after was made ſmall, [183]
By *Scipio* the Roman General;
Fourth *Seleucus*[s] *Antiochus* ſucceeds,
And next[t] *Epiphanes* whoſe wicked deeds,
Horrid Maſſacres, Murthers, cruelties,
Amongſt[u] the Jews we read in *Machabees*.*
Antiochus Eupater was the next,
By Rebels and Impoſtors dayly vext;
So many Princes ſtill were murthered,
The Royal Blood was nigh[v] extinguiſhed;
Then[w] *Tygranes* the great *Armenian* King,
To take the Government was called in,
Lucullus, Him, (the Roman General)
Vanquiſh'd in fight, and took thoſe Kingdomes all;
Of *Greece* and *Syria* thus the rule did end,
In *Egypt* next, a little time wee'l ſpend.
Firſt *Ptolemy* being dead, his famous Son
Call'd *Philadelphus*, did poſſeſs[x] the Throne.
At *Alexandria* a Library did build,[y]
And with ſeven hundred thouſand Volumes fill'd;

r The next two lines are not in the first edition. s *Seleuchus* next.
t then. u Againſt.

* 1 Macc. i. 20-28; 2 Macc. v. 1-22, and elsewhere. After this, the first edition has, —

By him was ſet up the abomination
I 'th' holy place, which cauſed deſolation:

v quite. w That. x next ſat on.
y The Library at *Alexandria* built,

The ſeventy two Interpreters did ſeek,
They might tranſlate the Bible into Greek.*
His Son was *Evergetes* the laſt Prince,
That valour ſhew'd, virtue, or excellence,
Philopater was *Evergetes* Son,
After *Epiphanes* ſate on the Throne;
Philometor, *Evergetes*[z] again,
And after[a] him, did falſe *Lathurus* reign:
Then *Alexander* in *Lathurus* ſtead,
Next *Auletes*, who cut off *Pompeys* head.
To all theſe names, we *Ptolemy* muſt add, [184]
For ſince the firſt, they ſtill that Title had.
Fair *Cleopatra* next, laſt of that race,
Whom *Julius Cæſar* ſet in Royal place,[b]
She with her Paramour, *Mark Anthony*
Held for a time, the *Egyptian* Monarchy,
Till great *Auguſtus* had with him a fight
At *Actium*, where his Navy's put to flight;[c]
He ſeeing his honour loſt, his Kingdome end,
Did by his Sword his life ſoon after ſend.[d]

* This account, which is that of Archbishop Usher, of the origin of the Greek version of the Old Testament, known as the "Septuagint," is not now credited. The translation was made at Alexandria, and was probably begun as early as about 280 B.C.

[z] then *Evergetes*. [a] next to.

[b] After this, the first edition has, —

Her brother by him, loſt his trayterous head
For *Pompey's* life, then plac'd her in his ſtead.

[c] At *Actium* ſlain, his Navy put to flight.

[d] This and the preceding line are not in the first edition.

His brave *Virago Aſpes* ſets to her Arms,[e]
To take her life, and quit her from all harms;
For 'twas not death nor danger ſhe did dread,
But ſome diſgrace in triumph to be led.
Here ends at laſt the *Grecian* Monarchy,
Which by the Romans had its deſtiny;
Thus King[f] & Kingdomes have their times & dates,
Their ſtandings, overturnings, bounds and fates:
Now up, now down now chief, & then broght under,
The heavn's thus rule, to fil the world[g] with wonder
The *Aſſyrian* Monarchy long time did ſtand,
But yet the *Perſian* got the upper hand;
The *Grecian* them did utterly ſubdue,
And millions were ſubjected unto few:
The *Grecian* longer then the *Perſian* ſtood,
Then came the *Roman* like a raging flood;
And with the torrent of his rapid courſe,
Their Crowns their Titles, riches bears by force.
The firſt was likened to a head of gold.
Next Arms and breaſt of ſilver to behold,
The third, Belly and Thighs of braſs in ſight, [185]
And laſt was Iron, which breaketh all with might;
The ſtone out of the mountain then did riſe,
and ſmote thoſe feet thoſe legs, thoſe arms & thighs
Then gold, ſilver, braſs, Iron and all the[h] ſtore,
Became like Chaff upon the threſhing Floor.*

[e] Then poyſonous Aſpes ſhe ſets unto her Armes, [f] Kings.
[g] earth. [h] that. * Dan. ii. 31-35.

The firſt a Lion, ſecond was a Bear,
The third a Leopard, which four wings did rear;
The laſt more ſtrong and dreadful then the reſt,
Whoſe Iron teeth devoured every Beaſt,
And when he had no appetite to eat,
The reſidue he ſtamped under feet;*
Yet ſhall[i] this Lion, Bear, this Leopard, Ram,
All trembling ſtand before the powerful Lamb.†
With theſe three Monarchyes now have I done,
But how the fourth, their Kingdomes from them won,
And how from ſmall beginnings it did grow,
To fill the world with terrour and with woe;
My tyred brain leavs to ſome better pen,
This task befits not women like to men:
For what is paſt, I bluſh, excuſe to make,
But humbly ſtand, ſome grave reproof to take;
Pardon to crave for errours, is but vain,
The Subject was too high, beyond my ſtrain,
To frame Apology for ſome offence,
Converts our boldneſs into impudence:
This my preſumption ſome now to requite,
Ne ſutor ultra crepidum may write.

The End of the Grecian Monarchy.[j]

* Dan. vii. 3–7. [i] But yet. † Dan. vii. 12–14.
[j] This is not in the first edition.

After ſome dayes of reſt, my reſtleſs heart [186]
To finiſh what's begun, new thoughts impart,
And maugre all reſolves, my fancy wrought
This fourth to th' other three, now might be brought:
Shortneſs of time and inability,
Will force me to a confus'd brevity.
Yet in this Chaos, one ſhall eaſily ſpy
The vaſt Limbs of a mighty Monarchy,
What e're is found amiſs take in good[k] part,
As faults proceeding from my head, not heart.

[k] beſt.

The *Romane Monarchy*, being the fourth and laſt, beginning *Anno Mundi*, 3 2 1 3.

STout *Romulus*, *Romes* founder, and firſt King,
Whom veſtal *Rhea* to the[l] world did bring;
His Father was not *Mars* as ſome devis'd,
But *Æmulus* in Armour all diſguiz'd:
Thus he deceiv'd his *Neece*, ſhe might not know
The double injury he then did do.
Where ſheperds once had Coats & ſheep their folds [187]
Where Swains & ruſtick Peaſants kept[m] their holds,
A City fair did *Romulus* erect,
The Miſtreſs of the World, in each reſpect,
His brother *Rhemus* there by him was ſlain,
For leaping o're the wall with ſome diſdain.
The ſtones at firſt was cemented with blood,
And bloody hath it prov'd, ſince firſt it ſtood.

[l] into th'. [m] made.

This City built and Sacrifices done,
A Form of Government, he next begun;
A hundred Senators he likewiſe choſe,
And with the ſtyle of *Patres*, honoured thoſe,
His City to repleniſh, men he wants,
Great priviledges then to all he grants;
That will within thoſe ſtrong built walls reſide,
And this new gentle Government abide.
Of wives there was ſo great a ſcarcity,
They to their neighbours ſue for a ſupply;
But all diſdain Alliance, then to make,
So *Romulus* was forc'd this courſe to take:
Great ſhews he makes at *Tilt* and *Turnament*,
To ſee theſe ſports, the *Sabins* all are bent.
Their daughters by the Romans then were caught,
Then to recover them a Field was fought;
But in the end, to final peace they come,
And *Sabins* as one people dwelt in *Rome*.
The Romans now more potent 'gin to grow,
And *Fedinates* they wholly overthrow.
But *Romulus* then comes unto his end.
Some feigning to the Gods [a] he did aſcend:
Others the ſeven and thirtyeth of his reign, [188]
Affirm, that by the Senate he was ſlain.

[a] faining ſay, to heav'n.

Numa Pompilius.

NUMA *Pompilius* next choſe they King,[o]
Held for his piety ſome ſacred thing,
To *Janus* he that famous Temple built:
Kept ſhut in peace, ſet[p] ope when blood was ſpilt;
Religious Rites and Cuſtomes inſtituted,
And Prieſts and Flamines likewiſe he deputed,
Their Augurs ſtrange, their geſtures[q] and attire,
And veſtal maids to keep the holy fire.
The Nymph[r] *Ægeria* this to him told,
So to delude the people he was bold:
Forty three years he rul'd with general praiſe,
Accounted for a[s] God in after dayes.

Tullius Hoſtilius.

TULLIUS *Hoſtilius* was third Roman King,
Who Martial diſcipline in uſe did bring;
War with the antient *Albans* he did wage,
This ſtriſe to end ſix brothers did ingage.
Three call'd *Horatii* on the Romans ſide,
And *Curiatii* three *Albans* provide:
The Romans conquer, th' other yield the day,
Yet in[t] their Compact, after falſe they play.

[o] is next choſen King, [p] but. [q] habit,
[r] Goddeſſe. [s] ſome. [t] for.

The Romans ſore incens'd, their General ſlay,
And from old *Alba* fetch the wealth away;
Of Latin Kings this was long ſince the Seat,
But now demoliſhed, to make *Rome* great.
Thirty two years did *Tullus* reign, then dye, [189]
Left *Rome* in wealth, and power ſtill growing high.

Ancus Martius.

NEXT *Ancus Martius* ſits upon the Throne,
Nephew unto *Pompilius* dead and gone;
Rome he inlarg'd, new built again the wall,
Much ſtronger, and more beautiful withal;
A ſtately Bridge he over *Tyber* made,
Of Boats and Oars no more they need the aid.
Fair *Oſtia* he built this Town, it ſtood
Cloſe by the mouth of famous *Tyber* floud,
Twenty four years time of his Royal race,
Then unto death unwillingly gives place.

Tarquinius Priſcus

TARQUIN a Greek at *Corinth* born and bred,
Who from his Country for Sedition fled.

Is entertain'd at *Rome*, and in ſhort time,
By wealth and favour doth to honour climbe;
He after *Martius* death the Kingdome had,
A hundred Senators he more did add.
Wars with the Latins he again renews,
And Nations twelve of *Tuſcany* ſubdues,
To ſuch rude triumphs as young *Rome* then had,
Some State and ſplendor [u] did this *Priſcus* add:
Thirty eight years (this ſtronger born [v]) did reign,
And after all, by *Ancus* Sons was ſlain.

Servius Tullius. [190]

NEXT *Servius Tullius* gets into [w] the Throne,
Aſcends not up By merits of his own,
But by the favour and the ſpecial grace
Of *Tanquil* [x] late Queen, obtains the place.
He ranks the people into each degree,
As wealth had made them of ability;
A general Muſter takes, which by account,
To eighty thouſand Souls then did amount.
Forty four years did *Servius Tullius* reign,
And then by *Tarquin Priſcus* Son was ſlain.

u Much ſtate, and glory,
v Stranger borne.
w ſits upon.
x *Tanaquil*,

Tarquinius Superbus the laſt King of the Romans[y]

TARQUIN the proud, from manners called ſo,
Sat on the Throne, when he had ſlain his Foe.
Sextus his Son did moſt unworthily,
Lucretia force, mirrour of Chaſtity:
She loathed ſo the fact, ſhe loath'd her life,
And ſhed her guiltleſs blood with guilty knife
Her Husband ſore incens'd to quit this wrong,
With *Junius Brutus* roſe, and being ſtrong,
The *Tarquins* they from *Rome* by force[z] expel,
In baniſhment perpetual to dwell;
The Government they change, a new one bring,
And people ſwear ne'r to accept of King.[a]

*An Apology.** [191]

TO finiſh what's begun, was my intent,
My thoughts and my endeavours thereto bent;
Eſſays I many made but ſtill gave out,
The more I mus'd, the more I was in doubt:

y *Roman* King. z with ſpeed.

a After this the first edition has, —
The end of the Roman *Monarchy,*
being the fourth and laſt.

* This Apology is not in the first edition.

The ſubject large my mind and body weak,
With many moe diſcouragements did ſpeak.
All thoughts of further progreſs laid aſide,
Though oft perſwaded, I as oft deny'd,
At length reſolv'd, when many years had paſt,
To proſecute my ſtory to the laſt;
And for the ſame, I hours not few did ſpend,
And weary lines (though lanke) I many pen'd:
But 'fore I could accompliſh my deſire,
My papers fell a prey to th' raging fire.*
And thus my pains (with better things) I loſt,
Which none had cauſe to wail, nor I to boaſt.
No more I'le do ſith I have ſuffer'd wrack,
Although my Monarchies their legs do lack:
Nor matter is't this laſt, the world now ſees,
Hath many Ages been upon his knees.

* See page 40.

A Dialogue between Old *En-gland* and New; concerning their present Troubles, *Anno*, 1642.

New-England.

ALas dear Mother, fairest Queen and best,
With honour, wealth, and peace, happy and blest;
What ails thee hang thy head, & cross thine arms?
And sit i'th' dust, to sigh these sad alarms?
What deluge of new woes thus over-whelme
The glories of thy ever famous Realme?
What means this wailing tone, this mournful[b] guise?
Ah, tell thy daughter, she may sympathize.

Old England.

Art ignorant indeed of these my woes?
Or must my forced tongue these griefs disclose?
And must myself dissect my tatter'd state,
Which 'mazed Christendome stands wondring at?

[b] mourning.

And thou a Child, a Limbe, and doſt not feel
My fainting weakned body now to reel?
This Phyſick purging potion, I have taken, [193]
Will bring conſumption, or an Ague quaking,
Unleſs ſome Cordial, thou fetch from high,
Which preſent help may eaſe my[c] malady.
If I deceaſe, doſt think thou ſhalt ſurvive?
Or by my waſting ſtate doſt think to thrive?
Then weigh our caſe, if't be not juſtly ſad;
Let me lament alone, while thou art glad.

New-England.

And thus (alas) your ſtate you much deplore
In general terms, but will not ſay wherefore:
What medicine ſhall I ſeek to cure this woe,
If th' wound[d] ſo dangerous I may not know.*
But you perhaps, would have me gheſs it out:
What hath ſome *Hengiſt* like that *Saxon* ſtout
By fraud or force uſurp'd thy flowring crown,
Or[e] by tempeſtuous warrs thy fields trod down?
Or hath *Canutus*, that brave valiant *Dane*
The Regal peacefull Scepter from thee tane?
Or is't a *Norman*, whoſe victorious hand
With Engliſh blood bedews thy conquered land?
Or is't Inteſtine warrs that thus offend?
Do *Maud* and *Stephen* for the crown contend?

[c] this.
[d] wound's.
* A question in the first edition.
[e] And.

Do Barons rife and fide againft their King,
And call in foraign aid to help the thing?
Muft *Edward* be depos'd? or is't the hour
That fecond *Richard* muft be clapt i'th tower?
Or is't the fatal jarre, again begun
That from the red white pricking rofes fprung?
Muft *Richmonds* aid, the Nobles now implore? [194]
To come and break the Tufhes of the Boar,*
If none of thefe dear Mother, what's your woe?
Pray do you/ fear *Spains* bragging *Armado*?
Doth your Allye, fair *France*, confpire your wrack,
Or do the *Scots* play falfe, behind your back?
Doth *Holland* quit you ill for all your love?
Whence is the ftorm from Earth or Heaven above?
Is't drought, is't famine, or is't peftilence?
Doft feel the fmart, or fear the Confequence?
Your humble Child intreats you, fhew your grief,
Though Arms, nor Purfe fhe hath for your relief,
Such is her poverty: yet fhall be found
A Suppliant for your help, as fhe is bound.

* Richard III. He is called the "boar" several times in Shakespeare's tragedy of Richard III. "Richard's armorial supporters were white boars. A white boar was also his favourite badge. In his letter from York he orders "four standards of sarcenet and thirteen gonfanons of fustian, with boars." Richard's favourite badge of cognizance was worn by the higher order of his partisans appendant to a collar of roses and suns." — KNIGHT'S Shakspere: Histories, vol. ii. p. 239.

/ not.

Old England.

I muſt confeſs ſome of thoſe ſores you name,
My beauteous body at this preſent maime;
But forreign ſoe, nor feigned friend I fear,
For they have work enough (thou knowſt) elſewhere
Nor is it *Alcies* Son,* nor[g] *Henryes* daughter; †
Whoſe proud contention cauſe this ſlaughter,
Nor Nobles ſiding, to make *John* no King,
French Jews ‡ unjuſtly to the Crown to bring;
No *Edward*, *Richard*, to loſe rule and life,
Nor no *Lancaſtrians* to renew old ſtrife:
No Duke of *York*, nor Earl of *March* to ſoyle
Their hands in kindreds blood whom they did foil
No crafty Tyrant now uſurps the Seat,
Who Nephews ſlew that ſo he might be great;[h]
No need of *Tudor*,[i] Roſes to unite, [195]
None knows which is the red, or which the white;
Spains braving Fleet, a ſecond time is ſunk,
France knows how oft[j] my fury ſhe hath drunk:

* Stephen, son of Stephen of Blois, Count Palatine of Champagne, and Adela, fourth daughter of William the Conqueror. Her name is sometimes given as Adelicia, Adeliza, or Alice; and the contraction from one of these forms into Alcie would be simple.

[g] and.

† The Empress Matilda, or Maud, the daughter of Henry I. See page 331, last line.

‡ A misprint for "*Lewis*" in the first edition.

[h] No Crook-backt Tyrant, now uſurps the Seat,
Whoſe tearing tusks did wound, and kill, and threat:

[i] *Teder*. [j] of.

By *Edward* third, and *Henry* fifth of fame,
Her Lillies in mine Arms avouch the ſame.
My Siſter *Scotland* hurts me now no more,
Though ſhe hath been injurious heretofore;
What *Holland* is I am in ſome ſuſpence?
But truſt not much unto his excellence.
For wants, ſure ſome I feel, but more I fear,
And for the Peſtilence, who knows how near;
Famine and Plague, two Siſters of the Sword,
Deſtruction to a Land, doth ſoon afford:
They're for my puniſhment ordain'd on high,
Unleſs our [k] tears prevent it ſpeedily.*
But yet I Anſwer not what you demand,
To ſhew the grievance of my troubled Land?
Before I tell th' Effect, I'le ſhew the Cauſe
Which are my ſins the breach of ſacred Laws,
Idolatry ſupplanter of a Nation,
With fooliſh Superſtitious Adoration,
Are [l] lik'd and countenanc'd by men of might,
The Goſpel troden [m] down and hath no right:
Church Offices were [n] ſold and bought for gain,
That Pope had hope to find, *Rome* here again,
For Oaths and Blaſphemies, did ever Ear,
From *Belzebub* himſelf ſuch language hear;
What ſcorning of the Saints of the moſt high?
What injuries did daily on them lye?

[k] thy. * The Great Plague came in 1665, about twenty years after.
[l] And. [m] is trod. [n] are.

What falſe reports, what nick-names did they take [196]
Not for their own, but for their Maſters ſake?
And thou poor ſoul, wert jeer'd among the reſt,
Thy flying for the truth was[o] made a jeſt.
For Sabbath-breaking, and for drunkenneſs,
Did ever land profaneſs more expreſs?
From crying blood yet cleanſed am not I,
Martyres and others, dying cauſeleſly.
How many princely heads on blocks laid down
For nought but title to a fading crown?
'Mongſt all the crueltyes by great ones done[p]
Of *Edwards* youths,[q] and *Clarence* hapleſs ſon,
O *Jane* why didſt thou dye in flowring prime?
Becauſe of royal ſtem, that was thy crime.
For bribery Adultery and lyes,[r]
Where is the nation, I can't parallize.
With uſury, extortion and oppreſſion,
Theſe be the *Hydraes* of my ſtout tranſgreſſion.
Theſe be the bitter fountains, heads and roots,
Whence flow'd the ſource, the ſprigs, the boughs & fruits
Of more then thou canſt hear or I relate,
That with high hand I ſtill did perpetrate:
For theſe were threatned the wofull day,
I mockt the Preachers, put it far away;
The Sermons yet upon Record do ſtand
That cri'd deſtruction to my wicked land:

[o] I. [p] which I have done, [q] Oh, *Edwards* Babes,
[r] For Bribery, *Adultery*, for Thefts, and Lyes,

I then believ'd not, now I feel and ſee,
The plague of ſtubborn incredulity.[s]
Some loſt their livings, ſome in priſon pent,
Some fin'd, from houſe &[t] friends to exile went.
Their ſilent tongues to heaven did vengeance cry, [197]
Who ſaw their wrongs, & hath judg'd righteouſly[u]
And will repay it ſeven-fold in my lap:
This is fore-runner of my Afterclap.
Nor took I warning by my neighbours falls,
I ſaw ſad *Germanyes* diſmantled walls,
I ſaw her people famiſh'd, Nobles ſlain,
Her fruitfull land, a barren Heath remain.
I ſaw unmov'd, her Armyes foil'd and fled,
VVives forc'd, babes toſs'd, her houſes calcined.
I ſaw ſtrong *Rochel* yielded[v] to her Foe,
Thouſands of ſtarved Chriſtians there alſo.
I ſaw poor *Ireland* bleeding out her laſt,
Such crueltyes[w] as all reports have paſt; *
Mine heart obdurate ſtood not yet agaſt.

[s] Instead of this and the preceding line, the first edition has, —

These Prophets mouthes (alas the while) was ſtopt,
Unworthily, ſome backs whipt, and eares cropt;
Their reverent cheeks did beare the glorious markes
Of ſtinking, ſtigmatizing, Romiſh Clerkes;

referring probably to the persecutions of Prynne, Bastwick, and Burton. Prynne himself says of the letters "S. L." branded on his cheeks, —

"Bearing LAVD'S STAMPS on my cheeks, I retire,
Triumphing, God's sweet Sacrifice, by Fire."

[t] Some groſſely ſin'd, from.

[u] Who heard their cauſe, and wrongs judg'd righteouſly,

[v] yielding. [w] cruelty. * See page 164 and note.

Now ſip I of that cup, and juſt't may be
The bottome dreggs reſerved are for me.

New-England.

To all you've ſaid, ſad Mother I aſſent,
Your fearfull ſins great cauſe there's to lament,
My guilty hands in part, hold up with you,
A Sharer in your puniſhment's my due.
But all you ſay amounts to this effect,
Not what you feel, but what you do expect,
Pray in plain terms, what is your preſent grief?
Then let's joyn heads & hearts [x] for your relief.

Old England. [198]

Well to the matter then, there's grown of late
'Twixt King and Peers a Queſtion of State,
Which is the chief, the Law, or elſe the King.
One ſaid,[y] it's he, the other no ſuch thing.
'Tis ſaid, my beter part in Parliament [z]
To eaſe my groaning Land, ſhew'd [a] their intent,
To cruſh the proud, and right to each man deal,
To help the Church, and ſtay the Common-weal.
So many Obſtacles came [b] in their way,
As puts me to a ſtand what I ſhould ſay;

[x] hands. [y] ſaith. [z] My better part in Court of Parliament,
[a] ſhew. [b] comes.

Old cuſtomes, new Prerogatives ſtood on,
Had they not held Law faſt, all had been gone:
Which by their prudence ſtood them in ſuch ſtead
They took high *Strafford* lower by the head.
And to their *Laud* be't ſpoke, they held i'th tower
All *Englands* Metropolitane that hour; *
This done, an act they would have paſſed fain,
No Prelate ſhould his Biſhoprick retain;
Here tugg'd they hard (indeed,) for all men ſaw
This muſt be done by Goſpel, not by Law.
Next the Militia they urged ſore,
This was deny'd, (I need not ſay wherefore)
The King diſpleas'd at *York*, himſelf abſents,
They humbly beg return, ſhew their intents;
The writing, printing, poſting too and fro,
Shews all was done, I'le therefore let it go.
But now I come to ſpeak of my diſaſter,
Contention grown, 'twixt Subjects & their Maſter;
They worded it ſo long, they fell to blows, [199]
That thouſands lay on heaps, here bleeds my woes,
I that no wars ſo many years have known,
Am now deſtroy'd and ſlaught'red by mine own;
But could the Field alone this ſtrife [c] decide,
One Battel two or three I might abide:

* A play upon words is not often to be met with in the writings of our grave author. Archbiſhop Laud was committed to the Tower Feb. 26, 1641, and was confined there until his execution. His trial took place in March, 1644. He was beheaded Jan. 10, 1645.

[c] cauſe.

But these may be beginnings of more woe
Who knows, but this may be my overthrow.[d]
Oh pity me in this sad perturbation,
My plundred Towns, my houses devastation,
My weeping[e] Virgins and my young men slain;
My wealthy trading fall'n, my dearth of grain,
The seed-times come, but ploughman hath no hope
Because he knows not who shall inn his Crop:
The poor they want their pay, their children bread,
Their woful Mothers tears unpittied,
If any pity in thy heart remain,
Or any child-like love thou dost retain,
For my relief, do what there lyes in thee,
And recompence that good I've done to thee.[f]

New England.

Dear Mother cease complaints & wipe your eyes,
Shake off your dust, chear up, and now arise,
You are my Mother Nurse, and I[g] your flesh,
Your sunken bowels gladly would refresh,
Your griefs I pity, but soon hope to see,
Out of your troubles much good fruit to be;

[d] Who knows, the worst, the best may overthrow;
Religion, Gospell, here lies at the stake,
Pray now dear child, for sacred *Zions* sake,

[e] ravisht.

[f] For my relief now use thy utmost skill,
And recompence me good, for all my ill.

[g] nurse, I once.

To ſee thoſe latter dayes of hop'd for good,
Though now beclouded all with tears and blood:[h]
After dark Popery the day did clear,
But now the Sun in's brightneſs ſhall appear.
Bleſt be the Nobles of thy noble Land,
With ventur'd lives for Truths defence that ſtand.
Bleſt be thy Commons, who for common good,
And thy infringed Laws have boldly ſtood.
Bleſt be thy Counties, who did[i] aid thee ſtill,
With hearts and States to teſtifie their will.
Bleſt be thy Preachers, who do chear thee on,
O cry the Sword of God, and *Gideon*;*
And ſhall I not on them wiſh *Mero*'s curſe,
That help thee not with prayers, Arms and purſe?†
And for my ſelf let miſeries abound,
If mindleſs of thy State I e're be found.
Theſe are the dayes the Churches foes to cruſh,
To root out Popelings[j] head, tail, branch and ruſh;
Let's bring *Baals* veſtments forth[k] to make a fire,
Their Mytires, Surplices, and all their Tire,
Copes, Rotchets, Croſſiers, and ſuch empty traſh,[l]
And let their Names conſume, but let the flaſh

[h] Your griefs I pity much, but ſhould do wrong,
To weep for that we both have pray'd for long,
To ſee theſe latter dayes of hop'd for good,
That Right may have its right, though't be with blood;

[i] which do. * Judg. vii. 18, 20.

† "Curse ye Meroz, said the angel of the LORD, curse ye bitterly the inhabitants thereof; because they came not to the help of the LORD, to the help of the LORD against the mighty."—JUDG. v. 23.

[j] Prelates. [k] out. [l] ſuch traſh,

Light Chriftendome, and all the world to fee
We hate *Romes* whore, with all her trumpery.
Go on brave *Effex* with a Loyal heart,
Not falfe to King, nor to the better part;[m]
But thofe that hurt his people and his Crown,
As duty binds, expel and tread them down.[n]
And ye brave Nobles chafe away all fear,
And to this hopeful[o] Caufe clofely adhere;
O Mother can you weep, and have fuch Peers,
When they are gone, then drown your felf in tears
If now you weep fo much, that then no more [201]
The briny Ocean will o'reflow your fhore.
Thefe, thefe are they I truft, with *Charles* our King,
Out of all mifts fuch glorious dayes fhall[p] bring;
That dazled eyes beholding much fhall wonder
At that thy fetled peace, thy wealth and fplendor.
Thy Church and weal eftablifh'd in fuch manner,
That all fhall joy, that thou difplay'dft thy Banner;
And difcipline erected fo I truft,
That nurfing Kings fhall come and lick thy duft:
Then Juftice fhall in all thy Courts take place,
Without refpect of perfon,[q] or of cafe;
Then Bribes fhall ceafe, & Suits fhall not ftick long
Patience and purfe of Clients oft[r] to wrong:

[m] Go on brave *Effex*, fhew whofe fon thou art,
Not falfe to King, nor Countrey in thy heart,

[n] By force expell, deftroy, and tread them down:
Let Gaoles be fill'd with th' remnant of that pack,
And fturdy *Tyburn* loaded till it crack,

[o] bleffed. [p] will. [q] perfons. [r] for.

Then high Commiſſions ſhall fall to decay,
And Purſivants, and Catchpoles want their pay.
So ſhall thy happy Nation ever flouriſh,
When truth & righteouſnes they thus ſhall nouriſh
When thus in peace, thine Armies brave ſend out,
To ſack proud *Rome*, and all her Vaſſals rout;
There let thy Name, thy fame, and glory[s] ſhine,
As did thine Anceſtors in *Paleſtine*:
And let her ſpoyls full pay, with Intereſt be,
Of what unjuſtly once ſhe poll'd from thee.
Of all the woes thou canſt, let her be ſped,
And on her pour[t] the vengeance threatned;
Bring forth the Beaſt that rul'd the World with's beck,
And tear his fleſh, & ſet your feet on's neck;
And make his filthy Den ſo deſolate,
To th' ſtoniſhment of all that knew his ſtate:
This done with brandiſh'd Swords to *Turky* goe, [202]
For then what is't, but Engliſh blades dare do,
And lay her waſte for ſo's the ſacred Doom,
And do to *Gog* as thou haſt done to *Rome.*
Oh *Abraham*'s ſeed lift up your heads on high,
For ſure the day of your Redemption's nigh;
The Scales ſhall fall from your long blinded eyes,
And him you ſhall adore who now deſpiſe,
Then fulneſs of the Nations in ſhall flow,
And Jew and Gentile to one worſhip go;
Then follows dayes of happineſs and reſt;
Whoſe lot doth fall, to live therein is bleſt:

[s] thy valour. [t] Execute toth' full.

No Canaanite ſhall then be found i'th' Land,
And holineſs on horſes bells ſhall ſtand.*
If this make way thereto, then ſigh no more,
But if at all, thou didſt not ſee't before;
Farewel dear Mother, righteſt cauſe[a] prevail,
And in a while, you'le tell another tale.

* "In that day shall there be upon the bells of the horses, HOLINESS UNTO THE LORD; . . . and in that day there shall be no more the Canaanite in the house of the Lord of hosts." — ZECH. xiv. 20, 21.

[a] Parliament.

An Elegie upon that Honourable and renowned Knight *Sir Philip Sidney*, who was untimely ſlain at the Siege of *Zutphen*, *Anno*, 1 5 8 6.* [203]

WHen *England* did enjoy her Halſion dayes,
Her noble *Sidney* wore the Crown of Bayes;
As well an honour to our *Britiſh* Land,
As ſhe that ſway'd the Scepter with her hand;

* So many changes were made in this poem in the second edition, and so much of the original was omitted, that it is here given entire as it appeared in the first edition.

An Elegie upon that Honourable and renowned Knight,
Sir *Philip Sidney*, who was untimely ſlaine at the Seige of *Zutphon*,
Anno 1586.

By *A. B.* in the yeare, 1638.

WHen *England* did injoy her Halſion dayes,
Her noble *Sidney* wore the Crown of Bayes;
No leſſe an Honour to our *Britiſh* Land,
Then ſhe that ſway'd the Scepter with her hand:

Mars and *Minerva* did in one agree,
Of Arms and Arts he ſhould a pattern be,
Calliope with *Terpſichore* did ſing,
Of Poeſie, and of muſick, he was King;
His Rhetorick ſtruck *Polimina* dead,
His Eloquence made *Mercury* wax red;
His *Logick* from *Euterpe* won the Crown,
More worth was his then *Clio* could ſet down.
Thalia and *Melpomene* ſay truth,
(Witneſs *Arcadia* penned in his youth,)
Are not his tragick Comedies ſo acted,
As if your ninefold wit had been compacted.

Mars and *Minerva* did in one agree,
Of Armes, and Arts, thou ſhould'ſt a patterne be.
Calliope with *Terpſechor* did ſing,
Of Poeſie, and of Muſick thou wert King;
Thy Rhethorick it ſtruck *Polimnia* dead,
Thine Eloquence made *Mercury* wax red;
Thy Logick from *Euterpe* won the Crown,
More worth was thine, then *Clio* could ſet down.
Thalia, and *Melpomene*, ſay th' truth,
(Witneſſe *Arcadia*, penn'd in his youth)
Are not his Tragick Comedies ſo acted,
As if your nine-fold wit had been compacted;
To ſhew the world, they never ſaw before,
That this one Volumne ſhould exhauſt your ſtore.
I praiſe thee not for this, it is unfit,
This was thy ſhame, O miracle of wit:
Yet doth thy ſhame (with all) purchaſe renown,
What doe thy vertues then? Oh, honours crown!
In all records, thy Name I ever ſee,
Put with an Epithet of dignity;
Which ſhewes, thy worth was great, thine honour ſuch,
The love thy Country ought thee, was as much.

To ſhew the world, they never ſaw before,
That this one Volume ſhould exhauſt your ſtore;
His wiſer dayes condemn'd his witty works,
Who knows the ſpels that in his Rhetorick lurks,
But ſome inſatuate fools ſoon caught therein, [204]
Fond *Cupids* Dame had never ſuch a gin,
Which makes ſeverer eyes but ſlight that ſtory,
And men of moroſe minds envy his glory:
But he's a Beetle-head that can't deſcry
A world of wealth within that rubbiſh lye,
And doth his name, his work, his honour wrong,
The brave refiner of our Britiſh tongue,

Let then, none diſ-allow of theſe my ſtraines,
Which have the ſelf-ſame blood yet in my veines; *
Who honours thee for what was honourable,
But leaves the reſt, as moſt unprofitable:
Thy wiſer dayes, condemn'd thy witty works,
Who knowes the Spels that in thy Rethorick lurks?
But ſome infatuate fooles ſoone caught therein,
Found *Cupids* Dam, had never ſuch a Gin;
Which makes ſeverer eyes but ſcorn thy Story,
And modeſt Maids, and Wives, bluſh at thy glory;
Yet, he's a beetle head, that cann't diſcry
A world of treaſure, in that rubbiſh lye;
And doth thy ſelfe, thy worke, and honour wrong,
(O brave Refiner of our *Brittiſh* Tongue:)
That ſees not learning, valour, and morality,
Juſtice, friendſhip, and kind hoſpitality;
Yea, and Divinity within thy Book,
Such were prejudicate, and did not look:
But to ſay truth, thy worth I ſhall but ſtaine,
Thy fame, and praiſe, is farre beyond my ſtraine;

---

* See page 347, line 10, and Introduction.

That fees not learning, valour and morality,
Juftice, friendfhip, and kind hofpitality,
Yea and Divinity within his book,
Such were prejudicate, and did not look.
In all Records his name I ever fee
Put with an Epithite of dignity,
Which fhews his worth was great, his honour fuch,
The love his Country ought him, was as much.
Then let none difallow of thefe my ftraines
Whilft Englifh blood yet runs within my veins.
O brave *Achilles*, I wifh fome *Homer* would
Engrave in Marble, with Characters of gold
The valiant feats thou didft on *Flanders* coaft,
Which at this day fair *Belgia* may boaft.
The more I fay, the more thy worth I ftain,
Thy fame and praife is far beyond my ftrain.
O *Zutphen, Zutphen* that moft fatal City
Made famous by thy death, much more the pity:
Ah! in his blooming prime death pluckt this rofe
E're he was ripe, his thread cut *Atropos*.

Yet great *Auguftus* was content (we know)
To be faluted by a filly Crow;
Then let fuch Crowes as I, thy praifes fing,
A Crow's a Crow, and *Cæfar* is a King.
O brave *Achilles*, I wifh fome *Homer* would
Engrave on Marble, in characters of Gold,
What famous feats thou didft, on *Flanders* coaft,
Of which, this day, faire *Belgia* doth boaft.
O *Zutphon, Zutphon*, that moft fatall City,
Made famous by thy fall, much more's the pitty:

Thus man is born to dye, and dead is he,
Brave *Hector*, by the walls of *Troy* we ſee.
O who was near thee but did ſore repine [205]
He reſcued not with life that life of thine:
But yet impartial Fates this boon did give,
Though *Sidney* di'd his valiant name ſhould live:
And live it doth in ſpight of death through fame,
Thus being overcome, he overcame.
Where is that envious tongue, but can afford
Of this our noble *Scipio* ſome good word.
Great *Bartas* this unto thy praiſe adds more,
In ſad ſweet verſe, thou didſt his death deplore.
And *Phœnix Spencer* doth unto his life,
His death preſent in fable to his wife.
Stella the fair, whoſe ſtreams from Conduits fell
For the ſad loſs of her dear *Aſtrophel*.*

Ah, in his blooming prime, death pluckt this Roſe,
E're he was ripe; his thred cut *Atropos*.
Thus man is borne to dye, and dead is he,
Brave *Hector* by the walls of *Troy*, we ſee:
Oh, who was neare thee, but did ſore repine;
He reſcued not with life, that life of thine.
But yet impartiall Death this Boone did give,
Though *Sidney* dy'd, his valiant name ſhould live;
And live it doth, in ſpight of death, through fame,
Thus being over-come, he over-came.

* "Aſtrophel. A Paſtorall Elegie upon the Death of the moſt noble and valorous Knight, Sir Philip Sidney. Dedicated to the moſt beautifull and vertuous Ladie, the Counteſſe of Eſſex." Lady Sidney, three years after her husband's death, married the Earl of Essex, Queen Elizabeth's celebrated favorite. Child's Spenser. Boston. 1855. vol. iv. p. 415.

Fain would I ſhew how he fames paths did tread,
But now into ſuch Lab'rinths I am lead,
VVith endleſs turnes, the way I find not out,
How to perſiſt my Muſe is more in doubt;
VVhich makes me now with *Silveſter* confeſs,
But *Sidney*'s Muſe can ſing his worthineſs.*

Where is that envious tongue, but can afford,
Of this our noble *Scipio* ſome good word?
Noble *Bartas*, this to thy praiſe adds more,
In ſad, ſweet verſe, thou didſt his death deplore;
Illuſtrious *Stella*. thou didſt thine full well,
If thine aſpect was milde to *Aſtrophell;*
I feare thou wert a Commet, did portend
Such prince as he, his race ſhould ſhortly end:
If ſuch Stars as theſe, ſad preſages be,
I wiſh no more ſuch Blazers we may ſee;
But thou art gone, ſuch Meteors never laſt,
And as thy beauty, ſo thy name would waſt,
But that it is record by *Philips* hand,
That ſuch an omen once was in our land,
O Princely *Philip*, rather *Alexander*,
Who wert of honours band, the chief Commander.
How could that *Stella*, ſo confine thy will?
To wait till ſhe, her influence diſtill,
I rather judg'd thee of his mind that wept,
To be within the bounds of one world kept.†
But *Omphala*, ſet *Hercules* to ſpin,
And *Mars* himſelf was ta'n by *Venus* gin;
Then wonder leſſe, if warlike *Philip* yield
When ſuch a *Hero* ſhoots him out o' th' field,

---

* "*Although I know none, but a* Sidney's *Muſe,*
Worthy to ſing a Sidney's *Worthineſſe:*"

Dedication to 'An Elegiac Epiſtle on the deceaſe of Sir William Sidney, by Joshua Sylvester.

† See page 288.

The Muſes aid I crav'd, they had no will
To give to their Detractor any quill,
VVith high diſdain, they ſaid they gave no more,
Since *Sidney* had exhauſted all their ſtore.
They took from me the ſcribling pen I had,
(I to be eas'd of ſuch a task was glad)

Yet this preheminence thou haſt above,
That thine was true, but theirs adult'rate love.
Fain would I ſhew. how thou fame's path didſt tread,
But now into ſuch Lab'rinths am I led
With endleſſe turnes, the way I find not out,
For to perſiſt, my muſe is more in doubt:
Calls me ambitious fool, that durſt aſpire,
Enough for me to look, and ſo admire.
And makes me now with *Sylveſter* confeſſe,
But *Sydney*'s Muſe, can ſing his worthineſſe.
Too late my errour ſee, that durſt preſume
To fix my faltring lines upon his tomb:
Which are in worth, as far ſhort of his due.
As *Vulcan* is, of *Venus* native hue.
Goodwill, did make my head-long pen to run,
Like unwiſe *Phaeton* his ill guided ſonne.
Till taught to's coſt, for his too haſty hand,
He left that charge by *Phœbus* to be man'd:
So proudly fooliſh I, with *Phaeton* ſtrive.
Fame's flaming Chariot for to drive.
Till terrour-ſtruck for my too weighty charge.
I leave't in brief, *Apollo* do't at large.
Apollo laught to patch up what's begun,
He bad me drive, and he would hold the Sun;
Better my hap, then was his darlings fate,
For dear regard he had of *Sydney's* ſtate,
Who in his Deity, had ſo deep ſhare,
That thoſe that name his fame, he needs muſt ſpare,
He promis'd much, but th' muſes had no will,
To give to their detractor any quill.

Then to reveng this wrong, themſelves engage,
And drave me from *Parnaſſus* in a rage.
Then wonder not if I no better ſped,
Since I the Muſes thus have injured.
I penſive for my fault, ſate down, and then [206]
Errata through their leave, threw me my pen,
My Poem to conclude, two lines they deign
Which writ, ſhe bad return't to them again;
So *Sidneys* fame I leave to *Englands* Rolls,
His bones do lie interr'd in ſtately *Pauls.*

His Epitaph.

Here lies in fame under this ſtone,
Philip and *Alexander* both in one;

> With high diſdain, they ſaid they gave no more,
> Since *Sydney* had exhauſted all their ſtore,
> That this contempt it did the more perplex,
> In being done by one of their own ſex;
> They took from me, the ſcribling pen I had,
> I to be eas'd of ſuch a taſk was glad.
> For to revenge his wrong, themſelves ingage,
> And drave me from *Parnaſſus* in a rage,
> Not becauſe, ſweet *Sydney's* fame was not dear,
> But I had blemiſh'd theirs, to make 't appear:
> I penſive for my fault, ſat down, and then,
> *Errata*, through their leave threw me my pen,
> For to conclude my poem two lines they daigne,
> Which writ, ſhe bad return 't to them again.
> So *Sydney's* fame, I leave to *England's* Rolls,
> His bones do lie interr'd in ſtately *Pauls.*
>
> *His Epitaph.*
>
> *Here lies intomb'd in fame, under this ſtone,*
> Philip *and* Alexander *both in one.*

Heir to the Muſes, the Son of *Mars* in Truth,
Learning, Valour, Wiſdome, all in virtuous youth,
His praiſe is much, this ſhall ſuffice my pen,
That *Sidney* dy'd 'mong moſt renown'd of men.

Heire to the Muſes, the Son of Mars *in truth,*
Learning, valour, beauty, all in virtuous youth:
His praiſe is much, this ſhall ſuffice my pen.
That Sidney *dy'd the quinteſſence of men.*

In honour of *Du Bartas*, 1641.*

Among the happy wits this age hath ſhown,
Great, dear, ſweet *Bartas* thou art matchleſs known;
My raviſh'd Eyes and heart with faltering tongue,
In humble wiſe have vow'd their ſervice long,
But knowing th' task ſo great, & ſtrength but ſmall,
Gave o're the work before begun withal,
My dazled ſight of late review'd thy lines,
Where Art, and more then Art, in nature ſhines,
Reflection from their beaming Altitude,
Did thaw my frozen hearts ingratitude;
Which Rayes darting upon ſome richer ground, [207]
Had cauſed flours and fruits ſoon to abound;
But barren I my Daſey here do bring,
A homely flour in this my latter Spring,
If Summer, or my Autumn age do yield,
Flours, fruits, in Garden, Orchard, or in Field,
They ſhall be conſecrated in my Verſe,
And proſtrate offered at great *Bartas* Herſe;

* For an account of Du Bartas, see Introduction.

My muſe unto a Child I may[a] compare,
Who ſees the riches of ſome famous Fair,
He feeds his Eyes, but underſtanding lacks
To comprehend the worth of all thoſe knacks:
The glittering plate and Jewels he admires,
The Hats and Fans, the Plumes and Ladies tires,
And thouſand times his mazed mind doth wiſh
Some part (at leaſt) of that brave wealth was his,
But ſeeing empty wiſhes nought obtain,
At night turns to his Mothers cot again,
And tells her tales, (his full heart over glad)
Of all the glorious ſights his Eyes have had:
But finds too ſoon his want of Eloquence,
The ſilly pratler ſpeaks no word of ſenſe;
But ſeeing utterance fail his great deſires,
Sits down in ſilence, deeply he admires:
Thus weak brain'd I, reading thy lofty ſtile,
Thy profound learning, viewing other while;
Thy Art in natural Philoſophy,
Thy Saint like mind in grave Divinity;
Thy piercing skill in high Aſtronomy,
And curious inſight in Anatomy:
Thy Phyſick, muſick and ſtate policy, [208]
Valour in warr, in peace good husbandry.
Sure lib'ral Nature did with Art not ſmall,
In all the arts make thee moſt liberal.
A thouſand thouſand times my ſenſleſs ſences
Moveleſs ſtand charm'd by thy ſweet influences;

[a] I fitly may.

More ſenſleſs then the ſtones to *Amphions* Lute,
Mine eyes are ſightleſs, and my tongue is mute,
My full aſtoniſh'd heart doth pant to break,
Through grief it wants a faculty to ſpeak:
Volleyes of praiſes could I eccho then,
Had I an Angels voice, or *Bartas* pen:
But wiſhes can't accompliſh my deſire,
Pardon if I adore, when I admire.
O France thou did'ſt in him more glory gain
Then in thy *Martel*, *Pipin*, *Charlemain*,
Then in St. *Lewes*, or thy laſt *Henry* Great,
Who tam'd his foes in warrs, in bloud [b] and ſweat.
Thy fame is ſpread as far, I dare be bold,
In all the Zones, the temp'rate, hot and cold.
Their Trophies were but heaps of wounded ſlain,
Thine, the quinteſſence of an heroick brain.
The oaken Garland ought to deck their brows,
Immortal Bayes to thee all men allows.
VVho in thy tryumphs never won by wrongs,
Lead'ſt millions chaind by eyes, by ears, by tongues
Oft have I wondred at the hand of heaven,
In giving one what would have ſerved ſeven.
If e're this golden gift was ſhowr'd on any,
Thy double portion would have ſerved many.
Unto each man his riches is aſſign'd [209]
Of Name, of State, of Body and of Mind:
Thou hadſt thy part of all, but of the laſt,
O pregnant brain, O comprehenſion vaſt:

[b] foes, in bloud, in skarres.

Thy haughty Stile and rapted wit ſublime
All ages wondring at, ſhall never climb.
Thy ſacred works are not for imitation,
But Monuments to future Admiration.
Thus *Bartas* fame ſhall laſt while ſtarrs do ſtand,
And whilſt there's Air or Fire, or Sea or Land.
But leaſt mine ignorance ſhould do thee wrong,
To celebrate thy merits in my Song.
I'le leave thy praiſe to thoſe ſhall do thee right,
Good will, not skill, did cauſe me bring my Mite.

His Epitaph.

Here lyes the Pearle of France, Parnaſſus *Glory*;
The World rejoyc'd at's birth, at's death was ſorry.
Art and Nature joyn'd, by heavens high decree
Now ſhew'd what once they ought, Humanity:
And Natures Law, had it been revocable
To reſcue him from death, Art had been able.
But Nature vanquiſh'd Art, ſo Bartas *dy'd*;
But Fame out-living both, he is reviv'd.

In Honour of that High and Mighty Princeſs [210]

Queen Elizabeth

OF HAPPY MEMORY.[a]

The Proeme.

ALthough great Queen thou now in ſilence lye
Yet thy loud Herald Fame doth to the sky
Thy wondrous worth proclaim in every Clime,
And ſo hath vow'd while there is world or time.
So great's thy glory and thine excellence,
The ſound thereof rapts[b] every humane ſence,
That men account it no impiety,
To ſay thou wert a fleſhly Diety:
Thouſands bring offerings (though out of date)
Thy world of honours to accumulate,
'Mongſt hundred Hecatombs of roaring verſe,
Mine bleating ſtands before thy royal Herſe.
Thou never didſt nor canſt thou now diſdain
T' accept the tribute of a loyal brain.

[a] of moſt happy memory. [b] raps.

Thy clemency did yerſt eſteem as much
The acclamations of the poor as rich,
Which makes me deem my rudeneſs is no wrong,
Though I reſound thy praiſes [c] 'mongſt the throng.

The Poem. [211]

No *Phœnix* pen, nor *Spencers* poetry,
No *Speeds* * nor *Cambdens* † learned Hiſtory,
Elizahs works, warrs, praiſe, can e're compact,
The World's the Theatre where ſhe did act.
No memoryes nor volumes can contain
The 'leven [d] Olympiads of her happy reign:
Who was ſo good, ſo juſt, ſo learn'd ſo wiſe,
From all the Kings on earth ſhe won the prize.

[c] greatneſſe. [d] nine.

* "*THE* HISTORIE OF GREAT BRITAINE VNDER THE CONQVESTS OF THE ROMANS, SAXONS, DANES and NORMANS. Their Originals, Manners, Habits, VVarres, Coines, and Seales: with the Succeſsions, Liues, Acts, and Iſſues of the ENGLISH MONARCHS, from IVLIVS CÆSAR, to our moſt gracious Soueraigne, KING IAMES." "By IOHN SPEED." London, 1623.

† "ANNALES RERVM ANGLICARVM ET HIBERNICARVM, REGNANTE ELIZABETHA, *Ad* ANNVM SALVTIS M.D.LXXXIX. GVILIELMO CAMDENO AVTHORE. LONDINI, M.DC.XV."

"ANNALES OR, THE HISTORY OF THE MOST RENOWNED and Victorious Princeſſe ELIZABETH, *Late Queen of England. Contayning all the Important and Remarkable Paſsages of State, both at Home and Abroad, during her Long and Proſperous Reigne. Written in Latin by the learned Mr* WILLIAM CAMDEN. *Tranſlated into Engliſh by R. N. Gent. Together with divers Additions of the Authors never before publiſhed. The third Edition.*" London, 1635.

Nor ſay I more then duly is her due,
Millions will teſtifie that this is true.
She hath wip'd off th' aſperſion of her Sex,
That women wiſdome lack to play the Rex:
Spains Monarch, ſayes not ſo, nor yet his hoſt:
She taught them better manners, to their coſt.
The *Salique* law, in force now had not been,
If *France* had ever hop'd for ſuch a Queen.
But can you Doctors now this point diſpute,
She's Argument enough to make you mute.
Since firſt the ſun did run his nere run race,
And earth had once [e] a year, a new old face,
Since time was time, and man unmanly man,
Come ſhew me ſuch a *Phœnix* if you can?
Was ever people better rul'd then hers?
Was ever land more happy freed from ſtirrs?
Did ever wealth in *England* more [f] abound?
Her victoryes in forreign Coaſts reſound,
Ships more invincible then *Spain's*, her foe
She wrackt, ſhe ſackt, ſhe ſunk his Armado:
Her ſtately troops advanc'd to *Lisbons* wall [212]
Don Anthony in's right there to inſtall.
She frankly helpt, *Franks* brave diſtreſſed King,
The States united now her fame do ſing,
She their Protectrix was, they well do know
Unto our dread Virago, what they owe.
Her Nobles ſacrific'd their noble blood,
Nor men nor Coyn ſhe ſpar'd to do them good.

[e] twice. [f] ſo.

The rude untamed *Iriſh*, ſhe did quel,
Before her picture the proud *Tyrone* fell.[g]
Had ever prince ſuch Counſellours as ſhe?
Her ſelf *Minerva* caus'd them ſo to be.
Such Captains and ſuch ſouldiers never ſeen,
As were the Subjects of our *Pallas* Queen.
Her Sea-men through all ſtraights the world did round;
Terra incognita might know the[h] ſound.
Her *Drake* came laden home with Spaniſh gold:
Her *Eſſex* took *Cades*, their Herculean Hold:
But time would fail me, ſo my tongue[i] would to,
To tell of half ſhe did, or ſhe could doe.
Semiramis to her, is but obſcure,
More infamy then fame, ſhe did procure.
She built[j] her glory but on *Babels* walls,
Worlds wonder for a while, but yet it falls.
Fierce *Tomris*, (*Cyrus* heads-man) *Scythians* queen,
Had put her harneſs off, had ſhee but ſeen
Our Amazon in th' Camp of *Tilbury*,[k]
Judging all valour and all Majeſty
Within that Princeſs to have reſidence,
And proſtrate yielded to her excellence.
Dido firſt Foundreſs of proud *Carthage* walls, [213]
(Who living conſummates her Funeralls)
A great *Eliza*, but compar'd with ours,
How vaniſheth her glory, wealth and powers.
Profuſe, proud *Cleopatra*, whoſe wrong name,
Inſtead of glory, prov'd her Countryes ſhame:

[g] And *Tiron* bound, before her picture fell. [h] her.
[i] wit. [j] plac'd. [k] at *Tilberry*:

Of her what worth in Storyes to be ſeen,
But that ſhe was a rich Egyptian Queen.
Zenobya potent *Empreſs* of the Eaſt,
And of all theſe, without compare the beſt,
Whom none but great *Aurelius* could quel;
Yet for our Queen is no fit Parallel.
She was a Phœnix Queen, ſo ſhall ſhe be,
Her aſhes not reviv'd, more Phœnix ſhe.
Her perſonal perfections, who would tell,
Muſt dip his pen in th' *Heleconian Well*,
Which I may not, my pride doth but aſpire
To read what others write, and ſo [l] admire.
Now ſay, have women worth? or have they none?
Or had they ſome, but with our Queen is't gone?
Nay Maſculines, you have thus taxt us long,
But ſhe, though dead, will vindicate our wrong.
Let ſuch as ſay our Sex is void of Reaſon,
Know tis a Slander now, but once was Treaſon.
But happy *England* which had ſuch a Queen;
Yea [m] happy, happy, had thoſe dayes ſtill been:
But happineſs lyes in a higher ſphere,
Then wonder not *Eliza* moves not here.
Full fraught with honour, riches and with dayes
She ſet, ſhe ſet, like *Titan* in his rayes.
No more ſhall riſe or ſet ſo [n] glorious ſun [214]
Untill the heavens great revolution,
If then new things their old forms ſhall [o] retain,
Eliza ſhall rule *Albion* once again.

[l] then. [m] O. [n] ſuch. [o] muſt.

HER EPITAPH.

Here sleeps THE Queen, this is the Royal Bed,
Of th' Damask Rose, sprung from the white and red,
Whose sweet perfume fills the all-filling Air:
This Rose is wither'd, once so lovely fair.
On neither tree did grow such Rose before,
The greater was our gain, our loss the more.

Another.

Here lyes the pride of Queens, Pattern of Kings,
So blaze it Fame, here's feathers for thy wings.
Here lyes the envi'd, yet unparalled Prince,
Whose living virtues speak, (though dead long since)
If many worlds, as that Fantastick fram'd,
*In every one be her great glory fam'd.**

* This is dated 1643 in the first edition.

*Davids Lamentation for Saul and Jonathan.**

2. Sam. 1. 19.

ALas ſlain is the Head of Iſrael,
Illuſtrious *Saul* whoſe beauty did excell,
Upon thy places mountainous and high,
How did the Mighty fall, and falling dye?
In *Gath* let not this things be ſpoken on,
Nor publiſhed in ſtreets of *Askalon*,
Leſt daughters of the Philiſtines rejoyce,
Leſt the uncircumcis'd lift up their voice.
O *Gilbo* Mounts, let never pearled dew,
Nor fruitfull ſhowres your barren tops beſtrew,
Nor fields of offrings ever on you grow,
Nor any pleaſant thing e're may you ſhow;
For there the[a] Mighty Ones did ſoon decay,
The ſhield of *Saul* was vilely caſt away,

* This is the last piece but one in the first edition. The last, "*Of the vanity of all worldly creatures*," is printed on pages 233–235 of the second edition, under the title of "*The Vanity of all worldly things.*" All the following poems, with this exception, were published for the first time in the second edition.

[a] For the.

There had his dignity ſo ſore a foyle,
As if his head ne're felt the ſacred oyle.
Sometimes from crimſon, blood of gaſtly ſlain,
The bow of *Jonathan* ne're turn'd in vain:
Nor from the fat, and ſpoils of Mighty men
With bloodleſs ſword did *Saul* turn back agen.
Pleaſant and lovely, were they both in life, [216]
And in their death was found no parting ſtrife.
Swifter then ſwifteſt Eagles ſo were they,
Stronger then Lions ramping for their prey.
O Iſraels Dames, o'reflow your beauteous eyes
For valiant *Saul* who on Mount *Gilbo* lyes,
Who cloathed you in Cloath of richeſt Dye,
And choice delights, full of variety,
On your array put ornaments of gold,
Which made you yet more beauteous to behold.
O! how in Battle did the mighty fall
In midſt of ſtrength not ſuccoured at all.
O lovely *Jonathan*! how waſt thou ſlain?
In places high, full low thou didſt remain.
Diſtreſt for thee I am, dear *Jonathan*,
Thy love was wonderfull, ſurpaſſing man,[b]
Exceeding all the love that's Feminine,
So pleaſant haſt thou been, dear brother mine,
How are the mighty fall'n into decay?
And warlike weapons periſhed away?

[b] paſſing a man.

To the Memory of my dear and ever honoured Father

Thomas Dudley Esq;

Who deceased, July 31. 1653. *and of his Age.* 77.

BY duty bound, and not by custome led
To celebrate the praises of the dead,
My mournfull mind, sore prest, in trembling verse
Presents my Lamentations at his Herse,
Who was my Father, Guide, Instructer too.
To whom I ought whatever I could doe:
Nor is't Relation near my hand shall tye;
For who more cause to boast his worth then I?
Who heard or saw, observ'd or knew him better?
Or who alive then I, a greater debtor?
Let malice bite, and envy knaw its fill,
He was my Father, and Ile praise him still.
Nor was his name, or life lead so obscure
That pitty might some Trumpeters procure.
Who after death might make him falsly seem
Such as in life, no man could justly deem.
Well known and lov'd, where ere he liv'd, by most
Both in his native, and in foreign coast.

These to the world his merits could make known,
So needs no Testimonial from his own;
But now or never I must pay my Sum;
While others tell his worth, I'le not be dumb:
One of thy Founders, him *New-England* know, [218]
Who staid thy feeble sides when thou wast low,
Who spent his state, his strength, & years with care
That After-comers in them might have share.
True Patriot of this little Commonweal,
Who is't can tax thee ought, but for thy zeal?
Truths friend thou wert, to errors still a foe,
Which caus'd Apostates to maligne so.
Thy love to true Religion e're shall shine,
My Fathers God, be God of me and mine.
Upon the earth he did not build his nest,
But as a Pilgrim, what he had, possest.
High thoughts he gave no harbour in his heart,
Nor honours pufft him up, when he had part:
Those titles loath'd, which some too much do love
For truly his ambition lay above.
His humble mind so lov'd humility,
He left it to his race for Legacy:
And oft and oft, with speeches mild and wise,
Gave his in charge, that Jewel rich to prize.
No ostentation seen in all his wayes,
As in the mean ones, of our foolish dayes,
Which all they have, and more still set to view,
Their greatness may be judg'd by what they shew.

His thoughts were more ſublime, his actions wiſe,
Such vanityes he juſtly did deſpiſe.
Nor wonder 'twas, low things ne'r much did move
For he a Manſion had, prepar'd above,
For which he ſigh'd and pray'd & long'd full ſore
He might be cloath'd upon, for evermore.
Oft ſpake of death, and with a ſmiling chear, [219]
He did exult his end was drawing near,
Now fully ripe, as ſhock of wheat that's grown,
Death as a Sickle hath him timely mown,
And in celeſtial Barn hath hous'd him high,
Where ſtorms, nor ſhowrs, nor ought can damnifie.
His Generation ſerv'd, his labours ceaſe;
And to his Fathers gathered is in peace.
Ah happy Soul, 'mongſt Saints and Angel s bleſt,
VVho after all his toyle, is now at reſt:
His hoary head in righteouſneſs was found:
As joy in heaven on earth let praiſe reſound.
Forgotten never be his memory,
His bleſſing reſt on his poſterity:
His pious Footſteps followed by his race,
At laſt will bring us to that happy place
Where we with joy each others face ſhall ſee,
And parted more by death ſhall never be.

His Epitaph.

Within this Tomb a Patriot lyes
That was both pious, juſt and wiſe.

To Truth a ſhield, to right a Wall,
To Sectaryes a whip and Maul,
A Magazine of Hiſtory,
A Prizer of good Company
In manners pleaſant and ſevere
The Good him lov'd, the bad did fear,
And when his time with years was ſpent
If ſome rejoyc'd, more did lament.

An EPITAPH [220]

On my dear and ever honoured Mother

Mrs. Dorothy Dudley,

who deceaſed Decemb. 27. 1643. *and of her age,* 61 :

Here lyes,

A *Worthy Matron of unſpotted life,*
A loving Mother and obedient wife,
A friendly Neighbor, pitiful to poor,
Whom oft ſhe fed, and clothed with her ſtore;
To Servants wiſely aweful, but yet kind,
And as they did, ſo they reward did find:
A true Inſtructer of her Family,
The which ſhe ordered with dexterity.
The publick meetings ever did frequent,
And in her Cloſet conſtant hours ſhe ſpent;
Religious in all her words and wayes,
Preparing ſtill for death, till end of dayes:
Of all her Children, Children, liv'd to ſee,
Then dying, left a bleſſed memory.

CONTEMPLATIONS.

SOme time now paſt in the Autumnal Tide,
When *Phœbus* wanted but one hour to bed,
The trees all richly clad, yet void of pride,
Where gilded o're by his rich golden head.
Their leaves & fruits ſeem'd painted, but was true
Of green, of red, of yellow, mixed hew,
Rapt were my ſences at this delectable view.

2

I wiſt not what to wiſh, yet ſure thought I,
If ſo much excellence abide below;
How excellent is he that dwells on high?
Whoſe power and beauty by his works we know.
Sure he is goodneſs, wiſdome, glory, light,
That hath this under world ſo richly dight:
More Heaven then Earth was here no winter & no
night.

3

Then on a ftately Oak I caft mine Eye,
Whofe ruffling top the Clouds feem'd to afpire;
How long fince thou waft in thine Infancy?
Thy ftrength, and ftature, more thy years admire,
Hath hundred winters paft fince thou waft born?
Or thoufand fince thou brakeft thy fhell of horn,
If fo, all thefe as nought, Eternity doth fcorn.

4 [223]

Then higher on the gliftering Sun I gaz'd,
Whofe beams was fhaded by the leavie Tree,
The more I look'd, the more I grew amaz'd,
And foftly faid, what glory's like to thee?
Soul of this world, this Univerfes Eye,
No wonder, fome made thee a Deity:
Had I not better known, (alas) the fame had I.

5

Thou as a Bridegroom from thy Chamber rufhes,
And as a ftrong man, joyes to run a race,
The morn doth ufher thee, with fmiles & blufhes,
The Earth reflects her glances in thy face.
Birds, infects, Animals with Vegative,
Thy heart from death and dulnefs doth revive:
And in the darkfome womb of fruitful nature dive.

6

Thy ſwift Annual, and diurnal Courſe,
Thy daily ſtreight, and yearly oblique path,
Thy pleaſing fervor, and thy ſcorching force,
All mortals here the feeling knowledg hath.
Thy preſence makes it day, thy abſence night,
Quaternal Seaſons cauſed by thy might:
Hail Creature, full of ſweetneſs, beauty & delight.

7

Art thou ſo full of glory, that no Eye
Hath ſtrength, thy ſhining Rayes once to behold?
And is thy ſplendid Throne erect ſo high?
As to approach it, can no earthly mould.
How full of glory then muſt thy Creator be?
Who gave this bright light luſter unto thee:
Admir'd, ador'd for ever, be that Majeſty.

8 [222]

Silent alone, where none or ſaw, or heard,
In pathleſs paths I lead my wandring feet,
My humble Eyes to lofty Skyes I rear'd
To ſing ſome Song, my mazed Muſe thought meet.
My great Creator I would magnifie,
That nature had, thus decked liberally:
But Ah, and Ah, again, my imbecility!

9

I heard the merry grashopper then sing,
The black clad Cricket, bear a second part,
They kept one tune, and plaid on the same string,
Seeming to glory in their little Art.
Shall Creatures abject, thus their voices raise?
And in their kind resound their makers praise:
Whilst I as mute, can warble forth no higher layes.

10

When present times look back to Ages past,
And men in being fancy those are dead,
It makes things gone perpetually to last,
And calls back moneths and years that long since fled
It makes a man more aged in conceit,
Then was *Methuselah*, or's grand-sire great:
While of their persons & their acts his mind doth treat.

11

Sometimes in *Eden* fair, he seems to be,
Sees glorious *Adam* there made Lord of all,
Fancyes the Apple, dangle on the Tree,
That turn'd his Sovereign to a naked thral.
Who like a miscreant's driven from that place,
To get his bread with pain, and sweat of face:
A penalty impos'd on his backsliding Race.

12 [224]

Here sits our Grandame in retired place,
And in her lap, her bloody *Cain* new born,
The weeping Imp oft looks her in the face,
Bewails his unknown hap, and fate forlorn;
His Mother sighs, to think of Paradise,
And how she lost her bliss, to be more wise,
Believing him that was, and is, Father of lyes.

13

Here *Cain* and *Abel* come to sacrfiice,
Fruits of the Earth, and Fatlings each do bring,
On *Abels* gift the fire descends from Skies,
But no such sign on false *Cain's* offering;
With sullen hateful looks he goes his wayes.
Hath thousand thoughts to end his brothers dayes,
Upon whose blood his future good he hopes to raise

14

There *Abel* keeps his sheep, no ill he thinks,
His brother comes, then acts his fratricide,
The Virgin Earth, of blood her first draught drinks
But since that time she often hath been cloy'd;
The wretch with gastly face and dreadful mind,
Thinks each he sees will serve him in his kind,
Though none on Earth but kindred near then could he
find.

15

Who fanceyes not his looks now at the Barr,
His face like death, his heart with horror ſraught,
Nor Male-factor ever felt like warr,
When deep diſpair, with wiſh of life hath ſought,
Branded with guilt, and cruſht with treble woes,
A Vagabond to Land of *Nod* he goes.
A City builds, that wals might him ſecure from ſoes.

16 [225]

Who thinks not oft upon the Fathers ages.
Their long deſcent, how nephews ſons they ſaw,
The ſtarry obſervations of thoſe Sages,
And how their precepts to their ſons were law,
How Adam ſigh'd to ſee his Progeny,
Cloath'd all in his black ſinfull Livery,
Who neither guilt, nor yet the puniſhment could fly.

17

Our Life compare we with their length of dayes
Who to the tenth of theirs doth now arrive?
And though thus ſhort, we ſhorten many wayes,
Living ſo little while we are alive;
In eating, drinking, ſleeping, vain delight
So unawares comes on perpetual night,
And puts all pleaſures vain unto eternal flight.

18

When I behold the heavens as in their prime,
And then the earth (though old) ſtil clad in green,
The ſtones and trees, inſenſible of time,
Nor age nor wrinkle on their front are ſeen;
If winter come, and greeneſs then do fade,
A Spring returns, and they more youthfull made;
But Man grows old, lies down, remains where once
he's laid.

20 [19]

By birth more noble then thoſe creatures all,
Yet ſeems by nature and by cuſtome curs'd,
No ſooner born, but grief and care makes fall
That ſtate obliterate he had at firſt:
Nor youth, nor ſtrength, nor wiſdom ſpring again
Nor habitations long their names retain,
But in oblivion to the final day remain.

20 [226]

Shall I then praiſe the heavens, the trees, the earth
Becauſe their beauty and their ſtrength laſt longer
Shall I wiſh there, or never to had birth,
Becauſe they're bigger, & their bodyes ſtronger?
Nay, they ſhall darken, periſh, fade and dye,
And when unmade, ſo ever ſhall they lye,
But man was made for endleſs immortality.

21

Under the cooling ſhadow of a ſtately Elm
Cloſe ſate I by a goodly Rivers ſide,
Where gliding ſtreams the Rocks did overwhelm;
A lonely place, with pleaſures dignifi'd.
I once that lov'd the ſhady woods ſo well,
Now thought the rivers did the trees excel,
And if the ſun would ever ſhine, there would I dwell.

22

While on the ſtealing ſtream I fixt mine eye,
Which to the long'd for Ocean held its courſe,
I markt, nor crooks, nor rubs that there did lye
Could hinder ought, but ſtill augment its force:
O happy Flood, quoth I, that holds thy race
Till thou arrive at thy beloved place,
Nor is it rocks or ſhoals that can obſtruct thy pace

23

Nor is't enough, that thou alone may'ſt ſlide,
But hundred brooks in thy cleer waves do meet,
So hand in hand along with thee they glide
To *Thetis* houſe, where all imbrace and greet:
Thou Emblem true, of what I count the beſt,
O could I lead my Rivolets to reſt,
So may we preſs to that vaſt manſion, ever bleſt.

24 [227]

Ye Fish which in this liquid Region 'bide,
That for each season, have your habitation,
Now salt, now fresh where you think best to glide
To unknown coasts to give a visitation,
In Lakes and ponds, you leave your numerous fry,
So nature taught, and yet you know not why,
You watry folk that know not your felicity.

25

Look how the wantons frisk to tast the air,
Then to the colder bottome streight they dive,
Eftsoon to *Neptun's* glassie Hall repair
To see what trade they great ones there do drive,
Who forrage o're the spacious sea-green field,
And take the trembling prey before it yield,
Whose armour is their scales, their spreading fins their
shield.

26

While musing thus with contemplation fed,
And thousand fancies buzzing in my brain,
The sweet-tongu'd Philomel percht ore my head,
And chanted forth a most melodious strain
Which rapt me so with wonder and delight,
I judg'd my hearing better then my sight,
And wisht me wings with her a while to take my flight.

28 [27]

O merry Bird (ſaid I) that fears no ſnares,
That neither toyles nor hoards up in thy barn,
Feels no ſad thoughts, nor cruciating cares
To gain more good, or ſhun what might thee harm
Thy cloaths ne're wear, thy meat is every where,
Thy bed a bough, thy drink the water cleer,
Reminds not what is paſt, nor whats to come doſt fear

28 [228]

The dawning morn with ſongs thou doſt prevent,
Sets hundred notes unto thy feathered crew,
So each one tunes his pretty inſtrument,
And warbling out the old, begin anew,
And thus they paſs their youth in ſummer ſeaſon,
Then follow thee into a better Region,
where winter's never felt by that ſweet airy legion

29

Man at the beſt a creature frail and vain,
In knowledg ignorant, in ſtrength but weak,
Subject to ſorrows, loſſes, ſickneſs, pain,
Each ſtorm his ſtate, his mind, his body break,
From ſome of theſe he never finds ceſſation,
But day or night, within, without, vexation,
Troubles from foes, from friends, from deareſt, near'ſt
Relation

30

And yet this ſinfull creature, frail and vain,
This lump of wretchedneſs, of ſin and ſorrow,
This weather-beaten veſſel wrackt with pain,
Joyes not in hope of an eternal morrow;
Nor all his loſſes, croſſes and vexation,
In weight, in frequency and long duration
Can make him deeply groan for that divine Tranſlation.

31

The Mariner that on ſmooth waves doth glide,
Sings merrily, and ſteers his Barque with eaſe,
As if he had command of wind and tide,
And now become great Maſter of the ſeas;
But ſuddenly a ſtorm ſpoiles all the ſport,
And makes him long for a more quiet port,
Which 'gainſt all adverſe winds may ſerve for fort.

32 [229]

So he that ſaileth in this world of pleaſure,
Feeding on ſweets, that never bit of th' ſowre,
That's full of friends, of honour and of treaſure,
Fond fool, he takes this earth ev'n for heav'ns bower.
But ſad affliction comes & makes him ſee
Here's neither honour, wealth, nor ſafety;
Only above is found all with ſecurity.

33.

O Time the fatal wrack of mortal things,
That draws oblivions curtains over kings,
Their sumptuous monuments, men know them not,
Their names without a Record are forgot,
Their parts, their ports, their pomp's all laid in th' dust
Nor wit nor gold, nor buildings scape times rust;
But he whose name is grav'd in the white stone *
Shall last and shine when all of these are gone.

The Flesh and the Spirit.†

IN secret place where once I stood
Close by the Banks of *Lacrim* flood
I heard two sisters reason on
Things that are past, and things to come;
One flesh was call'd, who had her eye
On worldly wealth and vanity;
The other Spirit, who did rear
Her thoughts unto a higher sphere:
Sister, quoth Flesh, what liv'st thou on
Nothing but Meditation?

* Rev. ii. 17.

† This poem seems to be an expansion of the idea of Saint Paul, of the strife between the Flesh and the Spirit, or the law of the members and the law of the mind.

Doth Contemplation feed thee ſo [230]
Regardleſly to let earth goe?
Can Speculation ſatiſfy
Notion without Reality?
Doſt dream of things beyond the Moon
And doſt thou hope to dwell there ſoon?
Haſt treaſures there laid up in ſtore
That all in th' world thou count'ſt but poor?
Art fancy ſick, or turn'd a Sot
To catch at ſhadowes which are not?
Come, come, Ile ſhew unto thy ſence,
Induſtry hath its recompence.
What canſt deſire, but thou maiſt ſee
True ſubſtance in variety?
Doſt honour like? acquire the ſame,
As ſome to their immortal fame:
And trophyes to thy name erect
Which wearing time ſhall ne're deject.
For riches doſt thou long full ſore?
Behold enough of precious ſtore.
Earth hath more ſilver, pearls and gold,
Then eyes can ſee, or hands can hold.
Affect's thou pleaſure? take thy fill,
Earth hath enough of what you will.
Then let not goe, what thou maiſt find,
For things unknown, only in mind.
Spir. Be ſtill thou unregenerate part,
Diſturb no more my ſetled heart,

For I have vow'd, (and ſo will doe)
Thee as a foe, ſtill to purſue.
And combate with thee will and muſt, [231]
Untill I ſee thee laid in th' duſt.
Siſters we are, ye twins we be,
Yet deadly feud 'twixt thee and me;
For from one father are we not,
Thou by old Adam waſt begot,
But my ariſe is from above,
Whence my dear father I do love.
Thou ſpeak'ſt me fair, but hat'ſt me ſore,
Thy flatt'ring ſhews Ile truſt no more.
How oft thy ſlave, haſt thou me made,
when I believ'd, what thou haſt ſaid,
And never had more cauſe of woe
Then when I did what thou bad'ſt doe.
Ile ſtop mine ears at theſe thy charms,
And count them for my deadly harms.
Thy ſinfull pleaſures I doe hate,
Thy riches are to me no bait,
Thine honours doe, nor will I love;
For my ambition lyes above.
My greateſt honour it ſhall be
When I am victor over thee,
And triumph ſhall, with laurel head,
When thou my Captive ſhalt be led,
How I do live, thou need'ſt not ſcoff,
For I have meat thou know'ſt not off;

The hidden Manna I doe eat,
The word of life it is my meat.
My thoughts do yield me more content
Then can thy hours in pleaſure ſpent.
Nor are they ſhadows which I catch,
Nor fancies vain at which I ſnatch,
But reach at things that are ſo high,
Beyond thy dull Capacity;
Eternal ſubſtance I do ſee,
With which inriched I would be:
Mine Eye doth pierce the heavens, and ſee
What is Inviſible to thee.
My garments are not ſilk nor gold,
Nor ſuch like traſh which Earth doth hold,
But Royal Robes I ſhall have on,
More glorious then the gliſtring Sun;
My Crown not Diamonds, Pearls, and gold,
But ſuch as Angels heads infold.
The City* where I hope to dwell,
There's none on Earth can parallel;
The ſtately Walls both high and ſtrong,
Are made of pretious *Jaſper* ſtone;
The Gates of Pearl, both rich and clear,
And Angels are for Porters there;
The Streets thereof tranſparent gold,
Such as no Eye did e're behold,
A Chryſtal River there doth run,
Which doth proceed from the Lambs Throne:

* Rev. xxi. 10–27; and xxii. 1–5.

Of Life, there are the waters ſure,
Which ſhall remain for ever pure,
Nor Sun, nor Moon, they have no need,
For glory doth from God proceed:
No Candle there, nor yet Torch light,
For there ſhall be no darkſome night.
From ſickneſs and infirmity, [233]
For evermore they ſhall be free,
Nor withering age ſhall e're come there,
But beauty ſhall be bright and clear;
This City pure is not for thee,
For things unclean there ſhall not be:
If I of Heaven may have my fill,
Take thou the world, and all that will.

*The Vanity of all worldly things.**

AS he ſaid vanity, ſo vain ſay I,
Oh! vanity, O vain all under Sky;
Where is the man can ſay, lo I have found
On brittle Earth a Conſolation ſound?
What is't in honour to be ſet on high?
No, they like Beaſts and Sons of men ſhall dye:
And whil'ſt they live, how oft doth turn their fate,[a]
He's now a captive,[b] that was King[c] of late.
What is't in wealth, great Treaſures to obtain?[d]
No, that's but labour, anxious care and pain,
He heaps up riches, and he heaps up ſorrow,
It's his to day, but who's his heir to morrow?
What then? Content in pleaſures canſt thou find,
More vain then all, that's but to graſp the wind.
The ſenſual ſenſes for a time they pleaſe,
Mean while the conſcience rage, who ſhall appeaſe?
What is't in beauty? No that's but a ſnare, [234]
They're foul enough to day, that once were fair.
What is't in flowring youth, or manly age?
The firſt is prone to vice, the laſt to rage.

* See note to page 215. [a] State? [b] ſlave, [c] a Prince. [d] for to gain?

Where is it then, in wiſdom, learning arts?
Sure if on earth, it muſt be in thoſe parts:
Yet theſe the wiſeſt man of men did find
But vanity, vexation of[e] mind.
And he that knowes the moſt, doth ſtill bemoan
He knows not all that here is to be known.
What is it then, to doe as *Stoicks* tell,
Nor laugh, nor weep, let things go ill or well.
Such *Stoicks* are but Stocks ſuch teaching vain,
While man is man, he ſhall have eaſe or pain.
If not in honour, beauty, age nor treaſure,
Nor yet in learning, wiſdome, youth nor pleaſure,
Where ſhall I climb, ſound, ſeek ſearch or find
That *Summum Bonum* which may ſtay my mind?
There is a path, no vultures eye hath ſeen,
Where Lion[f] fierce, nor lions whelps have been,
Which leads unto that living Cryſtal Fount,
Who drinks thereof, the world doth nought account
The depth & ſea have ſaid tis not in me,
With pearl and gold, it ſhall not valued be.
For Saphire, Onix, Topaz who would[g] change:
Its hid from eyes of men, they count it ſtrange.
Death and deſtruction the ſame hath heard,
But where & what it is, from heaven's declar'd,
It brings to honour, which ſhall ne're[h] decay,
It ſtores[i] with wealth which time can't wear away.
It yieldeth pleaſures far beyond conceit, [235]
And truly beautifies without deceit,

[e] of the. [f] lions. [g] will. [h] not. [i] ſteeres.

Nor ſtrength, nor wiſdome nor freſh youth ſhall fade
Nor death ſhall ſee, but are immortal made.
This pearl of price, this tree of life, this ſpring
Who is poſſeſſed of, ſhall reign a King.
Nor change of ſtate, nor cares ſhall ever ſee,
But wear his crown unto eternity:
This ſatiates the Soul, this ſtayes the mind,
And all the reſt, but Vanity we find.[j]

[j] The reſt's but vanity, and vain we find.

FINIS.

The Author to her Book.

THou ill-form'd offspring of my feeble brain,
Who after birth did'ſt by my ſide remain,
Till ſnatcht from thence by friends, leſs wiſe then true*
Who thee abroad, expos'd to publick view,
Made thee in raggs, halting to th' preſs to trudg,
Where errors were not leſſened (all may judg)
At thy return my bluſhing was not ſmall,
My rambling brat (in print) ſhould mother call,
I caſt thee by as one unfit for light,
Thy Viſage was ſo irkſome in my ſight;
Yet being mine own, at length affection would
Thy blemiſhes amend, if ſo I could:
I waſh'd thy face, but more defects I ſaw,
And rubbing off a ſpot, ſtill made a flaw.
I ſtretcht thy joynts to make thee even feet,
Yet ſtill thou run'ſt more hobling then is meet;
In better dreſs to trim thee was my mind,
But nought ſave home-ſpun Cloth, i'th' houſe I find
In this array, 'mongſt Vulgars mayſt thou roam
In Criticks hands, beware thou doſt not come;

* See pages 82–90 and notes.

And take thy way where yet thou art not known,
If for thy Father askt, ſay, thou hadſt none:
And for thy Mother, ſhe alas is poor,
Which caus'd her thus to ſend thee out of door.

Several other Poems made by the Author upon Diverſe Occaſions, were found among her Papers after her Death, which ſhe never meant ſhould come to publick view; amongſt which, theſe following (at the deſire of ſome friends that knew her well) are here inſerted

Upon a Fit of Sickneſs, *Anno.* 1632.
Ætatis ſuæ, 19.

TWice ten years old, not fully told
Since nature gave me breath,
My race is run, my thread is ſpun,
lo here is fatal Death.
All men muſt dye, and ſo muſt I
this cannot be revok'd
For Adams ſake, this word God ſpake
when he ſo high provok'd.
Yet live I ſhall, this life's but ſmall,
in place of higheſt bliſs,
Where I ſhall have all I can crave,
no life is like to this.
For what's this life, but care and ſtrife?
ſince firſt we came from womb,
Our ſtrength doth waſte, our time doth haſt,
and then we go to th' Tomb.

O Bubble blaſt, how long can'ſt laſt? [238]
that alwayes art a breaking,
No ſooner blown, but dead and gone,
ev'n as a word that's ſpeaking.
O whil'ſt I live, this grace me give,
I doing good may be,
Then deaths arreſt I ſhall count beſt,
becauſe it's thy decree;
Beſtow much coſt there's nothing loſt,
to make Salvation ſure,
O great's the gain, though got with pain,
comes by profeſſion pure.
The race is run, the field is won,
the victory's mine I ſee,
For ever know, thou envious foe,
the foyle belongs to thee.

Vpon ſome diſtemper of body.

In anguiſh of my heart repleat with woes,
And waſting pains, which beſt my body knows,
In toſſing ſlumbers on my wakeful bed,
Bedrencht with tears that flow'd from mournful head.
Till nature had exhauſted all her ſtore,
Then eyes lay dry, diſabled to weep more;
And looking up unto his Throne on high,
Who ſendeth help to thoſe in miſery;
He chac'd away thoſe clouds, and let me ſee
My Anchor caſt i'th' vale with ſafety.

He eas'd my Soul of woe, my flesh of pain,
And brought me to the shore from troubled Main;

Before the Birth of one of her Children. [239]

All things within this fading world hath end,
Adversity doth still our joyes attend;
No tyes so strong, no friends so dear and sweet,
But with deaths parting blow is sure to meet.
The sentence past is most irrovocable,
A common thing, yet oh inevitable;
How soon, my Dear, death may my steps attend,
How soon't may be thy Lot to lose thy friend,
We both are ignorant, yet love bids me
These farewell lines to recommend to thee,
That when that knot's unty d that made us one,
I may seem thine, who in effect am none.
And if I see not half my dayes that's due,
What nature would, God grant to yours and you;
The many faults that well you know I have,
Let be interr'd in my oblivions grave;
If any worth or virtue were in me,
Let that live freshly in thy memory
And when thou feel'st no grief, as I no harms,
Yet love thy dead, who long lay in thine arms:
And when thy loss shall be repaid with gains
Look to my little babes my dear remains.
And if thou love thy self, or loved'st me
These O protect from step Dames injury.

And if chance to thine eyes ſhall bring this verſe,
With ſome ſad ſighs honour my abſent Herſe;
And kiſs this paper for thy loves dear ſake,
Who with ſalt tears this laſt Farewel did take.

A. B.

To my Dear and loving Husband. [240]

IF ever two were one, then ſurely we.
If ever man were lov'd by wife, then thee;
If ever wife was happy in a man,
Compare with me ye women if you can.
I prize thy love more then whole Mines of gold,
Or all the riches that the Eaſt doth hold.
My love is ſuch that Rivers cannot quench,
Nor ought but love from thee, give recompence.
Thy love is ſuch I can no way repay,
The heavens reward thee manifold I pray.
Then while we live, in love lets ſo perſever,
That when we live no more, we may live ever.

A Letter to her Husband, abſent upon Publick employment.

My head, my heart, mine Eyes, my life, nay more,
My joy, my Magazine of earthly ſtore,
If two be one, as ſurely thou and I,
How ſtayeſt thou there, whilſt I at *Ipſwich* lye?

So many ſteps, head from the heart to ſever
If but a neck, ſoon ſhould we be together:
I like the earth this ſeaſon, mourn in black,
My Sun is gone ſo far in's Zodiack,
Whom whilſt I 'joy'd, nor ſtorms, nor froſts I felt,
His warmth ſuch frigid colds did cauſe to melt.
My chilled limbs now nummed lye forlorn;
Return, return ſweet *Sol* from *Capricorn*;
In this dead time, alas, what can I more [241]
Then view thoſe fruits which through thy heat I bore?
Which ſweet contentment yield me for a ſpace,
True living Pictures of their Fathers face.
O ſtrange effect! now thou art *Southward* gone,
I weary grow, the tedious day ſo long;
But when thou *Northward* to me ſhalt return,
I wiſh my Sun may never ſet, but burn
Within the Cancer of my glowing breaſt,
The welcome houſe of him my deareſt gueſt.
Where ever, ever ſtay, and go not thence,
Till natures ſad decree ſhall call thee hence;
Fleſh of thy fleſh, bone of thy bone,
I here, thou there, yet both but one.

A. B.

Another.

Phœbus make haſte, the day's too long, be gone,
The ſilent night's the fitteſt time for moan;
But ſtay this once, unto my ſuit give ear,
And tell my griefs in either Hemiſphere:

(And if the whirling of thy wheels don't drown'd)
The woful accents of my doleful ſound,
If in thy ſwift Carrier thou canſt make ſtay,
I crave this boon, this Errand by the way,
Commend me to the man more lov'd then life,
Shew him the ſorrows of his widdowed wife;
My dumpiſh thoughts, my groans, my brakiſh tears
My ſobs, my longing hopes, my doubting fears,
And if he love, how can he there abide?
My Intereſt's more then all the world beſide.
He that can tell the ſtarrs or Ocean ſand, [242]
Or all the graſs that in the Meads do ſtand,
The leaves in th' woods, the hail or drops of rain,
Or in a corn-field number every grain,
Or every mote that in the ſun-ſhine hops,
May count my ſighs, and number all my drops:
Tell him, the countleſs ſteps that thou doſt trace,
That once a day, thy Spouſe thou mayſt imbrace;
And when thou canſt not treat by loving mouth,
Thy rayes afar, ſalute her from the ſouth.
But for one moneth I ſee no day (poor ſoul)
Like thoſe far ſcituate under the pole,
Which day by day long wait for thy ariſe,
O how they joy when thou doſt light the skyes.
O *Phœbus*, hadſt thou but thus long from thine
Reſtrain'd the beams of thy beloved ſhine,
At thy return, if ſo thou could'ſt or durſt
Behold a Chaos blacker then the firſt.

Tell him here's worſe then a confuſed matter,
His little world's a ſathom under water,
Nought but the fervor of his ardent beams
Hath power to dry the torrent of theſe ſtreams.
Tell him I would ſay more, but cannot well,
Oppreſſed minds, abrupteſt tales do tell.
Now poſt with double ſpeed, mark what I ſay,
By all our loves conjure him not to ſtay.

Another. [243]

As loving Hind that (Hartleſs) wants her Deer,
Scuds through the woods and Fern with harkning ear,
Perplext, in every buſh & nook doth pry,
Her deareſt Deer, might anſwer ear or eye;
So doth my anxious ſoul, which now doth miſs,
A dearer Dear (far dearer Heart) then this.
Still wait with doubts, & hopes, and failing eye,
His voice to hear, or perſon to diſcry.
Or as the penſive Dove doth all alone
(On withered bough) moſt uncouthly bemoan
The abſence of her Love, and loving Mate,
Whoſe loſs hath made her ſo unfortunate:
Ev'n thus doe I, with many a deep ſad groan
Bewail my turtle true, who now is gone,
His preſence and his ſafe return, ſtill wooes,
With thouſand dolefull ſighs & mournfull Cooes.
Or as the loving Mullet, that true Fiſh,
Her fellow loſt, nor joy nor life do wiſh,

But lanches on that ſhore, there for to dye,
Where ſhe her captive husband doth eſpy.
Mine being gone, I lead a joyleſs life,
I have a loving phere, yet ſeem no wife:
But worſt of all, to him can't ſteer my courſe,
I here, he there, alas, both kept by force:
Return my Dear, my joy, my only Love,
Unto thy Hinde, thy Mullet and thy Dove,
Who neither joyes in paſture, houſe nor ſtreams,
The ſubſtance gone, O me, theſe are but dreams.
Together at one Tree, oh let us brouze, [244]
And like two Turtles rooſt within one houſe,
And like the Mullets in one River glide,
Let's ſtill remain but one, till death divide.

Thy loving Love and Deareſt Dear,
At home, abroad, and every where.

A. B.

To her Father with ſome verſes.

MOſt truly honoured, and as truly dear,
If worth in me, or ought I do appear,
Who can of right better demand the ſame?
Then may your worthy ſelf from whom it came.
The principle might yield a greater ſum,
Yet handled ill, amounts but to this crum;

My flock's ſo ſmall, I know not how to pay,
My Bond remains in force unto this day;
Yet for part payment take this ſimple mite,
Where nothing's to be had Kings looſe their right
Such is my debt, I may not ſay forgive,
But as I can, I'le pay it while I live:
Such is my bond, none can diſcharge but I,
Yet paying is not payd until I dye.

A. B.

In reference to her Children, 23. *June*, 1656.* [245]

I Had eight birds hatcht in one neſt,
Four Cocks there were, and Hens the reſt,
I nurſt them up with pain and care,
Nor coſt, nor labour did I ſpare,
Till at the laſt they felt their wing.
Mounted the Trees, and learn'd to ſing;
Chief of the Brood then took his flight,
To Regions far, and left me quite: †
My mournful chirps I after ſend,
Till he return, or I do end,
Leave not thy neſt, thy Dam and Sire,
Fly back and ſing amidſt this Quire.
My ſecond bird did take her flight,
And with her mate flew out of ſight;
Southward they both their courſe did bend,
And Seaſons twain they there did ſpend:
Till after blo'wn by *Southern* gales,
They *Norward* ſteer d with filled ſayles.

* This date is clearly wrong, as events are referred to in the course of the poem which took place more than a year later. It is probably a misprint for 1658.

† Samuel, who sailed for England Nov. 6, 1657 (see page 24), and returned home July 17, 1661 (see page 28).

A prettier bird was no where ſeen,
Along the Beach among the treen.*
I have a third of colour white,
On whom I plac'd no ſmall delight;
Coupled with mate loving and true,
Hath alſo bid her Dam adieu:
And where *Aurora* firſt appears,
She now hath percht, to ſpend her years; †
One to the Academy flew [246]
To chat among that learned crew:
Ambition moves ſtill in his breaſt
That he might chant above the reſt,
Striving for more then to do well,
That nightingales he might excell. ‡
My fifth, whoſe down is yet ſcarce gone
Is 'mongſt the ſhrubs and buſhes flown,
And as his wings increaſe in ſtrength,
On higher boughs he'l pearch at length.
My other three, ſtill with me neſt,
Untill they'r grown, then as the reſt,
Or here or there, they'l take their flight,
As is ordain'd, ſo ſhall they light.

* Dorothy, who married the Rev. Seaborn Cotton, June 25, 1654. In 1655 her husband preached at Wethersfield, Conn., but in 1660 he became the second minister of Hampton, N.H.

† Sarah, who married Richard Hubbard, of Ipswich, a brother of the Rev. William Hubbard, the historian.

‡ "June 25, 1656, I was admitted into the vniverſity, Mr Charles Chauncy being Preſident."—Rev. Simon Bradstreet's Manuscript Diary.

For an account of him, and of Mrs. Bradstreet's other children, see Introduction.

If birds could weep, then would my tears
Let others know what are my fears
Leſt this my brood ſome harm ſhould catch,
And be ſurpriz'd for want of watch,
Whilſt pecking corn, and void of care
They fall un'wares in Fowlers ſnare:
Or whilſt on trees they ſit and ſing,
Some untoward boy at them do fling:
Or whilſt allur'd with bell and glaſs,
The net be ſpread, and caught, alas.
Or leaſt by Lime-twigs they be foyl'd,
Or by ſome greedy hawks be ſpoyl'd.
O would my young, ye ſaw my breaſt,
And knew what thoughts there ſadly reſt,
Great was my pain when I you bred,
Great was my care, when I you fed,
Long did I keep you ſoft and warm, [247]
And with my wings kept off all harm,
My cares are more, and fears then ever,
My throbs ſuch now, as 'fore were never:
Alas my birds, you wiſdome want,
Of perils you are ignorant,
Oft times in graſs, on trees, in flight,
Sore accidents on you may light.
O to your ſafety have an eye,
So happy may you live and die:
Mean while my dayes in tunes Ile ſpend,
Till my weak layes with me ſhall end.

In ſhady woods I'le ſit and ſing,
And things that paſt, to mind I'le bring.
Once young and pleaſant, as are you,
But former toyes (no joyes) adieu.
My age I will not once lament,
But ſing, my time ſo near is ſpent.
And from the top bough take my flight,
Into a country beyond ſight,
Where old ones, inſtantly grow young,
And there with Seraphims ſet ſong:
No ſeaſons cold, nor ſtorms they ſee;
But ſpring laſts to eternity,
When each of you ſhall in your neſt
Among your young ones take your reſt,
In chirping language, oft them tell,
You had a Dam that lov'd you well,
That did what could be done for young,
And nurſt you up till you were ſtrong,
And 'fore ſhe once would let you fly, [248]
She ſhew'd you joy and miſery;
Taught what was good, and what was ill,
What would ſave life, and what would kill?
Thus gone, amongſt you I may live,
And dead, yet ſpeak, and counſel give:
Farewel my birds, farewel adieu,
I happy am, if well with you.

A. B.

In memory of my dear grand-child Elizabeth Bradſtreet, who deceaſed Auguſt, 1665. being a year and half old.*

FArewel dear babe, my hearts too much content,
Farewel ſweet babe, the pleaſure of mine eye,
Farewel fair flower that for a ſpace was lent,
Then ta'en away unto Eternity.
Bleſt babe why ſhould I once bewail thy fate,
Or ſigh the dayes ſo ſoon were terminate;
Sith thou art ſetled in an Everlaſting ſtate.

2.

By nature Trees do rot when they are grown.
And Plumbs and Apples throughly ripe do fall,
And Corn and graſs are in their ſeaſon mown,
And time brings down what is both ſtrong and tall.
But plants new ſet to be eradicate,
And buds new blown, to have ſo ſhort a date,
Is by his hand alone that guides nature and fate.

* The eldest child of her son Samuel.

In memory of my dear grand-child [249]

Anne Bradſtreet.*

Who deceaſed June 20. 1669. *being three years and ſeven Moneths old.*

WIth troubled heart & trembling hand I write,
The Heavens have chang'd to ſorrow my delight.
How oft with disappointment have I met,
When I on fading things my hopes have ſet?
Experience might 'fore this have made me wiſe,
To value things according to their price:
Was ever ſtable joy yet found below?
Or perfect bliſs without mixture of woe.
I knew ſhe was but as a withering flour,
That's here to day, perhaps gone in an hour;
Like as a bubble, or the brittle glaſs,
Or like a ſhadow turning as it was.

* "June. 20. 69 My B[r] Samuel[s] eldeſt child which was a daughter, between 3 & four yeares old dyed. He buried y[e] first y[t] euer had (w'ch alſo was a daughter) about 4 yeares ſince. The Ld teach him, and me, and all who it eſpec. concernes good thereby."—REV. SIMON BRADSTREET'S Manuscript Diary.

More fool then I to look on that was lent,
As if mine own, when thus impermanent.
Farewel dear child, thou ne're ſhall come to me,
But yet a while, and I ſhall go to thee;
Mean time my throbbing heart's chear'd up with this
Thou with thy Saviour art in endleſs bliſs.

On my dear Grand-child Simon Bradſtreet,* [250]
Who dyed on 16. Novemb. 1669. *being but a moneth, and one day old.*

NO ſooner come, but gone, and fal'n aſleep,
Acquaintance ſhort, yet parting caus'd us weep,
Three flours, two ſcarcely blown, the laſt i'th' bud,
Cropt by th' Almighties hand; yet is he good,
With dreadful awe before him let's be mute,
Such was his will, but why, let's not diſpute,
With humble hearts and mouths put in the duſt,
Let's ſay he's merciful as well as juſt.
He will return, and make up all our loſſes,
And ſmile again, after our bitter croſſes.
Go pretty babe, go reſt with Siſters twain
Among the bleſt in endleſs joyes remain.

A. B.

* The fourth child of her eldest son, Samuel.

To the memory of my dear Daughter in Law, Mrs. Mercy Bradstreet, who deceased Sept. 6. 1669. *in the* 28. *year of her Age.**

AND live I still to see Relations gone,
And yet survive to sound this wailing tone;
Ah, woe is me, to write thy Funeral Song,
Who might in reason yet have lived long,
I saw the branches lopt the Tree now fall,
I stood so nigh, it crusht me down withal;
My bruised heart lies sobbing at the Root,
That thou dear Son hath lost both Tree and fruit:
Thou then on Seas sailing to forreign Coast;
Was ignorant what riches thou hadst lost.
But ah too soon those heavy tydings fly, [251]
To strike thee with amazing misery;
Oh how I simpathize with thy sad heart,
And in thy griefs still bear a second part:
I lost a daughter dear, but thou a wife,
Who lov'd thee more (it seem'd) then̄ her own life.
Thou being gone, she longer could not be,
Because her Soul she'd sent along with thee.

* "Sept. ( ) 1670 My Br Samuel Bradstreet his wife dyed, wch was a soar affliction to him, and all his friends. May god giue us all a sanctisyed vse of this, and all other his Dispensations."—REV. SIMON BRADSTREET'S Manuscript Diary. She was a daughter of William Tyng. It appears from this poem that she died soon after the premature birth of a child, which did not long survive her. This child was Anne, born Sept. 3, 1670, so that the date of the mother's death, as given in the heading, must be a misprint for 1670. See N. E. Hist. Gen. Register, vol. ix. p. 113, note ‡‡.

One week ſhe only paſt in pain and woe,
And then her ſorrows all at once did go;
A Babe ſhe left before, ſhe ſoar'd above,
The fifth and laſt pledg of her dying love,
E're nature would, it hither did arrive,
No wonder it no longer did ſurvive.
So with her Children four, ſhe's now a reſt,
All freed from grief (I truſt) among the bleſt;
She one hath left, a joy to thee and me,*
The Heavens vouchſafe ſhe may ſo ever be.
Chear up, (dear Son) thy fainting bleeding heart,
In him alone, that cauſed all this ſmart;
What though thy ſtrokes full ſad & grievous be,
He knows it is the beſt for thee and me.

A. B.

* A daughter, Mercy, born Nov. 20, 1667. Governor Bradstreet, in his will, signed Feb. 20, 1688, O. S., mentions her as one "whom I have been forced to educate and maintain at considerable charge ever since September 1670." — Suffolk Probate Records, Lib. xi. Fol. 277–8. She afterwards married James Oliver, a physician in Cambridge. See N. E. Hist. Gen. Register, vol. viii. p. 314, and vol. ix. p. 113.

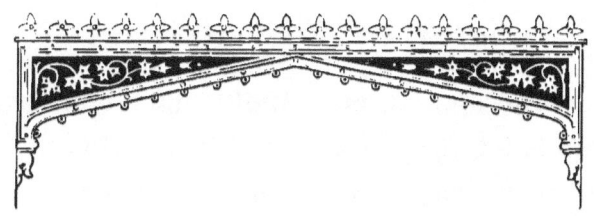

A Funeral Elogy, [252]

Upon that Pattern and Patron of Virtue, the truely pious, peerleſs & matchleſs Gentlewoman

Mrs. Anne Bradſtreet,

right Panaretes,*

Mirror of Her Age, Glory of her Sex, whoſe Heaven-born-Soul leaving its earthly Shrine, choſe its native home, and was taken to its Reſt, upon 16th. Sept. 1672.

ASk not why hearts turn Magazines of paſſions,
And why that grief is clad in ſev'ral faſhions;
Why She on progreſs goes, and doth not borrow
The ſmalleſt reſpite from th' extreams of ſorrow,
Her miſery is got to ſuch an height,
As makes the earth groan to ſupport its weight,
Such ſtorms of woe, ſo ſtrongly have beſet her,
She hath no place for worſe, nor hope for better;
Her comfort is, if any for her be,
That none can ſhew more cauſe of grief then ſhe.

* Gr. πανάρετος, all-virtuous.

Ask not why ſome in mournfull black are clad;
The Sun is ſet, there needs muſt be a ſhade.
Ask not why every face a ſadneſs ſhrowdes;
The ſetting Sun ore-caſt us hath with Clouds.
Ask not why the great glory of the Skye [253]
That gilds the ſtarrs with heavenly Alchamy,
Which all the world doth lighten with his rayes,
The *Perſian* God, the Monarch of the dayes;
Ask not the reaſon of his extaſie,
Paleneſs of late, in midnoon Majeſty,
Why that the palefac'd Empreſs of the night
Diſrob'd her brother of his glorious light.
Did not the language of the ſtarrs foretel
A mournfull Scœne when they with tears did ſwell?
Did not the glorious people of the Skye
Seem ſenſible of future miſery?
Did not the lowring heavens ſeem to expreſs
The worlds great loſe, and their unhappineſs?
Behold how tears flow from the learned hill,
How the bereaved Nine do daily fill
The boſome of the fleeting Air with groans,
And wofull Accents, which witneſs their moanes.
How doe the Goddeſſes of verſe, the learned quire
Lament their rival Quill, which all admire?
Could *Maro*'s Muſe but hear her lively ſtrain,
He would condemn his works to fire again.
Methinks I hear the Patron of the Spring,
The unſhorn Diety abruptly ſing.

Some doe for anguifh weep, for anger I
That Ignorance fhould live, and Art fhould die.
Black, fatal, difmal, inaufpicious day,
Unbleft for ever by *Sol*'s precious Ray,
Be it the firft of Miferies to all;
Or laft of Life, defam'd for Funeral.
When this day yearly comes, let every one, [254]
Caft in their urne, the black and difmal ftone.
Succeeding years as they their circuit goe,
Leap o're this day, as a fad time of woe.
Farewell my Mufe, fince thou haft left thy fhrine,
I am unbleft in one, but bleft in nine.
Fair *Thefpian* Ladyes, light your torches all,
Attend your glory to its Funeral,
To court her afhes with a learned tear,
A briny facrifice, let not a fmile appear.
Grave Matron, whofo feeks to blazon thee,
Needs not make ufe of witts falfe Heraldry;
Whofo fhould give thee all thy worth would fwell
So high, as 'twould turn the world infidel.
Had he great *Maro*'s Mufe, or *Tully*'s tongue,
Or raping numbers like the *Thracian* Song,
In crowning of her merits he would be
fumptuoufly poor, low in Hyperbole.
To write is eafie; but to write on thee,
Truth would be thought to forfeit modefty.
He'l feem a Poet that fhall fpeak but true;
Hyperbole's in others, are thy due.

Like a moſt ſervile flatterer he will ſhow
Though he write truth, and make the ſubject, You.
Virtue ne're dies, time will a Poet raiſe
Born under better Starrs, ſhall ſing thy praiſe.
Praiſe her who liſt, yet he ſhall be a debtor
For Art ne're feign'd, nor Nature fram'd a better.
Her virtues were ſo great, that they do raiſe
A work to trouble fame, aſtoniſh praiſe.
When as her Name doth but ſalute the ear, [255]
Men think that they perfections abſtract hear.
Her breaſt was a brave Pallace, a *Broad-ſtreet*,
Where all heroick ample thoughts did meet,
Where nature ſuch a Tenement had tane,
That others ſouls, to hers, dwelt in a lane.
Beneath her feet, pale envy bites her chain,
And poiſon Malice, whetts her ſting in vain.
Let every Laurel, every Myrtel bough
Be ſtript for leaves t' adorn and load her brow.
Victorious wreathes, which 'cauſe they never fade
Wiſe elder times for Kings and Poets made.
Let not her happy memory e're lack
Its worth in Fames eternal Almanack,
Which none ſhall read, but ſtraight their loſs deplore,
And blame their Fates they were not born before.
Do not old men rejoyce their Fates did laſt,
And infants too, that theirs did make ſuch haſt,
In ſuch a welcome time to bring them forth,
That they might be a witneſs to her worth.

Who undertakes this fubject to commend
Shall nothing find fo hard as how to end.

Finis & non. John Norton.*

Omnia Romanæ *fileant Miracula Gentis.*

* This clergyman was a nephew of the Rev. John Norton, of the First Church in Boston. He graduated at Harvard College in 1671. and was ordained pastor of the First Church in Hingham, Nov. 27, 1678, as successor of the Rev. Peter Hobart. He died Oct. 3, 1716, in the 66th year of his age, after a ministry of nearly thirty-eight years. — "LINCOLN'S History of Hingham," pp. 24–25.

It has been suggested that he edited the second edition of Mrs. Bradstreet's "Poems." — N. E. HIST. GEN. REGISTER, vol. ix. p. 113, note ‡‡.

INDEX.

INDEX.

A.

B.

D.

E.

I.

J.

K.

L.

N.

O.

P.

Q.

T.

CAMBRIDGE: PRESS OF JOHN WILSON AND SON.

www.ingramcontent.com/pod-product-compliance
Lightning Source LLC
Chambersburg PA
CBHW032005110726
47901CB00004B/973